ROYAL TREATMENT . . .

"Do you have any idea what could happen to you if I were the kind of man to take advantage of an innocent?" Jared asked.

"I can imagine," she said quickly. *I can more than imagine.*

"Can you imagine such a rogue would first put his arms around you, like this." Jared wrapped his arms around her and pulled her to him. Her heart thudded in her chest at the unexpected contact.

"He would hold you close and claim he was merely providing needed warmth in the chilling breeze. He would compare your face to the finest marble sculpture in the Louvre, eclipsing the beauty of the works of Michelangelo himself. And your eyes . . ."

"My eyes," she sighed.

His voice was as deep with meaning as his words. "He would say your eyes are like molten pools of midnight. So deep and dark and inviting that a man could forfeit his very soul and be grateful for the loss. And then he would bend his lips to yours." His lips brushed against hers and his breath stopped. "Lightly at first." His lips, firm and warm with promise, met hers again and she fought from sagging against him. "And then, perhaps, he would kiss you fully and thoroughly until you knew you'd been well and truly kissed."

"The fiend," she breathed.

"Indeed," he said softly and his lips claimed hers.

By Victoria Alexander

VICTORIA ALEXANDER

The Princess and the Pea

AVON

An Imprint of HarperCollins*Publishers*

This is a work of fiction. Names, characters, places, and incidents are products of the author's imagination or are used fictitiously and are not to be construed as real. Any resemblance to actual events, locales, organizations, or persons, living or dead, is entirely coincidental.

AVON BOOKS
An Imprint of HarperCollins*Publishers*
195 Broadway
New York, New York 10007

First Avon Books mass market printing: September 2014

Avon Trademark Reg. U.S. Pat. Off. and in Other Countries, Marca Registrada, Hecho en U.S.A.
HarperCollins® is a registered trademark of HarperCollins Publishers.

Printed in the U.S.A.

10 9 8 7 6 5 4 3 2 1

This book is dedicated with affection
and gratitude to:
Diane, Pam, and Sandi
Carol, Deb, and Mary.
All firm believers that fairy tales do come true.

Chapter 1

Chicago, 1895

"**H**ow pretentious! How terribly rude! Positively insufferable! The man's a cad! A beast! Why he's—" Cece White stopped in midpace, drew herself up to her imposing five-feet-six inches, and stared haughtily down a nose she acknowledged was too annoyingly pert to properly carry off the level of righteous outrage in her tone—"a snob!"

"Oh, he is indeed." Marybeth Anderson sniffed prettily and dabbed at the nonexistent tears at the corners of her watery blue eyes. "They all are."

"I hardly think it's fair to indict an entire country merely because of the actions of one or two of its male inhabitants," Emily White said mildly, glancing up from the embroidery that occupied her hands.

"Emily," Cece said, widening her eyes in astonishment, "I can't believe you would stand up for the man."

"I'm not." Emily cast her sister a quelling glance. "I'm simply pointing out that just because one Englishman's actions have been less than acceptable—"

"He toyed with her affections," Cece said indignantly.

"Broke my heart." Marybeth dabbed once again.

Emily ignored the interruption. "—does not mean they are all like that."

"Hah." Cece crossed her arms over her chest and glared. "They're no better than common fortune hunters, the lot of them. They're all only interested in the wealth of young, inexperienced Americans."

Marybeth nodded emphatically. "He as much as admitted it."

"You see, Emily," Cece said with satisfaction. "They don't even have the common courtesy to pretend they're interested in anything but our money."

Emily shrugged and returned her attention to her handiwork. "It's never been a secret. American heiresses have flocked to England for the past twenty years to trade their inheritances for titles. I don't see why you are so irate that this one has deigned to confess what is common knowledge." She glanced at Marybeth. "Since he did have the temerity to admit the truth, why is it you aren't even now planning your wedding to this scoundrel?"

Marybeth sighed dramatically. "It was his mother. She decided I was simply not good enough for her beloved son." A dreamy look glazed her eyes. "I could have forgiven him that. I could have forgiven him anything. He was truly magnificent. Tall, with shoulders that stretched forever and hair the color of midnight. And his eyes . . ." she sighed again, ". . . and he had a castle."

"A castle?" Cece snorted in derision. "Unheated, drafty, and no doubt crumbling about his ears. Precisely why he needs the money of an American heiress." She plopped down in an overstuffed armchair, a note of unfashionable discord in the perfectly appointed sitting room the girls shared between their bedchambers, but worn and comfortable and a favorite nonetheless. "What really bothers me is the way they all seem to think they're somehow better than Americans."

"Well," Marybeth rose to her feet, gathered her gloves and parasol, and said with newfound determination, "I wash my hands of them all. If Mother wants a title in the family, she'll have to get it herself. I'll not step from the shores of this country again to seek a husband. There are more than enough eligible men right here in Chicago." A wistful expression drifted across her face. "Still, he was charming . . ."

"Pity you couldn't live up to the high standards of his mother," Cece said sarcastically. "I think you've had a narrow escape."

Marybeth nodded reluctantly and took her leave. Poor girl. When she had left for London several months ago Marybeth had thought surely she would be the next American heiress to capture a British lord. Cece hated to see her friend return in so defeated a state, even though privately she suspected it was for the best. The mere idea of "Lady Marybeth" was enough to send Cece into spasms of laughter. She'd known Marybeth most of her life, and while the girl could handle the social rigors of Chicago, Cece doubted she could survive life in the rarified, rigid society of the English aristocracy.

Of course, who could? And who would want to? Still, for a young woman whose parents were pressing her to choose a husband . . .

"It would get me out of Chicago," she said, more to herself than to Emily, the seed of a scheme growing in the fertile soil of a highly inventive mind.

"Did you say something?"

"No . . . Emily," Cece said casually, "I have an interesting idea."

Emily's head jerked upright, her eyes wide with apprehension. "Oh no, Cece, not an 'interesting idea.'"

Cece toyed with a frayed spot on the arm of her chair. "I was just thinking . . ."

Emily groaned. "You always get in such trouble when you think."

Cece waved the chastisement aside. "Mother and Father have made no secret of their eagerness for me to marry. I suspect they would leap at the possibility of a marriage involving an English lord. Mother still gets that funny, far-off look whenever she talks about her trip there as a girl."

"But you said they were all fortune hunters, only interested in American money."

"And I meant it." Cece leapt to her feet and paced the room, the excitement in her voice matching the beat of her footfalls. "That's the very thing that makes this idea so delightful. Marybeth was no match for them. She's a darling girl but lacks the kind of cunning necessary for a challenge like this." Cece grinned. "I, however, do not."

Emily shook her head. "You can't seriously expect me to believe you actually want to marry an Englishman."

"Of course not, Emily. It's absurd, the way they have used their titles to rob this country of the flower of American womanhood, all the while considering us inferior."

"You've been reading the *Times* again," Emily muttered.

Cece ignored her. "Americans have trounced the British in every conflict since this country was born.

We lead the world in innovation and invention. It's time we put them firmly in their place." Her voice rose. "We shall convince Mother and Father to take us to London. We will meet the British head on and, in the best American tradition, we shall defeat them." She turned to her sister. "What was that beastly man's name again? The Duke of Blackrock?"

Emily stared with the look of one watching a runaway carriage and unable to do more than pray the innocent would get out of its careening path. "The Earl of Graystone."

"Only an earl?" Cece smiled smugly. "Well, I am the daughter of a captain of industry. The child of American ingenuity. He doesn't stand a chance."

"What are you planning?" Caution edged Emily's voice.

Cece favored her with a confident glance. "I shall meet this high-and-mighty earl and charm the aristocratic pants off him. Then, when he is mine to do with as I wish, I'll simply inform him he does not meet my standards, or the standards of my family or my country. Then we'll see who is too good for whom."

Emily shook her head slowly. "This is ridiculous. Aside from the obvious difficulties of selecting a particular man and setting your cap for him, you could actually end up married."

"Nonsense." Cece tossed her head confidently. "I will be in complete control."

"It's a dangerous game you're proposing."

Cece shrugged. "No more so than the ones we play here. I have already experienced more than my share of American fortune hunters. It can't be that different. Besides—" she sank back in her chair, her voice abruptly serious—"if I don't leave Chicago, I shall surely end up married to Clarence Hillsdale. Father sees such a wedding as more a business merger than a marriage. With his family's railroad holdings and Father's meatpacking interests . . ." Her voice hardened. "I refuse to marry Clarence."

"He's a nice boy," Emily said helpfully.

Cece scoffed. "He has no chin."

"His family has nearly as much money as ours. You can't claim he wants you for your inheritance."

"That's virtually his only asset."

"Still . . ." Emily cast about for words and her eyes brightened. "What about love?"

"Love? Emily, I am nearly twenty-one. If I was going to find love, I would have found it by now. I doubt the emotion even exists." She sighed in theatrical exaggeration. "I have given up on love."

"I haven't," Emily said firmly, her gaze dropping back to her embroidery.

Cece considered her younger sister in silence. Emily was just seventeen and had a great deal to learn about the world. But she was far too accommodating and proper for her own good and could be quite stubborn about what one should and shouldn't do. The girl simply had no spirit of adventure. It was such a pity. Emily was almost ethereally lovely, with light brown hair, amber eyes, and a delicate face and figure. Cece, on the other hand, considered herself far too bold, both in spirit and appearance. Her hair and eyes were a deeper, darker version of the younger girl's, her bosom a shade too full, her hips a bit too curved. Cece had long thought it a shame there wasn't a third sister who combined the characteristics of the other two.

"I'm not really interested in love anymore; or marriage, for that matter."

Emily looked up in mute surprise.

"I know it's what's expected of me, but . . . I have other plans."

"What other plans?" Suspicion colored Emily's voice.

Cece debated the wisdom of revealing her ambitions, even to Emily. It was a secret she'd held close for years, a desire she'd nearly given up on. Now, this idea of going to London, allegedly to look for a husband, could well give her the opportunity she longed for.

She drew a deep breath and leaned toward her sister. "Promise me you won't say a word."

Emily nodded warily.

Cece hesitated, then plunged ahead. "I want to travel the world. I want to float down the Amazon, climb the pyramids, see the Taj Mahal. I want to meet fascinating people and see amazing sights and do remarkable things. I want to be an independent woman. On my own. And I want to write about my experiences and adventures."

Emily shook her head skeptically. "I rarely see you write so much as a letter."

"I've been saving myself," Cece said loftily. "Regardless, I want—" she paused, considering the impact of her words and deciding once and for all to reveal everything—"I want to be a newspaper reporter. A journalist. Like Nellie Bly."

Emily stared. Stunned silence stretched between them.

"It's a wonderful idea. Practically flawless. Don't you see?" Cece's words tumbled out in an eager, rushing stream. "If we go to Europe and I don't marry, perhaps even cause a minor uproar, just the tiniest scandal, Mother and Father will surely see the futility of continuing their quest for a husband. And if I stretch it out long enough, say six months for an engagement and another year to get over my broken heart—"

"Your broken heart?" Emily said in disbelief.

"Well, I can't very well let our parents know my true purpose at that point." She threw her sister an exasperated glare. Sometimes Emily could be so annoyingly practical. Where did she get it from? "At any rate, by then I will be past my prime for marriage, practically a spinster. Oh, they will no doubt rant and rave for a time, but they won't bring me back home. It would be far too embarrassing to admit the meatpacking king's daughter couldn't snare a mere British lord. Then I can very likely do as I wish."

"They'll never agree with your plans. Why, you're talking about working for a living. About making your own way." Emily's face paled, and Cece feared she'd made the wrong decision in divulging her dream. "And Nellie Bly? She's so . . . so . . ."

"Daring? Courageous? Intrepid?"

"Scandalous!"

"Emily, she's positively wonderful. I have saved every article she wrote for the *Times-Herald* here, and quite a few from the *New York World*, as well."

"Do Mother and Father even suspect this absurd ambition of yours?"

"No, and they won't find out until it's too late," Cece said. "Remember, you promised."

Emily swallowed visibly, her tone grim. "I won't tell."

"Good," Cece said briskly and nodded. "Now, the first thing we must do is convince Mother and Father of the need to go to England. I'll talk to them in the morning. Father's always so wonderfully easy to manipulate at breakfast. Then we shall have to devise our campaign carefully. Draw up a sort of battle plan."

She steepled her fingers under her chin and grinned. "We are, after all, Americans. We defeated the English in the War for Independence and the War of 1812. We have the blood of George Washington and Andrew Jackson flowing in our veins. Nothing will stand in the way of showing them, once and for all, that Americans are not merely their equals but their betters. And I, Cecily Gwendolyn White, vow right here and now to best them on their own ground. On my own terms."

Emily stared at her sister in amazement, her words faint with disbelief. "God help the British."

JARED GRAYSON PROWLED the edges of his mother's parlor, cluttered with the treasures and trophies of generations. His restless gaze skimmed the opulent setting, its flaws apparent only to the knowing eye. Visitors never noticed the chip in the Ming vase strategically turned toward the wall, the fraying edges of the Persian carpet, the cracks in the ornate plaster ceiling. He stepped to the marble-topped table bearing a crystal brandy decanter amid its other offerings. At least the liquor was still the best. He poured a generous glass and swiftly downed a hefty swallow. The satisfying burn of the amber liquid steeled him to the inevitable confrontation ahead.

"So, Mother," he said casually, "what was wrong with the last one?"

"Did you say something, dear?" Lady Graystone, Olivia, glanced up from her position behind a delicate ladies' writing desk strewn with calling cards, notes, and invitations. Strands of graying hair escaped the confines of her perfectly arranged coiffure. Spectacles perched on her nose. She was the picture of harmless domesticity. Jared knew better.

"I said what was wrong with the last one?"

"The last what, dear?" Olivia said innocently.

Jared downed another pull of the potent liquor and resolved to remain patient, no matter how difficult that would prove to be. "The last heiress, Mother? The last potential Countess of Graystone? What was wrong with her?"

"Which one was that? Let me think . . ." Olivia drew her brows together in a pouting expression of thoughtfulness. "I remember now: It was the girl from that odd sounding place. Oh yes, Chicago." She tossed him a delighted smile, as if applauding herself for remembering.

Olivia's deliberately vague manner would have softened the resolve of anyone not thoroughly familiar with her tactics. The uninitiated would have, at once, taken pity on this still charming but obviously bubble-headed vision of mature femininity. Jared, however, was all too accustomed to his mother's tricks. When she behaved as if there was nothing in her head but cotton, as if her mind was clouded and feeble, as if she was not as sharp as a woman half her age, Jared's senses stiffened like a hound picking up a scent. The Dowager Countess of Graystone was up to something.

He drew a deep breath. "Yes, Mother, the one from Chicago. Her finances were exceptional, her background acceptable, and she was not unappealing. In point of fact, I found her quite an inviting little morsel."

"She would have gone to fat." Olivia's eyes snapped, her attitude at once keen and discerning. "She was already well on the way to having not one but two chins."

Jared suppressed an impudent grin. Olivia Grayson was no longer a sylphlike figure herself.

"I saw that, Jared."

He allowed the grin to escape. "I know you did,

Mother. That's what makes it so delightful." He swirled the brandy in his snifter and considered his next words. "All right, Mother. While I hardly think that's a suitable reason to eliminate a young woman worth millions from my quest for a suitable wife, I will accept your reasoning. But I remain curious about the others. The chit from San Francisco, for example." Jared leveled a steady gaze at his unruffled parent. "She had no lack of fortune and the proper amount of chins."

Olivia smiled serenely. "Insipid. Shallow. Possibly stupid. I would not rule out inbreeding somewhere in her background."

He swallowed a laugh and nearly choked on the effort to retain his composure. "What of the girl from Baltimore?"

She sighed with feigned regret. "Flighty. Absolutely no sense of decorum. And her brows nearly met above her nose." Olivia shook her head. "Simply not becoming in a countess."

Jared stared. Annoyance battled with amusement. His mother was far more perceptive than even he gave her credit for. Why hadn't he noticed that brow business? More than likely he simply hadn't cared enough. This search for a wife was an unavoidable necessity, nothing more.

He narrowed his eyes. "Very well, then. Tell me what was lacking in the New York heiress. She was lovely, one chin, two separate and distinct brows. She seemed neither too reserved nor too forward. Her ancestry was outstanding, her wealth excessive. What on earth was wrong with her?"

Olivia spread her hands before her in a gesture of inevitability and shrugged. "The poor child could not sit a horse to save her soul."

He widened his eyes in stunned disbelief. "You are telling me that every one of those women, young, for the most part lovely, and each with a dowry that could revive the legacy of Graystone, has been disregarded because of the most minuscule, insignificant reasons it has ever been my misfortune to hear?"

"Jared." Olivia frowned and rose to her feet. "They are not insignificant. Besides, there are other reasons why they were not suitable. Each and every one of them failed to pass my te—" her eyes widened in dismay— "er . . . my requirements. My standards."

Abruptly, his failures in these last months of tentative flirtations and cautious courting made sense. Amazement swept through him. "You've been testing them?"

"In a manner of speaking . . ." Olivia paused, as if groping for words, and Jared suspected for once her hesitation was not an act.

"What kind of tests?" he said through clenched teeth.

"Oh, the usual. This and that." Olivia gestured vaguely. "Questions only a mother could properly judge coupled with quite a bit of basic observation. You understand."

"I most certainly do not." He clenched his fists at his sides in an effort to keep his growing outrage under control. "Regardless of their faults—and it is fair to say those faults are minimal—reach and every one of my prospective brides has had the one inestimable quality I need in a wife. Money. Resources. Vast wealth. It is not a whimsical desire, an idle wish. You and I both know survival is questionable without a substantial infusion of funds, and the sooner the better."

"Of course I know all that." Olivia's eyes sparked. "But I refuse to settle merely because some young woman is the highest bidder. And an American no less. Why can't you find a nice British heiress?"

Jared sighed wearily. "British heiresses are few and far between these days. There is an agricultural depression you know, Mother."

"Nonetheless, your title is your inheritance, much the same as the wealth of some American heiress is hers. There has been an Earl of Graystone for nearly five hundred years."

"Indeed," he said sharply, "and marrying for money seems to have been quite a family tradition for most of them. I am simply carrying on a heritage."

She glared. "Still, you are the proud bearer of a legacy far more valuable than mere money. You are the twenty-first Earl of Graystone. No price can be put on that."

"I beg to differ, Mother." Sarcasm rang in his voice. "There is a price today and it is fairly reasonable. It's merely the amount needed to sustain this building, my townhouse, the estate and Graystone Castle." He laughed bitterly. "An American heiress with a shrewd eye for a bargain will have little trouble seeing she is getting her money's worth."

"If James hadn't died—" Olivia clapped her hand to her mouth, her eyes wide with obvious distress. "Jared, I—"

"Never mind, Mother." He ran his fingers through his hair in a gesture of futility and resignation. "I know. If James hadn't died . . ."

Until James's death, barely a year ago, neither Jared nor Olivia had suspected the dire depths to which the family fortune had sunk. With adept juggling and clever management his older brother had somehow maneuvered to allow Jared and his mother to continue their affluent styles of living. Olivia had remained ensconced in the Berkeley Square mansion. Jared had occupied his own townhouse in a less distinguished but still eminently respectable neighborhood and proceeded to dally with actresses and dancers until his public reputation was both impressive and exaggerated. James had even managed to come up with the extra blunt to support Jared's secret passion, his private dream.

"I am sorry, Jared," Olivia said quietly. "I know how difficult it is for you to take your brother's place. You were so close as children."

"We were close as adults as well." James was not merely the holder of the title and head of the family; he was an elder brother to look up to and the only person, outside of his partner, who knew Jared's secret. "I could tell James anything. Apparently he did not feel the same, at least in regard to the family finances."

Jared wished he could talk to James now. Wished he could ask how in the bloody hell he could avoid this specter of imminent financial ruin. Marriage seemed the only possible solution. He could see another answer, but it was too far in the distant future, too unlikely, too much of an implausible illusion to provide more than a dim glimmer of hope.

He shook his head slowly. "He would have known what to do. I just wish I was half as competent and capable as he was."

"You are, Jared," she said softly.

He flashed her a brief smile. "Thank you, Mother." His tone hardened. "I want you to understand one thing: I shall tolerate no more interference in this marriage business. I am twenty-seven, an adult; the earl, as you've pointed out. The next moderately acceptable American heiress to come along will be my bride for better or worse. And remember, I will not be the first to wed an American. Already, a new generation of off-spring of British-American matches is making its presence known." He grinned reluctantly. "I suspect the American influence will be a factor in England well into the next century."

Olivia expelled a sigh of acquiescence and smiled bravely. "God help the British."

"LONDON? POPPYCOCK," HENRY White said gruffly from behind his morning paper. "I see no need to travel halfway across the world to find a husband. There are plenty of good prospects right here in Chicago. Take that fine young man Clarence Hillsdale. Why, he's—"

"He has no chin, Father," Cece blurted.

"No chin?" The unconcerned voice remained hidden by the *Times-Herald*. Cece suspected her father paid far more attention to the financial section than to her. "I hadn't noticed, but it doesn't seem a critical factor in a husband. A chin isn't necessary to get an heir."

"Oh no, Father." She winked at the maid hovering behind her father's chair. An earnest tone colored her words. "Without a chin his collar creeps right up his face. Why, half the time I have no idea what Clarence is saying, his mouth is so muffled by his shirt. A chin would anchor his collar in place quite nicely."

"Just so, my dear. . . . What did you say?" The paper collapsed in a crush of newsprint and Henry stared at his oldest daughter in confusion. Cece favored him with an innocent smile. "I see. Sorry." Her father's expression shifted to a look of amused chagrin. "You now have my complete and undivided attention."

"Thank you," she said primly.

"Henry, I think a trip to London is a wonderful

idea." Phoebe White glanced pointedly at her daughter. "I think it's exactly what Cece needs and Emily, too, for that matter." A wistful expression flashed across her face. "I still remember my sojourn in London as if it was yesterday. A truly delightful season."

Henry's dark brows drew together in annoyance. "Delightful seasons can be had right here at home."

"Of course they can, Father," Cece said quickly. This was not the time to irritate her father by casting aspersions on his favorite city. "Chicago is one of the very best places anywhere. And didn't we prove that with the World Exposition?"

"By George, we certainly did." Satisfaction rang in his voice. "Two years later and they're still talking about it."

"Exactly." Cece nodded.

"Exactly . . . what?" The look of confusion had returned. Cece smiled to herself. She was thoroughly familiar with her father's expressions. The more befuddled she managed to get him, the better her chances of achieving what she wanted.

"Exactly why going abroad is such a wonderful idea." She tossed him a smug smile.

Henry glanced at his wife, who simply shrugged in resignation. She, too, was used to her daughter's convoluted way of thinking.

"I must be a little muddleheaded this morning," he said, his words cautious and deliberate. "Explain to me the reasoning behind this wonderful idea. In words your poor, stupid father can understand."

"Well." She breathed deeply and prayed for inspiration. "You and I both know this is the best country in the world, even if England and the rest of Europe are ever so much older. But since we are young we don't have silly little things like nobility and titles and such." Her words came faster and faster, in the belief that sheer speed alone would counter any flaws in her argument. "Still, it would be great fun, don't you think? To have one, I mean. And quite exciting for you and Mother, too, to have a prince or a duke in the family."

"Thank you for your concern for your mother and me." Sarcasm dripped off Henry's words. "But I scarcely think 'fun' is an appropriate reason to head to the other side of the globe."

Cece threw her mother a silent appeal for help. Phoebe merely smiled in encouragement. She was on her own.

"Very well, Father," she said, in her best no-nonsense voice. Henry's brow quirked upward at her tone. "Let's look at this realistically."

A smile tugged at the corners of his mouth and he gestured for her to continue. "Please, go right ahead."

"Thank you." Her voice was brisk. "I fear I shall never find a husband in Chicago." Henry opened his mouth in protest and she waved him aside. "Oh, I know what you're going to say. I've had offers, dozens in fact. And that's true. But no one, I felt, who could live up to the standards you'd expect from a son-in-law."

"There's Clarence."

"He has no chin," Mother and daughter chorused.

Henry rolled his eyes heavenward. Cece ignored him.

"I simply feel that my chances might be better in a new city, another country." She threw her father a mournful look. "I fear otherwise," she sighed deeply, "I shall never marry."

Henry stared in amazement for a long moment. He shook his head in disbelief. "That was good. Very good. Excellent." He glanced at his wife. "Does she get that from your side of the family or mine? Although I doubt my side has ever seen dramatics quite this impressive."

"Father!" Cece resisted the urge to stamp her foot.

"Henry," Phoebe said mildly, "haven't you always said you wanted to take me to Paris one day?"

Henry groaned. "First London, now Paris. What's next? China?"

"China would be interesting," Cece murmured.

"Don't be silly, Henry," Phoebe chided her husband. "No one said anything about China. But England is more than respectable for a young lady, and the prospects here do seem to be getting dimmer day by day. I don't relish the idea of a spinster for a daughter, and I quite like the thought of a title in the family. It would do Emily good, as well, to see what life is like in a stimulating world capital of culture and society. And Paris is practically next door to London. Besides, I could see my dear friend Millie." Phoebe leaned toward Cece in a confidential manner. "I haven't seen her in—my goodness, it must be more than twenty years now. We do exchange letters though."

Cece smiled patiently. "I know, Mother."

"Henry," Phoebe's manner was abruptly decisive. "The more I think about it, the more I like the proposal."

Surprise washed over Henry's face. Phoebe rarely insisted on anything. Cece stifled a triumphant grin. With her mother on her side, her father might as well give up right now.

"I have business to attend to here," he growled.

"Nonsense." Phoebe waved away the objection. "You have hundreds of highly qualified people more than capable of taking over for a few months. It's past time you took a good, long holiday."

"But I hardly think—" Henry's gaze flicked from wife to daughter and back.

"I think we should start packing." Phoebe threw him a challenging glare.

Henry had the look of a man realizing his fate was sealed.

"Please, Father." Cece held her breath.

He threw up his hands in defeat. "I give up; you win." He glared at his wife. "Both of you."

"Of course we do," his mate said pleasantly.

Cece sprang from her chair and threw her arms around her father. "Thank you, Father. You won't be sorry."

"I suspect I'll be very sorry," he grumbled.

Mother and daughter exchanged satisfied smiles, and Cece turned to go find Emily. Her sister had agreed not to tell their parents Cece's ultimate purpose but had refused to come help her talk her father into the trip. Just wait till she heard how very easy it had been after all, thanks to Mother.

She tossed a final comment over her shoulder. "We'll have a wonderful time, all of us. And I'm sure I shall find someone suitable, someone who would do us all proud."

Cece stepped out of the breakfast room and for a fleeting moment wondered just how broad the Earl of Graystone's shoulders really were. She barely heard her father's last words trailing after her.

"God help the British."

Chapter 2

". . . . they arrived late last night for a nice, relaxing stay here in the country before the mad rush of London, and I expect you to be pleasant to them." Lady Millicent Templeton drummed her fingertips on the polished mahogany dining table and glared at her nephew, who appeared far too busy piling his plate with breakfast items from the sideboard to pay her proper attention. "And do sit down, Quentin. I simply detest it when you plow through your food without even the slightest concession to civilization."

"Sorry, Aunt Millicent." Quentin grinned and plopped down in the nearest chair. "And by the way, I might point out, I am unfailingly pleasant, and also well-mannered, kindhearted and thrifty."

"Thrifty?" She snorted with disbelief. "You, Quentin Allister Bainbridge, may well be thrifty when dealing with your own money, but you seem to go through mine as if it were as free and plentiful as the very air you breathe."

"Ouch." Quentin adopted an injured tone. "That stings, Aunt Millicent, it really does. You know I shall pay you back every penny someday."

"It's the someday that concerns me." Millicent sighed with exasperation. "I daresay your father would not approve of the vast and unending amounts of money your project seems to require on virtually a daily basis."

"Of course he wouldn't," Quentin said cheerfully, slathering marmalade on a bun still steaming from the oven. "But as long as he is stationed in India, or wherever the Crown sends him on Her Majesty's Service, we needn't fear his displeasure." He popped the bread into his mouth.

"It's not just the money. Lord knows, I have more than enough to spare. And with no children of my own I have always thought of you as something of a son." She tossed him a fond glance. He smiled in return and reached for another bun. "Still, I can't help but think this tinkering of yours will lead to no good. Imagine a member of the aristocracy . . . Why, if society ever learned you were actually working with your hands . . ." She shook her head in anticipation of the dire consequences. "Really, Quentin, it's so terribly . . ."

"American?" he suggested.

"I was going to say democratic."

He shrugged. "I scarcely think there's much difference. And I like Americans. Especially the way they think about inventions and creativity and forging ahead into the next century."

Millicent huffed. "Well, it's simply not acceptable here."

"I'm half American, Aunt Millicent."

"I know that only too well." She shook her head mournfully. "I have tried my best through these years to overcome that flaw."

"You're American," he said gently.

She waved away his comment, her tone lofty. "That's

entirely different, my boy. I have adapted. Today, I am as thoroughly British as anyone, even if my family does not date back to the Crusades. If your mother had lived past your infancy, she too would have adjusted." She narrowed her eyes and glared. "I have long suspected you use that claim of American blood merely to excuse unacceptable behavior."

"Aunt Millicent!" Again, he assumed a wounded look that belied the twinkle in his eye. "I'm shocked you would think such a thing of me."

She selected a scone from her plate and buttered it lightly. "No, Quentin, you would be shocked if I did not."

"Touché." He saluted her with a crust of bread and an all-too-contagious grin. "Now, tell me about these friends of yours."

"An admirable way to change the subject. Very well. Let's see." She paused to sort and sift through the memories of what seemed a lifetime ago or, perhaps, only yesterday. "Phoebe and I met during my first season in London. We were both young and American and, while we were accompanied by our families, without the kind of female companionship one tends to take for granted until it's absent. Of course, I had the company of your father, graciously presenting his American sister-in-law to society. I believe you were five that year."

"I was seven."

"Whatever." She waved away the interruption. "Where was I? Oh, yes. Phoebe and I became bosom chums. Even when she returned home we kept up our friendship. Scarcely a month goes by without my posting a letter to her or receiving one from her.

"Shortly after her return she met and married

Henry White. He made a fortune in cows or beef or something along those lines; I forget what exactly. I was introduced to him on their arrival last night, and he is as charming in person as her letters had led me to believe." She grinned wickedly. "And still quite a handsome figure of a man."

"Aunt Millicent!" A note of shocked amusement rang in his voice.

She cast him a withering glance. "I am no longer a sweet, young innocent but I'm far from doddering on my last legs. One can, after all, appreciate a fine specimen of horseflesh without an urgent desire to ride the beast for oneself."

He laughed. "Now, who is shocking whom?"

"I suspect there are still lingering traces of America in my blood as well as yours," she said curtly. "At any rate, Phoebe has come to give her daughters the pleasure of a London season, just as we had. I suspect the ultimate goal is to find the older girl, and possibly the younger one as well, a husband."

"What are they like?" he said cautiously.

"Do not take that tone," she said reproachfully. "They are not cross-eyed and splay-legged. In fact, I am rather perplexed as to why the eldest has not wed before now. Both girls are lovely. Cecily, they call her Cece, in a somewhat striking, vivid sort of way, and Emily in a more delicate, graceful fashion." She studied him thoughtfully. "They are heirs to a quite impressive fortune."

He stopped in midbite and stared. "I do not need an heiress."

"Stuff and nonsense," she said airily. "Everyone needs an heiress."

"Then let me rephrase my comment." He slanted her a serious gaze. "I do not need a wife."

"Wrong again." She smiled pleasantly. "A wife is exactly what you do need and have needed for a long time. You are, how old now? Twenty-six?"

"Twenty-eight."

"Whatever." She continued without pause, "It is high time for you to marry, time for you to accept the responsibilities of your position in society, and past time for you to give up this folly upon which you insist on squandering your life and my money."

"What kind of folly?" a lilting female voice asked. Cece and Emily stood framed in the doorway like a Renaissance portrait. For a moment, a long unfelt patriotic pride glowed in Millicent. American girls were indeed enchanting, the very picture of health and vitality. No wonder their British counterparts never seemed to warm up to these cousins from across the pond.

"Good morning." Quentin sprang to his feet, a look of appreciation in his eye. Excellent; there was hope for the boy yet.

"Good morning, girls. Please, join us." Millicent gestured to the food-laden sideboard.

"Wonderful. I'm famished." Cece headed toward the feast with a determined step. "I feel as if I haven't eaten in weeks."

"She has, you know." Emily smiled. "She tends to exaggerate, but—" she glanced at the sideboard—"it does look good."

The girls quickly filled their plates.

"Now then," Cece said as soon as they were seated. She fixed Quentin with a steady stare. "Who are you and what is this folly of yours?"

"Cece!" Emily gasped in obvious dismay at her sister's lack of restraint.

Quentin grinned, and hope surged through Millicent. It was a rare woman who could resist the boyish charm of that smile. Or the blond, blue-eyed good looks of the man it belonged to.

"I'm Quentin Bainbridge. Aunt Millicent's sister was my mother. As for my folly—"

"There will be no talk of follies until the two of you have finished your breakfast," Millicent said firmly.

"Of course," Cece said but there was a distinct look in her eyes that said she was not about to let this go.

"Well," Cece said the moment she had finished eating. "Tell me about your folly."

Quentin's eyes sparkled. "I could show you if you wish."

"Even I haven't actually seen it," Millicent murmured.

"You've never asked," Quentin chided. "Well, ladies?"

Cece's eyes widened with interest, her tone teasing. "Oh, I do so love a good folly. What about you, Emily?"

Emily smiled halfheartedly. "A folly? How . . . nice. Don't you think, Cece, we should perhaps find out exactly what kind of folly this is before we—"

"Don't be such a stick, Em." Excitement rang in Cece's voice. "What better way to start our trip to England than with a folly? Any folly." She cast Quentin a suspicious look. "It is a good folly, isn't it? Well worth our time, I mean."

Quentin nodded somberly. "If I do say so myself, it is an excellent folly."

Cece jumped to her feet. "Well then, shall we go?"

Millicent groaned. "If you insist on going to see this creation of his, at least call for a carriage. He has arranged to use the abandoned stables of a neighbor for his project, just beyond the borders of my estate."

"Is it too far to walk?" Emily said hopefully.

Quentin stood and shrugged. "Not for me."

Cece nodded. "It's a glorious day out. A brisk walk will do us all a world of good."

Emily sighed and rose to her feet. "I hope you know what you're doing. The last time you wanted to see some kind of folly we ended up—"

"Emily!" Cece warned.

Emily smiled innocently.

Quentin quirked a puzzled brow. "You have seen follies before?"

"Oh, once or twice," Cece said lightly. "There's nothing like a good folly, I always say." She headed toward the door, Quentin and Emily trailing in her wake.

"And there do seem to be no shortage of follies these days," Emily said under her breath.

Quentin ushered her through the doorway. "Well, my dear, it *is* 1895. We're on the dawn of a new century. Think of all the wonders that lie ahead. This is the most exciting period in the history of mankind. And what is a folly today may well be commonplace tomorrow. By the by, tell me about that other folly you referred to . . ."

They strolled out of sight and their voices faded.

Millicent reached for her tea and smiled with satisfaction. Even if she had failed to make a match between Quentin's father and Cece's mother during that first season so long ago, perhaps, now, with the son and the daughter—either daughter—she had another chance.

THE DOORS OF the old stables were opened wide. Cece stood on the threshold, dividing the sunshine of the day behind her from the dark shadows within, and squinted in an effort to speed her eyes' adjustment to the change of light.

"Gracious!" Emily gasped. "What on earth are those contraptions?"

"My dear lady," Quentin said, a teasing note in his voice, "they are not contraptions. They are what you so callously called my folly."

Before her stood three—or at least it appeared to be three—separate and distinct mechanical creations, all in various stages of repair or, possibly, disrepair. What on earth were they? All metal and wire and spokes . . .

"Hell and damnation," Cece said under her breath.

"Cece!" Emily said sharply.

Cece barely heard her. She moved forward without thinking, a hand outstretched to touch—"Horseless carriages! How wonderful!" She circled the center vehicle eagerly, an odd crossbreed of a small two-seater buggy and a bicycle. With wheels out of all proportion to its size, it appeared a fanciful confection of levers and gears and ingenuity. Excitement quivered through her blood. "Does it work?"

"Of course it works." A deep, laughter-filled voice sounded behind her. She whirled at the words and stared at the figure framed in the doorway. Bright sunlight behind him blinded her to anything but his silhouette; tall and broad-shouldered, he seemed to fill the space in the now somehow smaller stable. "Have you seen one before?"

"I've seen pictures, of course, but only once in person. It didn't look anything like this, though. The horseless carriage I saw was more like an old wagon with a motor." She narrowed her eyes and peered at the dark form. "It was at the Exposition."

"Really? What Exposition? Where? How did they—"

"Jared," Quentin said with a laugh, "don't quiz the girl unmercifully."

"Right; sorry." She could hear a grin in his words. The shadowed figure stepped aside and sunlight dappled his strong and handsome face. A dimple danced in one cheek and his eyes sparkled as dark and intense as the nearly black hair that curled softly around his ears. The man seemed to shimmer with barely bridled energy. "I tend to get carried away by all this." He waved toward the work.

She pulled her gaze from his and studied the vehicles. "I can certainly see why. What part do you play in—" she repeated his gesture—"all this?"

"This is my partner." Quentin nodded at the stranger. "Jared Grayson, the E—"

"The brains of the entire endeavor," Jared cut in with a flourish and a bow. "At your service." His words were for everyone but his eyes were on Cece.

"Brains, hah," Quentin said. "Don't forget it was my idea to substitute the petrol powered—"

"Quite." Jared picked a rag off a wheel and wiped his hands casually. "It was also your convoluted design for a cooling mechanism that very nearly cost us our lives."

"My goodness." Emily's eyes widened. "What happened?"

"Nothing of consequence. Little more than a minor inconvenience." Quentin shrugged. "One has to expect to pay a certain price for progress."

Jared leaned toward Cece, bringing the warm scents of sun and wind enticingly nearer. He lowered his voice confidentially. "We blew up three motors before we got it right." He glanced upward toward a nearby section of sloping roof with a less than modest patch of wood, scorched black and shiny. "Had a bit of a flame there one day. Petrol, you know; highly flammable." He nodded at a back portion of the wall, covered with a huge canvas cloth. "There's a lovely hole behind that, the result of a few difficulties with steering mechanisms."

Awed, Cece gazed from the canvas to the vehicle and back into the incredibly dark centers of his blue eyes. "You wouldn't think something that small could do that much damage."

Quentin grinned. "It was bloody well impressive."

"It's amazing just how much power we've managed to harness." Jared's eyes twinkled and a flutter of excitement settled in her middle. "Now if we can only learn to properly control it . . ."

"How does it work?" Cece ran her hand along the rim of the wheel and cast him a glance of genuine curiosity.

Jared raised a dubious brow. "Do you really want to know?"

"Oh my, yes." Cece nodded eagerly.

"Don't get him started," Quentin warned.

Jared ignored his partner. "We began working with steam power. It's been tried for years and is moderately successful, but boilers tend to be cumbersome and heavy. Frankly, I think steam is outdated. Then we considered electricity. Battery-powered vehicles." He warmed to his subject and his words came faster, his tone intense.

Cece tried to concentrate on his words, but her mind kept getting lost, watching the movement of his mouth. What sort of man had a mouth like that anyway? Lips that were neither too full nor too thin. Kissed with a pale burgundy blush and corners that betrayed a propensity to smile.

"Some designers have had moderate success running off a battery for as much as thirty miles. But again, you run into a weight and space problem. So we discarded that in favor of this."

Something about his enthusiasm stirred her, wrapped excitement around her, like the silken ribbon on an unexpected present, and left her breathless. Jared gestured at the exposed motor, the movement pulling the fabric of his shirt taut across the muscles of his broad chest.

"We're using petrol for fuel. There are a number of problems we have yet to work out. We are still undecided on whether to use one or two cylinders, but the beauty of this idea is that, in a strictly practical way of course, the . . ."

It was interesting in a wonderfully boring sort of way. But she'd lost herself in the far more fascinating way his strong, expressive hands seemed to caress the lines and edges of his vehicle like a sweetheart. Far more appealing was the supple power apparent in the length of arm revealed beneath the rolled-up sleeves and the way his shirt opened wide at the collar for a tantalizing glimpse of muscled chest. And far more exciting was the rich timbre of his voice, the deeply textured tones that seemed to reverberate in the stable and wrap around her very soul.

But it was his eyes that held her spellbound. As dark blue as the sky at midnight and just as endless, they flashed with a fire spurred by imagination, a passion born of creativity. This was no insipid English lord, no down on his luck aristocrat willing to sell his title for financial security. This was a man destined by sheer force of will alone to make his mark on the world. A man well worthy of loyalty and respect and love. If, of course, she believed in love.

". . . and the French are doing a bang-up job, making great strides. There's a road race in Paris in two weeks. We're not entered, but I shall be there just to get an idea of their progress."

"Paris? Two weeks?" Cece cast him her sweetest smile. "What a marvelous coincidence. We'll be in Paris in two weeks."

"Paris?" Confusion stamped Emily's face. "I thought we were next going to L—" A sharp jab to her ribs stopped her in midsentence.

"Paris," Cece said quickly. "Paris first, then London."

"Of course," Emily glared. "How foolish of me to forget."

"I'm certain it simply slipped your mind." Cece threw her a swift, appeasing glance, then returned her attention to Jared. "You've explained how it's supposed to work, but does it?"

"Naturally it works," Quentin said with a huff of wounded pride.

A slow smile spread across Jared's face. "Would you care to see for yourself?"

Excitement surged through her. "A ride?" He nodded. "I'd love it." She turned to her sister. "Emily?"

"No, thank you." Emily shook her head vehemently. "I should think the most difficult horse alive preferable to that metallic beast."

Cece sighed tolerantly. "Em, you have absolutely no sense of adventure." Cece often wondered how the same parents could have raised such different daughters. Her sister's nature was no doubt the product of the finishing school both girls had at one time attended, although Cece had resisted all attempts to mold her own character into something considered more acceptable. And obviously Cece had shirked her duties as an older sister and failed to show her sibling life was far more interesting when one was not as concerned with behavior as excitement. She definitely needed to do something about that.

Emily crossed her arms over her chest. "Perhaps not, but I have a highly developed sense of safety." She eyed the vehicle skeptically. "Is that safe?"

Quentin and Jared exchanged glances.

"Relatively," Jared said.

"More or less," Quentin added.

"I suspected as much." Emily stared pointedly at Cece. "Are you certain you want to risk your neck in that thing?"

"This is to be my first venture in a horseless carriage and I—"

"Automobile," Jared said.

Cece pulled her brows together in confusion. "Pardon me?"

"We call it an automobile." He pronounced the word slowly, as if he was unaccustomed to its sound. "Or a motor car."

"I see. Automobile." She rolled the word around in her mind. "How appropriate. Very well. This is my first venture in an automobile and I'm not going to miss it." Cece extended a hand to Jared. "Mr. Grayson?"

He took her hand and helped her into the vehicle. His innocent touch sent a current of lightning skating up her arm and down her spine.

"It's Jared," he said firmly, gazing into her eyes.

"Jared," she repeated, noting with surprise the

somewhat airy quality of her voice. She drew a steadying breath that even to her own ears sounded more like a sigh, and reluctantly withdrew her hand. "Since we are obviously not going to be formally introduced . . ." She tossed Quentin a look of chastisement.

He groaned. "I hate formal introductions."

"Apparently." Jared sank down beside her. The seat was small, with barely enough room for the two of them, and her hip crushed against his in a most intriguing manner. She smiled. "If it's Jared, then you must call me Cece."

He regarded her for a long moment and nodded, as if she had somehow passed some kind of test. "It suits you."

"I know," she said primly.

"No introductions. No chaperons. First names." Emily released an exasperated sigh. "This is all so completely improper."

"Well, it just seems to me that modern inventions require modern behavior, not old-fashioned rules." Cece glanced at Jared. "Don't you agree?"

"Indeed," he said solemnly.

"You'd best put these on." Quentin handed her a heavy pair of leather and glass goggles.

She struggled into the cumbersome eyewear. "What are these for?"

Jared too sported a pair of the ungainly glasses. "Bugs," he said, his manner matter of fact.

"I'm so glad I asked." She cocked her head to one side and surveyed the odd picture he presented. "You look quite a bit like a frog in those. It suits you."

He laughed. "I know. Ready?"

"Ready." Her voice rang with confidence, but her

heart fluttered in her throat. Excitement sparred with apprehension. After all, she had never ridden in a beast like this before.

Quentin carried a large metal crank and stepped to the front of the automobile. Like the wind-up key to a child's toy, he inserted the crank and turned it.

The contraption shivered and coughed and sputtered like an old man with the ague. She tensed in anticipation. Perhaps this was indeed a folly. Perhaps she should get out now while there was still time. Perhaps . . . it was already too late.

With a roar, the machine sprang to life. Jared skillfully manipulated three metal tillers that rose from the floor between his long legs. The vehicle lurched forward and out through the stable doors.

The noise was unbelievable, the ride jolting and, except for the inadvertent contact of his body with hers, distinctly uncomfortable. Cece gritted her teeth. A lesser woman would no doubt be cowering in terror by this time. She was made of sterner stuff and determined to show no fear and enjoy the frightful ride.

"How do you like it?" Jared's yell was barely audible above the clamor of the machine.

"It's lovely," she yelled back.

He nodded and smiled.

After a few moments the automobile settled into an even gait. The ride smoothed and Cece relaxed enough to survey the scenery. They were on an overgrown country lane not substantially more than a footpath. On one side, a meadow fell away in a gentle downward slope. At the bottom, a charming pond glittered like a sapphire in a lush, green setting. It was a lovely, bucolic scene, pastoral and peaceful. And best of all, for the first time in her life, Cece saw it without having to peer around the backside of a horse.

Exhilaration filled her. "This is wonderful!"

Jared grinned. "Do you want to try it?" he yelled.

"Buy it?" What on earth did he mean? Of course she didn't want to buy this thing.

"No, no." He shook his head violently and bellowed. "I said try it. Drive it. Do you want to drive?"

"Hive? What hive?" She glanced about quickly. Why was he talking about bees? She didn't see any hives.

He pulled his brows together and shook his head again. "Put your hands here."

She strained to catch his words. "Where?"

"Here." He patted the middle lever. "On this tiller."

She tried to place her hand where he indicated but couldn't seem to reach.

"Wait," Jared hollered. He slid closer and slipped an arm around her. Her back pressed firmly against his hard chest. His arms wrapped around her. His mouth lingered a bare few inches from her ear. He took her hands in his and placed them on the levers between his legs. *Dear Lord, her hands were between his legs!* "This is how to control the machine. . . ."

She tried to concentrate on his words.

". . . use this lever to . . ."

Did his heart beat against her or was that just the tremble of the vehicle?

". . . the turning mechanism . . ."

Did his skin seem unusually hot, or was that just the warmth of the motor?

". . . to the right shift . . ."

Did his lips brush her ear, or was that just the wind in her hair?

". . . now it's all yours."

Without warning, his hands left hers and she searched her mind frantically. What did he say? Something about one lever doing this and another doing that? What on earth was she supposed to do? Why hadn't she paid attention? What was it he had done? Pushed this lever that way?

She pulled a deep breath, closed her eyes and pushed the center tiller.

At once the motorized beast swerved sharply, plunged off the road and careened wildly down the hillside that no longer seemed a placid slope but a precipitous mountain.

"What are you doing?" Jared yelled and struggled to regain control of the unchecked vehicle. "Let me get—"

With a jolt that cracked her teeth together, the machine hit a hole or a rock or something unknown and they were airborne. Seconds stretched to eternity, and Cece muttered a silent prayer, vowing to curb her impulsive tendencies and learn to embroider like Emily if only given a second chance.

The vehicle landed hard and bounced once, then again. Cece held on for dear life, one hand gripping the carriage seat. Instinctively she reached for Jared with the other and grabbed—nothing.

He was gone.

"Jared!" She screamed and twisted on the seat until she knelt facing back the way they'd come. Her panicked gaze searched the hillside and finally found Jared running after her. His lips moved, but she couldn't hear a word.

"What?" No doubt her call was effort wasted. Surely he could hear her no better than she could hear him.

Her only hope lay in mastering the controls of this renegade beast. She swiveled forward and stared at the meager display of levers and not much else. How had Jared worked this thing? Should she try this? Or that? She had to do something. It was not as if she could make things much worse.

Cece glanced up and stared in frightened fascination. Directly before her loomed a boulder. Small as boulders went, she was still fairly certain it could devastate the carriage and anything or anyone in it. Decisively, she reached forward, grabbed the right lever with one hand, the left with the other, gritted her teeth, closed her eyes once again and pushed.

Perhaps it was her actions, perhaps she indeed hit the oncoming rock; whatever the case, the runaway vehicle groaned and shuddered and jerked. Her hands were ripped from the levers and she flew through the air for a long, endless moment.

With an icy splash she landed, sank hard beneath the water, smacked the bottom with her posterior and bounced back to the surface. She pulled herself to her feet, drenched and gasping for breath, grateful the pond was barely waist deep.

"Are you injured?" Jared splashed through the water to reach her, a hint of fear shading his eyes, an oddly strained tone in his voice. On the side of the slope, Quentin ran toward them, Emily laboring to keep up.

"Only my pride," she said, pulling the askew goggles off her dripping, sodden hair and peering sheepishly at him. There was a look of fierce panic on his face she found out of place, and she unexpectedly felt the need to reassure him as she smiled ruefully.

He seemed to breathe a sigh of relief, his obvious concern replaced by amusement. He cocked his head and surveyed her thoughtfully. "Now, who looks like a frog?"

Speechless, Cece stared for a long moment until she noted the twinkle in his eye and the smile tugging the corners of his lips. She shrugged. "I think it suits me."

He laughed and she joined him until tears ran down both their faces. He had a wonderful laugh, full of life and joy. The unexpected thought flashed through her mind: What would it be like to hear his laughter often?

He wiped his face and eyed his vehicle. Mired in mud at the edge of the pond, it tilted precariously at an odd angle. "It's extremely fortunate you swerved in time to miss that rock."

She glanced at the boulder that had assumed the proportions of the Rock of Gibraltar when she approached it at breakneck speed but did not look nearly as large or lethal from a stationary point of view. "I'd say fortunate is something of an understatement."

"Still, this is a minor disaster. I just hope when we get it out of the mud there's no serious damage." He circled the carriage. "It's my own fault, of course. I should never have let you drive. A woman behind the controls of an automobile," he shook his head, "it's just ridiculous."

Cece trudged toward the edge of the pond, wet skirts trailing in the water behind her. The smile faded from her face. "Why is that so ridiculous?"

"Why?" He stared at her as if she had just said something remarkably stupid. "Surely even you would admit women clearly have no head for things mechanical."

She clenched her teeth and forced a note of calm to her voice. "I think I would have done quite an acceptable job if you'd only instructed me properly."

He pulled his brows together in a manner stern and

annoyingly superior. "I attempted to give you complete instruction. Apparently you were not paying as much regard to my directions as you should have."

"Complete instruction? Hah!" Her voice rose in accompaniment to her growing irritation. "If you had paid as much attention to making sure I understood the workings of your infernal machine as you did to wrapping your arms around me—"

"Wrapping my arms around you?" Jared stared in obvious astonishment.

"Don't you dare bother to deny it." She waded past him with as much dignity as she could muster in the now knee-deep water. "I know a flirtation, possibly even a seduction, when I see it."

Jared's mouth dropped open. "Seduction. How can you possibly believe I would try to seduce you while traveling in a horseless carriage?"

"That's what makes it so devious." She splashed the final steps out of the pond. "It's completely unexpected."

"Women." He practically spit the word. "Women make no sense at all. And I'm beginning to suspect that's especially true for impulsive, improper American women."

"What on earth is that supposed to mean?" She smacked her hands on her hips and glared furiously. "You're trying to tell me I'm . . . I'm . . . I'm stupid because I'm American?"

Confusion shone in his eyes. "I did not say stupid. Did you hear me say stupid?"

"You didn't have to say it." She waved away his objections with an angry gesture. "It was implied."

"I didn't imply stupid. I didn't even mean stupid." He paused for a moment. "Foolish perhaps, but not stupid."

"Foolish?" Irrational, unreasonable fury swelled within her. How dare he insult her intelligence? Her gender? Her country? "Very well, Mr. Grayson, but let me tell you one thing. I'd much rather be a foolish American than a stuffy Englishman."

"Stuffy?" Bewilderment settled on his features as if she spoke a language he did not understand, and satisfaction surged through her. "Who said anything about stuffy?"

"I did." She cast him a haughty glance. "Stuffy and snobbish and straitlaced."

His eyes flashed. "I scarcely think you can accuse me of being straitlaced when you've just finished charging me with attempted seduction. It seems not being able to make up your mind is the very definition of foolish."

Cece gasped with fury. "Nonetheless I'm not foolish enough to stay here one moment longer and be insulted by an arrogant Englishman." She turned and marched up the hill.

"Arrogant?" he called after her. "At least the English have something to be arrogant about."

Quentin reached him and followed Jared's irritated gaze glaring at Cece's stalk up the hill. "I thought you liked Americans."

"Quentin," he said grimly, "as much as they may protest it, the behavior of women has nothing to do with nationality. This creature is a female first and an American second. American men are sane, rational, inventive and energetic." He raised a brow at his now grinning friend. "But women, all women, are either the most insipid, boring beings on the face of the planet or," he gazed in Cece's direction, "they are lunatics."

Quentin laughed and turned his attention to the

leaning vehicle, tossing a comment over his shoulder. "I thought the short one was quite lovely, charming and relatively sane."

Cece met Emily halfway up the hill. The infuriating woman walked with the grace of a princess. Here was a female with no lack of confidence. A woman who could, no doubt, hold her own in many, if not most, situations. A woman who could easily rule an empire. Jared narrowed his eyes thoughtfully. "Who is she?"

"I believe her name is Emily." Quentin's voice came from behind the vehicle.

"Not her," Jared said impatiently. "The other one. Cece."

"She's the daughter of an old friend of my aunt's." Quentin bent to check the carriage wheels, his words muffled, his manner vague. "Father's some kind of butcher, I believe."

Jared's mood darkened. Quentin's words brought back his own financial status and his urgent need to marry an heiress. Working with the automobile always distracted his attention from his problems and responsibilities. His heart always lightened here.

Dismally, he noted a vague disappointment at Quentin's words. It would have been interesting had Cece been an heiress. No, not interesting—irresistible. Still, the very idea of marrying Cece for her money twisted something inside him. A bare hour in her presence and he knew she deserved to be more than the mere instrument of what came perilously close to a business transaction.

He pulled his gaze from her retreating figure and turned to help Quentin right the vehicle.

"Pity," he said, and realized with a shock just how very much of a pity it was.

* * *

EMILY GREETED CECE halfway up the hill. Cece threw her an angry glance.

"Well," Emily said slowly, "I gather we'll be going on to London now."

"Don't wager on it." Cece squared her shoulders and glared straight ahead. "I'm going to Paris."

Chapter 3

"EXPLAIN to me again exactly why we've come to Paris." Emily trailed in the wake left behind by Cece's determined push through the throng.

"We're in Paris, Emily," Cece said patiently, "because Mother has always wanted to see Paris and Father always promised to take her." She scanned the crowded park in the shadow of the Eiffel Tower. "It's as simple as that."

Emily shook her head. "Nothing is ever as simple as you make it sound. Even if I believed you—and I'm quite sure I don't—that still doesn't explain why you've dragged me into the midst of this ill-mannered mob."

Armed with her effortless American smile, imposing, beribboned hat and lethal parasol, Cece worked her way through the swarm. "Why, to see the start of the race, of course."

"What race?" Emily said cautiously.

"Paris to Bordeaux and back." Cece glanced behind her as if to confirm that Emily followed and proceeded with her relentless forward progress. "Seven hundred and thirty-two miles. The article in the *Herald* said it follows an ancient Roman route. It's all terribly exciting. It's history in the making and we shall be a part of it."

Suspicion narrowed Emily's eyes. "Do Mother and Father know we're here?"

"Don't be absurd." Cece's manner was nonchalant. "They'd never allow us to come alone." Her gaze skimmed the multitude. "They think we've gone back to the Louvre."

Emily gasped. "You lied to them."

"Not quite," Cece said absently, still searching the crowd. "If you recall, we did drive past the Louvre on our way here. We simply didn't stop."

"It's the same thing," Emily said, her words colored with indignation.

"Emily"—Cece stopped forging her way through the assembly and turned toward her sister, her tone tolerant—"I am nearly twenty-one, and you are fast approaching eighteen. We are grown women. Adults. If I had told Mother and Father, they would have treated us like children and forbidden us to come. And since I would have come anyway, it seems best if they are unaware of our little venture here. They can't possibly be upset about something they know nothing about." She raised a brow. "You won't tell them, will you?"

Emily released an exasperated sigh. "Of course I won't tell. But I am getting tired of keeping all these confidences of yours. You have more plots and plans simmering in your head than Mr. Jules Verne."

Cece smiled. "What a lovely thing to say. Thank you."

"It was not meant as a compliment," Emily muttered.

"I know. Now," Cece said briskly, "let us continue to make our way through this mass of people." Cece started off and Emily struggled to catch up with her.

"What on earth are you looking for anyway?" Emily

panted with the effort to match Cece's much longer and far more determined stride.

"I just wish to get a good look at the automobiles," Cece said vaguely. They broke through the crowd into a cleared space. Automobiles were lined up in anticipation of the start of the race. Spectators and drivers and the curious milled around. "Oh, look, Emily, aren't they magnificent?"

Emily shoved through the assembly to join her sister and examined the vehicles with disdain. "They're machines, Cece. I hardly think magnificent is the appropriate word."

"Well, I think they're quite wonderful." She stepped closer and eyed the line of metallic steeds. "They certainly appear polished, don't you think? They make Mr. Grayson's vehicle look positively primitive."

"It is primitive," Emily said wryly.

"Not primitive," Cece corrected, "merely unique. Rare. What's new is always somewhat uncomfortable. It's progress, Emily. I think it's splendid." She stared at a particularly attractive vehicle, crossed her arms over her chest and tilted her head thoughtfully. "I'd wager these are more advanced than his. Look at them."

She walked along the line of automobiles, gesturing with a gloved hand. "They are obviously much more expensive than his as well. I doubt if Mr. Grayson has any money of his own at all. You know, Quentin's aunt is funding the development of their vehicle. And she's apparently never even met Mr. Grayson. She knows Quentin has a partner but isn't the least bit curious about him." She shook her head in a pitying manner. "Imagine, no curiosity."

Emily cast her sister a wary glance. "How do you know all this?"

Cece smiled. "Servants."

Emily groaned. "You've been gossiping with servants?"

"I don't consider it gossip," Cece said airily. "It wasn't merely idle chatter. My discussions were for the express purpose of soliciting information. Interviews, if you will."

"Like Nellie Bly?"

"Exactly." Cece smiled, as if pleased with her sibling for understanding.

"Ladies, what an unexpected pleasure."

The sisters turned at the interruption.

"If it isn't the arrogant Englishman." Cece's gracious manner and extended hand belied her sharp words.

"And the lovely, foolish American." Jared took her fingers in his and raised them to his lips in a charmingly romantic gesture. "I gather you suffered no ill effects from our last meeting?"

"None whatsoever." Cece favored him with a smile and a twinkle in her eye. "Have you tried to seduce anyone else in your automobile?"

Emily sucked in her breath. Jared's eyes widened in obvious astonishment. How on earth could Cece be so . . . so . . . so brazen?

"No." He pulled a watch from his waistcoat and flipped open the cover. "But the day is still young."

His comment hung in the air. Emily's gaze shifted in abject disbelief from Jared to Cece and back. Did these two have no sense of propriety? Was this duel of words some outrageous flirtation, or did they mean each other actual bodily harm?

Without warning, Cece's laughter snapped the tense moment. Jared joined her and the couple shook with mirth. Emily released a breath she hadn't realized she held.

"So, all is forgiven?" Jared said.

Cece flashed him a radiant smile. "It is indeed." She nodded toward her sister. "You remember Emily."

Jared tipped his black silk hat. "Delighted to see you again, my dear." He returned his gaze to Cece. "What brings you to Paris?"

"That's what I keep asking," Emily said under her breath. No one seemed to notice.

"Paris is one of the great cities of the world. We're simply tourists. I believe I mentioned our intention to visit when we first met. And now with all this," Cece waved at the line of automobiles, "I scarcely think anyone with the opportunity to witness such an event would pass it up."

"It is impressive." Jared surveyed the motorcars with a knowing eye. "I have noted a number of refinements Quentin and I should try to incorporate into our own design."

"Really?" Cece said curiously. "What kind of refinements?"

He studied her for a moment, as if assessing her sincerity. "I must say I find your interest surprising."

"Why?" A challenge rang in her voice.

"Well, I find most women . . . that is to say, many women . . ." An expression akin to that of a drowning man trying to reach the water's surface crossed his face. He drew a deep breath. "Women, in general, do not seem to be mechanically inclined."

"Mr. Grayson . . . Jared," Cece said coolly, "I am not like most women, many women or even women in general. I find automobiles fascinating. I firmly believe they are the wave of the future. The vehicle of the twentieth century. Now," she smiled sweetly, "we would love for you to show us some of the observations you've made here. Wouldn't we, Em?"

"We'd love it," Emily said weakly.

"Excellent." Jared grinned, as if he couldn't believe his good luck, and offered one arm to Cece and the other to Emily. Emily waved him away, but Cece linked her arm through his and the trio took off.

Jared paused before the first vehicle. "This automobile has a steering tiller operated from the rear seat. If you remember, mine has only a single seat and some of us believe . . ."

Emily smiled politely and fell back a few paces. She preferred to walk behind the couple; it was so much easier to pretend she was even mildly interested in his explanations that way. Cece might not be like most women, but Emily freely admitted she was. And she considered automobiles, and anything and everything associated with them, unbearably dull.

Emily narrowed her eyes reflectively and studied the pair in front of her. Jared's energetic tone drifted past her. Cece listened with rapt attention, occasionally posing an obviously astute question, if the look on Jared's face was any indication. The two were absorbed in discussing the intricacies of the horseless carriage.

Ever since the Exposition, Cece had been intrigued by inventions and new ideas and anything that smacked of progress. But she typically ignored the specific details of innovation. Odd that she was so engrossed in the particulars of these creations . . .

Realization struck Emily like a bolt from above and she stopped dead in her tracks. How could she have been so blind? Her brash, daring, impulsive sister, the same sister who had proclaimed her skepticism of the very existence of love, the same sister who had broken countless hearts back home, was obviously smitten with this man. There was no other rational explanation for her behavior.

Emily grudgingly admitted she could see his appeal. Certainly he was handsome and quite dashing in the morning coat he sported today, as opposed to the casual garb he'd worn on their first meeting. But far more important than appearance was the fervor and intensity he displayed when discussing his silly machine. Cece always had been drawn to passion and excitement.

Half the time Emily wished she could be more like her sister. The rest of the time she was grateful she wasn't. Emily was a firm believer in the rules and requirements of proper behavior, of doing precisely what was expected of her. Cece didn't believe in rules at all and reveled in the unexpected. No doubt it would be her undoing one day.

Perhaps this man could actually be good for her. Perhaps he could channel Cece's unbridled zest for life into his own enthusiasm for automobiles and dissuade her from her desire to be a newspaper reporter. A working woman. Emily shuddered at the thought.

A gunshot jerked her from her musings and she rushed to catch up with Cece and Jared. She pushed her way to their side amid the cheers of the crowd. The automobiles rolled down the boulevard, their occupants waving with the thrill of the start or staring solemnly at the road ahead. It took but a few minutes for the vehicles to be nothing more than a cloud of dust and a minor rumbling in the distance.

"My, that was grand." Cece's eyes shone with excitement. "Which motorcar do you think will win?"

Jared pondered the question briefly. "They have a frightfully long course. The race is as much a test of endurance as speed. I doubt it will take less than three days." His eyes narrowed in thought. "Peugeot has a good vehicle, but I'd bet on Levassor. The man is a brilliant engineer."

"Well, if we are quite finished here . . ." Emily said hopefully.

"Do you have plans for the rest of the day?" Jared said, as if he had little interest in the answer.

Cece shrugged in an equally nonchalant manner. "As I said before, we are merely tourists. I should think we shall spend the rest of the day seeing the sights."

"I would be honored to accompany you." A smile touched the corners of his lips. "I haven't been to Paris for a few years and there are some sights I would very much enjoy seeing again. Perhaps the Louvre?"

Emily shook her head. "Oh, we've already seen—" Once again Cece's elbow jabbed into her ribs.

"We've seen the palace from the street," Cece said quickly, "but we've not yet had the chance to venture inside. And Emily, especially, loves art."

Emily cast a swift glare at her sister and forced a smile to her lips. "I love art."

"It's decided then." Jared nodded sharply, turned and hailed a cab.

Cece tossed Emily a look of apology. Emily sighed to herself and tried to discover a ray of hope in the long afternoon that stretched before her.

Jared helped them both into the cab and Emily settled beside Cece. She glanced at her sister. She did not relish the idea of tagging along after Cece and Jared, although she suspected a chaperon would be an excellent idea.

A chaperon.

Abruptly, her mood brightened. The hours ahead no longer seemed quite so bleak. In fact, they could well be quite amusing. She beamed a smile at her sister. Cece's brows drew together in a curious frown. Emily chuckled to herself.

After all of Cece's convoluted plans and schemes, it was so wonderfully ironic to realize she was more than likely in love. And in this man Cece might finally have met her match.

"DARLING, ARE YOU certain it's all right to leave you alone?" Worry colored Phoebe's voice.

"It's fine, Mother," Cece called weakly from beneath the bedclothes. "I just have a headache. I didn't want to go to the opera anyway. No doubt I'll be asleep in a few moments."

"Still . . ." Phoebe said, "I hate to go without you."

"Go, Mother, really." Cece struggled to keep the impatience from her voice. "I prefer to be alone. I'm sure I'll be fine after a good night's rest."

"If you're certain . . ." Phoebe did not sound at all convinced.

"I'm sure, Mother." Would she never leave? "Now, please, I must get some sleep."

"Very well." Phoebe placed a motherly kiss on her daughter's forehead. Cece closed her eyes in a feeble gesture of suffering.

"Emily, hurry and collect the rest of your things or we shall surely be late. Your father and I will meet you in the lobby. Cece, I shall cheek on you when we return."

"Mother, please don't worry," Cece said quickly. "I'll be fine in the morning."

An indecisive pause followed her words. Finally

her mother sighed in surrender. "All right then; good night, darling."

"Good night, Mother." Cece resisted the urge to grit the words through her teeth. Phoebe's heels clicked across the floor. The door to the parlor that separated Cece and Emily's hotel room from their parents' swished open and closed. Silence fell in the bedchamber for one . . . two . . . three seconds.

"Is she gone?" Cece said cautiously.

"She's gone," Emily said. "But the real question is, what are you up to?" Cece threw back the linens and bounded out of bed. Emily's eyes narrowed warily. "I suspected as much. Where are you going?"

"Out." Cece pulled a dress from the wardrobe. "Help me get into this, please."

Emily shook her head stubbornly. "Not until you tell me what you're planning."

Cece threw her an impatient glare. "It's really none of your concern."

"Oh?" Emily's voice was deceptively casual. "Then I suppose you won't mind if I tell Mother and Father you're going out?"

"Don't be ridiculous," Cece snapped. "Of course you can't tell."

"If you expect me to keep yet another of your endless secrets," Emily smiled sweetly, "then you'll have to take me into your confidence. Otherwise . . ." The threat hovered in the room.

"I thought you were tired of keeping my secrets."

"I am. But since you are bound and determined to act the way you do, I feel someone in this family ought to know exactly what mischief you're getting into." Emily released a forebearing sigh. "And I suppose it might as well be me."

"What a wonderful sister you are." Cece grinned and stepped into a modest gown, far more suitable for daytime than evening wear. "Help me with these buttons."

Cece turned her back to her sister and Emily worked on the long row of tiny mother-of-pearl studs. "You still haven't told me where you're going. Or with whom, although I daresay I can guess."

"I'm meeting Jared. He's going to show me the sights of Paris by night." Anticipation shivered through her.

"Why are you wearing this dress? It's quite nice but definitely not for evenings. Why aren't you wearing one of the new Worth gowns?"

"Emily," Cece said patiently, "we are both agreed that Jared is not financially well off. I would hate for him to feel uncomfortable if I were to appear in a dress that cost an indecent amount of money."

"You don't want him to know about Father's wealth, do you?"

"Heavens, no."

"Why on earth not?"

"I told you; I do not want him to be ill-at-ease." Cece's tone hardened. "And even at home I have found men are more often than not as interested in a girl's dowry or inheritance as they are the girl herself. I would prefer to enjoy myself without having to worry whether he is attracted to me or to Father's money. Besides, just one of the gowns Mother has purchased would likely finance work on his automobile for months."

"There." Emily finished the last button. "It's quite scandalous, you know."

"His automobile?"

"No; you meeting him this way. Mother and Father would never approve."

"Exactly." Cece nodded. "That's precisely why—"

"I know, I know," Emily said impatiently, "I won't tell. But I honestly don't understand why you insist on going behind their backs. This man may not have a title, or a penny to his name for that matter, but he's obviously intelligent and ambitious. He seems quite passionate about that horseless carriage of his, absurd though it may be. I think he is very much like Father must have been when he was first starting out to build his business. I suspect Father would like, possibly even admire, Mr. Grayson's drive and aspirations. Why don't you just introduce him to Mother and Father?"

"Oh, I could do that, I suppose, and I probably will at some point. But for now," Cece shrugged and grinned, "I prefer to keep him to myself. It's much more fun and exciting this way. Why, I'm getting to know him—the real him—without all the rigid rules and regulations society imposes on men and women."

Emily crossed her arms over her chest and leaned against the wardrobe. "You're in love with him, aren't you?"

"In love?" Astounded, Cece stared. "I surely would not call it love. I'm intrigued by him. I find him extremely interesting. But love? Why, I don't even—"

"Don't tell me again how you don't believe in love."

" 'Love is the yoke of slavery that binds women to the servitude of men,' " Cece quoted.

Emily groaned. "Where did you come up with that?"

"I don't recall," Cece said vaguely. "I read it somewhere."

"Well, it's silly." Emily glared. "I don't see why you're so adamant about not being in love. Especially since you've never acted this way about any other man.

Why, from the moment you first met him your behavior has been even more outrageous than usual."

"In what way?" Cece's voice rang with challenge.

"First of all"—Emily ticked the points off on her fingers—"you risked your life in that infernal machine of his."

"It was simply a matter of sampling progress, nothing more," Cece said loftily.

Emily threw her a skeptical glance. "Secondly, you chased him here to Paris—"

"I did not chase him," Cece said indignantly. "I told you; we came to Paris because Mother's always wanted to."

"Forgive me, that slipped my mind." Emily's words dripped with sarcasm. "Third, you let him drag us all over the Louvre, a museum we had already spent hours at, and you hung on every boring word he said."

"I did not hang on his every word," Cece said defensively. "It's simply that I found his discussions extremely interesting and enlightening. You should have paid more attention," she said pointedly.

"Hah." Emily rolled her eyes toward the ornate plaster ceiling. "You two were so wrapped up in talking to each other, neither of you even noticed I was there."

"Of course we knew you were there." Cece pulled her brows together in an annoyed frown. Now that she thought about it, she couldn't remember Emily being along, although she must have been. "You were there, weren't you?"

"That's exactly what I mean." Emily grinned. "You're in love."

Cece stared, an uncomfortable realization growing inside her. "I have been acting odd lately, haven't I?"

"Even more so than usual." Emily's tone softened.

"I think it's delightful if you have finally found love, whether you want to admit it or not. And as tedious as I find all this horseless carriage nonsense, I can see how much you enjoy it. But you simply cannot continue the kind of disgraceful behavior in which you've been engaged."

"You're right, of course," Cece said thoughtfully. "And I won't continue." She nodded with newfound resolve. "I shall introduce him to Mother and Father. Then everything will be aboveboard and we'll see what happens."

"Excellent." Emily breathed a sigh of relief. "Shall I call Mother back?"

"Heavens, no!"

Confusion crossed Emily's face. "Why not?"

"I shall introduce Jared, but not tonight." Cece shook her head. "No, the time is not quite right."

"When?" Emily demanded.

Cece spread out her hands before her in a gesture of uncertainty. "I don't know exactly. But not until I'm certain of my feelings. I would hate to get up their hopes that I have finally found an acceptable man."

"I suppose I shall have to settle for that," Emily muttered. "But don't take too long. I am close to bursting with all the confidences you have entrusted to me."

"Thank you." Relief rang in Cece's voice. This whole idea of actually being in love was new to her. She did like Jared, of course, and he did have an odd, but not unappealing, effect on her. She needed time, not only to get to know him better, but to come to grips with whatever this unexpected emotion was he inspired in her. "You'd better go on downstairs; Mother and Father will be waiting and I'd hate for them to return looking for you."

Emily nodded and studied her sister for a moment.

"I'm going, but please be careful. You're accompanying a man, almost a stranger, at night, in Paris of all places. If you were to see anyone you know, the scandal would quite destroy Mother. And Father would more than likely destroy your young man."

"That's the delightful thing about Paris, Emily," Cece said saucily. "We don't know anyone here. The very possibility of scandal is minimal. It's an evening almost without risk, an escapade without danger. It should be great fun."

"Fun." Emily snorted in disdain. "Fun will surely get you in a great deal of trouble one day."

Cece threw her a teasing glance. "Sometimes, Emily, a great deal of trouble is the price one pays. And sometimes it's well worth it."

Emily groaned. "I doubt that. As much as I hate to say it, go ahead and have your fun tonight, but if you don't tell Mother and Father soon, I shall."

"I will tell them . . . eventually." Cece nodded solemnly. "I promise. In the meantime, I'll continue my efforts to know the fascinating Mr. Grayson better. I'd hate to stir up our parents over him unless I'm certain he's worth the trouble." She paused and widened her eyes, struck by an unexpected detail. "He should get to know me somewhat better as well. I just realized, he doesn't even know my last name."

"At this point," Emily said wryly, clasping the crystal doorknob and opening the door, "that may be for the best." She stepped out of the room and shut the door firmly behind her.

Cece stared at the closed door for a long moment, then smiled slowly to herself. Emily was no doubt right in one respect whether she knew it or not: Whatever else might happen, tonight was definitely for the best.

* * *

JARED HANDED CECE down from the landau he'd engaged for the evening. She'd brushed away his suggestion of a bite to eat or a stop at one of Paris's more
notorious nightspots, insisting instead that they simply drive the boulevards and enjoy the nighttime am-
bience of this fascinating city. Cece was all too aware
of his lack of funds and determined not to embarrass
him in any way—although she did note his fashionable attire, especially for someone with so little money,
and ignored a twinge of annoyance that she had not
dressed a bit more impressively herself.

He offered his arm and they strolled along the Pont-
Neuf, the lights from the bridge's lamps reflected in
the twinkling waters of the river.

"It's been a lovely evening, Jared." Cece sighed with
contentment.

He raised a skeptical brow. "I'll agree the company
was certainly lovely, but we did nothing save drive the
streets."

"Jared," she chided, "this is Paris—an ancient city
facing the future head on. You can almost feel the
spirit of progress in the air. Besides, it's truly beautiful.
And at night . . . why, it's almost like magic."

"You're right, it is beautiful." The words were casual
but the gaze that met hers was intense. "And very
much like magic." He paused for a moment and then
smiled, his mood again lighthearted. "I've never actually believed in magic."

"I find that difficult to accept."

He raised his brows in surprise. "Why? If I remember, you have accused me of being stuffy. I hardly
think being stuffy and a belief in magic go hand in
hand."

"Don't be silly, Jared." Cece tilted her head and cast him a teasing glance. "Anyone who believes in horseless carriages surely has a touch of magic in his soul."

He laughed, with a flash of dimpled cheek. "So you've ascertained my secret."

She nodded solemnly. "That's not all I've learned about you."

"Really?" He raised a skeptical brow. "What exactly have you discovered?"

She leaned against the stone balustrade and studied him casually. "A great deal, I think. I know you are surprisingly well versed in art. I know you are obviously quite clever with machines. You should go far." A question flashed through her mind. "What are you planning to do with your automobile?"

His expression hardened. "It's a pipe dream, Cece, nothing more."

"Tell me about it, about your dream," she said gently.

"No doubt you'll think it foolish," he warned.

"No doubt." She shrugged. "But since you have already proclaimed me a foolish American, who better than I to determine what's foolish and what isn't?"

He stared at her for a long moment, then nodded slightly, as if reaching a decision.

"Very well." Those two words sent a rush of pleasure through her heart that he would trust her enough to share the confidence of his dream.

"I wish to build not just one automobile but hundreds, eventually thousands. I'm firmly convinced motorcars are the vehicles of the future." His eyes glowed with the light cast by the bridge lamps and an inner fire, a fire she'd glimpsed briefly before.

He leaned forward eagerly, and the masculine scent of bay rum enveloped her, drawing her closer to the intoxicating warmth of his body. "Once we refine our design, I see no reason why automobiles cannot be manufactured easily and at a reasonable cost. Mass production would make them accessible and affordable for the public." His voice rang with his vision, strong and determined and . . . irresistible, much like the man himself. "I should like to see an automobile in front of every manor house and cottage in England."

"I don't think that's foolish at all," she said staunchly. "I think it's admirable for a man to have ambition. To strive for success in a venture untried before. To want to make his presence known in the world. I find it deplorable that many men these days seem to feel the way to make their fortune is to marry a girl who already has one."

A startled expression darkened his handsome features. "You do?"

"Indeed." She nodded firmly. "Far too many men seem to want nothing more from marriage than a sizable dowry and the prospects for a significant inheritance."

"Perhaps they have no other choice," he murmured.

"Stuff and nonsense." Indignation rang in her voice. "I see absolutely no reason why a man should not work to get ahead in this life." She paused to consider her next words, then recklessly plunged onward. "Or a woman either, for that matter."

"Women? Work?" His startled expression intensified.

"Oh dear, now I've shocked you," she said.

"I'm beginning to believe nothing you say could shock me," Jared said wryly. "Please, do continue."

"It simply makes sense." Enthusiasm colored her words. "Women are every bit as good as men." She hesitated at the look of doubt on his face. "Not physically, of course, but intellectually. Why, your own country has been ruled by a woman for nearly sixty years now."

"I can't argue with that. But why on earth would a woman want to work? Isn't marriage and motherhood the dream of every female?"

She sighed at this strictly masculine interpretation of life. "Not every female. Most have no other options."

"Why aren't you married?"

The unexpected change of subject caught her by surprise and she shrugged. "I've simply never met anyone I wished to be shackled to for the rest of my life." *Not, perhaps, until now.*

"Shackled?" He laughed.

"Yes, shackled," she said, a resolute tone in her voice.

"I doubt your parents are in agreement with you on that topic." His eyes narrowed suspiciously, and she resisted the temptation to reach out her hand to smooth the wary expression from his face. "That reminds me: Do your parents know where you are?"

"I certainly hope not." Cece shook her head. "Mother would no doubt have some sort of apoplectic fit and Father would surely shoot you or worse." She grinned. "I discovered long ago that they are ever so much happier when they're not informed of my activities."

Jared groaned. "Bloody hell, Cece. You've gone out, at night, to meet a man who's practically a stranger." His forehead furrowed in a forbidding frown. "A stranger, I might add, who doesn't even know your surname."

"Jared, there's more than enough time for mundane details at some later point. Besides," she said primly, "we still have not been properly introduced."

"Properly introduced?" He gazed at her in astonishment. "I believe my original assessment of you was accurate. Even you must realize it's extremely foolish to engage in clandestine meetings with men you barely know. Men whose primary purpose might well be to take advantage of your virtue."

"Jared." She laughed softly. "Now you're being foolish."

"Foolish," he sputtered.

"Yes, indeed." She nodded vigorously. "You see, I already know one more thing about you that I've failed to mention. You are undoubtedly a man of honor."

"A man of honor?" He repeated her words as if he couldn't quite grasp their meaning.

She sighed patiently. Evidently, he was going to need a bit more of an explanation. "A man of honor would never take advantage of me. Although I am obviously intelligent, and noticeably self-assured, it is also painfully apparent that in the ways of men and women I am an innocent."

"An innocent." His voice was little more than a strangled gasp.

"I've shocked you again, haven't I?"

"My dear woman," Jared said slowly, "I believe we have gone past simple shock and into the realm of sheer astonishment."

"Do you need to sit down?" she said anxiously.

"No." He pulled a deep breath. "I'm quite all right. But tell me, how can you be so sure that I am an honorable man?"

"I have always been an excellent judge of character," she said confidently. *And I do know you, Jared Grayson. You may well be my destiny.*

"Do you have any idea what could happen to you

if you were wrong?" His eyes glittered in the lamp-light. "If I were the kind of man to take advantage of an innocent?"

"I can imagine," she said quickly. *I can more than imagine.*

"Can you? Can you imagine such a rogue would first put his arms around you, like this?" Jared wrapped his arms around her and pulled her to him. Her heart thudded in her chest at the unexpected contact. She hadn't fully realized how much taller he was than she, or the hard, muscled strength belied by the gentleness of his embrace. "He would hold you close and claim he was merely providing needed warmth in the chilling breeze."

"I don't feel any breeze," she said faintly.

"Ah, that's part of his diabolical plan. Next he would no doubt fill your head with pretty phrases." He gazed at her with an intensity that sparked a shiver in her blood. "He would tell you your hair catches the star-light and puts even the splendor of the moon to shame. He would compare your face to the finest marble sculp-ture in the Louvre, eclipsing the beauty of the works of Michelangelo himself. And your eyes . . ."

"My eyes," she sighed.

His voice was as deep with meaning as his words. "He would say your eyes are like molten pools of mid-night. So deep and dark and inviting that a man could forfeit his very soul and be grateful for the loss."

"He would say that?" Caught in the spell of his words, his touch, his gaze, her voice was little more than a whisper.

Jared nodded gravely. "He would. And then he would bend his lips to yours." His lips brushed against hers and her breath stopped. "Lightly at first." His lips, firm and warm with promise, met hers again, and she fought to keep from sagging against him. "And then, perhaps, he would kiss you fully and thoroughly until you knew you'd been well and truly kissed."

"The fiend," she breathed.

"Indeed," he said softly, and his lips claimed hers.

The touch of his mouth was scarcely more than gossamer on the night air, and she marveled at the excitement it triggered within her. The pressure of his lips increased and she swayed toward him, an unknown need urging her closer. Her lips opened beneath his, and their breath met and merged. It was as if the world ground to a stop. As if nothing else mattered now and always. As if her very core dissolved to a puddle of aching heat and forbidden desire.

It was not as if she had never kissed a man before. But if this was what love did to a simple kiss . . . She snaked her arms around his neck, tunneled her fingers through the hair that curled over his collar and pulled him tighter.

She tasted vaguely of honey and spice and the sweetness of life itself. His blood pounded in his ears and he wanted nothing more than to mark her as his forever. She was light and laughter and unimagined fire, and he throbbed with unquenched need.

He had, of course, kissed other women before her. Dozens. Even hundreds. A few quite innocent, but most significantly more experienced than she. But never had he known the sheer exhilaration and insistent demand for something far beyond a taste, a tantalizing glimpse, a mere suggestion of a passion he had not dared to dream could exist. What on earth had she done to him?

He pulled away, and even a vague disappointment

failed to fully penetrate the haze of mysterious emotions that shrouded her.

Jared stared down at her, a somewhat bemused smile on his lips. "I think perhaps we have seen enough of Paris for one night." He released her, turned and hailed a passing cab.

"It was a delightful evening, Jared," she said softly. "Beautiful. Almost . . . like magic."

He handed her into the cab. "You were right, I think. I believe in magic far more than I ever suspected." He hesitated, an odd, haunted look flashing across his eyes, his tone abruptly serious. "May I see you again tomorrow?"

She tilted her head and smiled. "I have not yet seen the city from the top of the Eiffel Tower. Perhaps we could meet there? Late morning?"

He nodded sharply, closed the cab door and signaled to the driver.

Cece leaned back against the worn leather seat and savored a sense of anticipation. Tomorrow, perhaps, he would tell her of his feelings for her. She hadn't the least doubt his emotions were as deep and intense as her own. One could not possibly share a kiss like that without feeling something far greater than mere lust.

He was unlike anyone she'd ever met. She didn't doubt he would one day achieve his dream. She could see his commitment in the deep blue of his eyes, touch his strength of purpose in the power of his arms around her and hear the fervor of his dedication in every word he spoke. This was a man one could willingly sacrifice one's own dreams for to help him achieve his. This was a man with whom to share a life. A future. A love.

She sighed with contentment and rested her head on the back of the seat. A smile from somewhere deep within her blossomed slowly on her face. She had never known sensations like this before. But then, never before had she been well and truly kissed.

JARED STRODE TOWARD the Champ de Mars, the Eiffel Tower looming before him. He spotted Cece's unmistakable figure some distance ahead and his determined step faltered, then slowed.

He pulled to a stop and studied the scene, far enough away to watch the sisters without fear of detection. Cece, tall and lithe, sported a stylish if somewhat absurd hat, and he smiled at the sight of it. She stood over her sister's seated form beside what appeared to be an artist's easel.

At once his smile faded. He clenched his jaw and fisted his hands at his sides. A leaden weight lay in the pit of his stomach. A heavy vise gripped his chest. For all he wanted to hear her voice, revel in her smile, hold her in his arms, his courage failed him.

He did not fear what he had come to tell her, although it was perhaps the most difficult thing he'd ever had to do. Now that he saw her, at most a few strides away, he suspected—no, he *knew*—that if he spoke to her face-to-face he would not be able to resist taking her in his arms. And then he would never let her go.

Jared had spent a long, sleepless night wrestling with unanswered questions of responsibility and honor and desire and, God help him, even love. With the dawn came the inescapable truth that this new and previously unknown feeling was surely love. What else could be so compelling? What else could be so painful?

Cece laughed, and even at this distance the sound

tugged at his heart, a sound resonant with energy and the sheer joy of living. This was a woman who could be more than a mere wife; this was a woman who could be a partner. His partner. A mate not simply for his life but for his soul.

Together, they could make his dreams come true. Together they could build his lone automobile into an empire. Together, they could share what would surely be as close to what he, or any other man, could ever come to paradise on this earth.

Jared didn't care if she was the daughter of a butcher or a king. And perhaps in another time, another place, love alone would be enough. Today . . . it was not.

Slowly, he withdrew an envelope from his waistcoat. He had written the note it held by the first light of day in the event he did not have the fortitude to do what he must. It was not so much a question of strength, or even courage, but rather honor. With Cece's blatant disregard of convention, enthusiastic response to his kiss, and trusting innocence, he had no doubt he could make her his, take her for his pleasure alone. But given the depressed state of the family finances, he was not free to offer her more. He could not make her his wife.

He turned, and his gaze fell on a group of small boys playing on the grass. He gestured to the oldest, a lad of about eight. "Boy?"

"Oui, monsieur?"

Quickly Jared explained the errand, pointed out Cece to the child and handed him the note and a coin. The boy grinned slyly and winked. It seemed even at this tender age a Frenchman was a Frenchman, and well versed in the little intrigues of love.

Jared sent the child on his way. He cast one last

greedy glance in Cece's direction, as if to burn her image into his mind forever, then quickly strode away.

Putting her behind him, figuratively and literally, also meant an end to his ambitions for his automobile. His own dreams were inconsequential compared to his family's need for him to marry wealth and guarantee their financial survival. There wasn't a chance in hell that the heiress he so badly needed to find and wed would understand her husband, a member of one of England's noblest families, dabbling like a common tinkerer in the development of motorcars. Not like Cece.

His resolve hardened and his step quickened. There would be no more delay in his marriage plans. Jared meant what he'd said to his mother; he would make every effort to win the next American heiress to come along, regardless of who she was or what she was like. It was past time to put away foolish dreams of automobiles and a tall, dark-eyed nymph.

If nothing else, he had been fortunate to at least taste that curious, intriguing ache artists exalted and poets wept over. Fortunate . . . or cursed? He didn't know and didn't care. Each step carried him farther from her, and he acknowledged one searing truth.

Jared Grayson, the twenty-first Earl of Graystone, would never be the same again.

"WHY DIDN'T YOU just tell them we were going to the Louvre again?" Emily gazed suspiciously at the canvas set before her.

"Don't be silly, Emily," Cece said airily. "Even Mother and Father would have questioned yet another museum jaunt." And it was imperative that she not arouse the suspicions of her parents at this point. Soon, perhaps, she would reveal everything to them. Well, not quite everything.

She had decided to tell Jared of her feelings for him. It was what a modern woman, a woman headed firmly toward the twentieth century, a woman who believed in progress, would do.

"But this . . ." Emily gestured helplessly at the artist's paraphernalia confronting her.

"This is perfect." Cece's tone rang firm. "I simply told Mother after all the masterpieces you had seen you wanted to attempt to paint yourself. To discover the artist within you. After all, you love—"

"I know, I know." Emily gritted her teeth. "I love art." She shook her head. "I still can't believe Mother accepted this farfetched story of yours about my sudden interest in smearing paint on canvas." She glared at her sister through narrowed eyes. "She didn't even ask me about it."

"I told her not to." Cece beamed smugly. "I must admit it was quite clever. I simply suggested that she not make a fuss over your artistic endeavors until you knew whether or not you had any real talent." She shrugged in a modest manner. "I told her it would embarrass you."

Emily's mouth dropped open in astonishment. "Embarrass me? What could be more embarrassing than sitting here, in front of the Eiffel Tower—and all of Paris, I might add—and attempting to paint? I don't know how to paint."

"Honestly, Em." Cece sighed in exasperation. Why couldn't the child be a bit more cooperative? And where on earth was Jared? He should have been here by now. "How difficult can it be? Lord knows, when I was incarcerated at Miss Rutherford's Finishing School

for Young Ladies they had us painting anything that
didn't move. We were forced to commit to paper for all
eternity everything from that astonishingly ugly
building to leftover fruit from the day's luncheon.
Didn't they teach you to paint?"

"Watercolors," Emily said under her breath.

"There, you see," Cece said triumphantly. "I knew it."

It was Emily's turn to sigh. "Perhaps you were unaware of this, but at Miss Rutherford's I was far better
known for spilling paint than placing it on paper."

"Oh, dear." Cece drew her brows together in a
thoughtful frown. "That could well explain Mother's
obvious astonishment when I explained your artistic
aspirations."

"No doubt," Emily said dryly.

Cece brightened. "Be that as it may, you are older
now and perhaps talent is something that can be developed even if one has no natural gift."

Emily tossed her a pointed stare. "I thought this was
simply a ruse for this morning only, so that you would
be able to meet your Mr. Grayson." Her eyes widened
with horror. "Surely you do not intend for me to continue with this cultural farce? This travesty against the
very world of art itself?"

"Only so long as is necessary. Now," she said briskly,
"why don't you begin?"

Emily turned helpless eyes to her. "How?"

"How? Well . . ." Cece surveyed the materials she'd
had the hotel concierge purchase for her. Emily had
worried needlessly. These were oil paints, not watercolors. No doubt this would be much simpler, not at all
difficult, easy as pie. And Emily needed to begin her
efforts; otherwise Cece would feel at least a twinge of
guilt when Jared arrived and she left her sister to her

own devices. She wished he would appear. It grew increasingly difficult to concentrate on something as insignificant as art when her future with the man she loved was at stake. "Here."

She selected a tube of paint and squeezed a black glob onto a small wooden palette.

"Oh, that is artistic," Emily said sarcastically.

Cece ignored her. She dabbed a brush in the rich, shiny goo and slashed several quick strokes on the canvas.

"There." Satisfaction rang in her voice. She handed the brush to Emily. "I told you it was easy."

"Easy, yes." Emily's tone was dubious. She stared at the elongated triangle. "But what is it?"

Cece gazed critically at the attempt. "Why, it's the Eiffel Tower, of course."

Emily crossed her arms over her chest. "If it is, it's leaning."

Cece tilted her head. "Not if you look at it properly."

The girls exchanged glances, and then burst into laughter.

"Mademoiselle?"

Cece turned at the unexpected interruption. A young boy, slightly grubby and more than a little impish, thrust an envelope into her hands. The child tipped his hat, grinned cheekily and skipped off.

"What was that all about?" Emily said curiously.

Cece laughed. "Probably just a fledgling art critic." She turned over the envelope. There was nothing written on it, not even her name. Odd. Who could . . . Jared.

Jared was to meet her here even now. Why would he . . . ? Her breath caught. Slowly, she ripped open the envelope, noting, in the back of her mind, the slight trembling of her hands.

She withdrew a single folded sheet. The vague scent of bay rum drifted up from the paper.

My dearest Cece,

I regret the formality of a note instead of speaking to you directly, but it is perhaps for the best.

Her heart fell.

I have been remiss in not informing you of certain responsibilities and duties that weigh heavily in my life. Obligations I dare not ignore.

Her throat tightened.

You accused me of being an honorable man, and for the first time in my life it is a claim I regret. Honor demands truth, and truth dictates that I inform you that I can never offer you the future you so richly deserve. Therefore, our association is at an end.

Pain stabbed through her.

You will remain in my heart forever.

Jared.

She stared mutely at the words before her, then instinctively crushed the note in her hand.

Emily's brows furrowed in concern. "What is it?"

"Nothing." Cece struggled to keep her voice level, fought the hysterical desire to weep, to vent the ache that threatened to overwhelm her. "It appears my plans have changed."

Instant understanding shone in Emily's eyes. "Oh dear," she murmured.

Cece blinked back insistent tears and forced a light tone, as if she hadn't a care in the world, as if her soul had not shattered. "It's quite unimportant. Nothing to worry about. Now," she adopted her best businesslike manner, "why don't you see if you can capture some of those lovely blossoms on canvas?"

"But—"

"No, Em, it's fine," Cece said with a firmness that belied the growing misery within her.

Emily cast her an appraising glance, tinged with sympathy, then silently turned back to her work. Cece watched her dab paint on canvas and the sisters fell silent for long moments. Cece murmured an occasional appreciative comment, but her mind was far from artistic pursuits.

Never before had she lost her heart to a man. Never before had she even considered sacrificing her own dreams to support and encourage those of a man. Never before had she suspected the existence of pain like this.

How could he? How could he callously toss her aside after they'd shared their thoughts, their hopes, their desires in life? And beyond that, how could she have been so completely wrong to believe, even for an instant, that he shared her feelings?

Jared. His very name burned somewhere deep in the core of her being with a fiery ache.

If this was the price one paid for love, she wanted no part of it. She squared her shoulders in an unconscious gesture and determination flowed into her. She would pursue her own desires of the independent life of a journalist. But first they would return to London, where she would do everything in her power to entice and conquer Marybeth's earl in a duel of hearts.

For a moment she almost pitied the man. He had no idea that an obstinate American was about to storm the castles of his life. No idea of the fury triggered by his arrogance to one woman and the arrogance of a fellow countryman to another. No idea he was the object of a complete stranger's unrelenting ire.

It was no longer a question of British snobbery

toward Americans, nor even of her disdain for men who married for money. No, now it was a crusade for any woman who had ever been duped in the name of love, for every tear wept and every heart broken. She would make an example of the earl he would not soon forget.

Her fists tightened by her side in an instinctive acknowledgment of her resolve. Only then did she realize that Jared's crushed words were still clasped in her hand.

And in her heart.

Chapter 4

"THERE she is. She's the one I told you about." Millicent nodded at the tall, walnut-haired beauty on the opposite side of the dance floor, surrounded by an impressive throng of obvious admirers. "She's quite lovely, isn't she?"

"Indeed," Olivia said, casting a speculative glance at the young American. "And you say she's an heiress?"

"Oh my, yes." Millicent's voice rose with enthusiasm. "Her father has a substantial fortune. Built a virtual empire on beef. They call him the meatpacking king."

"She does carry herself well," Olivia murmured approvingly.

"Doesn't she, though?" Millicent sighed. "I had so hoped she and Quentin would make a match of it, but he seems far more interested in the younger sister—the girl standing beside her."

Olivia's gaze swept the smaller figure. "She's quite young for a gathering like this, isn't she?" Olivia said, a touch of disapproval in her tone.

"Not at all," Millicent said defensively. "She is nearly eighteen and quite mature for her age." She narrowed her eyes pointedly. "If I recall, there are somewhat legendary stories about another younger woman who, at approximately the same age, cut a rather wide swath through society, including balls like this one."

Olivia laughed and held up a gloved hand. "Please, don't remind me. It took a great deal of determination and hard work to erase the provocative reputation of my youth."

"You've accomplished it quite well," Millicent said mildly.

Olivia cast her a sharp glance. "One does what one must." She smiled ruefully at her friend. "It was all long ago, and talk of the past only serves notice of how very much time has gone by. For both of us."

Millicent sighed wistfully at the memory of lost youth; then, with a mental shake of her head, she returned firmly to the here and now. "At any rate, her mother, Phoebe, has decided she can make her official debut next month here in London, so the girl was permitted to attend tonight. I am planning the event; a grand ball, I should think. Something wonderfully spectacular."

She leaned toward Olivia in a confidential manner. "I haven't hosted a party like this in years. It should be great fun. Phoebe is, by the way, one of my oldest friends."

Olivia's attention returned to the elder girl. "Well, her daughters definitely do her credit. The tall one; what is her name?"

"Cecily. Cecily Gwendolyn White."

Olivia nodded in appreciation. "Very nice." She studied Cece for a long moment. "She certainly appears quite composed. Not at all intimidated by this rather illustrious gathering. She does not strike me as having that flighty exuberance of so many young Americans."

"No, not at all," Millicent said thoughtfully. It did seem extremely odd. Cece's behavior since they'd returned from Paris last week had been quite restrained, nothing at all like the young woman who'd originally sailed into her breakfast room in eager pursuit of follies. Cece was now extremely subdued, preoccupied and positively listless.

Emily, on the other hand, seemed to have undergone a transformation quite as dramatic as her sister's. She was far more animated, enthusiastic, even downright chatty than before their trip. Millicent wondered if perhaps Emily's behavior was an attempt to distract the older girl from whatever it was that seemed to prey so heavily on her mind.

Millicent had, of course, mentioned her observations to Phoebe. But her friend had just shrugged helplessly and explained that she had long ago abandoned trying to understand the children she had given birth to. Either of them.

Phoebe's behavior, as well, had been a bit unusual. She seemed somewhat pensive and reserved, as if here in England, memories buried in the past were abruptly fresh and vivid. Millicent was not surprised. Returning to the scene of emotional turmoil, no matter how long ago, would surely give anyone pause.

It was not as if Phoebe and Henry were unhappy with each other. On the contrary, the private glances exchanged between the two were more than enough to make Millicent sigh with envy.

"I believe Jared should meet her," Olivia said, steely determination underlying the offhand tone of her voice.

Millicent brightened. An interesting suitor might be just what Cece needed to shake her out of her doldrums. "A wonderful suggestion. Although," she paused thoughtfully, "now that you mention it, Emily had asked if he would be here tonight."

Olivia raised a brow. "Really? Have they met?"

"I don't believe so." Millicent shook her head. "Emily simply asked if the Earl of Graystone frequented gatherings of this nature. Apparently a friend of Cecily's from Chicago is acquainted with him."

"Chicago?" Olivia frowned in concentration. "Of course; I remember now. The buxom blonde with the annoying giggle."

"I gather she did not meet with your approval?" Millicent said dryly.

Olivia shrugged. "She would not have been a good match for Jared. But this one . . ." Her considering gaze returned to Cece, and Millicent's followed.

Cece did meet Olivia's prime requirement for a daughter-in-law: a sizable inheritance. In that need, the Grayson family was not alone these days. Millicent was more than grateful that the economic conditions that left so many of England's venerated families tottering on the brink of financial disaster had not touched the fortune amassed by her late husband.

But for Olivia to seriously consider Cece as a wife for Jared was to pursue more than a mere heiress; it was to court disaster. Once the child snapped out of the strange mood she'd been in, Olivia would surely consider her anything but suitable.

"You will introduce them for me, won't you?"

"I should like nothing better." Millicent suppressed an impudent grin. She'd been friends with Olivia for years, and even though she loved her dearly, she could well see the other woman's flaws. Prominent among them was a simple fact of Olivia's nature: She was something of a snob, especially where her sons were concerned.

In spite of her best efforts, Millicent's grin slipped out. If Olivia settled on Cece as the next Countess of Graystone, she would get far more than she bargained for.

And just what she deserved.

CECE SMILED POLITELY at the young men surrounding her and murmured an occasional appropriate comment. She had no idea exactly what they said and cared even less. In spite of her love of excitement and the unexpected, Cece White was nothing if not well trained.

Under other circumstances the glittering ballroom, handsome, formally attired gentlemen and beautifully gowned ladies would have captured her wholehearted attention and full-fledged participation. She would have sparkled with enthusiasm, flirted outrageously, danced every dance. Tonight, however, she couldn't muster the minimal energy demanded for even the tiniest bit of fun.

She glanced around the crowded room and sighed silently to herself. Even Emily's information that the Earl of Graystone would attend the gathering tonight failed to lift her spirits. While initially she'd directed every bit of rage, every morsel of fury triggered by Jared's defection at the unsuspecting earl, her desire to wreak her revenge on him had vanished. It simply wasn't worth the effort. Even her ambition to follow in the footsteps of Nellie Bly had lost its appeal. All she seemed to want to do these days was sleep. And, when finally alone, in the privacy of her own bed, to weep.

The gentleman next to her proclaimed some bit of wisdom that the others of the group decreed humorous and she laughed lightly. What on earth had he said? Recent days were reminiscent of the time when she was twelve and had been thrown from a horse. The pain in her head had fogged her waking hours and turned sleep into a welcome escape to the nothingness of oblivion. The only real difference between then and now was that the pain today was not in her head but in her heart.

"You are not having the least bit of fun, are you?" Emily frowned by her side and drew Cece a step away from those around them.

"You've always claimed that I have far too much fun," Cece said, faintly amused by her sister's concern.

Emily sighed. "I know, but it appears I was wrong." Her eyes clouded with worry. "It seems I like you a great deal more when you are the rash, high-spirited sister who uses me to disguise your own highly improper pursuits." She shrugged. "At least I know to expect that virtually the unlikeliest things can happen with you. Now . . ."

"It's sweet of you to worry, but I'm fine," Cece said gently, and for a fleeting moment wondered if she would ever be really fine again.

Emily shook her head and cast her glance around the ballroom. Abruptly, she gasped, and Cece looked at her with mild surprise. "Whatever is the matter?"

Emily directed eyes wide with shock toward her sister. "Cece . . . I think you'd . . . or rather . . . perhaps it would be best if . . ."

Confusion pulled Cece's brows together. "What are you babbling about?"

"Dear girl, I'd like you to meet someone." Lady Millicent tapped briskly on her shoulder. Cece composed a pleasant smile and gracefully turned to face her mother's friend. A tall figure shadowed the older woman's back. "Cece, this is the Earl of Graystone." The shadow stepped forward.

Cece's heart stilled. Her breath caught in her throat. Her hands trembled. Her knees threatened to collapse.

"Jared Grayson, this is Cecily Gwendolyn White." Lady Millicent smiled encouragingly.

Cece stared, unable—unwilling—to believe her eyes. It was as if the room had faded into a dim, vague blur. As if nothing existed on the face of the earth but the two of them. As if they were isolated in a world all their own. He returned her stare, apparently as dumbfounded as she.

Jared Grayson.

The Earl of Graystone.

She pulled a deep, steadying breath. "You!" she said, in a voice barely audible.

A myriad of emotions flashed through the dark blue of his eyes. Shock. Disbelief. Acknowledgment. His eyes narrowed.

"Miss White," he said, his manner composed, his tone cool.

Surely he was not going to pretend they were strangers? Apparently he was. The ache she'd lived with since Paris abruptly blossomed to sheer, unadulterated fury. She grit her teeth and lifted her chin a notch. Two could play this ridiculous game. For the first time in nearly two weeks, she welcomed the challenge.

She extended her hand. "Your . . . lordship."

His eyes snapped at the subtle sarcasm implicit in her tone, and satisfaction surged through her blood. He grasped her hand and lifted it to his lips, his gaze never leaving hers. "Have you been in London long, Miss White?"

Even now she steeled herself against the warmth of his hand, a heat that seemed to burn through her glove and sear into her very soul. It took every ounce of will-power she possessed to resist the desire to snatch her hand away. Instead she pulled back smoothly, as if contact with the man did not threaten to break her defenses, as if she cared nothing for him, as if he were indeed a stranger.

She shrugged nonchalantly and kept her voice controlled, reserved, aloof. "We've been back in London about a week. We were in Paris before that. Do you know Paris, Mr.—pardon me—your . . . lordship?" she said sweetly, favoring him with a pleasant smile.

"I am well acquainted with the city." A muscle jerked subtly in his jaw, just above the point where his teeth were obviously tightly clenched, and she brightened her smile at the sight.

"Are you?" She kept her tone light, insignificant. This was no more than strangers discussing a mutual interest. "While there, we were fortunate to watch the start of a wonderful automobile race. Are you familiar with automobiles, your . . . lordship?"

His navy eyes stormed, that intriguing muscle ticked again, but his voice was politely noncommittal. "I have seen one or two."

"Really? How interesting." What a lying cad! She could almost understand why he wouldn't acknowledge knowing her—their meetings had been substantially less than proper—but why wouldn't he admit his familiarity with automobiles? Unless . . . realization struck her abruptly, and a smug sense of power flooded through her. He obviously didn't want anyone to know the Earl of Graystone tinkered with horseless carriages. "Well, I find them fascinating, don't you?"

His voice was strangled, as if he could barely choke out the words. "They are, no doubt, intriguing."

"No doubt," she said blithely. "But what I found equally alluring was the place itself: Paris. A truly marvelous city. Of course I did not get to see as much of it as I would have liked." If she were a cat toying with a wounded bird, this would, no doubt, be the moment to go in for the kill. "For example, I was quite prepared to go to the top of the Eiffel Tower when suddenly my plans changed and I—"

"Miss White," he said sharply, through a tight smile, "would you care to dance?"

"Dance?" she said, as though she'd never heard the word before.

"Dance with him, Cece," Emily said in a strained voice.

"Do dance with him, dear," Millicent urged, although the puzzled expression on her face indicated that she was more than a little confused by the odd turn her introduction appeared to have taken.

"I suppose now that we've been properly introduced . . ." It was all she could do to keep the formal tone in her voice and not spit the words at him. He nodded crisply and led her to the dance floor to the opening strains of a waltz.

For a long, silent moment neither spoke. They whirled about the floor with an effortless ease, as though they belonged in each other's arms. Cece pushed the traitorous thought firmly out of her mind.

She mustered her most charming expression. "I would suggest you practice that smile somewhat, your . . . lordship. And try to look as if you were enjoying this first dance with a virtual stranger."

"We must speak," Jared said tersely.

"Must we?" She snapped the words through clenched teeth. "Why don't we just write each other notes? Long enough to get one's point across, but far too short to explain anything beyond the nebulous claims of responsibility and duty."

"I can explain," he said firmly.

"Hah!" She glared at him scornfully. "As you explained how to operate your automobile?"

His eyes smoldered, and for a moment she feared she'd pushed him too far, but only for a moment. They danced to the opposite corner of the room, and abruptly he marched her off the floor and out French doors onto a flagstone terrace.

"Why did you drag me out here?" She clamped her hands on her hips and shot him a scathing glance.

"I said before, we have to talk." His words came short and clipped.

"You lied to me," she said, her voice rising.

"I most certainly did not."

She pointed a gloved finger straight at his heart, as though taking aim. "I thought you were a penniless inventor." Her voice rang with accusation.

"And I was under the impression you were a butcher's daughter." His tone was as indignant as hers.

She gasped. "I never told you my father was a butcher."

"Quentin did." His eyes narrowed suspiciously. "What made you think I was a penniless inventor?"

"It wasn't difficult. You certainly made it appear that way. Quentin's aunt is paying most of the cost of developing that machine of yours." She eyed him disdainfully. "None of these people know about your automobile, do they?"

"They do not," he said stiffly.

"Of course not." She shook her head in disgust. "No one in this stuffy British society would accept your tinkering with motorcars. Oh, they would no doubt consider it amusing for you to purchase one someday, or even encourage a discreet investment." She cast him a pitying look. "In my country, men who dream and have the courage to go after those dreams are respected and admired."

He clenched his fists by his sides. "This is not your country."

"To my regret." She jerked her chin high, swiveled to return to the ballroom, then abruptly turned back. "You broke my heart."

The accusation hung in the night air.

Jared spread his hands helplessly before him. Pain glittered in his eyes, and she steeled herself to its effect on her. His voice was quiet and she nearly melted at the sincerity that rang through the deep tones. "No more than giving you up broke my own."

She struggled to keep her voice under control. "You wrote that I would remain in your heart forever. Did you mean it?"

He nodded. "I never said it before to anyone. I love you, Cece."

She swallowed the sudden lump in her throat. "I love you too."

Their gazes locked, as if the acknowledgment of their true feelings was far too fragile to bear anything more than the most cautious of movement. Then, at once, she was in his arms.

His lips crushed hers with a passion born of pain and a need spurred by denial. The heat of his body radiated through her, his scent clouded her mind and the strength of his embrace nearly undid her. Joy surged in her blood. He pulled away and she gasped softly. "Oh Jared, I have missed you terribly."

"And I, you." He held her tightly and her heart beat against his.

The pure bliss of being in his embrace filled her, and for a moment she could do nothing but revel in the exquisite sensation. She could go on like this forever. But first . . . "Why didn't you meet me? Why did you send that note?"

He chuckled. "Fear, my love."

"Fear?"

He nodded solemnly. "I feared if I faced you, I would be unable to resist taking you in my arms. And then, no doubt, something like this would surely happen."

He bent his lips to hers and she met them eagerly. Desire rushed through her in a swell of carnal excitement and insistent demand. She pressed closer to him and he drew her tighter. Her breasts were crushed against his chest and his breath seemed to come in synchronous rhythm with her own. She wanted nothing more than to be held by him throughout eternity. Nothing more than to taste his lips on hers. Nothing more than to know the one man in all the world she'd ever loved did indeed love her back.

She pulled her lips from his with a sigh of pleasure and a touch of disappointment that in this garden, at this moment, a kiss was all they could share. She rested her head against his chest. "That would have been unforgivable."

He laughed softly. "Indeed."

They fell silent. She stood wrapped in his arms for a moment or a lifetime, content to do nothing more than absorb the warmth of his body next to hers. Cece wondered how the very same emotion that had so devastated her life now lifted her to heights of exhilaration she'd never imagined possible.

"Good Lord, Cece." Discovery rang in Jared's voice. "I just realized what this means."

She lifted her head and gazed curiously into his midnight eyes. "What *what* means?"

"The fact that you are an heiress." Excitement colored his words. "Don't you see? This means we can be married. I love you and you have money. It's perfect."

A cold hand gripped her heart and set her teeth on edge. She pulled out of his arms and eyed him cautiously. "Explain that phrase, 'it's perfect.'"

"Cece, don't be obtuse. You are an intelligent woman. Surely you understand the implications of all this."

"Perhaps," she said softly, "I simply wish to hear it in your own words."

"I need to marry an heiress; you are heir to a rather impressive fortune." With every word his enthusiasm grew, as did her outrage. "The beauty of it is, I've fallen in love with you. This shall not be the least bit distasteful after all."

He tossed her a confident glance. "I don't mind telling you, I was not looking forward to this marrying-for-money business. Every time I met a new prospect it seemed that one or the other of us was on display in a shopkeeper's window."

He shook his head and expelled a sigh of relief. "I can't tell you how much better I feel about everything now. An heiress and you in the bargain. It's bloody marvelous."

"Is it?" she said quietly.

It might have been that in the scheme of things, Jared did not know her as well as he assumed. It might have been that in his excitement he failed to notice her increasing ire. It might have been that he was simply too wrapped up in his own delight at the turn of events to note his intended heiress and potential bride growing steadily more irate.

She stepped away from him and primly folded her hands together. "Let me make quite sure I understand this as well as you seem to. First, you could not marry me when it appeared I did not have, as you so charmingly put it, an impressive fortune. Is that correct?"

Confusion crossed his face. "Well, yes, but—"

"No, please." She held up a white-gloved hand to stop him. "Allow me to continue. When you believed I was not an heiress, even though you admit you love me, it was quite all right to leave me standing at the Eiffel Tower, clutching a terse—and badly written, I might add—note, with my heart broken and my life in ruins."

"It was not badly written," he said indignantly.

"Hah!" She glared, fury building within her. "And now that you know my true financial status, all that can be swept under the nearest rug and blithely forgiven and forgotten. You expect me to leap into your arms without a second thought. You anticipate my fortune will shore up your sagging family worth." She narrowed her eyes suspiciously. "Just how broke are you, anyway?"

"We are not completely without funds," he said defensively. "We are nowhere near begging in the streets. But the estate does not bring in nearly what it once did. We are having to sell bits and pieces of our heritage; a painting here, a tapestry there, to make ends meet. There is, of course, credit, but that too has a limit. And the cost of maintaining my mother's home, my townhouse, Graystone castle—" his tone brightened—"did you know I have a castle?"

"Cold, ugly and out-of-date, no doubt," she said, contempt chilling her voice.

He threw her a puzzled frown. "Odd; I thought Americans loved castles."

"This American does not." She fairly spat the words at him.

Jared shrugged. "Well, we needn't spend much time there. The townhouse here in London is quite nice. I'm sure you'll like it."

She stared in stark disbelief. "After all this, what on earth makes you think I'll marry you?"

He gazed at her in genuine bewilderment. "You love me. And I love you. For many people that's the only basis for marriage. We happen to have an added benefit: I need money and you have it." He crossed his arms over his chest, his brows pulling together in an obvious lack of perception. "I don't see the difficulty."

How could he be so . . . so . . . so dense? Didn't the man understand anything? Couldn't he see how his whole attitude went against everything she believed in? How on earth could she be in love with a man this dim?

"The difficulty is my firm belief that a man—any man—should not marry for money. I find it disgusting and ill-bred."

"Not in my country," he said staunchly. "Here it is in the best tradition to marry for financial gain. It has been accepted, condoned, and more, encouraged in aristocratic circles for generations, hundreds of years. It's a perfectly acceptable way of propping up sagging fortunes. I can think of worse things on which to base a marriage."

"Well, no marriage of mine will be based on money," she said haughtily.

"Of course not." Relief crossed his face. "Ours will be based on love."

She glared in astonishment. "Ours will be based on nothing!"

"Nothing?" He shook his head, as if unsure of the meaning of the word.

"Nothing," she repeated coldly, "because there is not the slightest chance I will marry you for love or money. Not now, not ever."

"But I love you and you bloody well love me!" His voice rose in unrestrained irritation.

"I detest the very ground beneath your feet." She cast him a final disdainful glance and stalked toward the ballroom.

"I was right when we first met," he called after her. "I thought you were a lunatic then, and now I know the accuracy of my observation."

She stopped in her tracks, turned and glared, sparks shooting from her eyes. Her voice rang heavy with righteous indignation. Cece was nothing short of magnificent.

"I would rather be considered a lunatic than a fortune-hunting beast. And to think, I called you a man of honor." Chin high, she headed for the ballroom.

He snorted in disgust. "Honor? This has nothing to do with honor. It's about money," he said, adding under his breath, "and love."

The woman was infuriating. He had no idea why she didn't share his delight in the knowledge that all impediments to a union between them no longer existed.

He glared at her retreating figure and a slow grin spread across his face. Whether she wished it or not, eventually she would be his wife. He would have her in his life and in his bed. It no longer had anything to do with money. She'd no doubt never believe him, but the moment he saw her again he knew she was well worth whatever price he might have to pay.

Jared chuckled to himself and strode after her. Whether she was willing to acknowledge it or not, Cecily Gwendolyn White would indeed be the next Countess of Graystone and his wife forever.

If, of course, they could each survive the courtship.

CECILY SWEPT BACK into the ballroom with a touch more energy than was necessary but well within the bounds of propriety nonetheless. Jared followed a discreet few steps behind her. Olivia observed the scene with a speculative eye.

Odd, that Jared had escorted the girl to the garden after just one dance. One would have thought he was already well acquainted with the young woman, unless . . . of course—the answer was obvious. Jared had meant it when he said he would waste no time in pursuit of the next American heiress to come along. His determination to wed would also explain his unusually quiet demeanor of late. They no longer shared a household, but Olivia was still acutely attuned to her son's moods. And each time she'd seen him these past two weeks he'd been extremely reserved, melancholy, even cross.

Now, however, she could see his grin from across the room. Good; he obviously liked the girl. And so far she met Olivia's requirements. Jared's mother narrowed her eyes.

"We shall see," she said under her breath.

It was as if the next few moments happened in a dream, as if time slowed nearly to a standstill. She

watched her son approach Cecily, saw the girl swivel
to face him. Then Olivia spotted that clumsy oaf of a
son of Lady Charleton's stumble over his own overgrown feet on the dance floor. The idiot knocked into
Lord Pemberly, who in turn tottered several steps out
of the range of the dancers and into the oncoming path
of a servant: a waiter bearing a very large, very full,
crystal punch bowl.

Olivia opened her mouth to cry a warning but could
not seem to do more than stare in speechless horror.
Pemberly sprawled in the path of the waiter, who then
tripped headlong over the stout aristocrat splashing—
no, flinging—every drop of punch in the bowl on which
he still maintained a grip, over the closest innocent figure. And in a moment Cecily White stood dripping a
champagne and fruit concoction.

"My goodness," Olivia murmured, more to herself
than anyone else. "How will the child handle this?" She
hurried to the scene of the disaster.

A sticky pool puddled at Cecily's feet. Her gown,
obviously a Worth creation, was ruined. Her hair was
a shambles, her evening destroyed. Olivia reached the
girl and the crowd forming about her in time to hear
the hapless servant stammering abject apologies.

Cecily's eyes snapped, but her demeanor remained
calm, serene, even gracious. "It's quite all right. A simple accident, nothing more." She mustered a sincere
smile and directed it at the panicked waiter. "Really, I
shall dry." She cast a regretful look at the ruined dress.
"Eventually."

Olivia would have destroyed with a single glance
anyone who even suggested she had a democratic
bone in her body. And whether you chose to call it de-
mocracy or simply the responsibility of the upper

classes to set an example, Olivia never could abide anyone who dressed down servants in public.

On the mental list she carried in her head for the purpose of evaluating potential brides for her son, she placed a tiny check next to the lines marked *grace* and *deportment*. This child obviously knew how to carry herself in public. She was a young lady whose behavior one certainly would not have to worry about.

"Lady Millicent," Cecily said, apparently struggling to avoid any expression of discomfort. "If you could manage to find my parents, I should like to leave now." She shrugged ruefully. "I'm beginning to get a bit chilled."

"Miss White . . ." Jared said quickly.

Cecily turned eyes wide with disbelief toward him. "Do you wish to say anything further, your . . . lordship? This is perhaps not an appropriate moment."

Jared appeared to be conducting his own battle at stifling amusement. What on earth was the matter with the man? If he laughed at the girl she would never forgive him, and with good reason. Olivia would have to have a long chat with her son on public behavior, although she'd never noticed conduct like this before.

Jared's eyes twinkled. "I simply wished to ask if I might call on you?"

Cecily's composure remained unruffled, but the muscle around her jaw seemed to tense, as if she clenched her teeth. "I don't think that would—"

"Of course you may call on her, your lordship," the girl's younger sister said. What was her name? Oh, yes, Emily. She appeared nearly as well behaved as her sister.

"Em . . ." Cecily said under her breath.

"I think that's an excellent idea," Millicent chimed in. "Cecily and her family are staying at my home while they are here in London. Jared, you know you are welcome any time."

"I was counting on that, Lady Millicent." He lifted Millicent's hand to his lips and dropped a charming kiss there. Millicent actually seemed to blush at the attention. He turned to Cecily and reached to take her hand, then abruptly drew back, as if he thought better of the action. "I do hope you suffer no ill effects from this drenching, Miss White. Although I daresay one gets used to being soaked, don't you think?"

"I shudder at the thought, your . . . lordship." Was that a note of sarcasm in the girl's voice? Was she referring to something other than this punch fiasco? Surely not. The young people had just met. They'd not spent nearly enough time together for their words to have hidden meanings.

Cecily nodded sharply and, accompanied by her sister and Millicent, made her way to the door. Jared stared after her, a satisfied grin growing on his face. Dripping with punch or not, apparently the boy liked what he saw.

This Miss White had made a favorable first impression, but futures were built on more than one night. And more than one test. Olivia glanced from her son to Cecily's retreating figure and back. The man still had that silly smile on his face. Olivia shook her head in disbelief.

One sometimes wondered if the question should be whether a young lady was good enough for her son, or if he was good enough for her.

Chapter 5

"You told me she was a bloody butcher's daughter!" Jared paced the length of the modest library, for once refusing to be soothed by the vague scent of leather and tobacco and all things solid and male.

"I thought she was." Quentin lounged in a wing chair in the well-appointed room that had obviously seen better days and idly swirled the brandy in the snifter in his hands. "Something like that, anyway."

Jared glared at his partner. "'Something like that'? Her father has a meatpacking empire. A virtual kingdom of cattle. That's a far cry from a butcher shop on the corner."

Quentin shrugged. "I don't see what difference it makes."

"I believe the difference can be measured in millions," Jared said dryly.

"Congratulations." Quentin lifted his glass in a toast. "That solves all your problems."

"My problems are just beginning," Jared muttered.

"Really?" Quentin raised a curious brow. "I thought you needed an heiress. And you obviously like the girl."

"Like her?" He downed the last swallow of the liquor

in his glass and strode to his desk, where the decanter beckoned like an amber lighthouse. Quickly he poured a second healthy draught of the pungent spirits and pulled another long draw. The brandy burned rich and satisfying, and he reveled in the strong, hard taste of it. "I more than like her."

Quentin jerked upright and stared. "Surely you're not saying what I think you're saying?"

Jared met his friend's gaze solemnly. "Love, Quent. I am bloody in love."

"The world, as we know it, is at an end." Quentin laughed. "I never thought I would hear you utter that blasphemous word."

Jared smiled wryly. "Neither did I."

"Wait." Quentin cupped his ear with his hand. "Do you hear that?"

"What?"

"That sound." Quentin clasped his hand over his heart in an exaggerated gesture of dismay. "The sound of hearts breaking all over London. Perhaps throughout all of England itself." He slumped back in his chair and peered over the rim of his glass. "They'll be crying in their sherry when word of this gets out."

Jared snorted in derision and sank into the chair behind the mahogany desk. "I think, my friend, you overestimate my impact on the fair sex."

It was Quentin's turn to snort. "Hardly. Through the years, you've cut a rather wide swath through the ladies of this city and elsewhere. Both the sweet, young daughters of the best families as well as those, shall we say, somewhat less innocent but no less enchanting creatures of a more worldly persuasion."

Jared couldn't suppress an acknowledging grin. "I have had a good time of it."

Quentin nodded pointedly. "You clearly enjoyed being the second son with no expectations and fewer obligations."

Jared chuckled. "Ah, it was a difficult reputation to live up to, but I did my best. And, I must admit, it was not at all unpleasant. Now, however, I am the bearer of the title, with all the headaches that go along with it." He settled back in his chair and considered his friend thoughtfully. "You've never seemed particularly bothered by that position, and you're the lone son and heir of your family."

"Don't forget, old man, my father is a mere knight. There is no title involved here; all he can pass on to me is money." Quentin grinned. "Besides, we have an excellent arrangement. He expects very little from me and in return I do not sully the family name with scandal and disgrace."

"I can't help but envy you." Jared tilted his glass to his lips, as if the sheer potency of the brandy alone would dissolve his difficulties. "I now find myself charged with responsibilities I never before realized existed. Prime among them, putting this family's financial affairs back in order."

"As I said before, your problems are solved. You love the girl and she has money."

Jared shook his head slowly. "It's not that simple. When we were together in Paris—"

"Paris?" Admiration swept over Quentin's expression. "Excellent. You never told me you saw her in Paris. That's the perfect place to press your suit."

Jared stared at the brandy in his glass. "It did not end well."

Quentin studied him through narrowed eyes. "I see. That explains quite a bit. You've been extremely churlish ever since you returned. Exactly what happened?"

Jared caught the other man's apprehensive gaze and grimaced. "I'm afraid I severed our relationship." He took another pull on the liquor. "With a note."

"A note? A note is something you give a discarded mistress." Quentin shook his head in astonishment. "For a man who is practically a mechanical genius, with one of the cleverest minds it has ever been my pleasure to encounter, that sounds remarkably stupid."

"It was." Jared sighed. "But that appears to be the least of it." He smiled slightly at the thought. "She seems to have forgiven me that little error in judgment. Even admitted tonight that she loves me."

"Well, then . . ."

"Our problems go considerably beyond that." He reached for an intricately carved wooden box, flicked open the top and selected a cigar. Picking up a small knife, he deftly clipped off the end. "It seems my beloved has a deep and abiding dislike of men who marry for money."

He flipped the cigar toward his partner, and Quentin caught it with his free hand. "Then don't tell her."

Jared cast him a morose look. "She already knows."

Quentin stared in obvious amazement. "And to think I once admired your exploits with women."

"Those days are behind me." Jared selected a second cigar and rolled the cylinder between his fingers. "Cece is all I ever dared to dream of and far more than I'd hoped for. I find I desire only her, with or without her fortune." He eyed the tobacco ruefully. "I simply need to convince her of that."

"With your considerable skills"—Quentin got to his feet and ambled to the fireplace—"I shouldn't think that would be overly difficult." He thrust a long match into the blaze, then touched the flaming end to the cigar clamped between his lips. "Just do what you always do: flowers, expressions of devotion, an expensive, appropriate gift here and there."

Quentin stepped to the desk and offered his partner a light. Jared leaned forward and puffed until the cigar's tip glowed cherry red. "You know, for a man whose finances aren't what they once were, you certainly know how to live well."

"Thank you." Jared blew wobbly rings of pungent smoke and watched them drift lazily upward. "Appearances, Quent; it all comes down to appearances." He dipped the end of his cigar in his brandy and took an appreciative puff. "That and a little bit of credit. It makes all the difference. For example, I noticed in Paris several automobiles that look better than ours. Are their designs more sophisticated? Is their development more advanced? I suspect they simply seemed more impressive by virtue of their appearance."

Quentin dropped back in his chair. "That reminds me; have you noticed that no matter what kind of innovation we come up with, others seem to be no more than a step or two behind?"

Jared nodded and leaned forward, punctuating his words with his cigar and puffs of blue-gray smoke. "I've had thoughts along the same lines myself, although it's been months since I noticed anything specific. No doubt we're a bit more suspicious than is warranted. Since we are all heading in the same general direction, it's inevitable we should all come up with the same general ideas."

Quentin eyed the end of his cigar thoughtfully. "I wonder . . ."

Silence settled over the room. Jared reluctantly admitted, at least to himself, that it was inordinately difficult these days to concentrate on the automobile. He suspected he would be unable to think of much of anything but Cece until he had resolved their conflicts and finally won her over.

He shook his head slowly. "I don't think traditional methods will sway Cece. She is far too clever to fall for a few pretty phrases, and I doubt even a garden full of flowers will set this right."

Quentin rested his head on the back of the chair and puffed in a contented manner. "I like the girl. You have excellent taste."

"I do, don't I?" Jared smiled smugly.

"I've gotten to know her a bit while her family's been staying with my aunt." Quentin paused for a sip of liquor and a puff on his cigar. "She's quite unique. Very forward-thinking. Remarkably interested in progress—"

"She believes women should work," Jared said confidentially.

"No!" Quentin stared in genuine shock.

"It's true." Jared shook his head in disbelief.

Quentin frowned. "You will have to squash that idea without hesitation. As to her other qualities, aside from her rather questionable taste in hats, I find her unusually intelligent. Witty. Far too impulsive for her own good. Stubborn—"

Jared squinted through the smoky haze. "Are you listing her attributes or her character flaws?"

Quentin ignored the interruption. "What I mean is, even as she seems to spurn tradition, she appears quite well bred. She does know how to behave properly."

"Well, naturally," Jared huffed.

Quentin waved his cigar absently. "Let me put this

a different way. Take that unfortunate incident to-night. Another woman would have no doubt thrown a fit; berated the servant and probably the hostess as well. Your Cece handled it like—"

"A princess?" Jared smiled at the memory.

"Well, at least a countess," Quentin said wryly.

Jared puffed on the cigar and gazed thoughtfully at the curls of aromatic mist. "Even my mother noticed. She wants to meet Cece. I believe she was impressed by her behavior."

"My point exactly." Quentin nodded in obvious satisfaction.

"What are you trying to say?" Jared peered at his nearly empty snifter and reached for the decanter.

Quentin sighed in exasperation and pulled himself to his feet. He stepped the short distance to the desk and held out his glass. Jared obligingly refilled it. Quentin returned to his chair and settled in.

"What I am trying to say, old chap, is Cece has a certain set of values that have nothing to do with any of her beliefs about modern life." Quentin aimed his cigar like a weapon. "And therein lies your answer."

Jared stared in complete bewilderment. "I still haven't the vaguest notion of your point."

"Seduction," Quentin said in a solemn manner.

"Seduction?" Had the brandy muddled his brain? Or Quentin's?

"Seduction." Quentin nodded sagely. "It's perfect. If you seduce her, she'll have to marry you."

Jared glared at his partner in amazement. "I can't casually seduce Cece. This isn't some trollop we're talking about, some doxy off the street. This is the woman I plan to marry. The future Countess of Graystone. The mother of my children." He pulled his brows together in an annoyed frown. "The very idea is absurd. It's insane. It's—"

"It's brilliant." Quentin's grin was wicked. "Think about it for a moment. If indeed you get her in your bed, she'll be obligated to marry you. For the sake of her honor and yours."

"But I love her," Jared protested.

Quentin's eyes glinted in the lamplight. "Some people consider seduction much better when love is involved."

"Still . . ." Jared puffed thoughtfully on his cigar. Would it really be so wrong? "It's not as if I plan to abandon her."

"Not at all."

"I do intend to make her my wife," Jared said slowly.

"No question there."

"It might just work . . . but only as a last resort," Jared said firmly.

"Indeed." Quentin nodded. "A last resort."

"I must apologize, Quent. The more I consider this outrageous idea of yours, the more I agree with your original assessment." He lifted his glass in an unsteady salute. "It is indeed brilliant."

"I thought so," Quentin said modestly.

The men drifted into a companionable silence. The thought of seducing Cece was not at all unappealing. In fact, the more he pondered the idea, the more he hoped, for the first time in his life, to have to face . . .

. . . the last resort.

"HE'S A BEAST, I tell you, an absolute beast." Cece stepped out of her sodden gown and kicked the ruined garment across the room allocated to her in Lady Millicent's London mansion.

"I thought he was intriguing, interesting." Emily perched on the edge of a satin-covered chaise. "A man destined to make his mark on the world, I believe you said."

Cece glared. "He'll make his mark, all right, but he wishes to do it with Father's money." She grabbed the silk wrapper laid out on the end of the bed. "I simply cannot tolerate a man who marries for money."

"Lots of men marry for money or property or power." Emily shrugged. "History is full of marriages made to cement alliances between countries or to forge new relationships between warring parties. When you look at it that way, wedding simply for money seems positively minor, especially here in England."

"Well, it does not seem minor to me." Righteous indignation colored her words.

Emily cast her a worried frown. "I thought you loved him?"

Cece waved off the observation with a dismissive flick of her hand. "We have already established that fact."

Confusion furrowed her sister's brow. "But you won't marry him?"

"Oh, I shall marry him," Cece said lightly.

"But how—I mean—don't—" Emily's puzzled frown deepened.

"You're confused, aren't you, Em?" Cece said sympathetically. "I must admit I too am a bit perplexed." She sank down on the bed. "This business of love is most unsettling. I find myself forlorn and wretched without him, yet his presence is nothing less than maddening." She shook her head in amazement. "It defies all logic and sensibility."

"But you do plan to marry him?" Emily said cautiously.

"Of course." Cece shrugged. "I believe I should much rather be infuriated with him than miserable without him."

"I thought the whole idea behind your original scheme was to make Jared—or, rather, the Earl of Graystone—miserable?"

"That was before love entered the picture." She threw her sister a teasing grin. "I rather suspect I can do a far better job of making his life miserable as his wife than as a mere fiancée."

Emily stared, disbelief in her eyes. "Let me see if I understand all this. Even though you find this man irritating—"

"Only when it comes to this business of marrying for wealth," Cece said pointedly, "which I whole-heartedly disagree with."

Emily glared at the interruption. "Very well, I'll amend that. His reasons for marriage go against your own beliefs . . ." she quirked a questioning brow at her sister. Cece nodded for her to continue. "However, you are willing to overlook that rather significant conflict in order to spend the rest of your life with him and be . . . happily miserable. Is that correct?"

"Very good." Cece cast her sister an approving smile.

"It makes no sense whatsoever. Although . . ." Emily eyed her sister thoughtfully. "I suppose love is not supposed to make sense."

"I don't know," Cece said confidentially. "It's my first experience with love. I must say it's somewhat exciting, given the confusion and all."

"I suppose this means you'll give up that ridiculous idea of becoming another Nellie Bly," Emily said, as if her sister's answer was of no interest.

"My goodness, of course not. Whatever would make you think that?"

"Cece," Emily said with exasperation, "no man in his right mind would allow his wife to work for a living. Especially not as a journalist and certainly not a countess. It's simply not done. It would be absurd. Ridiculous. Positively scandalous."

"Why?" Cece's tone was light, and she smothered the impulse to laugh at her sister's expression. She could practically see the panic flitting through the girl's eyes in her struggle to come up with a good argument to sway her older sister.

Cece had already accepted the very real possibility that, with marriage, her dream would die. But that no longer seemed as tragic as it once would have. After all, she would have Jared, and if she'd learned nothing else about love she recognized he might well be enough to satisfy her ambitions—if, of course, she could help him achieve his goals with the automobile. The lure of the motorcar, the attraction of progress, the enticement of the modern world, was every bit as irresistible as the call of journalism. Why, she and Jared could work hand in hand to build his vision. Together, they could drive into the future on his wire-and-metal noxious-fumed steed. She would be more than a mere wife; she would be a helpmate, a partner—

"Children," Emily said triumphantly.

"What about children?"

"You cannot have children and be a journalist at the same time." Emily tossed Cece a smugly victorious smile. "Nellie Bly has no children."

"You may have a point there," Cece said slowly, resisting the desire to grin. "Children would definitely put a crimp in the life of a girl reporter. But I shall cross that bridge when, and if, I come to it. For now . . ."

"For now what?" Apprehension flickered across Emily's face. Cece sighed to herself at the expression. The poor child really needed to learn not to take everything in life quite so seriously.

"For now I need to decide how best to proceed with this courtship." Cece rose and paced the room, furrowing her brow in thought. She barely noticed her sister's anxious gaze following her every step.

"What is there to decide? You love him. You've already said you'll marry him. I don't see that there are any decisions left to make."

"Honestly, Em." Cece tossed her a pitying glance. The dear girl was so young and had so much left to learn. Cece might be new at this game of love, but she was an old hand at the ins and outs of the contest called courtship. "I simply can't fall into his arms just because he quirks his little finger and declares undying devotion. Not that he actually did," she said thoughtfully.

"Quirk his little finger?" Emily said, obviously confused once again.

"Don't be silly. He hasn't declared his undying devotion. Though he has admitted to love, so I suppose it's probably much the same thing." Cece shrugged. "At any rate, anything achieved too easily is valued too lightly. Why do you think emeralds are so terribly expensive?"

"Why, they're beautiful, of course," Emily said confidently.

"Certainly, but beyond that they're exceedingly rare. It is their uniqueness, the difficulty in obtaining them, that gives the jewels their true worth. If one could simply pluck them up off the street, they would be as trivial as pebbles." Cece shook her head. "No, Em, this match requires a great deal of sacrifice on my part. It diminishes any hopes I have of the independent life of a reporter."

Emily sighed her relief.

Cece ignored her. "It also requires my giving up my home and my country."

Emily frowned. "Your country?"

"I can't very well remain an American citizen and be a British countess at the same time. At least I don't think I can. I shall have to look into that." Cece paused to collect her thoughts. The realization of just what marriage to Jared would mean struck her abruptly. "No doubt he will expect to live here in England, rather than in Chicago."

"No doubt," Emily said dryly.

"We shall probably spend a great deal of the time at that drafty old castle of his."

"How do you know it's drafty?"

"Castles are always drafty, Em," Cece said loftily. "It's part of their charm."

Emily smirked. "It's no doubt haunted as well."

"That would be interesting, wouldn't it?" Cece brightened; then her mood fell. "I fear I cannot count on something so exciting as a spirit." Her tone was wistful. "It seems love costs a very great deal. I never even considered how high a price one would have to pay for it."

"Perhaps," Emily said gently, "because it's so rare."

Cece widened her eyes in appreciation. "How very perceptive." Her momentary twinge of doubt and self-pity vanished. "Loving Jared also requires that I overlook my conviction that a man should not profit by marriage alone. That he should have to work for his fortune. I further believe—"

Cece stopped short and stared at her sister. "Em," she said slowly, "I have an interesting idea."

Emily's eyes grew wide and an odd strangling noise came from her throat. "No, Cece, please. Not another 'interesting idea.' An 'interesting idea' is what got us here in the first place."

"And look at how delightfully this has turned out." Cece beamed at her sister. "At least it will be delightful. Eventually."

Emily threw up her hands in a gesture of surrender. "I give up. Don't keep me in suspense. Tell me the latest diabolical plot your fiendish mind has come up with. Get it over with."

"Emily," Cece chastised, "that's not fair. Fiendish and diabolical?" She cast her sister a wicked grin. "Well, perhaps just a little."

Emily groaned. "What are you planning?"

"If I truly believe a man should have to work for his fortune," Cece paused to choose the proper words, "then I see no reason why Jared should not have to work for his. Or rather, for me."

"Work?" Emily choked out the word. "What do you mean, work?"

"I'm not exactly certain." Cece narrowed her eyes, clasped her hands together and steepled her fingers. Thoughtfully, she tapped her chin with the tips of her nails. "It can't be anything too easy."

"Oh no, we wouldn't want to make this easy for him," Emily mocked.

"But it can't be too difficult either."

"Why not?"

Cece threw her an impatient glance. "Well, we wouldn't want him to give up altogether."

"So what are you planning?" Emily was plainly intrigued in spite of herself.

"It should be something near and dear to him. Something he feels strongly about. Something—" Cece's eyes widened. "Of course! That's it! It's so obvious, I can't believe I didn't see it immediately."

"What? What?" Emily said, with the frantic tone of one whose curiosity has been pushed to the limit.

The older girl sank onto the bed and beamed. "It's the perfect answer. I shall insist that he teach me to drive."

Confusion crossed Emily's face. "But you are an excellent driver. There are few other women in Chicago who can match your skill with the reins. I don't—" Emily gasped. "You're not talking about carriages, are you? You mean—"

"I do indeed." Cece nodded smugly and cast her a triumphant grin. "His automobile."

OLIVIA PUSHED OPEN the door of the third-floor nursery and cautiously stepped inside. She placed the gas lamp she carried on a small table to her right and waited a brief moment for its glow to fill every corner of the room.

Her hesitation had nothing to do with the possibility of an unexpected meeting with an errant mouse or other beast that might have made its home in the closed room. Those were distinct, real possibilities. Her wariness, her diffident manner, her doubtful first step, were a product of a far more bittersweet encounter. In this room, above all others, lived the ghosts of the past. Here, the memories of happier times with her boys assailed her with a nearly physical force.

Her gaze swept the room past the child-sized beds shrouded in linen and the long-unused playthings. Tension ebbed from her shoulders and she smiled softly. How odd to feel the least bit of apprehension here. When filled with the laughter of children this was always the nicest place in the house.

Few would have suspected the fierce love the eminently proper Countess of Graystone had for her sons. Fewer still knew of the moments stolen from disapproving governesses to play with her children or romp with them or read to them stories of fair princesses and noble knights and deadly dragons. Even her husband Charles had expressed mild disapproval over her dedication to her offspring. But then, as now, Olivia had behaved precisely as she wanted, exactly as she thought best.

She meandered slowly around the fringes of the room, stepping aside to avoid a carved wooden horse here, an insistent recollection there. Lord, they'd grown so fast. Regret stabbed her heart. Childhood had lasted such a short while. It seemed she'd barely had time to enjoy them before they'd relinquished the trappings of children altogether and moved into their own rooms downstairs and then off to school, to responsibilities, to adulthood.

With Charles's death five years ago, James had remained living here. As holder of the title, this was his rightful place. Now it was Jared's. Olivia sighed with heartfelt exasperation. She did wish he would finally return home. That unacceptable little flat of his was fine for a second son with no responsibilities, even though privately she had not been at all pleased with his choice right from the beginning, but now that he was the head of the family, he did need to be ensconced in more suitable surroundings.

Olivia trailed her fingers over dust-covered soldiers, standing in metal readiness for an order that never came. It was sad, somehow, to see these and the other toys waiting here for children who no longer existed. She shook her head in an effort to clear it of the foolish thought. Whatever possessed her to ponder such non-sensical things?

Perhaps it could be attributable to the same impulse that compelled her to visit the nursery tonight. She'd come up here once after James died. Then it was the sense that everything in her life, in her world, was in upheaval. But tonight was no different than any other night, this ball no different than any other. This company—

The thought hit Olivia like a bolt from above and she sank into a wooden rocker wedged amid shelves still burdened with the books of boyhood.

It's that girl. The American. It made perfect sense. Olivia prided herself on being an excellent judge of character. She'd had nothing to do with that incident with that poor child, but it did serve well as a first . . . test, of sorts. Very well. She had a good feeling about her. She liked the tiniest glint of steel she'd spotted in the girl's eye and the strength in her bearing. She wanted her son's wife to be more than an insipid, life-long burden. She wanted her to be a helpmate, a part-ner. Jared could, no doubt, use every bit of assistance available.

She leaned back in the rocker and narrowed her eyes thoughtfully. The child proved acceptable at a public gathering, but how would she fare in private?

And how could Olivia best evaluate this girl's suitability as a future countess?

Perhaps a house party? At Graystone Castle? That might well be the perfect setting. Olivia hadn't entertained on a large scale since before Charles died. The long-forgotten rush of excitement that accompanied planning for such an event surged through her, and newfound determination pulled her to her feet.

She cast one final glance around the nursery and wondered how long it would be before Jared's children were firmly established here. How long before she could once again steal precious time from an overprotective governess for games and stories? Her gaze fell upon the bookshelf. Without thinking, she reached for the book on the end and plucked it from its resting place.

Olivia smiled with delight. It was a long-neglected volume of tales by Hans Christian Andersen. She blew the dust off the leatherbound cover and remembered how Mr. Andersen's stories had enchanted her children and, secretly, herself. She riffled the pages and the book fell open to one of her favorites, *The Princess and the Pea*.

It struck her abruptly how very much she had in common with the prince's mother. The queen was so concerned that her son wed a true princess that she tested the applicant by placing a single pea under twenty mattresses and twenty featherbeds. In the charming tale, the princess passed the test. Olivia wondered if she'd somehow been influenced by the nearly forgotten story and, more, wondered if this American would do as well.

She snapped the book closed, replaced it on the shelf, and then paused and picked it up again, tucking it under her arm. She had much to do and little time to waste. Olivia picked up her lamp and briskly stepped out of the room, closing the door firmly behind her. She headed toward her bedchamber, her mind filled with plans and preparations. Still, she couldn't suppress a smile that bordered on the improper edge of a grin.

Olivia could scarcely blame the queen in Mr. Andersen's story for her interfering actions. After all, what mother wouldn't want the very best for her son?

Chapter 6

THE low murmur of excited voices greeted Cece on her way down the stairs. She stepped into the parlor and pulled up short.

"My goodness!" Her disparaging glance swept the room. "It looks like a flower shop in here."

"Isn't it lovely, dear?" Phoebe said, pleasure evident on her face. She and Lady Millicent stood in the center of the room, barely noticeable amid the greenery. Flowers covered every surface. Bouquets littered tabletops. Blossoms of all shapes and sizes and colors competed for attention in a display of glorious confusion. "They arrived this morning."

Emily stepped from one grouping to the next, poking among the buds in an apparently futile quest for cards. She threw her sister a disgusted glance. "And they're all for you. Every single one."

"Are they?" Cece said coolly and plucked a lone card from the nearest nosegay.

"From the Earl of Graystone, I suspect." Millicent nodded knowingly. Emily rolled her eyes toward the ceiling.

Cece glanced at the card. It bore what was obviously the Graystone crest and Jared's name, nothing more. Cece tapped the card thoughtfully with her finger. "Lady Millicent, perhaps you could explain to me—"

"I know what you're going to say, my dear." Millicent waved away the anticipated question.

Cece shook her head. "I'm afraid I simply don't understand how someone in his financial straits could afford a gesture as obviously expensive as this."

Millicent tossed her a tolerant smile. "I'm sure it's difficult to comprehend for someone of your background." She sank onto a settee nearly hidden by blooms and patted the seat beside her. "Sit down and I will attempt to explain."

Cece joined her and waited expectantly.

Millicent settled back and studied the younger woman. "You see, life is much different here than in America. When a family's name and fortune stretches through the centuries it is not uncommon for wealth to also ebb and flow with time. The earls of Graystone, just as nearly every other aristocratic family, have, through the years, had to cope periodically with economic uncertainty. But it's imperative that one still keeps up appearances. And all this—" she waved a hand airily at the fragrant array—"is no doubt provided in part because of the family's reputation, outstanding credit and excellent expectations, as well as the certain knowledge that few respectable English lords are truly penniless and down on their luck for long."

Millicent shrugged. "It's simply the way life has always been here. In America fortunes, especially these days, are more often the result of individual hard work as opposed to inheritance. You call them, I believe, self-made men. Why, your own father—" Millicent cast a questioning glance at Phoebe and received an encouraging nod in response—"built his substantial wealth himself. But here it's not unusual for a family to look toward a suitable marriage to rebuild the family coffers."

Emily tossed her sister a smug look. "That's what I said."

Millicent narrowed her eyes and pulled her brows together in a gesture of admonition. "I can see in your face, Cece, your opinion of such a match. But don't judge Jared too harshly. He is no worse than most men in this country, perhaps in the world, and far better than a great many I could name."

She leaned forward and grasped Cece's hand. "I suggest you give him a chance. You may find in spite of the fact that he needs your money, he has much to offer in return." Millicent grinned abruptly. "I could not help but notice the definite sparks between the two of you last night."

"Cece!" Phoebe gasped with delight. "Is this true? Are you already taken with this young man?"

Revealing heat rose in Cece's face. She pulled her hand from Millicent's grasp and sprang to her feet. "Of course not, Mother. How absurd. Why, we have only just met."

Emily grinned and Cece glared at her. She cast a quick glance at Lady Millicent, only to find her mother's friend smiling with a knowing air that indicated that she had few doubts about the accuracy of her observations.

A throat was cleared discreetly at the doorway.

"Milady?" Lady Millicent's butler strode to her side and offered her a small silver tray.

Millicent picked up the card it bore, glanced at it briefly and nodded. "Show her in, Frederick.

"How very interesting," Millicent murmured and rose.

"Millicent, how lovely to see you again." A small, rounded woman swept into the room like a diminutive ship in full sail.

"Olivia, I don't believe you've met my guests," Millicent said, inclining her head toward the girls and their mother.

The newcomer pulled off her gloves. "Not formally; I did notice them last night, however."

"No doubt," Millicent said under her breath. "May I present my dear friend Phoebe, Mrs. Henry White, and her daughters Miss Emily White and Miss Cecily White." A twinkle of amusement shone in her eye. "I should like to introduce you to Olivia Grayson, Lady Graystone, the mother of the Earl of Graystone."

Cece and Emily traded swift glances. It was all Cece could do to keep her expression composed, her manner controlled. So this was the ferocious dragon that had so crushed Marybeth's ambitions concerning Jared. She did not seem especially fierce. The woman was much shorter than Cece, full of figure but nowhere near plump, with a face the years had been especially kind to. Cece could well imagine a time when this woman was considered a great beauty.

"Lady Graystone, what a lovely coincidence," Phoebe said. "We were just—"

"We were just discussing what a wonderful time we all had at last night's ball," Cece cut in quickly. Somehow it seemed wiser right now not to let Jared's mother know he was responsible for turning the parlor into a greenhouse.

"Really?" Lady Graystone turned her gaze on the girl, and Cece nearly jumped with recognition. The woman's blue eyes were just a shade lighter, just a bit wider than her son's, but otherwise there was no doubt as to the family resemblance. The older woman perused Cece with an assessing glance. "I should think it ended rather badly for you, my dear."

Cece struggled not to squirm under Lady Graystone's studied inspection and forced a light tone to her voice. "Not at all. Accidents happen. One shouldn't let a minor mishap color the entire evening."

Lady Graystone nodded approvingly. "Excellent. I too firmly believe in not allowing a single incident to cast a shadow over what was otherwise quite an instructive evening."

"An instructive evening?" Phoebe said quizzically.

Lady Graystone's gaze locked with Cece's and she instinctively knew what her mother couldn't possibly understand, what Lady Millicent might well suspect, what would make Emily laugh out loud: Lady Graystone was already sizing up Cece as a prospective wife for her son. The very same way she had examined and discarded Marybeth as a potential daughter-in-law.

But Cece was not Marybeth. She, above most girls of her acquaintance, was well up to the challenge that might be issued by the protective mother of an English earl. After all, she had come to England in part to prove Americans were equal to, if not better than, the British. And the stakes of this enterprise were far higher than originally anticipated. Now she played for the man she loved. This was one contest she would not lose.

Cece raised her brow the barest notch. The corners of Lady Graystone's lips twitched, as if she suppressed a quick smile. Cece wondered if anyone else in the room noticed a gauntlet had been thrown down and accepted.

"Now then," Lady Graystone said briskly, turning toward Phoebe and Millicent. "I was going to send the invitation, but I thought it would be so much more pleasant to deliver it in person."

"Invitation?" Millicent said. "Don't tell me you are finally entertaining again?"

"It does seem like a long time, doesn't it?" Lady Graystone sighed. "I simply lost all desire for hosting social events after Charles—" she glanced at Phoebe— "my husband, passed away. And then my son James died just a year ago and . . . well, I'm certain you understand."

Phoebe nodded sympathetically.

"But now," Lady Graystone continued, in a tone that indicated bravely carrying on, "there is Jared to consider. He is the Earl of Graystone, with all the responsibilities and duties the title bears. And I have been remiss in my obligations for far too long as well.

"I have decided to have a small house party next weekend. Nothing elaborate, you understand. Something simple. Perhaps a dozen or so people." She addressed Phoebe. "Will your social obligations permit a few days in the country?"

Phoebe's brows drew together in a considering frown. "I believe so. We are extremely busy with plans for Emily's coming out, but I should think a few days away from London would be a welcome respite. The pace here can be so exhausting."

"Indeed." Lady Graystone nodded her agreement. "I believe you will enjoy Graystone Castle. It has a fascinating history and has been the family seat of the Graysons for centuries."

"I have always heard that castles are cold and drafty," Emily said innocently. Cece threw her a warning glare.

Lady Graystone laughed. "Why, my dear child, that's virtually the definition of a castle. Even so, they are far more comfortable today than hundreds of years ago. We do try to keep up with the times, particularly in our own homes. And whatever else it may be, Graystone Castle is home." She leaned toward Emily in a confidential manner. "Although we have noticed the various ghosts inhabiting the place don't seem at all happy about improvements that have been made through the years."

Obvious concern stamped Emily's face, and even Cece was taken aback until she noted the teasing light in Lady Graystone's eyes.

Lady Graystone turned to Millicent. "Naturally you and Quentin are invited to stay at the castle as well."

Millicent shook her head. "Oh my, no. My estate is but a short ride from yours, so we shall stay there. I cannot abide the thought of trekking to the country to stay in someone else's home when I can enjoy the comforts of my own with a minimal amount of difficulty. However, I assure you, we shall be present every day, for every entertainment."

"That will do, then." Lady Graystone moved toward the door. "I have a great number of errands to accomplish today. I shall send a servant around with further details on precisely what is planned for the weekend and look forward to seeing you all then." Her gaze swept the gathering, lingering a fraction of a second longer on Cece than on the others.

"Lovely flowers, my dear," she said softly.

"Allow me to accompany you to the door," Millicent said, stepping to the other woman's side. The two moved away and Cece barely heard Millicent's faint words: "Olivia, what on earth are you up to?"

Cece strained to catch more, but the voices trailed off. Still, she didn't need to hear the answer to Lady Millicent's inquiry. Cece was certain she already understood all too well exactly what Lady Graystone was up to.

LADY GRAYSTONE WAS not the only one to drop in unexpectedly. Through much of the afternoon a steady flow of visitors arrived, discreetly curious about Lady Millicent's American guests. Not a small number were young men eager to further their acquaintance with Cece and Emily, to the younger girl's obvious satisfaction. With each new male caller the floral display in the room grew, until Cece wondered wryly if the scent of flowers alone was enough to cause true suffocation, or at least a permanent ache in the back of her head.

The last admirer finally bid his farewell and Cece collapsed onto the settee with a weary sigh. She rubbed the throbbing point at the back of her neck and closed her eyes. "Goodness, Lady Millicent, do you face this constant stream of visitors every day?"

"Dear me, no." Millicent chuckled. "It seems you and your sister have made quite an impression."

Emily plopped onto the sofa beside her sister. Cece opened her eyes and slanted her a disgusted glance. Emily grinned in triumph. "We have, haven't we? I find it all extremely exciting."

"I find it exhausting," Cece muttered.

A concerned frown furrowed Phoebe's brow. "Are you quite all right, darling? It's not at all like you to be so fatigued by a simple afternoon of calls."

"It's not who came." Emily smirked. "It's who didn't."

"I'm fine, Mother." Cece glared at the younger girl, who knew her sister far too well for comfort. Most annoying of all was the simple fact that Emily was right.

With each new arrival Cece had expected to hear Jared's voice, see his tall, broad-shouldered figure, lose herself in the blue depths of his eyes. Disappointment stabbed her time and again through the interminably long day. It was all she could do to force herself to offer appropriately pleasant comments and idle chatter to young men whose names were forgotten a moment after their introduction.

Frederick entered the room, stepped to Lady Millicent's side and spoke softly into her ear. She glanced quickly at Cece and nodded to the butler. "It appears our list of guests is not yet complete."

"Lady Millicent." Jared's voice sounded from the doorway. Cece jerked upright on the sofa, weariness and aching head abruptly forgotten. She composed a pleasant smile on her face and folded her hands in her lap, hopefully presenting the perfect picture of serene disinterest. Only she could hear the thud of her heart in her chest at his approach.

"I hope you don't mind my unannounced visit." Jared strode to Lady Millicent, lifted her hand and brushed his lips against the back. Millicent favored him with an amused smile. "I found I was nearby and couldn't resist the impulse."

"My dear boy, you are welcome anytime." Millicent nodded toward Phoebe. "I don't believe you have met my friend and guest, Mrs. Henry White. Phoebe, this is Jared Grayson." Millicent raised a brow at her friend. "The Earl of Graystone."

"I see," Phoebe said thoughtfully and glanced at

Cece. "I gather you are already acquainted with my daughter?"

"Acquainted?" Emily said with a short laugh, shaking her head in exaggerated disbelief.

Cece tossed her a quelling glance.

"His . . . lordship and I have indeed met," Cece said coolly. She had no intention of letting him see how his mere presence affected her. Rising to her feet, she offered her hand. "Lovely to see you again. And so soon."

Jared took her hand in his and lifted it to his lips. His gaze never left hers. "Not soon enough."

She pulled her gaze, and her hand, from his. "Perhaps, too soon."

His eyes narrowed slightly. "Perhaps." He turned to her mother. "Mrs. White, I wonder if I might have the pleasure of escorting your daughter on a ride through the park?"

"Oh dear," Phoebe said with an expression of mild dismay. "Would it be proper, Millicent?"

"I think it would be acceptable." Lady Millicent nodded. "It is well past five o'clock. The park will be full of people at this hour. It's just the place to see and be seen." She glanced pointedly at Jared. "Especially if one wants one's intentions made clear."

Phoebe shook her head. "I do wish Henry was here."

"Where is Father?" Cece realized she hadn't seen him since late morning.

"I believe he had a letter of introduction to some club or other." Phoebe frowned in annoyance. "However, the hour is growing late and I hope he returns shortly."

"London boasts some of the finest clubs for gentlemen in the world," Jared said. "No doubt he's simply enjoying himself and has lost track of time. Now then,

Miss White," his gaze pinned Cece's, offering so much more than a mere carriage ride, "would you do me the honor of accompanying me to the park?"

His tone was confident, his attitude assured, but there was the tiniest flicker of doubt in his dark eyes. Cece smiled sweetly. "In a carriage?"

His brow rose slightly. "What else?"

Hers quirked in an answering response. The man was as good at issuing challenges as his mother, although meeting Lady Graystone's would, no doubt, be the more difficult. Cece could never expose Jared's passion for invention to the world, although privately she thought his reluctance nonsensical. Still, it did no harm for him not to know that he already had won her firm loyalty.

She shrugged with false innocence. "One always likes to be certain," she said for his ears alone, then turned to Phoebe. "Mother?"

"Do have a pleasant time, dear." Phoebe smiled brightly.

The amazingly efficient Frederick stood by the door bearing Cece's hat and parasol. She accepted the ribbon and floral concoction and deftly secured it to her dark curls, ignoring Jared's barely suppressed smile of amusement. She adored hats that were just a touch outrageous and he would simply have to learn to like them as well, or at least tolerate them. Frederick handed her the parasol and Jared offered his arm. With a genuine smile she received one, with a curt nod accepted the other, and she and Jared were on their way.

A fashionable phaeton stood in the street, drawn by a perfectly matched pair of dappled grays.

"Very nice," she said, a note of appreciation in her voice. Lady Millicent was right: The British nobility definitely knew how to keep up appearances.

Jared handed her into the carriage, seated himself by her side and took up the reins. She steeled herself to pay no attention to the beckoning heat of his body next to hers, to disregard his close proximity in the intimate seating of the rig.

"What?" she chided. "No driver in full livery? I'm surprised, Jared. I should think you would think that such a gesture would surely impress an American like myself."

Jared shrugged nonchalantly. "I simply preferred not to have an eavesdropping servant along. I believe there are a few things you and I need to settle. Alone. I hardly expected you to object, given our previous encounters." He guided the horses into the flow of traffic. "Do you?"

"Not at all," she said lightly. "In fact, I quite appreciate the opportunity for a frank discussion."

"You do?" His eyes narrowed in obvious suspicion. "I must say I'm somewhat surprised by your attitude. I expected you to be—"

"Annoyed? Upset? Livid?" she said pleasantly.

"At the very least." His tone was wry. "The way we parted last night, I assumed you would refuse to see me."

"Not at all." They pulled into Hyde Park and she glanced around curiously at the crowded flow of carriages and riders on horseback promenading through the lane. "Is it always this busy here?"

Jared expertly maneuvered the carriage into the slow-moving procession and nodded politely at a passerby. "Always at this hour. Hyde Park is the place to see and be seen."

"Oh?" Realization struck her abruptly. "That's what Lady Millicent meant with her comment about making one's intentions clear."

He slanted her a meaningful glance. "I don't wish there to be any doubts as to my intentions."

She raised a brow. "And they are?"

A startled expression crossed his face. "I thought I had made that perfectly clear. I want to marry you."

She adjusted her parasol and adopted a cool tone. "I don't seem to recall you asking. Nor do I remember you speaking to my father about the matter."

"Nonetheless . . ." His brows drew together in a frown of confusion. "I love you. And you said you loved me."

"Love," she said calmly, "has very little to do with it."

His eyes darkened. "Love has everything to do with it."

"No, Jared." She directed him a steady gaze. "That may well have been true when you were . . . a penniless inventor." She shrugged. "But now all has changed."

"Oh?" Skepticism colored his tone. He leaned closer and tipped her chin to face him, his thumb stroking the line of her jaw. His voice was low and intense. "Precisely how has everything changed?"

Cece widened her eyes and longing rushed through her. Still . . . she struggled to gather her wits about her. She was determined to carry this through with a cool, serene demeanor in spite of the way she quivered inside at his touch, the way his voice sapped the will from her resolve, the way his eyes plumbed hers with an untold intensity that melted something at her very core. She drew back from his skillful touch.

"I am beginning to understand that life here is much different than at home. In England there is apparently nothing wrong with marrying for financial benefit. In fact, it seems to be encouraged."

"You understand that now, do you?" His eyes twinkled annoyingly.

She slanted him a stern gaze. "However, understanding does not mean acceptance. My personal views have not changed. I still believe men should work for their fortune."

"Cece, I do not consider courting you work." He grinned. "Invigorating, exciting, exasperating perhaps, but definitely not work."

"It seems to me that a marriage to restore a family's wealth is not unlike a business arrangement. Yes, indeed," she nodded firmly, "it is definitely a business proposition."

"Business," he said, "is not at all how I'd characterize the proposition I'm interested in."

She ignored him pointedly. "Regardless, it is a business deal and I propose to go about it as such."

A teasing light glimmered in his eye. "Just what do you have in mind?"

"Well . . ." She chose her words with care. It was one thing to throw minor obstacles in the course of an easy courtship but quite another to discourage him altogether. While she could well declare love had nothing to do with the arrangement of their marriage, love was the only thing she could count on to compel him to agree with her proposal. She suspected he would not bother with the trouble of a difficult pursuit were it not for that heady emotion. "My father says a sound business deal is advantageous to both sides."

"A wise man, your father," Jared murmured.

"I think so," she said, pleased with his cooperation, or at least his attention, thus far. "Both parties need to benefit. Each needs to achieve what he, or she, desires. In this case, the gain on your side is obvious."

"So, I believe, is the benefit on yours. Most ladies of my acquaintance would consider your gain by our marriage more than sufficient reason for the, ah, merger." He tipped his hat to a carriage full of giggling young women presided over by a dour-faced matron who acknowledged Jared's attention with a condescending smile. "Let's see . . . you would acquire an old and respected title. You would assume an enviable position in British society. You would become mistress of Graystone Castle, as well as a somewhat impressive London mansion. Add to that a husband who loves—"

"Love," she said sharply, "has noth—"

"I know, I know," he said with an exasperated sigh, "love has nothing to do with it."

"There is no room in business for an emotion that befuddles the mind and clouds the senses," she said primly.

"Are your senses clouded?" His gaze held hers, and for a moment she wanted nothing more than to lose herself in the rich sapphire promise of his eyes.

"Not at all," she said, in a tone just a shade higher than she wished.

"What do you want, Cece?" How on earth could a voice be so soft yet so laden with meaning she could only guess at?

What did she want? She wanted the warmth of his lips on hers. She wanted to surrender to the odd ache that permeated her body whenever he so much as spoke her name. She wanted to be by his side and, God help her, in his bed for the rest of her days.

Anything achieved too easily is valued too lightly.

She wrenched her gaze from his and drew a deep,

steadying breath, resisting the impulse to shake her head to revive her senses. Resolve coursed through her. She really had to work harder at disregarding the traitorous emotions he triggered.

She smoothed an invisible wrinkle in her skirt. "In return for my allowing you to commence with this courtship—"

He raised a brow. "Am I to understand this business deal of yours only permits courtship, not necessarily marriage?"

"Honestly, Jared"—she shook her head in annoyance—"of course marriage naturally follows courtship. But, in the meantime, you are to proceed with a proper courtship as well as agree to my proposition. The two go hand in hand."

"I have yet to meet your father, but I suspect he must be proud of you. You obviously know how to drive a hard bargain." Jared laughed. "Please continue."

"I am quite serious about this, Jared," she said indignantly.

"And I am taking it quite seriously." The corners of his mouth quirked, as if he suppressed a smile, belying the solemn tone of his words.

She struggled against a rising tide of irritation at his obvious amusement. "What I want is something you alone can provide." She paused thoughtfully. "Well, no, I suppose someone else could do it, but if you're to become my husband, you're the only one I would even consider approaching. Especially to begin. I find the very thought terribly exciting, and I always knew one day the opportunity would arise. When you think about it, it's not such a big thing. Really a simple service of sorts."

"A service?" His eyes widened and he nearly choked the word.

She pulled her brows together in annoyance. "You needn't look like that. It's not as if I was asking you to risk life and limb. I merely wish for you to teach me to drive your automobile."

"My automobile." Relief suffused his face, followed slowly by a growing comprehension. "My automobile?"

"Yes, Jared. Your automobile." She cast him a pleasant smile that masked the satisfaction prompted by his response. Now he would take her concerns seriously. Now he was obviously no longer amused.

"My automobile?" Jared repeated the words in a stunned tone.

"I believe we have established that."

"But . . ." He had the trapped look of a child caught in the act of stealing a cookie and desperately trying to make the crime appear less than it was. Abruptly, his expression cleared and a smug note sounded in his voice. "I attempted to teach you once. If I recall, that did not turn out at all well. I hardly think a repeat performance is called for to convince both of us of the futility of such a task."

"Nonetheless," she said airily and smiled in response to a rider who tipped his hat, "that's what I want."

"But my automobile." Sheer panic shone in his eyes. "It's not a toy, Cece."

"Nor is this the request of a child." Patience colored her words.

"The last time I attempted to teach you to drive, you ended up in the pond. With my motorcar." His lips compressed to an unyielding line. "It took the better part of a week to clean it up and get it operating again."

"It is entirely possible I was not paying the proper amount of attention at the time. And I believe we've already established that your instructions were less than adequate."

"Cece, what you're asking is absurd. If nothing else, our initial experience should point that out." His voice held a note of desperation common to men who understand their arguments are fruitless. "Surely something else would serve as well as teaching you to drive? Some other task?" His expression brightened. "I say, I have an idea."

"An interesting idea?"

He nodded enthusiastically. "Undoubtedly. What about a nice, traditional quest?"

"A quest?"

"Yes, you know." He grinned cockily. "We British are excellent at quests. Why, we've been questing for centuries. Slaying dragons, rescuing damsels in distress, that sort of thing."

"Specifically, what kind of quest did you have in mind?" she said, intrigued in spite of herself.

"What kind of quest?" He echoed her words as if repeating her question gave him needed time to come up with an answer. She could almost see the tiny wheels and gears, similar to those of his automobile, churning in his head. "What kind of quest . . ."

"Indeed, Jared." She stifled a grin of delight. The man was definitely already working for his fortune. "What kind of quest?"

"The Earls of Graystone have partaken of countless quests through the ages; surely one of those would serve in our circumstance." He paused, as if to recall the details of his family history. "You must realize, Cece, while it is true that, through the centuries, many of my ancestors have married to bolster the family fortune or to cement alliances, they have nearly as often married for love. And that typically involves a quest of some sort to win the hand of the lady in question."

"And those quests?" she prompted.

"One earl was forced to defeat all comers at the king's tournament to claim his bride. Another found it necessary to rescue his lady love from the evil clutches of a rival."

"A rival." Cece tapped her bottom lip with the tip of her forefinger and adopted an expression of consideration. "That does show promise. A rival would certainly keep you on your toes. Yes, indeed, I can see how that might—"

"On further thought, a rival is not an option here." He narrowed his eyes and glared in irritation. "Isn't there anything else, Cece, I can do to save my life, my sanity and my automobile?"

"Well, I suppose you could slay a dragon for me." An immediate vision of his mother sprang to her mind and she pushed aside the unworthy thought.

"Dragons are a rare commodity these days." His voice was mournful and he heaved the heavy sigh of a man about to admit defeat. "Very well," a tone befitting a sacrificial lamb tinged his words, "I shall attempt to teach you to drive."

"Excellent, Jared." She leaned toward him and cast him an innocent glance. "Just try and think of it . . . as a quest."

"Quest? Hah! You prefer a man who acquires his wealth through hard work and you have set me the one task guaranteed to be the most difficult I've ever encountered. Teaching a woman to drive . . ." He shook his head, disgust evident on his handsome face. He glared at the horses before him, as if the well-trained beasts were to blame for his predicament.

Once again Cece was hard pressed to suppress a grin. She turned her face away from him and perused the passing scenery. This was all quite delightful. Jared's reaction was more than she'd dared hope for. Men certainly did overreact. Why, what would he have done if she'd insisted on that ridiculous dragon suggestion? Besides, teaching her to drive would probably not be nearly the chore he expected. She was, after all, rather quick witted and caught on to new ideas easily. Surely she could master a simple machine.

She glanced at him from beneath the rim of her hat. A slight, satisfied smile played around his lips. She drew her brows together in puzzlement. That subtle expression of masculine triumph did not bode well.

"Jared . . ." she said cautiously.

"Did you meet Lady Wilson last night?" He nodded toward an elegantly dressed woman in a nearby carriage.

"No, but . . ." What on earth was he up to?

"I shall introduce you, then. There is no time like the present to begin getting to know London society." He reined in the team and waited for Lady Wilson's arrival.

The next half hour was filled with the polite social niceties that apparently accounted for an afternoon in the park. Jared did not once mention her task or quest or whatever he chose to call it. In turn, Cece bided her time. Not until they were nearly at her door did she return to the subject.

She extended her hand to him. "In my country a business deal is very often agreed to with nothing more than a handshake."

He grasped her hand in his, his eyes gleaming with an unreadable emotion. "We do the same here. Although when the two parties are male and female . . ." He lifted her hand to his mouth, turned it palm up and drifted his lips along the sensitive flesh of her inner wrist, just above the protection of her glove. She sucked in her breath sharply at the unexpected intimacy of the contact.

The deep blue of his eyes seemed to see inside her very soul. His voice was resonant with purpose. "I intend to pursue you quite aggressively, Cece."

She gasped in a valiant effort to regain her shattered senses. "And I firmly intend to let you."

JARED LEANED BACK against the tufted leather seat of his brougham and gazed idly at the city streets passing by, confident in the skill of his driver at the reins. Once again he was on his way to attend yet another of the endless social events London society prided itself on.

It had become a pattern this past week. Jared did indeed throw himself headlong into courting Cece. He made it a point to be at every function she attended; he accompanied her on rides in the park, in carriages and on horseback, as often as possible, and he even attempted to create a good impression with her father.

Jared was surprised to discover he liked Henry White, and White seemed to return his regard, once the American got over his innate distrust of anyone who would dare to pursue his daughter. Jared could well see where Cece obtained her strong opinions about men having to work to achieve success. With this self-made millionaire as a model, how could she think anything else?

Henry White may well have been responsible for the obstinate streak in his offspring as well. Jared tried everything he could think of to dissuade her from the ridiculous notion of learning to drive his automobile. His efforts fell on ears not only deaf but every argument seemed merely to encourage her resistance. In spite of his continued irritation, he couldn't help but admire the strength of her will.

Still, the very thought of a woman at the controls of his machine was absurd. Certainly he had allowed her that privilege when they first met. But it had been a momentary lapse in judgment, nothing more. He could admit, if only to himself, that while his purpose in that venture had not been seduction, as Cece had so indignantly claimed, he had hoped to impress the enthusiastic and damned pretty American with his automobile.

Persistence was not all he admired about Cece. With every day, every hour, every moment spent in her company he fell more and more under the spell of a woman he found not only fascinating but irresistible. She had a wry wit that left him struggling for a quick retort or choked with laughter. She was surprisingly intelligent, an attribute he rarely noticed in women of her social class. And with each kiss stolen in a rare moment of privacy, he could taste the hint, the suggestion, the promise of an imprisoned passion he ached to release.

He would have this American as his own, forever. And if he had to risk his automobile in the process, he sighed to himself, it would be a small price to pay. The merest gaze into the deep chocolate of her eyes was enough to cause him to vanquish all thoughts of machines and progress and the oncoming twentieth century and agree to anything and everything she wished.

Still, he hoped it would be unnecessary. He had a trump card hidden well up his sleeve. If played correctly, it would assure her hand in marriage before he was forced to go through the farce of allowing her to touch his motorcar. Jared grinned at the thought.

Seduction was no longer a last resort.

Chapter 7

"I BELIEVE that's sufficient for our first lesson," Jared said, a note of finality in his tone.

"Sufficient?" Cece stared, astonished. "This is it? All you intend to do?" She gestured vigorously toward the vehicles standing untouched in the stables. "I haven't so much as placed a foot in one of your automobiles."

"Nor shall you," he said under his breath, so low she must have misheard. He shook his head firmly. "Regardless, it's getting late. It shall soon be time to dress for dinner. And the rest of Mother's guests should have arrived by now."

He leveled her a stern glance. "Surely you wouldn't want anyone to notice our absence, would you?"

"Of course not." She planted her hands on her hips and glared. "But for the past hour you have done nothing save lecture me on the workings of the automobile. You have thoroughly acquainted me with various theories of propulsion. You have familiarized me with the mechanical intricacies of your machine. You have droned on and on about which gear does what to what and why until I want nothing more than to shove the whole thing, and its owner, back into the blasted pond!"

"One needs to know how things work before one can master them," he said in a superior manner.

Her hand itched to smack the smug expression off his face. "Stuff and nonsense," she snapped. "I haven't the vaguest concept of the internal anatomy of a horse, yet I find I can handle the animal with ease."

"Horses," he smiled condescendingly, "are far different from automobiles."

"No doubt." Irritation rang in her voice. "Will an automobile balk if a dog runs across the road? Will an automobile bloat its stomach to ensure you end up thrown from your seat at an inopportune moment? Will an automobile totally disregard your direction and instead insist on going where it wishes to go? It seems to me driving an automobile would be quite a bit easier than riding a horse."

"Nonetheless . . ." he said, in a patient voice she would have thought reserved for small children or the feeble-minded. Her annoyance grew. "We are finished for today."

"Jared," she resisted the impulse to stamp her foot in exasperation, "I am no closer to learning to drive a motorcar now than when we got here. Although, I daresay, I could probably build one."

"Cece . . ." He leaned toward her ominously, his tall figure blocking out the late afternoon sun. His dark eyes gleamed and delicious fear shivered through her. His voice was little more than a growl. "I have agreed to your ridiculous demand to teach you to drive. I shall perform that heinous task my way in my own time. I do not intend to turn over the automobile I have spent years of my life developing to anyone without proper preparation.

"Furthermore, I am not fully convinced it is not

against nature to mix women and mechanics." A sly smile curved his lips. "For example, name one female inventor."

"That's not the point," she said loftily.

His smile blossomed to a smirk. "I thought as much. But for your next lesson I will allow you to sit behind the controls of an automobile." He gestured at the two vehicles flanking the center motorcar. "One of those perhaps."

"Jared!" She fairly sputtered his name, her throat choked with indignation. "You told me yourself those two are not completed." She narrowed her eyes and glared. "They don't run, Jared."

He shrugged casually. "They will serve quite well for your first experience in the driver's seat. Now . . ." He stepped away and closed the great doors of the stable. They shut with a shuddering thud that marked the end of her first session of instruction as surely as the final curtain on a three-act play. Cece stared in frustration.

Jared strode toward the lane and the long walk back. He paused and glanced over his shoulder. "I'm returning home. Are you coming?"

"I don't see that I have much of a choice," she muttered and scrambled to catch up with him.

Cece fell into step beside him and attempted to match his long strides with her own. She was unused to men being more than an inch or so taller than she. Jared's height and the length of his gait was both pleasing and a challenge. The return trek to Graystone Castle was a long one, and a silence Cece considered anything but companionable lay between them.

She fumed to herself. Obviously she had vastly underestimated Jared. Oh, certainly, the man had grudgingly acquiesced to her insistence on learning to drive, but at this rate she'd be in her dotage before she ever set a course at the helm of an automobile. This was not going at all well.

She stole a glance at Jared. The satisfied smile on his face was more than enough to confirm her suspicion that he had no intention of placing his precious automobile in her feminine clutches. No doubt he planned to stretch out his so-called lessons until she threw up her hands in despair and resignation.

What would Nellie Bly do?

The question hit her like a thunderbolt, and the answer came just as swift. Nellie Bly would never let a mere man get in the way of something she wanted. Why, she'd competed with men throughout her career and emerged triumphant as often as not. No, Nellie Bly would not give up, and neither would Cece.

She mirrored his smug smile with her own. The Earl of Graystone might have generations of history in his corner, but Cecily Gwendolyn White was a product of a country young, strong and dedicated. This was one American determined to show this one Englishman that in a battle of wits, she was far better armed than he.

She cast him another quick glance. Jared again wore the same kind of casual garb he'd had on when they first met, clothes more suitable to a penniless inventor than a lord of the realm. In this guise he was rugged and earthy, and her heart melted with the look of him. This was no earl beside her now; this was the passionate man who'd captured her imagination the moment he launched into his first speech about the benefits of gas power versus steam.

A thought struck her abruptly. "Do you still wish to manufacture automobiles?"

He laughed, a harsh, mirthless sound. His expression was set, resolved. "I told you in Paris, that was a foolish dream."

"I don't see why," she said stubbornly. "I don't see why you can't do anything you want to if you work at it hard enough."

"You are an innocent." He cast her a rueful glance. "Are you typical of Americans in general, or are you completely unique?"

"Both. My countrymen are very ambitious and truly believe in the benefits of labor." She tossed him an impish grin. "I admit I happen to be a tad more . . . shall we say *opinionated* than others. Now," her tone turned brisk, "you are avoiding my question."

He blew a heavy sigh and gazed at the road winding ahead of him. It was a moment before he spoke, his words thoughtful and resigned. "I can no longer spend the time I once did working on the automobiles. Moments here, these days, are stolen hours. When I was merely the younger son I was not expected to occupy my time with anything considered worthwhile. I was more or less left to my own devices."

"Which, in part, explains the rather impressive reputation you've achieved with the fairer sex. Or so I've heard," she said wryly.

He flashed her a quick grin and nodded. "But I spent as much time, if not more, developing the vehicles. Quentin and I have worked together for a number of years.

"Now all has changed." He waved at the land spread out before them. "With James's death, all this became my responsibility. Management of the estate, juggling of finances, even social position now falls to me."

His voice softened and his eyes reflected a pride

that brought a lump to her throat. "I love this land. I never dreamed someday I'd be charged with its custody. We have tenant farmers here. Free men, of course, who walk the same land trod by their fathers and their grandfathers before them. Men whose heritage here is as great as mine, whose roots go as deeply into the soil here as the ancient oaks. Just as their ancestors did, they look to the castle for leadership and direction. To me.

"When I took over I initiated the most modern, up-to-date methods of land management possible, but with agricultural prices being what they are these days, the estate still barely brings in enough to break even.

"When my father was a young man ownership of property was all one needed to ensure life would be prosperous." His eyes narrowed. "Things are very different today."

"But couldn't your idea to produce and sell automobiles return that prosperity?"

"Perhaps someday." He shook his head. "But I no longer have the luxury of time."

At once she understood his need to marry a wealthy wife went far beyond mere monetary benefits to the survival of a tradition of life tied to the very foundations of this venerable country itself. He carried a commitment to this land and the people who lived here that had been forged long before his birth. Her stern attitude toward men who married for money did not fade, but for this man she could make an exception.

She walked beside him silently, pondering how to help him achieve his dreams and live up to his obligations at the same time.

"I still don't see why you insist on keeping your

involvement with the motorcars a secret. Quentin doesn't."

"Quentin makes his own rules." Jared laughed. "He uses his claim of being half-American to excuse every outrageous thing he's ever done. I am the silent partner in our venture." He paused thoughtfully. "Actually, it was James's idea to keep my work on the automobile quiet."

"Really?" Surprise coursed through her.

"Indeed." Jared nodded. "I frankly did not care one way or the other, but it was James's opinion that my activity would cast a bad light on the family name—a Grayson working with his hands and all that, you know."

"God forbid," she said sarcastically.

He pointedly ignored her comment. "At any rate, James was the head of the family and I had always trusted his advice. He was clever and competent. James never lacked for confidence either. He always seemed to know the correct thing to do, the right path to take."

"You miss him, don't you?"

Jared sighed. "I miss his counsel and his guidance. I can't help but think, if he were still alive, he would not have to resort to marriage to solve the family's woes. Although," he threw her a mischievous grin, "I can't help but be grateful it has come to this."

He glanced at her and she tried not to smile. It wouldn't do to let him know she shared his gratitude. Not yet.

"There is a race at the end of the month," he said in an offhand manner. "Outside London to Bath and back, a mere two hundred miles. A trifling compared to the Paris–Bordeaux race. Still, even if we can match the pace set there, and that will be difficult at best, the contest should take at least a day."

Cece stopped short and stared in astonished delight. "Don't tell me you'll drive in the race?"

He shook his head. "I am the silent partner, remember?" Jared smiled ruefully. "I'll be there to cheer Quentin on, nothing more."

She narrowed her eyes in annoyed disbelief. "I don't understand you at all. Doesn't it bother you to let someone else take credit for your work?"

He studied her for a long moment. "I know what I've accomplished," he said quietly and shrugged. "I daresay that's all that really matters in life."

He turned and strode down the path. For a moment she stared motionless at his tall, retreating figure. With each new day she learned more and more about this man. And nearly each new facet of his personality, every unsuspected nuance of his character, only served to endear him to her. Even his reasons for marriage were quickly paling beside the nobler aspects of his nature.

Still, there was that bothersome attitude of his about teaching her to drive. Cece grinned abruptly and dashed to catch up with him. That was one character flaw she would neither forgive nor forget. She was more than willing to pit her determination against his. The more she thought about it, the more delightful the prospect. Jared might well have kept her far removed from his automobile today, but Cece would drive the motorcar, sooner or later, with or without his help.

"What do you think of Graystone Castle?"

Cece hadn't even noticed the turn in the lane that brought the castle into view. The massive structure loomed in the distance, a benevolent stone giant guard-

ing over the green fields, hills and valleys. The building was not exactly what she'd pictured in her mind.
She'd imagined the kind of fantasy creation that graced
the pages of children's fairy tales, all turrets and spires,
white marble walls and blue tile roofs. No, Jared's
seemed a very practical sort of castle.

With a fair amount of concentration, one could
dimly identify the original building, constructed in the
1300s, according to Lady Graystone. Succeeding generations, in the name of progress and modernization and
remodeling, had added addition upon addition, wing
upon wing, until the castle seemed more a title of en-
dearment than a definition. Nonetheless, every new
builder must have cared about the old place. Each an-
nex matched in material if not necessarily in style. Today, the castle squatted comfortably like an ancient
wise woman, with her own secrets and knowledge, in
silent observation of the world around her.

"I like it," she said decisively. "It's very much a home
and not at all what I expected. I find it quite charming."

"Oh?" He raised a skeptical brow. "I thought surely
you would dislike it. It's so—what is that phrase?—oh
yes, 'cold, ugly and out-of-date.'"

"Jared, if we are to get along together now and in the
future, you must remember one thing about me." She
leveled him her best no-nonsense look. "I simply hate it
when people throw my own words back in my face."

A smile quirked the corners of his lips. "Even when
you're wrong?"

She lifted her chin and cast him a pleasant smile of
her own. "Especially when I'm wrong."

"AN INTERESTING ASSORTMENT of people you've collected here, Olivia," Millicent said.

"Do you think so?" Olivia murmured.

Millicent studied the assembly gathered in the grand parlor to await the announcement for dinner. Henry and Phoebe chatted near the fireplace with Jared and Sir Humphrey Cresswell, a rotund, aging widower with an inflated opinion of his effect on the fairer sex. His daughter, Sofia, a somewhat overblown blond creature with a penchant for the type of seductive flirtation that would no doubt lead her to trouble one day, perched on the edge of a sofa perilously close to an obviously flattered Quentin. Emily stood beside the couple with a polite, strained smile on her lovely face.

Millicent narrowed her eyes in consideration. Could Emily be at all interested in Quentin? What a charming idea. She would have to pursue that thought at a later time.

In another corner of the room, Cece appeared to be in an animated discussion with Lady Linnea DeToulane and Lord Nigel Radcliffe. The red-haired beauty, now in her third widowhood, was notorious for choosing husbands extremely old, extremely wealthy and preferably infirm. Between marriages, in spite of all efforts toward discretion, she was as well known for her enthusiastic pursuit of pleasure as for her discriminating choice in spouses.

Nigel Radcliffe was rumored to be her latest paramour. A bit older than Quentin, the charming rogue was considered one of the most eligible bachelors in England, and one of the most evasive. He appeared not in the least bit close to settling down, to the chagrin of his family and the disappointment of hopeful young misses everywhere.

Millicent shook her head. "What is going on here, Olivia?"

"A simple gathering of houseguests, nothing more," Olivia said innocently.

"A simple gathering?" Millicent stared in disbelief. "This is anything but simple." She cast Olivia an assessing glance. "You do know about Nigel and that woman, don't you?"

Olivia shrugged. "Gossip, nothing more."

Millicent snorted in a most unladylike manner. "You know as well as I do, even the *Times* is not always as accurate as London gossip. As for your other guests . . ." She gestured toward the blonde cooing at her nephew. "Have you watched the way that off-spring of Cresswell's is attempting to sink her fangs into Quentin? And I've seen her casting the same sort of hungry looks toward Jared."

Olivia shook her head in reproach. "She's simply an extremely friendly and outgoing young lady."

"Friendly and outgoing?" Millicent could scarce believe her ears. "She is well on her way to becoming a genuine tart, if she's not one already."

"Millicent!" Olivia stared, eyes wide with apparent shock. "I cannot believe you would say such a thing about that charming child."

"I can say that and more," Millicent said sharply. "Although I must admit she comes by her manner naturally. That old goat of a father of hers has cast carnal glances at every feminine ankle here, including yours and mine."

"Isn't it nice to know we can still turn a head or two?" Olivia said lightly.

"Olivia!" Why on earth was the woman so obtuse

tonight? "I would not trust him around any of us, especially the girls."

Olivia patted her gently on the arm. "You really must keep your voice down."

Millicent fairly sputtered with indignation.

"Did I remember to thank you for encouraging Quentin to stay here with the other guests?" Olivia said. "I thought it would be best, with so many activities scheduled. Why, there is a hunt first thing in the morning, and I've planned a formal dinner for tomorrow night with a few additional guests from the neighborhood expected. It should be lovely. Tonight, of course, we are dining somewhat casually. By the way, do you think a room in the west wing would suit Quentin?"

"Whatever," Millicent said absently. She still could not figure out exactly what Olivia was up to. It gnawed at her mind like a rat with a crust of bread.

"With the exception of the Whites, I've put the other guests in the west wing as well," Olivia said casually.

Millicent barely noted her words, her thoughts too full trying to determine Olivia's plan. She'd known her friend far too many years not to recognize that she did very little without an ulterior purpose. But this odd mix of guests made no appreciable sense whatsoever. "Yes, yes, I'm sure whatever quarters you've arranged will be fine."

"With just the barest luck," Olivia said quietly, signaling her butler to announce dinner, "it should be very fine indeed."

"You do see, don't you, my dear, how marriage can ultimately ensure a woman's independence?" Linnea DeToulane said.

Cece leaned forward with interest. "But I thought

for a woman to be truly independent she had to throw off the shackles of marriage and face life on her own two feet."

"Her sister says she reads a lot," Jared said confidentially from his position at the head of the table. Cece sat to his right, Lady DeToulane to his left.

"Well, she is quite obviously reading the wrong thing," Linnea said firmly. "And believe me, I know what I'm talking about."

Jared leaned toward Cece. "Linnea has recently killed off her third husband."

"My, that is impressive," Cece murmured, not quite sure whether to believe him or not.

"Who's killed off whom?" Sir Humphrey said from Cece's other side.

"Jared," Linnea chided, "you will give the poor child a completely erroneous impression of me. I adored each and every one of my husbands. How many did you say?"

"Three," Quentin said with a grin, seated between Linnea and that obnoxious Cresswell girl.

"Are you certain?" Linnea's brows pulled together in a pondering expression. "Let me think, there was . . ." She fell silent, obviously preoccupied with the count of dead husbands. This woman no doubt lived her life perched precariously close to the edge of scandal. Cece stared with rapt fascination.

Linnea's expression brightened. "Three. He's right, it was three."

"I hope you do not plan on counting deceased husbands one day." Jared growled the words near Cece's ear. A tremor of delight shivered through her at the nearness of his lips.

"I don't know, Jared," she said lightly. "I have always

believed anything worth doing was worth doing to the best of one's ability. And I can count ever so much higher than three."

His eyes sparkled with amusement, his voice weighing heavy with his threat or his promise. "I plan on living a full and very long life."

"I shall count on it." Her words were little more than a whisper. His gaze captured hers. For a moment it was as if there was no one else in the room, in the world, but the two of them. Cece longed to lean forward, cup his chin in her hand and pull his lips to hers. She yearned to lose herself in his taste, his scent, his strength.

"See that you do." His eyes reflected her own desire. She wanted nothing more than to be in his arms again. She wanted what she'd sampled, ever so briefly, in Paris. She wanted the excitement of love and the sheer exhilaration of unabashed passion. And she had no doubt that, in that kind of lesson, Jared would be anything but a reluctant teacher.

Shrill laughter shattered the moment between them, and Cece started abruptly, as if she and Jared had been caught in a scandalous embrace. A knowing smile touched his lips and he glanced away, down the long table. She followed his gaze to the Cresswell girl, fluttering her eyelashes at Quentin, who appeared much more amused than aroused.

"Your mother certainly has selected an interesting array of guests," Cece said under her breath.

"Indeed." Jared narrowed his eyes thoughtfully and studied his mother at the far end of the table. "One wonders what she is planning."

"Planning?" Curiosity jabbed Cece. "Whatever do you mean? Surely this is no more than a cordial gathering?"

"I wonder . . ." Jared paused and continued to watch his mother. Olivia caught his eye and nodded pleasantly. "My mother never does anything without a great deal of forethought. And this assembly is not what I would have expected of her."

"What do you mean?"

"Just a suspicion . . ." Jared pulled his gaze from Olivia and back to Cece. "Cresswell and his daughter are not among my mother's most intimate friends. I would have thought them far too brash for her. And discretion is not a term one would apply to Sir Humphrey. They are acquaintances, nothing more. Nigel is an old friend of mine and, as such, his presence here is not unusual. But Linnea . . . while I have always been fond of her, I would never have imagined my mother felt the same. Linnea is rather—"

"Overwhelming?"

"Exactly." He shook his head, as if to clear the uneasy thoughts. "It's extremely odd . . . perhaps attributable to Mother's long absence from entertaining."

Cece cast him a wry smile. "You must admit, though, it does seem to be an intriguing assembly. I can scarcely wait to see how we all get on together."

Jared laughed and reached for his goblet. Cece took a quick sip of her wine to hide her own grin.

Linnea turned toward her, a gleam in the older woman's eye. "So, I gather Jared will be your first husband?"

A sputtered cough erupted from Jared and Cece struggled to swallow without choking.

Linnea nodded with satisfaction. "I thought as much. Rumors are flying."

"Rumors?" A tolerant smile played about Jared's lips, as if he didn't care one whit about gossip. Well, if he could act rational and nonchalant, so could she.

"Yes, indeed," she said sweetly, "what rumors?"

Linnea shook her head condescendingly. "It's been quite obvious. Everywhere you go, Jared shows up. The two of you have been seen together in the park and elsewhere." She shrugged a satin-covered shoulder. "People do talk, you know."

"What exactly have you heard?" Quentin said idly.

She cast him a withering glance. "My dear boy, if you would pull your head out of that machine of yours every now and then, you too would be abreast of the latest gossip, scandal and speculation." Linnea leaned toward Cece in a manner of one confidant to another. "Quentin is attempting to build horseless carriages."

Cece's gaze flicked to Jared. He adopted a patient, slightly bored look, as if to say he had heard this conversation before. "A horseless carriage? How very interesting."

"How very absurd, you mean. It's quite ridiculous, a grown man occupying his time with something far more suitable as a child's plaything than a vehicle for adults. Nothing will ever come of it." Linnea sighed dramatically. "You might as well try to fly."

Cece pulled her brows together in annoyance. While this woman's views on life in general might well be stimulating, she obviously could not see the potential in Jared's automobile. Or, for that matter, in the future. "Surely, with the onset of the twentieth century, the motorcar and numerous other machines will become more and more—"

"Miss White is quite enamored of the future," Quentin said with a grin.

"And dear Linnea is more than a little fond of all things past." Jared lifted his glass in a teasing toast. "From history to husbands."

"Yes, well . . ." Linnea appeared distinctly uncomfortable for a moment. She eyed Jared thoughtfully but addressed herself to Cece. "You know, he's not at all unattractive. Really quite handsome in a rugged, youthful sort of way."

"Thank you," Jared said modestly.

Cece stared in amazement. While extremely entertaining, this was not at all the sort of dinner conversation she expected. Was the discussion at Lady Graystone's end of the table anywhere near this uninhibited and intimate?

"Still, I wouldn't choose him as a husband, my dear. He's simply too young and far too healthy. He should last an inordinately long time. No"—Linnea shook her head firmly—"Jared would never do as a husband. However, I should think he'd make an excellent lover."

Jared grinned.

Quentin choked.

Heat rushed up Cece's face.

The Cresswell girl reddened, reached for her glass and knocked it over. Servants hurried to her side.

Goodness, did Lady DeToulane have no sense of propriety at all? Cece was well known back home for her outspoken candor, but even she realized there were certain boundaries one didn't cross. The slightest hint of such indiscretion was unthinkable, no matter how very provocative the idea might be.

All attention focused on the servants mopping up the mess before Cresswell's daughter, but Cece's gaze strayed to Jared. He watched the proceedings with a slight, crooked smile of amused disbelief. One strong, tanned hand rested lightly around the stem of his goblet, the other out of sight in his lap. He drew a quick swallow from his glass and responded to a comment of Quentin's with a nod and a light laugh. The wine moistened his lips with a faint, inviting sheen that begged to be tasted, savored, relished.

"If the rumors are to be believed—and I daresay only a fool would discount London gossip—then the boy's made quite a suitable match for himself," Sir Humphrey said, leapfrogging the conversation back to the somewhat personal question of her real or imagined relationship with Jared.

"Thank you," Jared said, a little less modestly this time, with just a touch of annoyance in his voice.

"Yes, indeed." Sir Humphrey nodded toward her father at the other end of the table. "She's bloody rich and dammed pretty too."

Sir Humphrey slanted her something that tottered between a grin and a leer, no doubt the result of one too many glasses of claret. She returned his expression with a polite, noncommittal smile and turned back to the others.

". . . and then he said, 'Well, my dear, if one finds it necessary to actually tally the score, one should never play in the first place.' And I said, 'I quite agree, my lord. Still, it never hurts to know exactly where one stands or, if you prefer, where one . . .'" Lady DeToulane chatted engagingly to a captive audience of those seated around her. No doubt the tale was amusing, but Cece's unfamiliarity with the subject or the main characters lent a certain difficulty to following the story.

A slight draft ruffled her gown at her knee. She ignored the tickling sensation and concentrated on Lady DeToulane's lighthearted banter. The draft returned, almost a caress this time, and she shifted her leg in mild irritation. Once more the fabric of her gown stirred. A hand clasped her knee.

Cece started slightly and stared at Sir Humphrey. This time there was no mistake; the expression on his face was definitely a smirk. She glared and he winked and removed his hand.

Cece glanced at Jared. Still engrossed in Lady DeToulane's clatter, he seemed not to have noticed the interchange between her and Sir Humphrey. She released a breath she hadn't realized she held. Jared would not take the older man's attentions to her lightly, and she preferred to avoid any kind of scene between the two of them, especially with Lady Graystone at the table.

"Damned pretty." Sir Humphrey's warm, wine-fumed breath puffed against her ear, and once again his hand grasped her knee.

She shoved it away firmly but without undue attention, dropped her linen napkin on the floor and bent to retrieve it. Sir Humphrey too leaned down.

"Sir," she whispered stiffly, "if you touch my person once more, I shall be forced to deal with you quite harshly."

"American girls have such spirit." A lecherous glint shone in his eyes. "I do so love spirit."

She glared and jerked upright in her chair. She refused to so much as glance in Sir Humphrey's direction, and minutes passed without incident. The old fool had no doubt received her message. The tension in Cece's shoulders eased and she joined eagerly in the ebb and flow of the conversation.

A pithy comment from Quentin prompted laughter all around. In the midst, Sir Humphrey's chubby hand once again settled on her knee and squeezed.

This was quite enough. Obviously the despicable man needed something more to the point to make it perfectly clear she had no interest in his amorous antics. She cast around for a suitable weapon. They were well into the meal, but a sterling dessert fork shimmered invitingly before her. Cece slipped the fork into her lap and, with the next gale of laughter, plunged it into the back of Sir Humphrey's flabby fist.

Sir Humphrey yelped in a most satisfying way, and Cece smiled smugly. He sputtered. He coughed. He choked, finally turning a most interesting shade of purple. Perhaps it was the color of the man's plump little face that finally drew the attention of the others. Or perhaps it was that horrible strangling sound emanating from him. Either way, Cece had no intention of going to his aid.

"Do you think something disagreed with him?" Cece said innocently, dabbing the corners of her mouth with her napkin.

"Good God!" Jared sprang from his chair and rushed to Sir Humphrey's side, Quentin a step behind him.

"Papa!" The Cresswell creature clapped her hands to her face and rose to her feet.

"I say, can I help?" Nigel Radcliffe called from the far end of the table.

"Smack him," Linnea said firmly. "Smack him sharply on the back. And don't be afraid to put some force into it."

"Oh yes, Jared," Cece nodded eagerly. "A good belt is precisely what he needs."

Sir Humphrey's eyes bulged, whether at the women's directions or his apparent lack of air, Cece wasn't sure. Jared and Quentin flanked him, traded swift glances, and then, in a stalwart effort to prevent what appeared to be his eminent demise, Jared pulled his hand back and let it fly.

The resounding smack reverberated in the great hall, and even Cece winced at the painful sound. The force propelled Sir Humphrey's bloated body forward like a full sail with a sudden gust of wind and an unidentified piece of half-chewed fare exploded from his mouth and soared across the room.

Stunned silence filled the hall.

Sir Humphrey gasped with exertion.

His daughter appeared appropriately mortified.

Cece stifled an irresistible impulse to giggle.

Shock colored the faces of nearly everyone at the other end of the table.

"I told you." Linnea favored the group with a superior smile. "A good smack on the back always works. Usually it's not quite so dramatic or—" she threw Sir Humphrey a disdainful look—"revolting."

"Sorry, my dear," Sir Humphrey muttered, his color gradually returning to its normal ruddy tone. "My apologies all around."

"Think nothing of it." Jared nodded. He and Quentin returned to their respective places.

"Most unfortunate," Sir Humphrey mumbled and sank into his seat. A quick angry glance shot toward Cece from narrowed eyes.

She smiled pleasantly and turned away, her gaze catching Jared's mother's. A hint of a smile quirked the corners of Lady Graystone's lips, and she nodded slightly, as if she approved of Cece's action.

Cece's eyes widened, unease tinging her smile. Lady Graystone turned away to speak to Cece's father. Surely Olivia could have no idea of what had occurred here? Cece had been extremely discreet. There was no conceivable way Olivia could even suspect Sir Humphrey's embarrassing moment had been the direct result of a fork imbedded in his hand prompted by his disgraceful actions. Unless . . .

Cece studied the older woman thoughtfully. It was difficult to believe Olivia was unaware of the man's obvious penchant toward licentious behavior and his apparent attraction to young women. Anyone watching the man for more than a moment or two could easily discern that. But why on earth would Olivia seat Cece next to him? Wouldn't she expect some kind of incident?

No, Cece was letting her imagination run rampant. Even if her farfetched thoughts were true, what possible motive would Jared's mother have to place Cece in such an awkward situation? She shrugged off the disquieting idea and turned to join in the banter around her.

She waited until once again her companions were distracted by laughter and, surreptitiously, slipped her fork back into place.

WITH THE CORNER of her mind Olivia reserved for social niceties, she chatted pleasantly with the guests at her end of the table. She could not resist a slight satisfied smile.

Granted this wasn't much of a first test for the American girl, but it had served its purpose. Olivia did not know the precise details but was astute enough to realize that Sir Humphrey had been up to his old tricks, precisely why she had seated him next to Cecily in the first place.

Any hostess would doubtless come up against men of Sir Humphrey's ilk now and again. It took a special touch to discourage them firmly while not creating a spectacle. Of course, in this case Cecily's response had triggered that disgusting display of choking, but even Olivia could not blame that on the girl.

No, Cecily had not created a scene. She had not called for her father or Jared to defend her honor. And, most importantly, she had not disrupted a social occasion. That charge fell squarely on the chubby shoulders of Sir Humphrey.

Olivia nodded to herself approvingly. This was proceeding quite nicely. She almost hoped the girl would succeed. Cecily had already leapt the first hurdle Olivia had set for her.

But could she leap them all?

Chapter 8

Cᴇᴄᴇ tossed and turned and turned and tossed until the fine linen sheets knotted about her legs and her pillow bunched beneath her head. No matter what contortions she performed in an effort to find an acceptable spot, sleep evaded her like an incessant insect buzzing just out of reach.

It wasn't as if she had fallen into bed reluctantly. On the contrary, between the trip from London, Jared's so-called driving lesson and the scandalous goings-on at dinner, the day had been extraordinarily busy. And tomorrow promised to be just as full. A hunt was planned for the morning and, while she had no interest in that activity, Jared, as host, insisted on attending. He only reluctantly agreed to meet her beforehand at the stable, where she expected he would do his level best to avoid instructing her in the operation of his precious automobile.

It wasn't the fault of her surroundings. The room allotted her in the castle's west wing was exceedingly comfortable and even quite charming in an old-fashioned sort of way, with massive antique furniture and wall hangings, and ceilings that seemed to soar perilously close to heaven itself. Even the mattress on the huge four-poster bed was as soft and inviting as a whispered caress. No bulges, bumps or lumps here.

She gave the pillow an unwarrantedly vicious punch, flipped over on her back and stared at the ceiling high above her. In the moonlight that filtered from the window she couldn't make out the intricate coffered design, only shapes and shadows that seemed to undulate in and out of her vision. At this moment, did sleep elude Jared as well? Did he too lay awake, staring at a ceiling very much like this one?

For not the first time she considered this very odd emotion called love. It was not the blissful, unquestioned happiness described by poets. Instead, it was much more like a constant state of anticipation punctuated by periodic bouts of frustration, annoyance and longing. It was that unquenched yearning for something still unknown that caused her restlessness tonight.

Every moment spent in his presence seemed to weaken her resolve to make him work for her hand. With every word, every glance and, Lord help her, every kiss, she seemed to fall more and more under his spell. And the chaste kisses they'd shared since Paris were simply not enough.

Cece prided herself on being a modern woman and as such was well aware of the physical intimacies that lovers shared. But it had always sounded somewhat odd, definitely awkward and just a touch distasteful. Now, her opinions faltered.

More and more in moments like this she wondered what it would be like to share newfound passions with a man. With Jared. His kiss alone had given her a glimpse of sensations she never dreamed existed.

What more could she expect when his lips refused to linger on hers and instead drifted down her neck to taste the sensitive flesh that even now trembled at the thought of his desire? When his strong, tanned hands refused to rest discreetly and instead explored the hills and valleys of her increasingly receptive body? When his hard chest crushed her breasts with an insistent demand she had never—

Cece gasped and sat upright, heat flashing up her face. She threw off the sheets and swung her feet over the side of the bed. This was quite enough. She stood decisively and grabbed her wrapper. Swiftly, she donned the silken robe and stalked to the door. She refused to spend the rest of the night mooning over Jared and succumbing to indecent thoughts, intriguing though they might be. A good book would occupy her traitorous mind. She grit her teeth and pulled her door open. At this point even a boring book would help. Anything to put herself, as well as images of Jared, to rest.

The gaslights in the broad hallway were turned down low and no one stirred in the corridor. Cece had only seen the castle's library while on a brief tour, but she'd always been quite proud of her unerring sense of direction. Courses and routes, whether in buildings, city streets or on open roads, seemed to stick forever in her mind. Once shown a direction she never lost it. It was admittedly an unusual gift, but Cece considered it a practical talent nonetheless.

Silently she slipped though the halls, down the stairs and into the library. She lit a lamp and gazed around the book-edged room. Volumes lined shelf after shelf; rows of tomes reached to a ceiling that disappeared in the shadows above. She perused the shelves nearest her and wrinkled her nose in disgust.

Chaucer, Balzac, Milton. Nothing of any interest whatsoever. No treatise on the rights of women. No publications detailing the latest inventions of Mr. Edison. No Twain, no Melville, no Alcott. How frightfully boring. She sighed. At least the writings she'd discovered thus far would not keep her awake. She couldn't imagine the words of Samuel Pepys capturing her attention to the point where she would not want to put it down.

Surely there was something of note here. Cece moved to the next wall and her gaze caught a promising shelf: Shakespeare. Not her first choice, but not altogether unacceptable.

Her fingers trailed along the gilded leather spines and paused for a moment on *Romeo and Juliet.* She shook her head firmly. She was in no mood for star-crossed lovers tonight. Cece bypassed the rest of the tragedies and the histories until her touch rested lightly on the Bard's more humorous offerings. *A Midsummer Night's Dream?* No; too fanciful. *Much Ado About Nothing?* No; the treatment of Hero by Claudio always infuriated her. *The Taming of the Shrew?* She grinned and plucked the book from its resting place. Now here was a story she could well appreciate.

She chuckled to herself and made her way back to her chamber. She would have to ask Jared what he thought of this particular play. Given their ongoing battle over her driving instruction, his views on this particular Shakespearian effort might well be amusing and insightful.

Cece turned the corner into the hall and pulled up short. Someone stood at the door to her room. She took another few cautious steps forward and peered into the dimly lit corridor. It was Sir Humphrey! What on earth was he doing with his hand on her doorknob? She started toward him indignantly, then stopped. No; far better to see exactly what the old lecher was up to than to confront him now. She flattened herself against the nearest recessed door and watched.

Sir Humphrey darted a quick glance up and down the hall. Even from here she could see his lascivious grin. Apparently even a fork imbedded in his hammy hand was not enough to dissuade this rotund suitor that his attentions were not merely unwanted but repugnant as well. Again she stifled the urge to confront him face to face. She was, after all, alone in the hall and, despite his rather ineffectual appearance, she had no idea how dangerous the nasty creature could really be.

Sir Humphrey turned the knob and tiptoed into her room and closed the door quietly behind him. Cece suppressed the desire to giggle at the thought of how any rational toes could truly support a bulk of Sir Humphrey's magnitude. She waited, her gaze fastened on the door. Moments ticked by. She shifted impatiently. Surely he had realized by now that she was not in her bed? Damnation! What if he decided to wait for her? What if at this very moment the lustful old coot was reclining in her own bed dreaming of her arrival? And what if, unaware, she had innocently walked in on him? Shivers of revulsion coursed down her spine.

She squared her shoulders. She would give Sir Humphrey a few moments more and then join Emily in her room. In the morning, she would decide what to do about his outrageous behavior.

The door to her room opened abruptly and she pressed her back into the shadows of her doorway hiding place. Sir Humphrey stepped into the hall, casting a cursory glance at the empty walkway. He appeared quite disgruntled and muttered under his breath. She strained to catch the words on his retreat down the corridor but failed to pick up more than "tart," "hussy" and "American."

The nerve of the man! How dare he be indignant because she was not available for his amorous advances? Impulsively, Cece marched after him, determined to give him a verbal thrashing he would never forget, when yet another door in the hall opened. Once again, Cece shrank into the shadows.

Lady DeToulane progressed down the corridor in a casual manner offset by the assessing glances she tossed this way and that. Linnea stopped directly before Nigel Radcliffe's room and Cece gasped. No doubt this was another attempt at assignation among the houseguests.

Lady DeToulane's head jerked upright, her hand dropping from the knob, and Cece's heart fluttered in her throat.

"Is anyone there?" Linnea whispered sharply.

"It's only me," Cece said, stepping from her hiding place.

"Oh." Linnea appeared at a loss but only for a moment. Her eyes narrowed. "Whatever are you doing, roaming the halls at this hour of the night?"

"I couldn't sleep." Cece shrugged and held up the book. "I thought reading might help." She affixed an expression of innocence on her face. "And what of you? Are you having difficulties sleeping as well?"

"Difficulties sleeping?" Linnea looked as if the very idea was foreign to her; then she brightened. "Yes, of course. That's it exactly."

Dramatically she brought the back of her hand to her forehead and heaved a heartfelt sigh. "I do have such troubles retiring at night. Rest constantly seems to evade me." Linnea peeked out from beneath her raised hand. "It is a difficult cross to bear."

Cece struggled to appear appropriately sympathetic. "I can well imagine."

"No, no, it's quite beyond imagining." Linnea swept her arms outward in a wide gesture to encompass an entire world of woes. "The inability to sleep dominates one's life. It preys on the mind, sapping one's will and energy."

She placed an arm around Cece's shoulder and gently steered her away from Nigel's room.

"It sounds quite horrible," Cece said, suspecting Linnea's growing tirade more a fiction to hide her true purpose in the hallway than a product of any real affliction.

"Indeed." Linnea nodded seriously. "Horrible is something of an understatement. You are so very lucky to still be young enough to avoid such ailments." She stopped before Cece's door. "This is your room, isn't it?" Cece nodded. "How old are you, my dear?"

"Nearly twenty-one."

"As old as that," Linnea murmured. "Well, you still have some good years left."

"Thank you," Cece said dryly.

"Not at all." Linnea waved a dismissive hand, then reached for Cece's doorknob. "I, on the other hand, am old enough to be . . . well, shall we say an older sister. An older and much wiser sister. Husbands, no matter how wealthy or amicable or mature, do tend to age a woman. Still . . ."

Linnea leaned toward Cece in a confidential manner. "I am scarce past my thirty-second year and I feel I too have some good years left."

Cece bit her lip to hide her grin. "Undoubtedly."

Linnea nodded and opened Cece's door. "I have never been one for reading, yet this idea of yours of using a book to get to sleep has definite possibilities."

Cece raised a curious brow. "I'm surprised you haven't thought of it before."

"Yes, well . . ." Linnea cast a surreptitious glance at Nigel's door, and Cece wondered what he would think of Linnea's newfound literary interest. "There is no time like the present to try something one has never experienced before. You run along to bed now."

Firmly, Linnea nudged Cece into her room. "Do try to get some rest, my dear. I simply could not bear it if I thought yet another person in this house was suffering the way I am."

"Do you need directions to the library?"

"The library?" Confusion colored Linnea's face.

"The room with the books?" Cece prompted.

"No, no." Linnea shook her head briskly. "No need for that. I'm sure I shall find it with no difficulties whatsoever." She pulled the door toward her. "If this works, you will have my undying gratitude. Good night." The door snapped closed behind her.

Cece's long-suppressed grin broke free. Wicked thoughts flew through her mind. *If I have her undying gratitude, just what does Lord Radcliffe receive?*

Cece counted slowly to ten, then quietly opened her door the barest crack. Linnea stood by the door to Nigel's room. She glanced around swiftly, turned the knob and stepped inside.

Cece's amusement at the nighttime antics was tempered by astonishment. Certainly she had heard of illicit arrangements like this between unmarried— and often married—ladies and gentlemen. She was a modern woman, after all. Still, coming face to face with Sir Humphrey's advances and now Linnea's indiscretions was contrary to her upbringing, to the beliefs and values she'd been raised to accept. She narrowed her eyes thoughtfully and considered what she'd observed thus far. Perhaps being a modern woman required some reassessment.

The sound of another door opening in the corridor brought her to her senses, and she stared to see who the latest player was in this late-night game of hide-and-seek. Emily came into sight. Cece gasped. No, not her sister! Emily was far too young and innocent to enter into such nocturnal activities. Sibling protectiveness surged through her. Cece threw open her door and pulled her sister into her room.

"What on earth are you doing?" Emily said indignantly.

"What am I doing?" Cece drew herself up in her best older-sister manner. "The question is, what are you doing?"

Emily threw her an annoyed glare. "I thought I'd try to find the kitchen and get something to drink. I couldn't sleep."

"That seems to be an epidemic tonight," Cece said under her breath.

"What?" Emily's eyes narrowed. "What did you think I was doing?"

Guilt at her initial suspicion flooded her. She really should have known better than to even question Em's activities. Why, of the two sisters, Cece was the one more likely to go forging ahead without a thought to propriety or good sense. Cece was the one most apt to throw caution aside and act on emotion. Cece was the one with the impulsive nature that had more than once gotten her in a great deal of trouble. Still, in this improper atmosphere it did no harm to look out for her younger sibling.

"Nothing of any consequence," Cece said airily. "But there is a great deal of activity going on in this hallway tonight and it would be prudent to be alert."

"What kind of activity?" Curiosity tempered with suspicion shone in Emily's eyes.

"You simply would not believe it, Em." Cece leaned forward eagerly. "First Sir Humphrey attempted to waylay me in my room—"

Emily gasped. "The beast! Are you all right?"

Cece waved aside her concern. "I wasn't there at the time. Then Lady DeToulane crept to Lord Radcliffe's room—"

"No!" Emily's eyes widened with shock.

"Yes indeed." Cece nodded. "She tried to tell me she had difficulties sleeping."

Emily snorted disparagingly. "The very idea. To think she would attempt to fool you with such a feeble excuse when her true purpose was so blatantly obvious."

"What on earth do you know of such goings-on?" Cece said warily.

Emily cast her sister a superior smile. "You're not the only one who is well aware of the realities of modern life, as well as the relationships between men and women. I do not agree with half of your so-called progressive ideas, but I think it's advisable to know what one is facing."

Cece's eyes widened in surprise. "You've been reading."

Emily nodded smugly. "Of course I have."

"I never suspected," Cece murmured, staring at her sister with newfound respect. "I am impressed."

"Thank you." Emily tossed her a self-satisfied grin.

"Obviously there is no need to explain to you why you cannot be wandering the halls at this hour."

"Obviously." Puzzlement drew Emily's brows together. "Just for the sake of clarification, explain it to me anyway."

Cece sighed. Regardless of what Em thought about herself, regardless of what she read, she was still an innocent. And Cece wanted to keep it that way. "We wouldn't want you caught up in any kind of disgraceful activity. Your mere presence among such indiscreet occurrences could involve you, however indirectly, in scandal."

For the first time Emily appeared distinctly apprehensive. "What should I do?"

"I suggest you give up any idea of going anywhere other than your own room, and when you get there lock the door behind you. I'll watch to make certain of your safety." Cece opened the door a crack and peered out. "I believe the coast is clear."

"Thank you." Emily breathed a grateful sigh. The sisters stepped cautiously into the hall and turned toward Emily's room. A door creaked farther down the corridor. The girls exchanged frantic glances and leapt for the sanctuary of Cece's room. Swiftly, they pulled the door nearly closed, leaving it open the merest inch; not wide enough to be seen, but more than sufficient to provide a clear view of the hall.

Sofia Cresswell crept quietly down the corridor, paused at a door, then silently turned the knob and entered the room.

A strangled gasp emanated from Emily.

"The hussy!" Emily threw open the door and indignantly started toward the room Sofia had just entered.

Cece grabbed the collar of her robe and yanked her back, snapping the door closed behind her.

"Where do you think you're going?" Cece demanded.

Emily planted her hands on her hips. Outrage stormed in her eyes. "Do you know whose room that tart went into?"

Cece racked her brain, but the answer eluded her. No doubt her sister's unexpected ire clouded her mind. "I don't—"

"It's Quentin's," Emily said sharply. "That—that—that creature is in Quentin's room."

Cece studied her sister carefully. "I know this kind of behavior is shocking, but why on earth—" Realization dawned on her abruptly. "You like him, don't you?"

Emily raised her chin a notch. "I more than like him."

"You're not telling me you're in love with him?" Cece stared in astonishment. Why hadn't she seen this coming?

Emily nodded slowly. "I don't know for certain. It does feel like it could be love. I'm not sure that he sees me as much more than a child. I certainly have the oddest sensations around him. A strange yearning, an annoying frustration, complete and total confusion—"

"Oh dear." Cece shook her head despairingly. "That's love, all right."

"It's not at all what I expected," Emily said forlornly.

"I'm sure it gets better," Cece said staunchly, adding under her breath, "it has to."

"What do I do about that?" Emily gestured helplessly in the direction of Quentin's room.

Cece furrowed her brow in concentration. "Obviously we must get her out of there before anything untoward occurs."

"How?" Emily nearly wailed the word.

Cece cast her a condescending smile. "Simple, Em. We knock on the door."

Cece pulled open her own door and took a resolute step toward Quentin's chamber just as the door to his room unexpectedly opened. This time it was Emily who jerked her sister back into their hiding place. Cece stood, Emily kneeling below her, and both girls watched the unfolding scene in rapt attention.

A sleep-ruffled Quentin ushered a protesting Sofia into the hall. "I am flattered, my dear, truly I am, but I choose to keep my chambers to myself on this occasion. When I wish a lady, even one with charms as noticeable as yours, in my bed I will let her know. In addition, I prefer to be the visitor, not the visited. I am not particularly fond of unexpected guests in the middle of the night."

"But, Quentin . . ." Sofia leaned against his chest and fluttered her eyelashes up at him in a gesture of coquettish adoration. Cece could have sworn a growl came from her sister, below. "I thought surely after all we shared tonight . . ."

Quentin gently but firmly disentangled her clasping arms. "Sofia, we sat next to one another at dinner. We chatted amicably before and afterwards. You and I shared little more than total strangers."

"But I thought . . ." Sofia pouted prettily.

"I believe you did not think at all." Quentin cast her a cool look. "I would suggest returning to your chamber at once before we attract any attention here. I cannot imagine what your father might say."

Sofia tossed her loose blond hair over her shoulder in a gesture of defiance, but even in the dim light Cece could see her face had paled. "My father lets me do what I wish. Still, perhaps it is best to end this." She lowered her head and peeked up at him flirtatiously. "Another time perhaps?"

"Sofia, I have run into my share of young ladies like you before," Quentin said patiently. "I have learned first-hand, and through the similar experiences of friends, precisely what the end result of an evening such as the one you propose would entail. I have no desire to acquire additional obligations or responsibilities, and I do not intend to satisfy any claim of dishonor with a forced marriage." He smiled politely. "Do I make myself clear?"

"Quite," Sofia said with an angry glare. She spun around and flounced down the hall.

"Good night," Quentin called softly, and chuckled at the retreating figure. He turned to step into his room, paused and swiveled back to the empty corridor. "Good night, Emily. Good night, Cece."

The sisters slammed the door shut and stared at each other with horror.

"How embarrassing," Emily said, a stricken look on her face. "I am mortified."

"Nonsense, Em, we did nothing wrong."

"We eavesdropped on a private conversation." Emily groaned.

"Don't be absurd," Cece said confidently. "It was quite inadvertent. Besides, this hallway tonight is more public than a train station, with all the comings and goings."

"It does seem to be busy." Emily frowned in concern. "Do you think we should tell Mother and Father about all this?"

"Dear me, no," Cece said quickly. "In fact, it would be best if we kept this entirely to ourselves."

"Do you really think so?" Emily asked dubiously.

Cece nodded briskly. "Yes indeed. I think the wisest course is to completely ignore it. I have no idea if this kind of activity is typical in British country houses, or if this is just an unusually licentious gathering. Regardless, for the moment let us pretend we have seen nothing."

"If you insist," Emily said doubtfully.

"I do." Cece opened her door and cast her glance up and down the hall. For now, it appeared quiet. She gestured at Emily to go ahead. "I will watch to make certain you reach your room unmolested. And, Em . . . be sure and lock your door behind you."

Emily nodded and hurried to her room. Cece waited until her sister disappeared behind the closed door and she heard the click of the lock, then turned, closed and locked her own door behind her.

She leaned against the solid barrier and smiled ruefully. This was an extremely enlightening evening. Who would have dreamed of such occurrences? The thought struck her again as to the odd makeup of this party of Lady Graystone's. It seemed a prescription for scandal. She shook away the disquieting idea. Surely a woman who was so concerned over the standards of a potential daughter-in-law would never deliberately throw such a combustible mix of guests together. It was coincidence, nothing more.

Cece picked up her book from the bed where she'd tossed it in the excitement of the evening and yawned. It seemed she no longer needed assistance to sleep. She placed the volume on a nearby table, extinguished the lamp and fell back into bed. Once-evasive sleep now seemed to welcome her like a long lost love.

She snuggled against the pillow and an unbidden

thought danced in her mind. What would she have done if Jared had come to her door tonight? Would she have turned him away or welcomed him into her bed? The man already had full claim on her heart. Would anything more truly be so wrong? The questions and possible answers brought an unthinking smile to her lips.

Just before oblivion claimed her, in a last corner of her mind still fighting the blissful lure of sleep, a tiny thought nagged at her.

Lady Graystone was not the type of woman to accept, or allow, coincidence.

Chapter 9

". . . therefore if I move the tiller like this, the automobile should . . ." Cece perched in Jared's motorcar in its usual spot in the stables, her brow furrowed in concentration.

It was a lovely brow, capping the most remarkable eyes he'd ever seen. Not unlike rich chocolate—and he did so love chocolate—they were a deep, bittersweet color with occasional smoldering flashes of fire. Her skin was a counterpoint of cream and peaches. It was something of a shame, how well her brains equaled her beauty. While intelligence was a quality he would grudgingly admit he could appreciate in a wife, it made his effort to avoid allowing her to drive his automobile far more difficult than anticipated. Why, he'd already taught her nearly everything he could without actually moving the vehicle, and had drilled her on most points repeatedly. There was nothing left to do but gracefully admit defeat. Unless . . .

She leaned forward, studying the instruments necessary to operation of the vehicle. A few errant tendrils of lush walnut hair escaped the confines of the coiffure high on her head and teased the back of her neck. It was an irresistible picture. A delightful scene. A siren call he could not ignore. And the perfect opportunity.

He bent toward her and lightly brushed his lips against a fascinating spot midway between her hairline and the neck of her dress. At first she seemed not to notice. He continued, his touch light and provocative.

She froze.

"Jared?" Her tone was cautious. "Whatever are you doing?"

"The last resort, my love," he said under his breath.

She jerked upright and swiveled toward him. "What did you say?"

"My favorite sport . . . my love," he said innocently, and tossed her a wicked grin.

"Oh." She flushed a most becoming shade. "I didn't quite hear you."

"No?" He edged closer to nuzzle her ear, and she shivered in response. "I would think these delightful ears would have exceptionally acute hearing."

"Yes . . . well . . ." she said faintly.

He ran his lips down the line of her neck from beneath her ear and back, then onward to trace the curve of her jaw. "I would further think this exquisite skin to be extraordinarily sensitive."

Her eyes widened and her breathing came fast and shallow. "It does seem to be." She fluttered her hand in front of her face. "Is it getting quite warm in here?"

"Quite," he murmured, continuing his sensual exploration. She shuddered slightly, her eyes drifted closed and her head fell back, exposing her graceful neck to his plundering mouth. His lips trailed lower, dipping into the hollow at the base of her throat to meet the neckline of her blouse and the first of a long row of tiny buttons. Skillfully he flicked the top one open and kissed the exposed flesh.

"Jared?" Her voice was barely a sigh.

"Yes?" He unfastened a second button and a third.

"Do you remember when we were in Paris?"

"Um-hum." His lips caressed every inch revealed by each succeeding button. A fourth . . . a fifth . . . a sixth, until her blouse lay open, baring a flimsy camisole and the succulent flesh straining above the corset it failed to hide. He ran his tongue along the edge of the undergarment and she quivered. "I remember Paris extremely well."

"And we talked . . . about the dangers . . . of a dishonorable man?" Tiny gasps separated her words.

He untied the ribbons of her camisole and pushed it low. Rosy-tipped breasts heaved above the confines of her corset and he cupped one luscious offering. Lightly he rubbed the flat of his thumb across the tip and watched it pebble at his touch.

"A rogue, I believed we called him," Jared said softly, and bent to take her breast in his mouth. She drew a sharp breath and uttered an unthinking moan.

"Jared?" Her fingers tunneled through his hair and she grasped his head mindlessly. "What else would a rogue do?"

He grinned against her skin at her words, sweet with the promise of success, and raised his head. His gaze caught hers and his smile faded, vanquished by the abrupt recognition that whatever game the two played with each other, this moment was something far more tangible . . . lasting . . . real.

Her eyes were endless with newfound desire, glazed with awakening passion. Her face was flushed, heated; her chest heaved. She bit her lower lip, full, lush and inviting, and stared at him with a look that said all he'd ever dreamed of, all he'd ever wanted, was his for the taking. His breath caught in his throat with the sure knowledge that she offered him not only her body but her soul.

"Jared?" Her voice was husky and intense. "Wouldn't he kiss me until I knew I'd been well and truly kissed?"

For a moment he could only stare at the blatant yearning revealed in her eyes. Then he pulled her to him, her bare chest crushed against his, his mouth descending to meet hers.

"The fiend," he breathed, and claimed her lips with his own. The pressure of his mouth on hers, the eager way her lips opened beneath his, destroyed any vestige of self-control that might have yet lingered at his command. His tongue swept inside her mouth, tracing the inner edge of her lips, dueling with hers in an urgent dance of need and fire. Gentleness was flung aside in a burning passion to devour and consume and make this woman his forever.

She responded to the demand of his lips with an unquenched ache that insisted on fulfillment. Her tongue met his eagerly, desperate for unknown sensations she could only guess at. Tenderness was discarded in her frantic quest to conquer and claim this man as her own.

Cece pulled him tighter and wrenched her lips from his, surrendering to the overpowering compulsion to rain kisses on his face, to bite the lobe of his ear, to taste the corded power of his neck. A thought popped to the surface of senses drugged with pleasure and desire: If this is what one could expect from a rogue, thank God Jared's reputation was not unfounded in that area! His mouth claimed her breast and coherent thought vanished in her frenzied struggle to satisfy a raging need she'd never suspected existed.

He could not get enough of her. Not her taste, not her scent, not the feel of her velvet skin beneath his touch, beneath his mouth. He ran his hand up her leg higher, ever higher, in an exploration of territory not known by man before. Her fingers dug into his back, the sharp pain spurring him onward. His hand reached the juncture of her thighs and only the thin fabric of her undergarments separated him from her damp heat.

She twisted on the small seat of the motorcar, struggling to increase the pressure of his touch on her most private places. The exquisite sensation stole her breath and her mind. The long, hard length of his manhood pressed against her, and she wondered blindly how much longer they could continue before sheer pleasure ripped them apart.

A corner of his mind screamed that this was not the place; this was not the time. The seat of an automobile was not where he wished to start a lifetime with the only true love of his life. But dear God, she was raging hunger, incessant fervor and heaven itself beneath his touch. If this was the reaction of an innocent newly awakened to the glories of passion, he could only thank the stars he was the first to storm the castle walls of her desire.

A hunting horn sounded in the distance.

"Bloody hell." The sound jerked him to his senses like a slap of icy water. He groaned and sagged against her.

"Jared, don't stop now." She moaned and clutched him tighter.

"Cece . . ." Reluctantly, he gathered his wits about

him and struggled to sit upright, firmly disengaging her arms from around his neck.

Cece sprawled across the seat, her blouse gaping open, her skirt bunching nearly around her hips. For a moment she gazed at him, unfulfilled passion simmering in her eyes. Then her dazed expression slowly cleared and awareness dawned on her face. She bolted upright, one hand grasping the edges of her blouse together and the other clapping to her cheek.

"Goodness, Jared." Her eyes were wide with what might have been embarrassment or, more than likely, curious excitement. "Did we . . . ? How could . . . ? That was . . ."

"That was without a doubt the most incredible . . . um, kiss I have ever experienced." He leaned forward and kissed the tip of her nose.

"Thank you." She smiled modestly and blushed with obvious pleasure.

"Now, however, I regret it's time to go." He regretted it more than he could say. He climbed stiffly out of the motorcar, Cece scrambling in his wake. Jared watched with pleasure her struggle to right the convoluted folds of her skirt. Even now she appeared so appealingly disheveled, enjoyment quickly turned again to desire, and it was all he could do not to take her back in his arms and finish what they had started.

Cece worked on fastening the long row of buttons that ran the length of her bodice and cast him a rueful glance. "This obviously means our lesson for today is over."

"Lesson?" What was she talking about? Certainly he was more experienced in these matters than she, but he would hardly term it a lesson.

She studied him for a long moment. A grin broke

across her face. "The automobile, Jared. Remember? The driving lesson?"

"Of course." He shrugged sheepishly. "For a moment there I thought—"

"I'm quite aware of what you thought," she said primly, her proper tone in comical contrast to her appearance: disorderly clothing, tousled hair, the high color of passion still in her cheeks. She finished with the last button and gestured toward the motorcar. "These lessons of yours are not going at all well. By now I assumed I would have mastered the controls—"

"Oh, you've mastered control, all right," he murmured.

She continued without pause. "—of the vehicle and be puttering about country roads. But I have yet to learn one practical thing about driving."

He stepped close to her and met her indignant gaze with his own. His words sounded low and fraught with meaning. "Have you learned anything at all?"

"Well, yes, I—" Her voice faltered. The annoyance in her eyes softened, melted and faded away, replaced by the smoldering flashes he now recognized and reveled in. "I've learned a great deal."

"About driving an automobile?" He was so close, he could smell the spicy floral scent that was uniquely hers. Another moment and he would forget all about his duties to his mother's guests and cast aside his responsibilities as the Earl of Graystone to lose himself in the intoxicating presence of this American vixen.

"Not entirely," she said breathlessly.

"What have you learned?" He stared into her eyes with an intensity that dared her to reveal the secrets of her very soul.

"Well, I've learned that in some subjects . . . you are an excellent teacher." An unexpected twinkle danced in her eyes, a spirited glint of amusement and something more, a challenge, perhaps, or a promise. She lifted her chin a notch.

"And I look forward to our next lesson."

CECE FLOUNCED INTO the empty breakfast room and headed straight for the bountiful offering laid out on the sideboard. One thing she would say for the British: They certainly knew to start the day.

She was famished, no doubt the result of her early morning lesson on motorcars and passion. Lust certainly did sap one's strength and drain one's energy. She popped a piece of sausage into her mouth. Still, it did seem well worth the trouble.

She had never let a man take such liberties before. Lord, she had never wanted to. But with Jared, not only did she make no move to stop him, her behavior could easily be called encouraging. The sensations he aroused were nothing short of magnificent, and she could scarcely wait until he attempted such indiscretions again—given, of course, that she would allow him such familiarity. She paused in the effort to fill her plate and grinned. There was no question she would allow him. They did plan to be married and, after all, she was a modern woman.

She piled her plate high with everything that appeared remotely edible, avoiding, of course, those odd-looking fish. Kippers, they called them. It wasn't that she didn't like fish; they simply did not appeal to her for breakfast. Just the sight of them lying there, staring accusingly, was somewhat distasteful first thing in the morning.

Cece turned toward the table and stopped dead in her tracks.

"Good morning, my child." Lady Graystone sat serenely at the head of the table, a stack of correspondence to one side, the remains of a modest, almost spartan meal to the other. Cece glanced at her own groaning plate and smiled weakly.

"Good morning, Lady Graystone."

"Please, do sit here beside me." Olivia gestured to the chair next to hers. Cece would have much rather placed substantially more distance between them, but there was no avoiding what sounded vaguely like a royal summons.

She drew a deep breath, mentally squared her shoulders and reminded herself who and what she was. She was Cecily Gwendolyn White, American heiress, a woman of the nineties with one foot firmly planted in the oncoming twentieth century and more than likely the next Countess of Graystone. No deceptively pleasant dragon in mother's disguise was going to get the best of her.

"Where is everyone this morning?" Cece said brightly.

"Oh, here and there." Olivia waved vaguely. "I believe your mother and sister have gone with Millicent to her home to spend much of the day making preparations for your sister's debut. Your father and most of the others are hunting. Odd though," Olivia pursed her lips thoughtfully, "Jared was not here when they began. He arrived several minutes late, quite out of breath and somewhat disheveled. He said he had been attending to some sort of business."

"Did he?" Cece said faintly and took a bite of a savory biscuit that tasted like dust in her mouth.

Olivia eyed her for a moment. "Forgive me for saying so, my dear, but you too appear somewhat unkempt. Have you been up and about for long?"

"I was up with the sun this morning." Cece cast Olivia her sincerest glance. "And I felt the need of a walk, a very long walk, to clear my senses."

"It must have been quite windy," Olivia observed mildly.

"Windy?" Cece drew her brows together in confusion.

Olivia nodded toward the younger woman's head. "Your hair, my child; it's in quite a state."

Cece sent her hands flying to her hair and she groaned to herself. She could tell from touch alone that she must look a fright. No mere wind could do that much damage. Still, it was an offered lifeline, and she grabbed it with enthusiasm. "It was quite brisk. Surprisingly so. Practically a cyclone."

Olivia glanced toward the French doors. "Yet it seems so calm out now."

"Well, certainly now it's calm," Cece said quickly. "That's the most terrifying thing about windstorms: They blow right up out of nowhere. One moment everything is tranquil and placid and the next," she snapped her fingers, "why, your home has been blown into another state and you're extremely lucky just to be alive."

"I see," Olivia murmured and took a sip of her tea. Did her lips quirk upward at the corner just before they were hidden by the cup? Surely Cece was mistaken.

Olivia patted her mouth lightly with a linen napkin. "Why did you rise so early this morning? I do hope you slept well?"

Another lifeline, and this one very close to the truth.

"Well, to be honest, I did not sleep at all well."

"I am so sorry." Sympathy and curiosity shone in Olivia's eyes. "Why not?"

"Why not?" Cece had decided last night it would serve no purpose to discuss the nocturnal activities to anyone not directly involved. If there was one thing her mother had taught her, it was that gossip never furthered anyone's cause. And if she had learned nothing else from the career of Nellie Bly, it was that one should indeed gather all the information available, but one should disseminate it wisely.

"I do hope your quarters were adequate? Your bed comfortable?" Concern etched Lady Graystone's face.

"My room is lovely," Cece said hurriedly. "And the bed is one of the most comfortable I've ever slept on."

"Then what was the problem, my dear?"

"The problem . . ." Cece hesitated for a moment and searched her mind for an answer, any answer. What would keep someone awake in an old castle, aside from houseguests playing musical bedrooms? A ghost? No, far too improbable. Unexplained creaks and bumps in the night? Certainly, but—the answer flashed into her mind and she leaned forward confidentially. "I believe it was mice."

"Mice?" Olivia said, surprise glimmering in her eyes.

"Mice."

"Could it have been anything else?" Olivia's voice rang with innocent curiosity.

"I'm quite certain it was mice." Cece nodded firmly. "Why, I could hear them nearly all night. Scurrying up and down the hallways."

"A lot of mice, do you think?"

"Definitely." Cece frowned in concentration. "At least four."

"Four?" Olivia again patted her lips with her napkin, and this time Cece was sure she hid a slight smile.

"Well," Olivia said briskly, "I shall have to have Watkins look into the situation. Although I daresay castles like this are bound to have a few extra unwanted guests now and again. Still, I wouldn't want to have those invited annoyed by those who aren't."

Cece waved a hand in an airy gesture of nonchalance. "I wouldn't worry about it. I suspect I was the only one the least bit bothered by the pitter-patter of little feet."

"Now, my dear"—Olivia rose—"I feel a bit of a headache coming on, so if you will excuse me?"

"Of course." Cece cast her a concerned glance. "I do hope you feel better."

"It all depends, my dear." Olivia smiled faintly. "It really all depends."

OLIVIA CHUCKLED TO herself and lightly climbed the stairs. Mice and cyclones. She had to give the girl credit; she was certainly creative when necessary.

Rodents in the hallways. Mice! Imagine! Some would no doubt call them rats. Olivia knew full well what kind of midnight games would be played among those particular guests. She ignored a twinge of guilt that Sir Humphrey could have posed a serious threat to Cecily or her sister. That was the very reason she had encouraged Quentin to stay at the castle and placed him across the hall. Surely he could be counted upon to act as rescuer should a scream ring out in the middle of the night. Nigel, too, would defend the girls if it had come to that. Her son's old friend was a rake, a rogue and a rascal, but she had known her share of that type of man in her youth and prided herself on distinguishing between those with flawed moral character and others who had strayed but still possessed a true sense of honor. No matter what else he might be, Nigel Radcliffe was an honorable man.

Cecily White appeared to have her own code of honor as well. Olivia nodded approvingly to herself. She had given the girl every opportunity to indulge in what was essentially harmless gossip and Cecily had not risen to the provocative bait.

While gossip did seem to be the lifeblood of London society, Olivia firmly believed it should never be spread idly. One should, on the other hand, always listen closely and, when necessary, use the flow of rumor and innuendo for one's own purposes.

But Cecily had nothing to gain from revealing what Olivia suspected was a rather active night in the west wing. If the girl was indeed to take her place in society as the next Countess of Graystone, she must know how to use gossip as a benevolent weapon, a weapon kept sharpened but rarely used, and never wielded simply as a source of amusement. This was an important test for the American, and Olivia was inordinately pleased with her response. Yet another check appeared on the mental list of qualities Olivia required for a bride for her son.

Olivia stepped into her chambers and paused momentarily, struck by a thought she had nearly overlooked. That windstorm nonsense might have passed muster to anyone other than a mother who had noted her son's own untimely and disorderly arrival. She knew precisely where Jared and Cecily had each passed the night, but where had they been earlier this morning? They were no doubt together; that much was obvious.

Olivia strode to the window and frowned, absently

gazing through the glass, ignoring the lush green of the rolling English countryside. Jared apparently already liked this girl and, judging from the state of her disarray, she liked him in return. Still, Olivia had no intention of permitting any kind of marriage because of an indiscretion between the two. And if Cecily did not pass the rest of Olivia's tests . . . well, there would simply be no wedding at all.

So far, the girl had done beautifully, and Olivia realized, in some small way, she was hoping the child would succeed. None of the others had made it nearly this far, and it was growing more and more difficult to dream up challenges for the American—challenges that would not alert Jared to his mother's activity. But Olivia still had a trick or two left to play.

Olivia smiled slowly at the verdant scene framed by the window. Cecily's penchant for creativity was definitely a beneficial attribute.

She was going to need it.

Chapter 10

CECE surveyed the remnants of her rather hearty breakfast and suppressed a small, quite dainty, extremely feminine and totally ill-advised hiccup. Even her chat with Lady Graystone hadn't diminished the appetite the formidable lady's son had helped build. She propped her elbows on the table and rested her chin on her intertwined fingers. The only crimp in an otherwise blissful day was Jared's continuing reluctance to allow her free rein behind the controls of his motorcar to pilot it on the open road.

Still, he had shown her how the machine worked. Indeed, his explanations were extremely thorough, to the point where she suspected she could take the vehicle apart and reassemble it herself, blindfolded. Thoughtfully, she sipped the last dregs in her teacup. She was so well versed on the principles and the practicalities of automobiles, perhaps she no longer needed someone to actually show her how to control the beast. Perhaps she could figure it out herself. . . .

A throat cleared behind her. "I beg your pardon, Miss White?"

Watkins, the butler, stood in the doorway.

"Yes, Watkins?" Cece cast him a friendly smile.

The servant's face remained expressionless. "It seems there is a problem."

"Oh?" How odd. What kind of problem would Lady Graystone's butler bring to her?

"Lady Graystone has a sick headache," Watkins said solemnly.

"I am sorry," Cece said sympathetically. "What a shame."

"She has retired for the remainder of the day."

"I see," Cece said slowly, not certain she saw anything at all. "And you're telling me because . . . ?"

"Lady Graystone said to inform you of the situation and request you take over preparations for tonight, since Lady Millicent and Mrs. White are otherwise engaged today."

Relief flooded through her. Whatever other quirks Phoebe White might have, she had raised both her girls to be flawless hostesses. Cece could handle an army of servants with the panache of a battlefield general. "I assume she has already prepared a menu? Informed the cook? Arranged for flowers? Music? Etcetera?"

"Her ladyship always arranges the flowers personally. She also selects them herself." The expression on the servant's face never wavered, but his voice held the slightest note of censure. "Her ladyship believes flowers express the soul of an estate, and she insists such a task should be handled by the family, not a gardener."

"Very well," Cece said brightly. If this was all there was left to arrange for tonight's dinner, she should be able to handle it with little effort. "I'm confident I can accomplish that to Lady Graystone's satisfaction."

"There is another problem." Watkins's voice seemed to echo in the close confines of the breakfast room.

"What is it?" Caution edged her tone.

"Her ladyship had arranged for a small group of musicians to play this evening." A gleam appeared in his eye. "Word arrived from London a few moments ago that they would not be able to attend."

She released an annoyed sigh. "What happened?"

Watkins shrugged ever so slightly. "Drunk, I think, miss, or dead. The message was not completely clear."

"Wonderful." Sarcasm dripped from the word. This was a bit more of a problem than flower arranging; still, nothing to panic over. "I shall have to think about that one for a while, but surely we can come up with some type of entertainment. And it is, after all, a small gathering."

"Small?" A glimmer of surprise shot through Watkins's eyes.

Apprehension tweaked her insides. "It is small, isn't it? I understood it was just the houseguests and a few neighbors."

"Lady Graystone has a significant number of neighbors."

Foreboding squeezed her stomach. "What precisely are we talking about here, Watkins? How many people are expected tonight?"

"Including the houseguests?"

"Most definitely including the houseguests."

"When last I checked I believe the final count had come in . . ." he paused, and she could have sworn his hesitation was strictly for dramatic effect, "at sixty-four guests."

She smothered a startled gasp. "Sixty-four people are expected here? Tonight? For dinner?"

His eminently proper butler eyebrow rose the barest fraction. "The dining hall comfortably seats one-hundred-and-twelve."

"One-hundred-and-twelve," she said faintly. "I suppose that's something to be grateful for, at any rate. We shall only be half full."

She drew herself up straighter in her chair and pulled a deep breath. "The flowers should not pose a problem. Music or entertainment will be a bit more of a challenge." She thought for a moment, then snapped her fingers. "Surely there are some musicians in the village? Someone who plays the piano? A minister's daughter? Better yet, with an estate this size and the vast number of servants employed here, I cannot believe there aren't a fair number who play some type of instrument. Fiddles, something of that sort?"

She rose from her chair and paced the room, her mind working in tandem with her step. "I would imagine a substantial percentage of those sixty-four souls play as well. We shall invite them to take part." She shot the butler a confidential glance. "I've never yet met anyone who would pass up the opportunity to show off his or her musical skills, no matter how feeble they may be."

She grinned triumphantly. "Why, we shall turn the evening into a musicale using the guests as part and parcel of their own entertainment. It should be quite a charming amusement and a great deal of fun."

"Excellent, miss," Watkins murmured. A tiny spark of appreciation twinkled in his eye. "However, I feel I should tell you—"

"Don't say it." Cece thrust her hands before her as if to stop the words from falling from his lips. "Please, don't tell me—"

"There is another problem." Watkins's tone rang like the voice of doom.

Cece squared her shoulders and raised her chin resolutely. "Watkins, I am an American. We are quite used to overcoming rather incredible odds. We are resourceful and self-sufficient. This is a party, not the end of the world." A short, anxious laugh skittered from her lips. "How bad can it be, anyway? It's not as if I were being called upon to prepare this meal myself. After all, we have a cook."

Watkins again lifted his eyebrow the tiniest bit. Her stomach plunged much further.

"We do have a cook, don't we, Watkins?"

For a moment what might have been sympathy glittered in Watkins's eyes.

"The cook is sick."

"HELL AND DAMNATION."

The three kitchen maids gasped at the rude indiscretion. Cece didn't care. She paced up and down the massive kitchen past huge warming ovens, a preparation table that seemed to go on forever, even a fireplace she could literally stand in. The castle kitchen was an intriguing mix of old and new. Copper pots and pans hanging from cast-iron hooks, their surfaces shined to mirror brightness, reflected her passage.

If only her mother was here to advise her. No, that would be the coward's way out of this dilemma. And if she was to become the Countess of Graystone, it was only right that she should be able to handle such a situation. Still, she wasn't the countess yet, and if her mother was available, Cece would be more than willing to thrust this entire endeavor into her parent's capable hands.

She pulled to a halt and studied the servants lined up before her. The two on the ends were similar in appearance, both dark-haired and short, with rounded figures. Like bookends, they flanked the middle maid. Taller and thinner than the others, the girl's fair hair was of that indefinable color somewhere between blond and brown. All three were of indeterminable ages, but she didn't think any were much older than she, or much wiser. And all three appeared, if not exactly terrified, then at least more than a little apprehensive.

"Do any of you know how to cook?"

They shook their heads quickly and nearly in unison. Cece sighed and tried to fight the panic rising within her.

"None of you knows how to cook anything?" Cece cast them a hopeful look designed to forge alliances and create the impression that servant and master alike were all in this together. "Anything at all?"

The maid on the far end raised a timid hand. "Cook 'as been lettin' me cook veget'bles of late. Carrots, onions, potatoes."

"Excellent!" Cece beamed and clasped her hands together. "And your name is?"

"Mary, miss." The maid bobbed a quick curtsy.

"'Scuse me, miss," the other half of the bookend maids said tentatively. "I pretty much bake the bread 'ere. 'Ave for a few years now."

"Splendid!" Cece said with a satisfied smile. "And you are?"

The girl dropped a curtsy exactly like the first maid. "Ellen, miss." She nodded toward Mary. "She's my sister."

"I thought as much," Cece murmured. She turned

to the middle servant. A head taller than the other two, she appeared a year or two older.

"Desserts, miss," she said sheepishly and dipped a curtsy. "I'm Willomena. Cook 'as been teaching me to do desserts."

"Did you have dessert planned for tonight?" Cece said hopefully. "If it's already made, that's one less thing to worry about."

The maids traded swift glances; then the tall one stepped forward, apparently the spokesperson by virtue of a silent vote. " 'Twere the oddest thing, miss. We all knew about the party. 'Er ladyship 'asn't 'ad a party 'ere since the old earl died. But aside from the dustin' and the moppin' and the scrubbin', and that more fer the 'ouseguests than anything else," she said confidentially, "there 'asn't been a lick'o preparation for this party."

"No bread," Ellen said somberly.

"No menu," Mary said soberly.

"Nothing," Willomena said solemnly. She shook her head in dismay. "What 'as the castle come to, I ask you? It's a disgrace."

"A scandal," Mary moaned.

"Oh, the shame of it," Ellen lamented. "The 'orrible shame."

For a moment Cece could only stare at the trio, the import of their words escaping her in the sheer absurdity of their dismay. It was exceedingly nice to have servants who held their positions with pride. Still, a party was nothing but a party, after all. And even in the rigid societal structure of 1890s Britain, a social disaster would, in time, be forgotten. Beyond that, it was still morning. She and this downhearted trio had the entire day to come up with some kind of miracle.

"Well," Cece drew a deep breath, "if there is nothing planned, then we can do nothing wrong. That is to say, anything we do should be quite acceptable."

The maids exchanged looks once again, seemed to reach a unified response and turned matching smiles toward her.

"Very good." Cece nodded. "Now we seem to have the ability to take care of some of the superficial details of this dinner. Still . . . none of you know how to cook . . ."

She directed her gaze to Mary ". . . beef?"

Mary shook her head. Cece turned to Willomena. "Lamb?"

Willomena's gesture mirrored Mary's. Cece faced Ellen with a sinking heart. Her voice held a note of last-ditch hope. "Poultry? Fish? Game?"

Ellen looked as if she wanted to say anything but what she did. "Just bread."

"Vegetables," Mary added.

"Dessert," Willomena sighed.

"That is a problem." Cece leaned back against the table and raised a skeptical brow. "Any ideas, ladies?"

"Don't you know 'ow to cook, miss?" Mary blurted.

"Me?" Cece snorted in derision. "Why on earth would you think I'd know how to cook?"

"You're from America, miss," Ellen said, as if that explained everything.

Willomena nodded eagerly. "We read a lot of stories about America, miss. About brave pioneer families crossin' the whole country—"

"About cowboys and Indians and scouts and gunslingers," Ellen said eagerly. "About the Wild West, mostly."

"With people named Dead Eye McCall and One-Shot

Willie and Sam the Serpent Saline." Mary released a heartfelt sigh. "It sounds bloody excitin'."

"Dime novels," Cece said under her breath.

"And you bein' from there and all, we thought sure a little thing like cookin' wouldn't present a problem." Unblemished faith shone in Willomena's eyes. "For an American."

"Yes, well . . ." How much better could things get? Not only was she expected to plan and execute an evening for sixty-four people, but the staff with which she had to pull it off apparently viewed her as a combination of Buffalo Bill and Lady Liberty.

She eyed the trio before her cautiously. Confidence practically glowed about them. It seemed that in their eyes, America—more specifically, the Wild West—was as close as one could get to heaven on earth. And anyone even remotely connected with that paradise was a virtual saint.

"I'm from Chicago, ladies," Cece said. "It's extremely civilized."

The expectant expressions before her did not fade. She tried again.

"I don't live in the Wild West. I'm not stout-hearted pioneer stock. I've never met a real Indian. And the only time I've ever even been around cooking was . . ."

Like lightning before a storm, unforgettable memories flashed through her mind.

". . . Fork Tongue Frank," she said softly.

The expectant faces in front of her faded and she was swept back to the summer she was twelve years old. The months her mother always referred to as "that unfortunate incident with your father." It was the most wonderful time of her life.

Henry White was indeed a self-made man, beginning his career as a cowboy on the open range. Henry quickly decided there was little future in the rugged life of cattle drives and working other men's herds. He suspected the way to make his fortune was closer to the market end of the beasts' progress from prairie to table. With the small amount of money he had saved he started his own meatpacking venture in Chicago.

Henry had a knack for beef and business. By the time Cece was born the Whites were quite prosperous. By the time she hit twelve he was proclaimed king of the meatpacking industry.

Perhaps it was his success that triggered the "unfortunate incident." Perhaps it was merely the realization that there would be no son to carry on the family business. Or perhaps it was simply his charming wife's penchant for spending his hard-earned money freely and without a second thought as to where it came from, and the same inclination he saw developing in his daughters.

With the declaration that "at least one of his children should damn well know where the money to support this family comes from," Cece was whisked from the eminently civilized world of Chicago to the last two months of a Wyoming cattle drive.

And she had loved it.

Her days were spent on horseback with men who were rough and rowdy, kind and funny. Men who tried to watch their salty language around her and failed. Men who looked on her less as the big boss's daughter and more as a little sister. Cowboys.

Her favorite was an old, gnarled gnome of a man: Fork Tongue Frank. Frank O'Malley ruled the chuck wagon with a wooden spoon in one hand and a barely hidden bottle of whiskey in the other. In spite of his short stature, the little Irishman was bigger than life and absolutely fascinating. His tongue indeed was forked a little. O'Malley claimed it was the legacy of his great-grandpa who was part rattler. Other cowboys said he'd actually fallen in a drunken stupor and slit the end of his tongue on a broken bottle, and that it just grew back that way. But Cece liked O'Malley's version best.

She hung around his wagon with a tenacity that he rewarded by spinning tales that mixed Emerald Isle leprechauns with frontier natives. He even took her into his confidence and shared some of his culinary secrets.

"If ya drop somethin' on the ground, wipe it off fore ya throw it back in the pot." Fork Tongue's gravelly voice still rang in her mind, as if he'd spouted his wisdom just yesterday. "Men don't mind a bit a grit, long as the vittles is nice and tasty.

"And remember, girl, nothin' fills the empty spot in a man's belly like beans. And a splash of this—" he held up his bottle with a twinkle in his eye—"makes even the worst food this side of kingdom come and back again mighty tasty."

Fork Tongue showed her how to bake corn bread over an open fire, and even the cook in the grand house in Chicago had, through the years, occasionally allowed Cece into her sanctuary for a blissful afternoon of baking corn bread and reliving memories.

The last day of the drive, right before the crew headed the cattle to the railroad in Cheyenne for the trip to Chicago, the cowboys marked the end of the long, arduous trail. She suspected now that the celebration had been more for the benefit of a twelve-year-old girl than anything else. With the wisdom of age, she had no doubt the real celebrating came after the cowboys had their pay firmly in hand and could take advantage of the saloon and whatever other forms of entertainment the cattle town had to offer.

But on that final day, under Frank's watchful eye, the men dug a pit, lit a huge fire that burned to slow, smoldering embers and patiently roasted a carcass. It took all day and was without a doubt the most delicious thing Cece had ever tasted.

Beef cooked over an open fire. Corn bread. A rather meager offering of culinary expertise. Still . . .

She narrowed her eyes and surveyed the trio of maids. If nothing else, they were eager and willing. "Willomena, what's the best dessert you can prepare? Your specialty, as it were?"

Willomena drew herself up with pride. "That would be trifle, miss. I make a trifle better than any one."

"Makes you think you'd died and gone to 'eaven," Mary said.

"Knocks your socks right off your feet, it does," Ellen added enthusiastically.

"It sounds perfect." Cece grinned. "Ellen, do you know how to bake corn bread?"

"I can bake anything, miss," Ellen said modestly.

"She knows her bread, all right," Willomena said.

"And a tasty job she does too," Mary chimed in.

"Never made corn bread, though." Ellen frowned, then brightened. "But if you can give me some 'elp as to the basics . . ."

"Basics, Ellen, are about all I can give you," Cece said wryly. "Now, ladies, with your able assistance I think we can pull off this evening."

She folded her arms across her chest and smiled slowly.

"I have an interesting idea."

"WHAT IN THE name of all that's holy is going on here?" Jared stopped dead in his tracks beside Lady Millicent at the top of the short flight of stone steps leading from the castle terrace to the formal gardens.

"It is quite impressive, isn't it?" Lady Millicent murmured, slanting him a sidelong glance to gauge his reaction. She was not disappointed.

"Impressive . . . and altogether unexpected." He stared, appreciation and astonishment rampant on his handsome face.

From their vantage point on the steps, the gardens and surrounding lawns were laid out like a carpet at their feet. Guests invited to Lady Graystone's gathering meandered amid roses and hedges and blossoms of all kind. Violinists strolled among ladies and gentlemen who greeted one another and chatted amicably like the old friends and neighbors most of them were.

On the lawns edging each side of the formal beds, rows of tables set with white linen and the castle's best silver and crystal glittered in the deepening twilight. Tapers twinkled from multi-armed candelabra and competed for attention with the gardener's best blooms, overflowing urns and vases in a lush display of light and beauty. Everywhere his gaze fell, lanterns winked from perches on trees and fountains and nooks and crannies he'd never imagined existed, competing for attention with the very stars in the heavens.

"Impressive may not do it justice." Jared offered Millicent his arm, and the couple proceeded down the steps.

Millicent nodded her approval. "It does look like something from a fairy tale."

"Doesn't it though. By jove, I didn't know Mother had it in her. Something this—" he gestured to the fantasy setting before them "—fresh. Creative. Original. I'll say this for her: It may take her a few years, but when she decides to finally rejoin society and entertain once again, she certainly does it up right."

"Jared . . ." Millicent stopped on the bottom riser and frowned at him reproachfully. "This is not your mother's doing."

"It's not?" Confusion colored his words. "Then who . . . ?"

"Cece did it."

His puzzled expression deepened. "What on earth do you mean 'Cece did it'?"

Millicent considered him for a long, thoughtful moment. "You really have no idea at all, do you?" He shook his head and she took his arm in the same manner she'd use to gently break news of a calamity to an unsuspecting innocent.

"My dear boy. . . ." She steered him away from the growing throng of guests to a bench secluded somewhat from direct view and settled herself as comfortably as possible. "It is my understanding—and mind you, Phoebe, Emily and I were at my home most of the day—that this entire affair was dropped in Cece's hands at the last possible minute. Or this morning, at any rate, which is the last moment if one is planning an event quite as extensive as this one." Millicent swept her hand dramatically in the direction of the partygoers. "Why, just look at how many people are in attendance."

"It does appear she invited half the village," Jared

said dryly, a suspicious glint in his blue eyes. "Please continue."

"When we arrived here—quite late too, I might add—Cece already had everything under control." Millicent raised her head and sniffed delicately. "Do you smell that?"

Jared dutifully inhaled and widened his eyes in appreciation. "I hadn't noticed it before now, but there is a most delicious aroma in the air. Beef perhaps?"

"Of course it's beef," Millicent said indignantly. "Beef is practically in her blood. I understand she sent to the village butcher for every joint of beef they had available, and a fair number of chickens as well. Then she had—I believe it was stable boys, but it might have been footmen or even undergardeners—"

"Had them what?" Impatience rang in Jared's voice.

"I am getting to that, Jared," Millicent huffed, "all in good time. Now, where was I . . ."

"Something about stable boys or footmen and beef joints?" Jared said encouragingly.

"If you would stop interrupting, I would be more than happy to conclude. As I was saying . . ." She shot him a sharp glare to stifle any interference on his part. He stared expectantly and, mollified, she continued. "At any rate, Cece instructed servants to dig a pit and roast the meat over the fire. It's been cooking all day. Beyond that, she has directed a number of other dishes for tonight's gathering."

Millicent leaned forward, her voice low and private. "I understand the cook was ill."

Jared drew his brows together in a puzzled frown. "How extremely odd. Cook is never ill."

"That's not all I've heard," Millicent said smugly. "Do you see that man over there playing the fiddle?"

Jared glanced in the direction she indicated. "And that one near the arbor?" Again Jared's gaze followed her lead. "Do they look at all familiar?"

Jared perused the men briefly and sat up straighter in recognition. "Good God! They're members of the castle staff. Why on earth does Cece have servants entertaining?"

"The musicians who were supposed to play tonight apparently died in some horrible drunken brawl. At least that's the story I heard. Whatever." She waved airily, as if the gesture brushed away any bothersome details. "The point here is that Cece was bright enough to commandeer staff as musicians, come up with a meal for—how many people do you think are here?"

"Quite a few," Jared said wryly.

"Provide sustenance for a significant number of people, decorate the grounds—I thought moving the whole soiree outdoors was a nice touch, don't you?"

"Very nice." Jared surveyed the scene thoughtfully. "What you have not yet explained is how this all ended up in Cece's lap."

"Haven't I?" Millicent frowned. "I did think I explained that part straightaway. Phoebe, Emily and I were at my estate all day, planning her coming out. It is next week, you know? The only ones who could have possibly assisted her at all were that twit, Sofia, and that tart, Linnea DeToulane. They were God knows where, not that they would be of any help in a crisis anyway. . . ."

"My mother?" His dark eyes flashed, but his words were quiet, controlled . . . ominous. "Where was my mother through all this?"

"Olivia," Millicent said, her tone innocent, her gaze assessing, "was confined to bed with a sick headache."

"My mother spent the day in bed?" Disbelief underlaid his words.

"That's what I heard. Of course, a great deal of my information comes from my maid, who got it from castle servants." Millicent smiled sweetly and laid one gloved hand on his arm. "I wouldn't worry too much, dear boy; I believe Olivia is quite recovered now. I saw her only a few minutes ago and she appeared the picture of health."

"Bloody hell." Anger flared on his face. "She did this deliberately, no doubt. Another one of her tests."

"Tests?" Millicent probed gently. She didn't want to push the boy too much, but curiosity gnawed at her like a hound with a bone.

"She's submitted every woman I've so much as looked at in the last few months to examinations devised by her Machiavellian mind." Jared clenched his jaw in an obvious effort to control his outrage. My, when angered the boy certainly was deliciously handsome in a wonderfully menacing sort of way. "I warned her it would have to stop."

"I see," Millicent murmured. All at once, Olivia's actions made sense. Millicent was unaware of Olivia's tests of previous bridal candidates. Obviously, none of those had come anywhere near acceptance. Cece, on the other hand, was closing in quickly on the matrimonial prize that included Jared, his title and all that went with it. "That explains quite a lot."

Jared barely acknowledged her presence, apparently speaking more to himself than to her. "She will not get away with it this time."

"You must give your mother some credit, Jared," Millicent chided. "This evening was a difficult trial. And Cece has carried it off with wit and charm. Olivia can have few complaints. I would say, if indeed this was a test, Cece has passed with honors."

Jared nodded, his angry expression fading to one of newfound pride. "She has done a damn fine job." He grinned abruptly. "She'll make an excellent countess, don't you think?"

Millicent beamed. "I do indeed. Now run along and find your future countess and tell her what you think."

Jared turned to go, but Millicent called him back. "And Jared, I would wait to talk to your mother." Millicent shrugged. "Why on earth spoil such a lovely evening?"

Millicent watched the boy hurry off. His mother was one of her oldest friends, but she'd wager Olivia had met her match this time. It was obvious to anyone with half a mind that Jared was already in love with Cece, and she no doubt returned his affection.

In this battle of wits she'd have to put her money, and her encouragement, behind the Americans. Still, Olivia never was one to give up easily. Millicent was hard pressed to remember when, if ever, her friend had lost any kind of skirmish. Millicent vowed to follow the progress of this contest closely. It promised the best entertainment she'd had in years.

She grinned wickedly.

It was indeed a lovely evening.

". . . AND I CAN'T thank you all enough for your tremendous efforts today." Cece stood in the midst of a brief lull of activity in the kitchen and beamed at her trio of helpers, flanked by assorted other members of the castle staff. "It was quite in the cooperative spirit of the Wild West. Americans could not have done it better."

Murmurs of appreciation rippled through the ranks like waves on the shore. The three kitchen maids blushed with pleasure.

"We couldn't 'ave down it without you, miss," Mary said.

Ellen nodded. "You were our inspiration."

"A virtual guidin' spirit as it were, miss," Willomena added.

"Thank you." Cece nodded her gratitude and heaved a sigh of relief. "It does appear we shall pull this off, although," she cast them an impish grin, "I doubt any of these guests have ever partaken of chuck-wagon fare."

"Then they're all in for a treat I'd say," Willomena said staunchly.

"Somethin' they'll not soon be forgettin', I'd wager." Ellen grinned.

"And not be gettin' again anytime soon neither," Mary said smugly. She leaned toward Cece and spoke under her breath. "Beggin' your pardon, miss, but in the stories they call it grub."

"Of course." Cece smiled apologetically. "Silly of me to forget. You're absolutely right. Tonight, in the heart of Britain, we serve chuck-wagon grub. It should be quite delightful."

"There's more than one appetizing item on the menu tonight." Jared stood in the entry to the kitchen, the landing a few stair steps above the main floor. Arms folded across his chest, he leaned lazily against the stone archway.

Cece tossed him an easy smile, then cast a quick glance at the assembled servants, who stared at Jared as if they'd never seen the earl before. No doubt they never had in the kitchen. This was their domain, less than a few steps away physically, but it might well have been a million miles away from Jared's world. With a subtle nod, she sent her troops back to their respective stations and they scurried like tumbleweeds in a desert wind.

She plucked her gloves off the table and stepped toward him. "I'm so glad you've seen something that meets with your approval."

"Everything meets with my approval." His voice rang low and seductive, a vivid reminder of this morning's passionate kiss. His tone shivered up her spine and through her blood. Hunger that had little to do with the evening's meal simmered in his eyes. "You look exquisite."

"Thank you." She favored him with a serene smile designed to hide her relief. Cece had spent far less time than usual at her toilet tonight. Between overseeing the meal, arranging the flowers, directing the staff and a haphazard roundup of anyone on the estate who had ever touched a musical instrument, there was scarcely a moment left to see to her own needs.

She'd decided to wear one of the new Worth gowns, less formal than the others; the striking lemon yellow creation complimented her dark hair and eyes. The admiration reflected in his eyes confirmed what the mirror had told her, and her confidence rose.

He sauntered down the steps and offered his arm with a gallant flourish. "If you are quite through spinning your magic . . ." he raised a questioning brow. "You are finished, aren't you?"

She cast a last look around the kitchen. Even though there had not been entertaining of this magnitude at the castle for some years, the staff was trained well enough to overcome the myriad of problems created by the absence of a cook and any advance planning.

"I just hope the magic holds throughout the evening and does not turn out to be a mere illusion." She took his arm and accompanied him up the stairs. "I would so hate for everything to vanish with a snap of someone's fingers."

"Judging by the enchanting scene outside and the savory aroma on the breeze, I suspect your efforts will definitely disappear . . . to the culinary satisfaction of all."

They stepped through a servant's exit and into the balmy night. The candlelight flickered like captured fireflies. Ladies in frothy summer gowns bantered with gentlemen in elegant formal attire. The scent of roses flirted with the aroma of roasting beef to tease the senses with a tantalizing suggestion of sweet and savory.

"It does appear to be going well . . ." She drew her brows together in a worried frown and swept her hand before her to encompass the entire gathering. "Still, I can't help but wonder what their reaction will be. This is definitely not what any of them expect. For one thing, supper will not have the proper number of courses. I had hoped, of course, the uniqueness of the setting and the food would overcome any—"

"The food will be wonderful," Jared said firmly.

"And then they will be called upon to join in afterwards as part of the evening's entertainment, and I'm not entirely—"

"This is the only thing I find truly unexpected about this evening." Jared laughed. "I never imagined the supremely confident Miss Cecily White would be worried about anything as mundane as a mere party."

Cece raised her chin a notch. "I am not worried," she said, a chill in her voice. "I am simply concerned all goes well." She cast him a weak smile. "I've never handled anything like this before. My mother plans all our entertaining."

"Never?"

She shook her head. "Never."

"Extraordinary." Jared stared, admiration coloring his words. "You certainly have done a bang-up job."

"It was definitely a challenge."

"It was possibly a test."

Cece stopped short. "What on earth do you mean by that?"

Jared released an exasperated sigh and gritted his teeth. His eyes darkened with annoyance. "A test. An examination. A little something devised by my meddling, somewhat devious mother to evaluate a future countess."

"She was testing me?" Cece stared in disbelief.

"I don't know for certain," Jared admitted. "It's just a suspicion I have, a very strong suspicion. You see, ever since I began this quest for a wife—"

"You mean an heiress," she said wryly.

"A wife," he said with a pointed glance. She raised her shoulders in a skeptical gesture. He ignored her and continued. "Every female I've shown the least bit of interest in has been put to some sort of test by my mother and found lacking."

"What kind of test?" she said, curious despite herself. "And how many females?"

A rueful smile quirked his lips. "Not many. Heiresses are not especially easy to find."

"Anything achieved too easily is valued too lightly," she said loftily.

"Indeed." He raised a brow in droll agreement.

"About those tests?" she prompted.

He shrugged. "I don't know exactly what they were. Little things, I suspect. Nothing like this."

"I see," Cece murmured. All the odd bits and pieces of the stay at the castle abruptly fitted together into an intriguing picture. It certainly made sense: Lady Graystone's unusual choice of guests, the quarters assigned, the party suddenly thrust upon her shoulders. Still, Marybeth had said nothing about being tested; only that Lady Graystone had decided the American was not good enough for her son. "I knew your mother had standards that were difficult to meet."

Jared stared sharply. "What makes you say that?"

Cece widened her eyes and willed the words back in her mouth. It would not do at all to let Jared know her original purpose for coming to England was to teach the high-and-mighty Earl of Graystone a lesson about the superiority of Americans.

She drew a steadying breath and smiled sweetly. "It's not a farfetched assumption to make, Jared. You are, after all, her only son."

"True." His brow furrowed in thought. "I suppose I should not be too harsh with her, if my theory proves correct. Her intentions were, no doubt, for the best. Still, I did warn her."

"Oh?" Cece suppressed a skeptical grin. "Just what did you tell her?"

Jared tucked her hand in the crook of his arm and the two strolled toward the other guests. "I simply informed her I would tolerate no more interference. I advised her the next moderately acceptable American heiress would be my bride."

"Indeed." Cece raised an incredulous brow. "Am I to gather then that I am moderately acceptable?"

He stopped and studied her lazily. His gaze drifted down her body, lingering here and there with a thoroughness that brought a rush of heat to her cheeks. The caress of his insolent glance continued until she wasn't sure if she wanted to slap his face or throw herself into his arms. Finally his gaze met hers.

His eyes twinkled with unconcealed amusement. "Moderately."

She gasped with indignation. "Moderately?"

"There you are." Lady Millicent bustled up to them, oblivious to the sparring match she interrupted. "Cece, my dear, you have done a marvelous job. The evening is off to an excellent start, and I've no doubt this is just the beginning."

Lady Millicent positioned herself between Jared and Cece, locking their arms with hers, and started toward the other guests, chatting all the while. "It's all so wonderfully creative and original. Who would have thought of moving everything out-of-doors? Even the cooking. Of course, everyone here is giving Olivia the credit for all this." Millicent shook her head in an exasperated manner. "It's dreadfully unfair."

Cece and Jared traded knowing glances.

"I quite agree," Jared said, "it is unfair."

"It's nothing," Cece said quickly. "This is, after all, Lady Graystone's party. I was simply helping out."

Millicent snorted disdainfully. "Olivia took advantage of your good nature. It was quite unsporting of her. Why, I—"

Millicent halted abruptly and gasped. "It can't be!"

Cece and Jared followed her gaze. A tall, distinguished-looking man stood on the edge of the gathering and appeared to be searching the crowd.

"He looks vaguely familiar," Jared said thoughtfully, "but I can't quite place him."

"Who is he, Lady Millicent?" Cece said, curiosity in her voice.

"This is completely unexpected. I didn't even know he was in England. How delightful." Millicent broke into a grin and a brisk walk. "That, my dear children, is my brother-in-law, Quentin's father, Sir Robert Bainbridge and—dear me."

Millicent pulled to a stop and stared at Cece. "I nearly forgot."

"What?" Concern, brought on by the odd look on Lady Millicent's face, underlaid Cece's word.

Millicent pulled a deep breath. "Robin is not only a member of my family, but he easily could have been part of yours.

"But for a quirk of fate, he would have married your mother."

Chapter 11

PHOEBE White's mind wandered and her gaze drifted. It was not as if Henry and the gentlemen he was in such an animated discussion with were boring, mind you. On the contrary, the impact of the value of the dollar versus the pound when it comes to something-or-other as it related to what-in-the-world was fascinating beyond words. Phoebe took a long sip of champagne and stifled the impulse to yawn.

Still, she had to give Henry his due. He no doubt knew she paid no attention whatsoever; regardless, every now and then, he'd nod in her direction, as if she were a legitimate part of the conversation. Henry was such a dear.

Her gaze meandered amid the guests. While none of them realized it, she was well aware this evening was the product of her daughter's hard work. Phoebe would have been more than happy to help Cece had the child only contacted her at Millicent's. But no, Cece was determined to manage this event by herself. That she did so splendidly filled Phoebe with pride and a touch of melancholy: Her daughter was obviously well prepared to stand on her own two feet. Her oldest babe was no longer a child.

Phoebe's casual glance caught on a tall figure near the edge of the crowd. Blond and broad shouldered, his very shape appeared reminiscent. She pulled her brows together in a considering frown. Surely she knew who this was, although she was certain she had not been introduced to him this evening. She observed him idly and sipped her wine. His features were still hidden in the shadows and her curiosity peaked. The stranger turned to accept a glass from a servant and stepped forward. Lantern light flickered on his face.

Phoebe's breath caught in her throat and time stood still.

"Robin," she said with a soft gasp.

For a moment she was no longer the mother of two nearly grown daughters and the wife of a millionaire but a green girl on her first trip abroad. For a moment twenty-three years of love and marriage and life fell away and she was again innocent and untried and trusting. And for a moment the first man she ever loved, the first man who ever made her heart sing and her hands tremble, waited once again for her across a crowded ballroom . . . or an ocean.

Just like that awkward girl, Phoebe stared, unable to pull her gaze away. Panic squeezed her heart. What would she say to him? What would she do? What would he do? It had been so very long. Did he miss her? Hate her? Love her? Had he been happy without her? Did he still want her? What would be her response if the answer . . . was yes?

It wasn't as if they hadn't ultimately cleared things up between them. But it had all been by letters. All the anger and sorrow and resignation had been dealt with by written words only. This would be their first face-to-face meeting since they parted, each vowing eternal dedication to the other.

He looked absolutely wonderful. Older, of course, but distinguished and handsome nonetheless. Her mirror told her she had aged gracefully. Her figure was still trim, her face still fair. Would he think so?

Robin's gaze flicked past her, then snapped back to mesh and lock with hers. Stunned disbelief washed over his face, followed quickly by resolve. He started toward her, and she fought an immediate impulse to run, whether toward him or away she didn't know. Shock rooted her to the spot.

He drew closer, and even at a distance she could see a steely glint of purpose in his eyes, a sense of determination in his step. What were his intentions?

Abruptly, someone stepped between them and she lost sight of him in the sudden wave of bodies milling about the grounds. Her heart thudded in her chest and she gulped a bracing swallow of champagne in a futile effort to quiet her unsteady nerves. The crowd shifted and she craned her neck to see around those still blocking her view.

"Phoebe." His voice was a dream from the past.

She tightened her fingers on the wineglass. Somewhere in the back of her mind she noted that her manner was exactly like her daughter's. Phoebe squared her shoulders and raised her chin. Pulling a slow, steady breath, she turned.

She held out her hand and cast him her most sincere smile. It was the smile of one acquaintance to another. Serene. Pleasant. Impersonal.

"Robin, how delightful. Millicent didn't mention that you were expected."

"I wasn't." His hand clasped hers. His gaze searched her face with an intensity that weakened her knees and her resolve. He brought her hand to his lips and brushed the back of it lightly. The skin beneath her gloved hand sizzled with the heat of his touch. "If I had known you were here I would have returned to England much sooner."

"We decided to come on a sudden impulse. The visit wasn't planned at all." What was she saying? Inane, everyday things. Social niceties. Polite conversation. What did it matter when his eyes blazed into hers with the fire of a man rediscovering a long-lost treasure? "It was my daughter's idea."

Gently she pulled her hand from his, but his gaze refused to release her.

"It has been a long time, Phoebe." Even today, she would have recognized his voice anywhere. Mellow and strong, it echoed in the depths of her soul.

"Almost forever," she said softly, abandoning all pretense at reserved behavior.

"I must speak to you." His tone rang with controlled passion. "Alone."

Shock, fear and excitement coursed through her veins. "I'm not certain that is—"

"Phoebe?" Henry's voice jolted her back to reality. To 1895. To who and what she was. Ladies Aid volunteer . . . accomplished hostess . . . proud parent . . . loving wife. "I don't believe I've met . . . ?"

"Henry," Phoebe said quickly, grateful for the opportunity to tear her gaze from Robin's and breathe freely again. "This is an old friend of mine, Sir Robert Bainbridge. Robin, this is my husband, Henry White."

"Your husband." Robin lifted a brow in a subtly superior manner.

"Robert Bainbridge," Henry said thoughtfully, as if he were trying to place the name. His eyes narrowed a fraction and he smiled a pleasant smile he reserved for particularly difficult business dealings.

Phoebe's heart sank. She had told Henry everything about Robin. After all, she'd met her future husband on the ship returning home from England. It was absolute foolishness to believe for a second he would have forgotten all about Robin.

No doubt no one but she noticed the interchange between the two men. How they seemed to size up the mettle of the other. They were of a similar height and breadth, but the differences were far more striking. Robin was fair, with hair still the color of sunshine on wheat and eyes blue and deep. Henry's eyes were a rich brown, so endless when aroused or angry, one could almost see one's soul in them. Even though his walnut hair was kissed at the temples by silver, he appeared far younger than his forty-eight years.

"Pleasure to meet you," Henry said and held out his hand.

Robin gripped it with a smile that never reached his eyes. "Quite."

Each man stared at the other with a kind of primal challenge Phoebe would have found fascinating had she been able to concentrate on that instead of noting how the knuckles of both men were white with the grip of the other.

For a long moment they stood, until breaking apart as if by mutual consent.

"If you will excuse me," Robin said politely, "I have yet to find my son."

"By all means." Henry nodded.

"Phoebe, my dear," Robin's gaze raked across her,

and she shivered with the message in his eyes. "It was delightful to see you. I'm certain I will see you again soon." He nodded at Henry. "White."

"Bainbridge." Henry's voice rang firm and cool. He watched Robin cross the lawn and greet his son, his gaze hard and considering. "Phoebe?"

"Oh, do look, Henry," Phoebe said, panic rushing her words. She had no desire to talk about Robin, at least not at this moment. She took his arm and steered him in the general direction in which she had last seen Cece. "Cece is right over here, I believe. I promised to—"

"Phoebe . . ."

She refused to look at him. "I do not wish to discuss Robin. I would prefer—"

"Phoebe . . ." He fairly growled the word.

She stopped and stared up at him. "Yes, dear?"

"Are you cold?"

His consideration touched her and guilt tweaked her conscience. How could she forget about Henry? Even for a moment? "Thank you, but I'm quite fine."

His eyes caught hers with an intensity that even after all these years never failed to send flutters through her midsection. "Then . . . why are you trembling?"

"I SUSPECT NONE of this is quite proper," Emily said condescendingly.

"No doubt." Cece nodded.

"Why, eating right here on the lawn . . ." Emily clicked her tongue in disapproval.

"Scandalous," Cece agreed, "simply scandalous."

"And encouraging guests to entertain themselves . . ." Emily shook her head in a mournful manner.

Cece sighed with resignation. "Disgraceful."

At the far end of the terrace servants had casually

scattered chairs in informal settings. Some guests sat in small groupings, while others stood in twos or threes or more. But all attention focused on those currently performing. Cece couldn't help but look on the success of the impromptu entertainment with satisfaction. She'd been right: No one, not here, not at home, could resist the chance to show their talent—even if said talent was minimal at best.

A particularly discordant note rang through the air, as if the singer was protesting her impending execution. Cece and her sister winced in unison.

"It's completely out of the ordinary, quite unexpected and . . ." Emily grinned, "absolutely delightful."

Cece stared with surprise. "Why, thank you, Em. I never dreamed you'd like my rather unorthodox effort."

"Neither did I." Emily shrugged and cast her sister a look of amazement. "I never imagined you could handle something like this. You are always so full of 'interesting ideas,' but they never seem to turn out precisely as you envision. This—" Emily gestured at the gathering "—is a genuine accomplishment. It's frankly something of a revelation."

"A revelation?" Cece laughed. "I'm glad I have somehow managed to exceed your expectations."

"So am I."

A revelation; imagine. Cece chuckled to herself, then sobered abruptly, struck by the cutting truth of her sister's observation. Of course Cece had hopes and dreams, prime among them following the path trod by Nellie Bly. But had she done a single, solitary thing to achieve those dreams? Short of her admittedly ill-advised idea to come to England, engage the affections of the Earl of Graystone and reject him in hopes of being allowed to do as she wished, she'd in fact done nothing to further her goals. Now the lure of journalism had faded, replaced by the fascination of automobiles and the attraction of Jared himself.

Jared. What if his suspicions about his mother's activities were correct? What if Lady Graystone actually was testing her? After tonight Cece's confidence in her ability to handle any trial Lady Graystone could devise was boundless. But what if, through no fault of her own, she failed a test she didn't even realize she faced? Would Jared's affection prove sufficient to overcome his mother's will? Would he still wish to marry her if she did not live up to Lady Graystone's standards? Would his love remain true?

"Have you met Quentin's father yet?" Emily said, with a nod in the man's direction. Sir Bainbridge stood some distance away, engaged in conversation with Jared's mother. "He's quite grand and extremely dashing."

"Like his son, perhaps?" Cece tossed her sister a teasing smile.

Emily blushed. "Perhaps."

Cece studied Robert Bainbridge thoughtfully. This was yet another revelation. The very idea of her mother's long-ago involvement with this stranger was unsettling, to say the least. It was impossible to picture Phoebe White with anyone other than Henry White. Ever. And harder yet to imagine her as a girl younger than Cece, in love for the first time. Still . . . she glanced toward her parents on the opposite side of the terrace.

They were a striking couple; one complemented the other. Each had dark hair and eyes. Henry was considerably taller than Phoebe, and she appeared delicate and fragile in his wake. With a start, Cece realized her mother was still extremely pretty, her father distinguished and handsome. For the first time Cece suddenly viewed her parents as people independent of spouses and children. It was an extremely disturbing thought.

This did indeed seem the evening for revelations. First there was the confirmation of her abilities and competence to the surprise of her family and her own relief. Next, there was the as yet unconfirmed idea of Lady Graystone testing her qualifications to be a countess. And finally there was the disquieting glimpse into her mother's past and the uncomfortable acknowledgment that, long before she was her mother, Phoebe had experienced the same awkward emotions Cece herself now knew.

"Shall we join the others?" Emily broke abruptly into her thoughts.

"My, yes." Cece linked her arm with her sister's and they started toward the terrace. "I would dearly hate for us to miss anything. Tonight has already been an enlightening evening. I can scarcely wait to see what will happen next."

"IT HAS BEEN a long time, Robert." Olivia held out her hand to Sir Bainbridge with genuine delight.

"Olivia." Robert's eyes sparkled in greeting. "You are looking even more lovely than usual."

"Robert!" Heat flushed up her face. Admittedly she had changed somewhat in the ten years since they'd last met. Her figure was a bit fuller. More than a few strands of gray had crept into her hair, but she thought they added a distinguishing touch to her features. Her face, however, showed few lines, and Olivia privately thought she had weathered her forty-seven years quite nicely. "You are a rogue."

Robert laughed. "Only for you, Olivia, only for you." His expression sobered. "I was quite sorry to hear about Charles and James."

"I received your notes." Olivia cast him a smile of appreciation. "They were most welcome. Now," she said brightly, "tell me what at long last brings you home."

"I am to be appointed to a position in London."

"Oh?" Olivia struggled to keep the blatant curiosity from her voice. "What kind of position?"

Robert shook his head and chuckled wryly. "You always did have a very direct nature."

"If you don't go after what you want, you will very likely miss it altogether," Olivia said, her manner firm.

"I see." Robert paused to sip his wine, and his glance slid beyond her to Phoebe. "Does that apply to everything?"

Olivia followed his gaze. "Oh dear; I had forgotten all about that."

Robert shrugged. "No reason for you to remember. I believe you and Charles were abroad during the months Phoebe was in England."

"Millicent told me what happened, of course." A pang of sympathy shot through Olivia at the barely concealed look of hopeless desire in Robert's eyes. Poor man. From what Millicent had said, he'd had quite a passion for Phoebe. She wasn't certain of all the details but recalled it had had something to do with messages not being delivered and a minor misunderstanding that grew out of control and destroyed their association. She hurried to change the subject. "You still haven't told me what kind of government position you might be accepting."

Robert smiled and shook his head. "It would be indiscreet for me to mention it before the formal announcement; therefore . . ."

Olivia waved a dismissive hand. "No matter. I have no wish to put you in an awkward position. I shall simply have to swallow my curiosity and wait with everyone else."

Robert raised a skeptical brow. "If memory has not failed me altogether, I believe curiosity was one of your most highly developed traits."

"One changes with the years," Olivia said airily. "Some things become far more important; others lose their appeal entirely."

"Do you think so, Olivia?" Robert's eyes gleamed intensely, and again his gaze skimmed past her to rest on Phoebe White. "Is there any secret, I wonder, to which things become less important with time and which grow ever stronger to the point where one would gladly give up a great deal for them?"

"I don't know, Robert," she said faintly. It was apparent Robert Bainbridge still had strong feelings for Phoebe White. What a shame. As much as she hated to interfere, Olivia would simply have to take this matter in hand, if only to avert the trouble she suspected could be brewing.

Robert had the look of a man considering the most dire of options. Any action on his part to win Phoebe back, and destroy her marriage in the process, would have to be firmly squelched. It could only lead to scandal, and that Olivia would not permit. If Cecily was indeed to become the next Countess of Graystone, the last thing any of them needed was sordid gossip about her mother and another man. Why, the entire affair could ultimately end in divorce, and that was an embarrassment that would no doubt color them all with the same brushstroke of dishonor.

Olivia would have to distract Robert from any thought of pursuing Phoebe. She considered him thoughtfully. It had been many years since she'd practiced the nuances of flirtation. Still, it must be very much like riding a horse: Learned once, it no doubt came back to one when needed. Olivia needed it now.

"Robert . . ." She favored him with her most charming smile. "It has been so long since you've visited; would you care to join me for a stroll around the castle grounds? We can catch up on our respective pasts."

Robert bowed slightly. "Olivia, I would be delighted." He offered his arm and she accepted it graciously. He cast one last look at Phoebe, then turned his complete attention to Olivia. "It seems I have a great deal to catch up on. But first—" he steered Olivia toward the rose garden—"tell me all you know about Henry White."

"You will cease this interference in my life at once!" Jared paced the length of the castle library, barely keeping his temper in check. His ire had simmered through the long evening, and now that the guests had finally bid good night and those staying at the castle had retired, it was past time to confront his mother. He relished the moment.

Olivia perched on a comfortably shabby wing chair and gazed at him innocently. "Jared, dear, I have no idea what on earth you are talking about."

Jared glared. "You know exactly what I am talking about."

Olivia's eyes widened with ingenuous candor. "Really, Jared, I am quite at a loss."

Jared rolled his eyes toward the distant ceiling and drew on every ounce of control at his command. He closed his eyes and, with a slow, measured manner, counted to ten. It always surprised him how this simple technique soothed even the nerves of a man plagued by meddlesome females. His composure restored, his gaze again fell on his mother.

"You expect me to believe you have no inkling of what I am justifiably furious about?" Jared's surprisingly calm tone belied the import of his words.

Olivia shrugged helplessly. "None whatsoever."

"Tell me about the party, Mother."

"The party?" Olivia's guileless manner would have convinced most people of her genuine innocence. Even Jared hesitated, wondering if his assumption as to his mother's tactics could possibly be wrong. "I think the party was an unqualified success. Of course I did so hate abdicating my responsibilities as hostess to Cecily. Still," she heaved a heartfelt sigh, "it could not be helped. I was altogether incapacitated."

That was it; Jared's momentary doubt vanished. Never in his entire life had his mother been "incapacitated."

"Millicent said it was a sick headache," he said, studying his mother closely.

Olivia peeked at him from beneath downcast lashes. "Yes indeed. It was quite awful. I am only grateful that I rallied in time to make an appearance this evening."

A note of compassion shaded Jared's words, and he gazed at his mother with his most understanding expression. "It was certainly noble of you."

Olivia lifted her chin in a gesture of courage and bravery. "It was not at all easy."

"I can imagine." In spite of his anger, Jared was

hard pressed not to burst into laughter. Her heroic act in the face of dire illness was impressive, to say the least. He didn't believe it for a second. "I thought Cece managed to handle the evening quite well. What did you think?"

"It was a bit unconventional, but all in all I think she did an excellent job." Olivia nodded her satisfaction.

"What do you think she handled best?" he asked in an offhand manner.

"Best?" Olivia pulled her brows together thoughtfully. "The entire evening was no doubt difficult. But I do think the cook's being sick provided the greatest—"

"Trial?" Jared said sharply.

"No, no." Olivia waved away his interruption with an absent flick of her hand. "I was going to say challenge. The entire incident was a—" She stopped short and her eyes widened with obvious dismay at what she had nearly admitted.

"A *what*, Mother?" Jared narrowed his eyes and glared. "A test, perhaps?"

"Jared, you can't possibly believe—"

"Oh, I can believe, Mother, and I do."

"It was an unfortunate coincidence, nothing more."

"Coincidence?" Jared scoffed disdainfully. "Coincidence is the one thing I would never believe." A sudden thought struck him. "I wonder . . . have there been other tests, as well?"

"I don't understand how you could possibly suspect me of such a thing," Olivia said in an indignant tone.

Jared raised a brow in disbelief. "Your record in such matters is indisputable. I was a fool not to have realized you would continue your meddlesome efforts. What do you plan next, Mother? Famine? Plague?

Perhaps you'll simply put a pea under her mattress to test her sensitivity."

"I always did like that story," she murmured.

He leveled her a stern glare. "I have a great deal of difficulty accepting the fact that after our last discussion, when I expressly forbade you to interfere in my affairs with any more tests of prospective brides—"

"I never actually promised . . ." she said under her breath.

He quelled her comment with a furious glance. Resting one hand on either side of his mother's chair, he leaned toward her, his manner brooking no argument. She appeared almost to shrink into the chair.

"While I cannot prove you were indeed testing Cece"—Olivia seemed to relax the slightest bit at his words—"I will give you one last warning."

His mother stared silently, apprehension mingling with stubborn determination in her eyes.

"If I so much as suspect you of tossing the tiniest obstacle, the merest difficulty, the slightest dilemma in Cece's path in the future, I will take action we will both regret." He narrowed his eyes slightly. "Do I make myself perfectly clear?"

"Jared . . ." She pushed him aside and rose to her feet with a fair amount of grace and dignity. Jared had to admit she could certainly be impressive, even regal, when she put her mind to it. "In the first place I simply haven't the vaguest idea what you're accusing me of."

Jared snorted skeptically.

She raised a brow and directed him the same quelling look he had often received as a child. Even as an adult it triggered a wave of discomfort. He was far too old for her tricks and his boyhood unease quickly turned to adult annoyance. He would not yield to her this time.

"In the second place," she said loftily, "I cannot fathom what the dire consequences would be if I were to simply . . . er . . . evaluate, as it were, Cecily's qualifications to share your life. It's in the best interest of all concerned to make certain she is worthy of your title."

"The consequences could be quite extensive, Mother." Jared smiled slowly. Olivia's expression remained adamant, but she paled visibly. "You see, I have already decided to marry Cece. Whether she meets your requirements no longer matters. She meets mine. If your meddling interferes at all with my courtship, I shall marry her at once."

"Well, I scarcely think—"

"That's not all, Mother," Jared said sharply. "Furthermore, I shall accompany Cece back to America and we will make our lives there. In addition, I will give up my title. This will be the end. After five hundred years I will be the last of the Earls of Graystone."

For a moment mother and son stared at each other. Silence, sharp as a razor, hung between them.

"Very well." Olivia's eyes flashed with irritation, but her voice was calm. "I shall certainly acquiesce to your request." She slanted him a pointed glance. "Not that I have done anything untoward up to this point, mind you."

"Of course not." Smug satisfaction surged through him at his success. Olivia could deny it all she wished but he had no doubts as to her activity.

"Now, I am quite fatigued. It has been an extremely long day." She speared him with a sharp glance. "And I have been ill, you know. Good evening." Olivia nodded briskly and swept from the room.

"Good evening." Jared chuckled to himself. Whatever else one could say about Lady Olivia Graystone, she might retreat but she never, ever surrendered. However, this was one time his dear mother would not win.

He stepped to a table that bore a decanter of brandy and two ready glasses and poured a healthy draught. A long swallow of the smooth, warming liquor increased his sense of triumph. He had a firm handle on the women in his life.

Jared swirled the brandy and idly watched the amber liquid coat the sides of the glass. Whether or not his mother was actually testing Cece, he was confident she would desist any such attempts in the future. Olivia would not risk his displeasure if it meant losing the title.

Would he—could he—give up all this?

A pang shot through him at the very thought. Oh, not the loss of the title. As a second son he had never expected it to be his in the first place. But this castle, this land had a grip on his heart he'd never suspected until it became his responsibility alone. In the year he'd been earl he'd discovered just how much his heritage meant to him, and how proud he was to be a part of it.

What kind of life could he build in America? In spite of a wealthy wife, he would be very much the penniless inventor Cece had first thought him. Could he follow in the footsteps of Vanderbilt and Rockefeller and Henry White himself and build a fortune out of nothing? Could he be the man Cece fell in love with? The irony twisted a smile on his lips. Without his title, and all that went with it, he would have no need for her fortune, no need to marry for money. Abruptly, he realized he would have to refuse any funding from her, even a dowry. If he was to succeed in America, he and his automobile would have to do it on their own.

Resolve coursed through him. The future he envisioned in America would be difficult at best, disastrous at worse. Could he risk all for the woman he loved? God help him. He didn't even have to ask the question twice. The answer was obvious.

He only hoped this was a decision he wouldn't have to make. Surely his mother understood his was not an idle threat. It would not be easy to leave, but it would be unavoidable.

As for Cece . . . Jared sank into the chair vacated by his mother and grinned. This morning's kiss was nothing short of spectacular. If the horn hadn't sounded . . . he had few doubts as to the end result of their encounter. He pulled another deep draw of the liquor.

Seduction was obviously the way to proceed. Why, the woman was putty in his hands. He suppressed the merest twinge of guilt, a twinge that had struck him more and more lately. She would indeed be his wife, sooner or later. Seduction was simply the best way to achieve that goal quickly and efficiently and keep her from his automobile at the same time. He could scarce be blamed if it was also the most delightful.

Jared leaned his head against the back of the chair and smiled smugly. Without a doubt he was in command of his women and in control of his life. At this moment, here in his family's ancestral home, Jared felt every inch the lord of the manor. Tonight, he was indeed the virtual king of his castle. He sipped more of the brandy and tried without success to ignore the lone thought nagging deep in the recesses of his brain.

Jared sighed with resignation. He should enjoy

these few moments of peace and harmony. No doubt between his future wife and his mother, this sense of calm and tranquility would be extremely short-lived.

OLIVIA MARCHED UP the stairs to her apartments in the east wing with an indignant step designed to assure any casual observer of her acute displeasure. She thrust her chin forward firmly, held her back ramrod straight and hoped, in the dim light, no one would notice the twinkle in her eye.

Olivia stepped into her chambers, pulled the door firmly behind her, leaned against it and laughed aloud. She couldn't believe how much entertainment this little game had provided. Not that the lively amusement had persuaded her to relinquish her original purpose. On the contrary, Cecily's continued successes simply spurred Olivia to greater levels of difficulty, challenges that were nearly as demanding to create as to meet. She hadn't had so much fun in years.

When had she lost that sense of gaiety?

The question popped into her mind without warning. Whatever had happened to that girl who cared only for soirees and promenades in the park and stolen looks across a crowded room? When had she become so concerned with what was acceptable and proper? At what point had her wish to merely influence those around her turned to a desire for control?

She moved to her dressing table and sank onto the matching bench. The woman who returned her gaze in the mirror looked almost like a stranger tonight. Odd; she certainly didn't feel any different now than she had when she was a girl. Oh, naturally she'd had to adapt to the strict social parameters of a countess. And she'd had to adjust her sense of fun and frolic to conform to proper behavior. There was nothing wrong with that. Was there?

Her reflection stared, her expression thoughtful and more than a little puzzled. Whatever had put her in such a strange mood? Perhaps . . . it had just been far too long since she thoroughly enjoyed herself.

The woman in the mirror grinned. And wasn't Jared amusing tonight? She did so love it when the dear boy put his foot down like that. Charles used to have exactly the same expression on his face, the same tone in his voice, the same furious gleam in his eye. Male indignation was obviously something passed on from father to son.

She pulled the pins from her hair and shook the tresses free. At least she hadn't admitted anything to him. There was even the slim possibility he believed her protestations. Not that it mattered. How could she possibly promise not to continue to do something she hadn't confessed to doing in the first place?

Olivia selected a silver-backed brush and ran it through her hair with an absent stroke. She hadn't counted on Jared actually caring for the girl. That would make matters far easier should the child pass her tests. But if she failed, it would complicate an already awkward situation.

So far, Cecily had performed impressively. Tonight's success was quite extraordinary, almost enough to declare her a winner. With this last achievement, the American had met every challenge Olivia had set before her. Still, she wanted to be certain this girl would be the kind of wife, countess and, ultimately, mother, her son and his heritage required. The survival of her family and its legacy depended on it.

Olivia's hand stilled and the woman in the mirror

narrowed her eyes pensively. There was perhaps one more test. A final test of loyalty and courage. If Cecily passed, Olivia would welcome her to the family with outstretched arms. If not . . .

Abruptly the lighthearted mood that had filled her evaporated. The blithe-spirited stranger in the mirror vanished, replaced by her own familiar image. If Cecily could not overcome this last challenge, Olivia would be forced to oppose their union with every weapon at her disposal.

Olivia stared at her reflection. Determination washed through her, restoring her confidence and her resolve. She was only trying to do what was best for Jared, his future and the future of his family. No price was too high to pay for that.

Even her son's broken heart.

"WHAT DID SHE say?" Cece stepped into the library and closed the doors behind her.

Jared glanced up from his intense study of the liquor in his glass and smiled a warm greeting. His gaze met hers and his eyes lit with a fire that brought a flutter to her insides. This morning's kiss still lingered in her mind and on her lips.

"It's very late." His voice was low and heated her blood with an odd craving. "I thought you had retired with the others."

His appreciative gaze skimmed over her. She still wore the yellow Worth gown and he was both grateful she had not yet changed into her nightwear and vaguely disappointed.

Firmly pushing aside all thoughts of desire and passion and the realization that they were very likely alone in this part of the castle, Cece settled into a soft leather sofa and surveyed him in a businesslike manner.

"I saw your mother leave. She seemed somewhat irate."

"Irate?" Jared chuckled wryly. "She's denied everything completely. She's very good; my mother has turned innocence into a fine art. Short of employing the rack and the iron maiden, I shall get nothing out of her."

"I see," Cece said slowly. "Do you honestly think she's been testing me?"

Jared shrugged. "I can't see that it matters now. I have told her of my feelings for you and forbidden her to present you with any further problems. If indeed my suspicions are correct, I am confident her interference is now at an end."

"Of course," she murmured. There was no doubt at all in her mind about either the guilt of Lady Graystone or the very distinct possibility that her activities would continue.

Jared had no way of knowing about the incidents with Sir Humphrey and the events of last night. While there was nothing that could be done to prove Lady Graystone's fine hand in all this, Cece would have wagered her father's last dollar on the lady's involvement. And in spite of Jared's sweet words and the gleam in his eye, the question of what he would do should she fail a test loitered tenaciously in a corner of her mind.

"Jared," she blurted in a surge of determination to know the answer.

"Hmm?" His eyes smoldered and he idly swirled the brandy in his glass. His strong, tanned hand cupped the snifter. Her knees weakened, her breath caught and images of this morning fired the heat in her face.

She could almost feel the touch of his hands on her feverish flesh.

"Should I meet you at the same time tomorrow for our driving lesson?" Damnation! That wasn't the question uppermost in her mind. It was only when he gazed at her with eyes so deeply sapphire she could lose herself in a single glance that she could think of nothing except the demanding pressure of his lips on hers, the charged touch of his hand on her surprisingly receptive body and her own wonderfully desperate responses.

His gaze locked with hers and she could read a hunger both terrifying and tempting. She wondered if their next session would follow the path of the last. Her heart throbbed at the thought.

"There will be no lesson tomorrow, at least not in the morning." His eyes, glorious, dangerous, hypnotic, seemed to draw her closer, even though she never actually moved an inch and his words barely registered on a mind too intoxicated with thoughts of sensual kisses and erotic caresses. "I have business to attend to in London, but I shall return by afternoon."

"We're leaving for London in the afternoon. Mother wants to get ready for Em's party." Cece noted vaguely that her voice was calm and her speech coherent, but she paid scant attention to what she in fact said. "It's only a week away."

The words emerged from her as if of their own accord. She could do little more than stare at the intriguing way his mouth moved when he spoke, when he sipped his brandy, when the liquor glistened on his lips in an unspoken invitation. Instinctively, she ran her tongue over her own lips.

"Capitol. Then I shall stay in London." Even his

voice, the superior British accent that had once annoyed her, now triggered ripples of anticipation. She could lose her soul to that voice. She could listen to him forever. "The race is next week as well. The day after Emily's coming out."

His words finally penetrated the heady haze of arousal that fogged her senses and she jerked her gaze to his. He smiled as if he read her thoughts and warmth flashed up her face. Goodness! When had she become so wanton?

"The race. I had nearly forgotten." She drew a deep breath for composure and pulled her brows together in a considering frown. "I don't imagine you've changed your mind and will be driving after all?"

He shook his head in a resolute manner. "No. Quentin will handle that chore. For all intents and purposes, I shall be there only as his friend. To provide moral support, as it were."

She sighed with exasperation. "I still think that's the most ridiculous thing I've ever heard. Why, in my country—"

"Yes, yes, I know." Jared's lips quirked upward in a tolerant smile. "In America a man with ambition and talent can go far. Creativity and invention is respected and admired. Men who dream are—"

"That is quite enough," she said coolly, all thoughts of passion vanishing beneath justified patriotic indignation. "I needn't stay here and hear my country maligned." She rose to her feet. "It is past time I retired."

"Cece . . ." Jared stood and quickly crossed the few steps separating them. He grasped her hands in his. His gaze met hers, meshed and held. "I would never malign a country that could create anything as marvelous as you."

"Oh?" His admission took her breath away, and once again she wanted nothing more than to melt in his arms. "Well, as long as you admit—"

"I would admit anything for you." He brought her hands to his lips and kissed the back of first one and then the other. "I would give up anything for you." He turned her hands over and placed a kiss in one palm and then the next. "I would do anything . . ." his midnight eyes burned into hers with the intensity of a single star on a cloudless night ". . . for you."

"Really?" Her voice was scarcely more than a sigh.

He nodded solemnly, but a twinkle lurked in the corner of his eye. "Really."

He pulled her close and gently drifted his lips across hers in a touch so light, it might have been little more than a dream. She strained toward him, eager to continue the instruction he had begun this morning. He released her abruptly, firmly stepping back and away. "You do need to retire. Now."

"Do I?" Her tone was sultry, inviting. A tiny voice somewhere in her mind argued that she was going far beyond the limits of proper behavior, far beyond the realm of safety, far beyond the possibility of stopping. She no longer cared.

Retiring was the last thing she wanted to do at this moment. What she wanted—what she needed—was Jared and everything that need entailed. A hundred reasons for restraint, for caution, for decorum demanded attention, and she shrugged them off like blossoms in the wind. There was no real reason why a modern woman should not be with the man she loved and planned to wed.

"Why?" she breathed.

He had the look of a man caught between honor

and temptation. An intriguing mix of emotions marched across his face: desire; indecision; regret. He drew a deep, shaky breath and laughed, a rough, ragged sound. Jared leaned forward, kissed her on the tip of her nose and withdrew. Disappointment flooded her.

"Because, at this point, I think it would be for the best." Jared shook his head. "I find it difficult to believe my own words, but"—he shrugged wryly and grinned—"it must have something to do with love."

". . . with love," she echoed. Yes, it had everything to do with love.

"Now." He grasped her shoulders, turned her toward the door and gave her the tiniest push. "Bid me good night and go to your room." He sighed deeply. "Before I change my bloody mind."

"There is nothing that says a man can't change his mind," she said, an encouraging note in her voice.

He steered her toward the door. "Nothing except common sense and one's own nagging conscience."

"Conscience?" She tried to stop her inexorable progress out of the room, but his touch was unyielding. "What on earth does conscience have to do with anything? You are not taking advantage of me. I am more than ready and extremely willing."

"I realize that," he admitted, but his grip did not ease. "Only an idiot would fail to realize that."

"You are not an idiot." Her protestations seemed to fall on deaf ears.

"No, but I am very likely a fool," he muttered. He opened the library door and firmly pushed her out of the room. "Your enthusiasm does not make this any easier."

"I don't understand you at all." Frustration and denial rang in her voice. "How can you do this to me? To us?"

"I have absolutely no idea." He closed the door with a sharp snap, and she swore she could hear a sigh of relief.

"You disappoint me, Jared." She glared at the door. "Your reputation as a rogue is greatly exaggerated!"

A hearty chuckle sounded behind the wooden barrier. "Thank you."

Cece sighed, crossed her arms over her chest and resisted the urge to kick the innocent door. She had clearly indicated to Jared her desire. Why, she had practically thrown herself at him. How on earth could he resist what she offered? And to use that ridiculous excuse about love! Still . . . her annoyance ebbed, and she absently turned and headed to the west-wing stairway.

A man truly in love just might be willing to forgo his own satisfaction to preserve a lady's honor. When one thought about it rationally, without a cloud of desire fogging one's mind, it made a great deal of sense. Wasn't that exactly what Jared had just done?

And how had she behaved in return?

The cold hand of chagrin gripped her stomach.

A tart. That's what she was, a tart. And a silly tart at that. With nothing better to say in response to his admissions of devotion but "really." She groaned aloud and started up the stairs. He had tried—in fact, he had obviously struggled—to be noble, to save her from himself. Or, more accurately, to save her from herself.

The man was truly wonderful. His only real flaw was his obnoxious view of the abilities of women in general and his attitude toward females and automobiles in particular.

She stopped short between steps, struck by a sudden idea. A sudden interesting idea. Just this morning the thought had occurred to her that Jared had admirably succeeded in educating her as to everything she could possibly know about the workings of an automobile. She had, after all, watched him and others behind the controls. Surely she could teach herself how to drive the vehicle. Abruptly, she realized that Jared was right in one respect: It was ever so much easier to operate a machine if one was acquainted with its inner mechanics. And, if truth were told, the motorcar was not nearly as complicated as she had initially envisioned.

Confidence brought a grin to her lips and she continued up the stairs with a lilt in her step. Teaching herself to drive would take a heavy burden off Jared. The poor man would no longer have to devise ways to keep her from his automobiles. Why, she was doing him a favor.

No doubt Jared would not see it in that light—but, with any luck, Jared would not know. At least not until she mastered his machine. And master it she would. He would be off first thing in the morning, but she had hours before her return to London. And once she was no longer eager for lessons on driving, she could permit—no, encourage—Jared to instruct her on a subject she found even more fascinating than motorcars. A subject in which just this morning he had demonstrated his expertise. And she had demonstrated enthusiasm and a willingness to learn. Her grin widened.

She wondered, for their next lesson, just who would be teaching whom?

Chapter 12

APPREHENSION mingled with anticipation, and Phoebe could scarcely keep her mind on the matters at hand. The twin emotions seemed her constant companions these days. She sat at the ladies' writing desk in Millicent's drawing room and stared at the papers before her. The lists of guests, of errands, of things still undone for Emily's party two days from now might well have been written in some exotic foreign tongue, for all the sense she made of them.

Phoebe set her pen aside with disgust and gave into the memories that had haunted her since Robin's arrival. She had avoided confronting those thoughts with the same determination she'd avoided the man himself. Neither was easy.

Robin hadn't lived in London for years, and it would be several weeks before his newly acquired townhouse was habitable. Naturally, he stayed here at Millicent's along with Quentin, Phoebe and the rest of the Whites. Millicent's house was every inch as grand as her own in Chicago, and there was no lack of space in which to elude another houseguest. There were the public meetings, of course, at meals and various other gatherings through the course of the week. And while Phoebe had managed never to be alone with him, she could not avoid those heart-stopping moments when his gaze would capture hers, and her breath would catch in her throat.

Today, however, she was completely alone. But solitude did nothing to ease her mind. Millicent was off, preoccupied with errands. The girls were driving in the park with Quentin and Jared. Robin was at some government office, and Henry was once again at the club he had grown so fond of. What men found so appealing at such places was beyond her.

She could have accompanied Millicent. She could even have insisted that the girls stay home. She could have surrounded herself with people, much as the superstitious surrounded themselves with amulets to avoid disaster. A confrontation with Robin was a disaster she was not prepared for.

She pushed her chair back from the desk and rose to her feet. Staying here, in this very communal room, was risking an encounter she did not want. With a speed born of renewed determination and constant anxiety, she gathered up her papers and headed toward the hall.

The sound of the front door opening grated across her senses and halted her in her tracks. The door thudded shut and the low murmur of a servant's voice mixed with a deeper tone too indistinct to identify positively. But her heart fluttered and she wondered—no—she knew. The tread of a man's footfall drew nearer, and she fought the panic-spurred impulse to run. She stilled, as if not moving would somehow allow her to remain undetected.

Robin strode through the wide doorway and

stopped abruptly. Surprise washed over his face, followed swiftly by delight.

"Phoebe." He said her name as if it were a gift or a prayer.

She drew a deep breath and resolved to remain cool and collected in spite of the emotions raging within her. Her voice was curt. "Robin."

He walked toward her, and she instinctively stepped back, but he paid no attention and passed her to reach a tray bearing several decanters and a number of glasses. He poured a glass for himself, then turned to her.

"Millicent always was wonderfully prepared." He raised a brow. "Would you care for something?"

Liquor? In the middle of the day? "Please. Sherry, I should think."

"You always preferred sherry, if I recall," he said softly and poured her wine.

He handed her the glass and their fingers touched with a shock that jerked her gaze to his. Deep, devouring; she thought surely he could see into her soul.

"You've been avoiding me."

"No. I—" She wrenched her gaze from his, afraid he'd read her emotions in her eyes. She quickly stepped away, the need to put distance between them stark and unyielding.

"Why?" The word was a gentle accusation.

"I—" She sighed and turned to stare out the window, clutching her lists and notes. It was so much easier to talk to him when she didn't have to face the mute appeal in his eyes. "I simply think it's best, that's all."

"There is still much unresolved between us." His voice reverberated in her blood.

"No, Robin, there is nothing unresolved." She shook

her head firmly. "It has been a very long time and life for both of us has continued."

"Has it?" His voice drew closer. "Sometimes I wonder if my life didn't stand still the moment you left, only to resume when I saw you again this week."

She forced a casual lilt to her words. "That's ridiculous, Robin. You've been extremely successful."

He laughed, a mirthless sound. "Success can be measured in many ways." He paused, as if gathering his thoughts. A long moment passed.

"Why didn't you return to me?" The quiet timbre of his voice belied the depth of emotion in his words. She'd dreaded his question but dreaded more her answer.

"It was too late," she whispered.

"That's not good enough." Barely controlled anger rang in his voice.

She whirled to face him, and the question that had hovered in the back of her mind for years sprang to her lips. "Why didn't you come after me?"

His gaze burned into hers with an intensity that stole her breath and perhaps her heart. "It was . . . too late."

Anger abruptly surged through her and she pushed him out of her path and stormed across the room, slamming her glass on a table along the way. "Not good enough, Robin. It's simply not good enough. I waited for you. I waited days and days in that dreary little inn. By the time I realized you were not coming I had very nearly destroyed myself with fear and worry and guilt."

"It was a simple misunderstanding." Her own anger reflected in his eyes. "I explained it all in my letter."

"Yes, I read your explanation over and over until I could recite it by heart, and then I burned it." She glared with the stored fury of more than two decades, emotion she didn't know she harbored. "I no longer remember it word for word, but its meaning is still clear in my mind."

"There was nothing I could do. I was sent out of the country on urgent business for the Crown the very day I was to meet you."

"So your letter said."

"How could I know the messenger with whom I had entrusted my dispatch to you would fail to deliver it?" His tone held a pleading note.

"You couldn't possibly know, Robin. Nor could you know I stayed in that wretched inn for four days. Four long, horrid days I waited for the man I was running off to marry. I died in that inn, Robin. And when finally I gave up all pretense and admitted to myself you had abandoned me—"

"I never abandoned you," he said sharply.

She shot him a withering glare. "When I was able to face that undeniable fact I managed to make my way back to London and to my parents. My parents . . ."

She shuddered at the memory. "I shall never forget it. The shock and anger and the sheer disappointment in their eyes that I would have done such a thing. And then there was their compassion and sympathy. They were wonderful, and I did not deserve such kindness. It broke whatever small part of my heart that remained whole."

"You certainly recovered quickly enough," he said sarcastically.

"What are you implying?" Fury underlaid her words.

"I am implying nothing." His eyes flamed with a rage that matched her own. "I am saying it directly. By the time I learned what had transpired, by the time I finally wrote to tell you what had happened, you were engaged and about to be married."

"It was six months, Robin. Six months without hearing anything from you." She threw the words at him like a weapon.

In two strides he was beside her. He grasped her arms roughly, her papers flying out of her hand, and he glared into her face. "You met White on the bloody boat!"

"Indeed I did," she said defiantly. "He was kind and good and strong, and he loves me and I love him."

"Do you?" His eyes burned with a fierce hunger that abruptly turned her anger into a need just as violent, just as aching. She stared in shock and silence and . . . surrender. "Do you?"

"Yes," she whispered, and for a single heartbeat he stared. Then he crushed her lips with his.

Her head swam and she clung to him with an urgency she hadn't known existed. The years vanished and it was as if they were both once again young and impetuous and in love. His tongue plumbed the depths of her mouth and she met his onslaught with one of her own. Passion spiraled between them, stealing her will, her mind. How would she survive this meeting of long-denied desires, this meshing of once-matched souls?

He pulled his lips from hers and ran his mouth along the edge of her ear and down her neck. She trembled beneath his touch and a moan slipped from her lips.

"Phoebe. Dearest Phoebe." His words whispered

against her skin. "I have dreamed of you for years. Forever."

"Forever." She sighed. Once before she'd offered him forever. Later, she'd promised—

"Henry!" she gasped, and struggled to free herself from Robin's arms.

"What of him?" Robin pulled back and met her gaze with his.

"He's my husband." She labored without success against the solid strength of his arms. "We mustn't, Robin. This isn't right."

"Isn't it?" He pulled her tight against him. His heart thudded beneath her cheek. "We belong together, Phoebe; we always have."

"Please, Robin," she said quietly. "Please unhand me. Now."

With obvious reluctance, he released her, and she quickly stepped back. Her mind was a jumble of conflict and confusion.

"Leave him, Phoebe." Robin's voice was rough and intent.

"Divorce?" She gasped. "I could never—"

"It's not the scandal it once was. We would survive. Together." His eyes burned with a fervor both frightening and exciting. "I shall not lose you again."

For a long moment she could only stare in shocked silence. A myriad of emotions crashed through her head and she struggled to sort one from the next.

She shook her head slowly. "I don't—"

A swift stride brought him to her side and he silenced her words with a gentle finger to her lips. "Not now, Phoebe. I do not want a rash, hasty answer one way or the other. There is far too much at stake here. You have much to lose should you choose my offer. I, on the other hand," he stared into her eyes with a passion that stilled her heart, "have everything to gain."

He nodded sharply, turned on his heel and strode from the room.

Words failed her, and Phoebe could only stare helplessly at his retreating figure. Leave Henry? She couldn't. She wouldn't. He was her life, the very air she breathed.

She sank into the nearest chair and buried her face in her hands. How could she have forgotten about Henry even for a moment? Oh, certainly his caresses through the years were not as urgent as they once were. And her heart no longer throbbed at his mere presence. But there was a warmth and a comfort and a deep, abiding love that surely meant their souls were destined for each other. How could she have risked all that? How could she have let herself be swept away by a foolish moment of passion? Perhaps Robin was right. Perhaps there still lingered between them emotions as yet unresolved.

She drew a deep breath and rose slowly to her feet. Without thinking, she moved to the papers scattered across the floor and picked them up from the intricately patterned carpet. She had a great deal of thinking to do.

About Robin.

About Henry.

And, most of all, about herself.

"IT IS A lovely party, Millicent." Olivia nodded approvingly. "I think you have done a splendid job."

"It is going well, isn't it?" Millicent beamed with pride. "I can't recall the last time I entertained on such a grand scale."

"You certainly have attracted an impressive gathering," Olivia said.

"It's nothing." Millicent modestly waved away the compliment, but satisfaction shone in her eyes.

Olivia cast her gaze over the crush of people crammed into Millicent's ballroom. There was no question that the younger Miss White's introduction to society was a complete success. Olivia caught sight of the child and couldn't help but suppress a sigh. It was so long ago that she too glowed with the excitement of her first adult assembly, yet it seemed like yesterday. Where had the years gone?

". . . add to that the fact that I do believe Quentin is quite fond of the girl," Millicent said, bringing Olivia firmly back to the present. "Phoebe agrees with me that a match between the two of them would be splendid. I have always wanted to cement our friendship with a marriage between our families. It simply was not meant to be before now."

"How are Robert and Phoebe getting along?" Olivia's level tone belied the curiosity churning within her. "I should think seeing one another after all these years . . ."

"I have noticed a distinct tension in the air whenever the two of them are in the same room," Millicent said confidentially. "Nothing overt, mind you, but Robin has seemed extremely intense, Phoebe is quite distracted and even poor Henry looks as if there are storm clouds hovering just above his head."

Olivia nodded sagely. "It doesn't sound at all pleasant."

"It really isn't. I don't believe the girls or Quentin have noticed anything, but I am quite uncomfortable." Millicent sighed. "The thing that is most upsetting is that Phoebe and Henry have always been so happy together; at least that's the impression I've always had from her letters. As for Robin, he is a dear man but, Lord knows, I can certainly see his faults. He is nearly as arrogant today as he was twenty-odd years ago."

Millicent cast a furtive glance around, as if to ensure their privacy, then leaned toward Olivia. "You know, he simply assumed Phoebe would remain here in England waiting for him back then. He never knew she didn't get the message that he was sent out of the country. Even so, to presume that she would put her life aside with the briefest of explanations . . ." Millicent shook her head. "I have always suspected that everything turned out for the best after all. Upon reflection, I rather think Phoebe would not have been happy with Robin. It is rather disloyal to admit it, family ties and all that, but there you have it."

Millicent's eyes narrowed, and she stared at the couples whirling across the dance floor. "Now, he's seen her again and I do not like the look in his eye. He's a man who has always pursued what he wants."

"Henry White does not strike me as a man who easily gives up what is his," Olivia observed mildly.

Millicent brightened. "No, he doesn't, does he? And he is such a fine figure of a man—"

"Millicent!"

A rosy blush crept up Millicent's cheeks, but she stared at her friend unflinchingly. "Don't 'Millicent' me. I am nowhere near my dotage yet. And I am thinking of remarrying."

Olivia gasped, shocked by the candid admission. "Who?"

"There actually isn't a 'who' right now, but it doesn't

matter," Millicent said airily. "It was Robin who gave me the idea. With his new position in London—"

"What new position is that?" Olivia asked, feigning ignorance.

"Whatever." Millicent's light tone dismissed the comment. Olivia wondered if she really didn't know Robert's new position or if she cared less. "At any rate, Robin now really needs a wife—not for an heir of course; there is Quentin and one wouldn't—"

"Millicent," Olivia said sharply, "get to the point."

Millicent tossed her a haughty glance. "The point is, I am still relatively in my prime; or at least that's the way I feel. There is no reason why I should not seek romance or, at the very minimum, male companionship. Or you either, my dear," she said pointedly.

Olivia's gaze drifted to Robert, on the other side of the hall. She'd been vaguely aware of exactly where he was all evening. Perhaps she was taking this idea of providing a distraction for him a bit too seriously. Still, from what Millicent said, scandal was very possibly brewing between Robert and the Whites.

"Do you really think so?" Olivia murmured.

"I do."

"Much as I hate to admit it," Olivia shrugged, "I quite agree."

Millicent stared in stunned silence.

Olivia laughed. "I do agree with you now and again, if you'll recall."

"Yes, but . . ." Millicent pulled her brows together with a considering expression. Olivia stood a shade taller under her perusal, confident in the new ivory lace-trimmed, wine silk evening gown designed to conceal her flaws and emphasize her attributes. "I thought I'd noticed something different tonight. You're not wearing mourning of any kind." She nodded. "You really do look quite charming."

"I can still pull myself together when the occasion warrants it," Olivia said dryly.

"Yes, dear friend, but—" Millicent raised a brow. "I can't remember the last time you decided an occasion—any occasion—deserved the effort."

"As you so subtly pointed out, it is indeed past time to immerse ourselves once again in all the foibles and follies of society. I for one do not relish the thought of turning into a bitter old crone." Olivia shrugged and smiled. "I can see no other way to prevent that than with a touch of flirtation here, a bit of teasing banter there, perhaps even a mild indiscretion or two."

"Olivia!" Millicent's mouth dropped open in astonishment. "I hadn't expected you to take to the idea quite this enthusiastically." She grinned abruptly. "I wonder if beneath that proper exterior beats the soul of a . . . well, a . . ."

"A tart?" Olivia suggested.

Millicent shook her head, her tone wry. "I was searching for a less condemning word."

Olivia lifted her shoulders in resignation. "*Tart* seems to fit so nicely. Perhaps it's maturity or simple boredom, but I quite like the idea of being termed a tart at my age."

Millicent's eyes twinkled. "It does feel very much like we are beginning something of a new life."

"Indeed." Olivia nodded firmly. "Now, where shall we start?"

"Let me think." Millicent surveyed the crowd, then nodded to a far corner. "Lord Collingsworth is an interesting prospect. A shade older than we are, but still quite functional. He is an excellent possibility. And over there I see Harold Sedgewick. He is . . ."

Olivia listened to Millicent's assessment of the various suitable gentlemen in the room with only partial attention. She had to admit, the idea of flinging herself headlong back into society had grown in recent weeks. Robert's reappearance and her decision to distract him from Phoebe had only solidified what had, up till then, been nothing more than a vague dissatisfaction with her life.

But before she could do anything about her own future, she had to resolve her son's. Cecily had mastered every task thus far with grace and intelligence. And while a countess did need to know how to handle any awkward situation that might arise, from indiscreet houseguests to clumsy servants to last-minute social disasters, the requirements for being a wife went well beyond those needed for a title holder.

There was no test on earth that Olivia could devise that could verify love, and ultimately that was what she wanted for Jared. But, since that was out of even Olivia's reach, she would have to depend on the next closest attributes: courage and loyalty.

How would Cecily react if, unexpectedly, Jared was the subject of unpleasant gossip? If someone used the river of rumor that raged through London society to reveal his intimate involvement with automobiles? An involvement that went beyond the eminently proper position of patron, or even investor, to the rather gritty title of inventor? Would Cecily stand beside him?

Guilt shivered through Olivia, but she resolutely pushed it away. Certainly Jared had warned her not to interfere again, capping it off with that ridiculous threat about giving up his birthright and moving to

America. She did not believe it for a moment. Even if he were serious—she squared her shoulders slightly— no risk was too great to ensure that her son married the proper woman.

Besides, the dear boy had no idea Olivia knew all about his automobiles, and had known nearly from the beginning. There was no possible way suspicion would fall on her. All she needed to do was drop a word here, an innuendo there, and before the evening was more than half through, rumor would roar through the room. She simply had to decide where to start. . . .

". . . so I believe he would be an excellent place to start." Millicent nodded toward an unidentified gentleman across the room.

Olivia's gaze flickered over the crowd and settled on Robert. He was the only one worth her interest. But first things first. Who was the biggest gossip in London?

". . . beyond that, I have heard his pockets are quite deep and he is obviously . . ." Millicent prattled on, apparently unaware of her friend's perusal. Millicent, of course, always knew everything, always had her finger on the pulse of society and was always innocently willing to pass on new information.

"Millicent," Olivia interrupted, "did you ever discover who Quentin's partner is in that absurd horseless carriage of his?"

"No, indeed," Millicent said regretfully, "and I do so wish I knew. Quentin plans to drive in some ridiculous race tomorrow, and I would feel ever so much better knowing who is involved in this with him."

Olivia shook her head slowly in a gesture of unease. "I'm quite afraid I may have the answer."

Olivia hooked her arm in Millicent's and steered her toward a private corner. Millicent's eyes widened with Olivia's every word.

"... and please, do promise you won't say a word about my suspicions. I know Quentin has no concerns about his involvement with this motorcar—"

Millicent sighed. "He is, after all, half American."

"Quite." Olivia nodded. "I fear any knowledge of the Earl of Graystone's activity would be quite scandalous."

"Olivia, you can certainly trust me not to say a word," Millicent said solemnly.

Olivia cast her a grateful smile. "Oh, my dear, I am certain I can trust you implicitly." Olivia bit her lip to keep her smile from blossoming into a satisfied grin.

"I'm confident you'll do exactly what needs to be done."

"AND SO YOU see, sir," Jared pulled a deep breath and held it, "I should very much like to marry her." He had no doubt as to Cece's willingness to wed him, but would the father share the opinion of the daughter?

Henry White leaned against the mantel in one of Lady Millicent's parlors, diffidently swirling brandy in his glass. The man seemed somewhat preoccupied, his mind anywhere but here. The moment stretched endlessly.

Jared cleared his throat. "Sir?"

"What is it, my boy?" Henry said absently.

Jared narrowed his eyes thoughtfully. He had run into White several times this past week, and always the American had appeared contemplative and very far away. Jared wondered what could be troubling him. Even though he had requested White's presence away from the party, and had spent an interminable amount of time gathering up the courage to do so, this was obviously not the right moment to ask for Cece's hand. No matter; it could wait. Odd; there was more disappointment than relief at the thought.

"Perhaps I could lend my assistance in resolving whatever problem you may have encountered?" Jared asked.

"Problem?" Henry took a deep pull of the liquor and shook his head. "I appreciate the offer." He shrugged. "But I'm afraid this is something I'll have to deal with by myself."

Again White seemed to sink deep into thoughts of his own. Whatever was bothering the man was no doubt quite personal and extremely private. Jared wondered if he should silently take his leave.

"How much a role does my money play in your interest in my daughter?" White said without warning.

Jared drew a deep breath. He'd expected just such a question from Cece's father. Obviously the man was paying far closer attention than it appeared. Was this ability to concentrate on one topic even while preoccupied with another a clue to the American's business success?

"To be honest, sir, initially it played a rather significant role. But now . . ."

"Now?" White raised a stern brow.

Jared shrugged. "Now it no longer matters."

"Why?" White shot the question like an arrow.

"I love her, sir," Jared said simply.

"Would you love her as well without her fortune?"

"Yes," Jared said without pausing so much as a heartbeat.

White's eyes narrowed slightly, his studied gaze intense and deliberate. Jared resisted the urge to loosen the collar around his neck, which seemed somehow tighter than only a moment ago. Abruptly the older man nodded, as if satisfied with what he'd found. Jared released a breath he hadn't realized he'd held.

"Love is a tricky emotion," White said quietly. "And women are dammed unpredictable creatures."

"I seem to have discovered that already, sir." Jared's tone was wry.

White drew a deep pull of the brandy. A droll smile quirked the corners of his mouth. "You appear to know my daughter far better than I expected."

Thoughts of Paris flashed through his mind, followed swiftly by memories of their encounter in the stable. He struggled to suppress a satisfied smile. "I have done my best, sir."

Again, White narrowed eyes that flashed an unspoken threat. "See that you do not grow to know her too well."

He could see by the look in White's eyes that any protestations of innocence would not be believed. He grinned weakly. "No, sir."

White nodded, as if certain his implied warning was understood. "There are some things you should know about my girl. You'd better sit down." White pulled two cigars from his waistcoat and handed one to Jared, who grinned his appreciation. "This might take a while."

He settled into a burgundy brocade wing chair and gestured to the younger man to take the matching chair. Jared sank into the comfortable seat and, for the first time since the two men had entered the room, relaxed. There was nothing like a good cigar and good company to do that for a man.

White struck a match and leaned forward to touch the tip of Jared's cigar, then lit his own. Long seconds passed in the companionable silence of men who shared an appreciation for the finer things in life.

"First of all," White blew a small, wobbly ring of blue-gray smoke, "Cece takes after her father in many respects."

"Really?" Jared blew a ring slightly larger than White's.

"Indeed." White puffed a circle, steadier and larger than the last. "She can be quite stubborn, extremely persistent and determined to have her own way."

"I have noticed those tendencies," Jared said idly.

"She is also impulsive, prone to leaping into matters without any consideration as to the possible consequences of her actions."

Jared gazed smugly at his latest, and most impressive, ring of smoke. "I have noticed that as well."

"Mark my words, Jared, Cece needs a husband with a firm hand." White pointed his cigar sternly at the younger man. "But like any good filly, she's worthless if her spirit is broken. I would not like to see that happen to any daughter of mine."

White puffed a large misty ring, followed quickly by a second that spun lazily through the first. "Do I make myself clear?"

Jared stared at the dissipating haze. White's point went well beyond any spur-of-the-moment smoke-blowing competition. He looked at the man with renewed respect and hoped he would remember this intimidating technique when he someday had daughters of his own.

"Very clear, sir."

"Excellent." White rose to his feet, and Jared followed suit. "I shall settle a considerable sum on Cece when you marry. And I will provide her with funds of her own on an annual basis."

"That's extremely generous, sir." Far better than Jared had hoped for. Cece's money would mean a rebirth of the estate and all that went with it. Even so, now that the deed was nearly done, it was more than a little distasteful. It must be that bloody love business rearing its annoying head again. If he had known how that persistent emotion would complicate everything, he might well have married the first heiress he'd found, even one whose brows met over her nose.

White tossed his half-finished cigar in the fireplace with a look of regret. "What do you plan on doing with that horseless carriage of yours?"

"My horseless carriage?" Jared said cautiously.

White leveled him a sympathetic gaze. "Surely you did not think Cece would keep such a secret?"

Jared groaned to himself. "Actually, sir, yes I did."

"Not when it comes to her father." A touch of triumph colored his smile. "Although she did tell me not to reveal your activity to anyone else. Some nonsense about society here not understanding—"

"Yes, sir," Jared interrupted. "I believe I've heard it all before."

White laughed. "No doubt you have, especially if I know my daughter." He paused and eyed Jared speculatively. "I find motorcars extremely interesting. If some of the kinks can be worked out, I suspect they will be the vehicles we shall all ride into the twentieth century."

"My thoughts exactly." Jared nodded eagerly.

"I should like to see this machine of yours."

"It would be my pleasure, sir."

"Perhaps . . ." a gleam twinkled in White's eye, and Jared noted how familiar that expression appeared, ". . . you would even permit me to . . ."

Jared's stomach sank.

". . . oh, say . . ."

At once he realized why he recognized that look of White's.

". . . drive the automobile?"

Bloody hell! The woman did indeed take after her father.

"Of course, sir." Jared forced a smile to his lips.

"You are a damn poor liar, my boy. I like that." White grinned. "I detest liars, especially good ones." He turned to go and reached for the door handle.

"Sir . . ." Jared blurted impatiently.

White raised a quizzical brow. "Yes?"

"You still have not answered my question."

"Your question?" White's brow creased with puzzlement, then smoothed. "Of course. Completely slipped my mind. Yes, yes, you can marry her, if she'll have you." White's gaze flicked over him in an assessing manner. "But I must admit you're much more acceptable than I ever expected from Cece. She's made a good choice."

The compliment was tossed out in an offhand manner, but White's words warmed Jared. He already had a great deal of respect for this self-made man, and knowing White considered him at least satisfactory for his daughter touched him in a way he never would have expected.

"Thank you, sir," Jared said sincerely.

White nodded shortly and pulled open the door. "It's high time we made our presence known at this fiasco."

"Fiasco?" Jared suppressed a grin.

White rolled his eyes heavenward. "Did I say fiasco?

Slip of the tongue." He leveled Jared a sidelong glance. "Remember that phrase, my boy, 'slip of the tongue.' It's saved my life with my wife more than once. It's convenient, easy to remember and almost impossible to argue with."

Jared's grin broke free. " 'Slip of the tongue,' yes, sir. I'll remember."

The men strode side by side down a long corridor, through a door and into a second-story foyer. To one side, a double stairway swept down to the first floor. On the other, a tall, wide arched entry framed the ballroom. White surveyed the room and his expression froze. Jared followed his gaze to where it rested on Quentin's father. Sir Robert appeared in idle conversation with a small gathering of gentlemen.

Was this what had the American so preoccupied? Lady Millicent had mentioned a long-ago relationship between Phoebe White and Robert Bainbridge, but surely the past had no bearing on the events of today. White's dark eyes narrowed, his face set as if carved in steel itself, and Jared pitied any man on the receiving end of that expression.

"Jared . . ." White's intense gaze never left his quarry.

"Yes, sir?"

"I told you I detest liars, didn't I?"

"Yes, sir."

"I also despise thieves and cheats."

"Yes, sir."

"And I protect what is mine."

"I can certainly understand that, sir."

"See that you do, my boy." White nodded sharply. "See that you do." White turned to leave, then turned back.

"By the way, Cece told me about your motorcar, but I've no doubt she kept your secret when it comes to anyone else. She has a highly developed sense of loyalty."

Jared grinned. "I am counting on that."

White shrugged. "Apparently others do not have the same qualities."

A sinking sensation settled in the pit of Jared's stomach. "What do you mean?"

White shook his head wryly. "I mean, I have heard about your automobile for the past hour, right here. Rumors, some quite unpleasant, have been flying all evening."

Jared groaned. "Bloody hell."

White quirked a brow, his manner mild. "I don't understand you British at all. Why, in my country—"

"I know, sir, I know." Jared pulled a deep breath and gritted his teeth. The rest of this evening would not be at all pleasant. "And believe me, right now I would just as soon rather be in your country.

"I'd rather be anywhere but here."

Chapter 13

"**W**HERE on earth is Jared?" Cece struggled to keep a peevish tone from her voice. "I have barely seen him all week, and now he seems to have vanished."

"I shouldn't worry," Emily said, her mind obviously elsewhere. "He's certain to be here somewhere."

Cece glanced critically at her sister. This was the first moment all evening she'd had a chance to speak with Emily. The girl had been surrounded by eager young men as soon as the festivities began.

Emily positively sparkled tonight. Her amber eyes glowed with excitement, high color warmed her cheeks, the frothy white gown she wore created a vision reminiscent of a fairy tale princess. Cece remembered the marvelous time she'd had at her own coming out and was inordinately pleased her sister was experiencing the same success.

"You seem to be having a pleasant evening," Cece said with a smile.

"Oh, Cece." The younger girl sighed. "Isn't this the most perfect night ever?"

Cece laughed softly. "Perhaps not ever, but I will agree it is a lovely evening."

"It's wonderful," Emily said with a bob of her head. "Simply wonderful."

Cece's gaze skipped over the multitude squeezed in the ballroom and continued her search for Jared. He was nowhere to be seen, but Cece vaguely noted what appeared to be a great deal of animated conversation taking place among ducked heads and behind protective fans. She wondered if some juicy tidbit of gossip was circulating through the room, then dismissed the inconsequential notion.

"I only wish I could find Jared. I wonder if he's with Quentin? Have you seen him at all lately?"

"Quentin?" Emily asked, as if the name was unfamiliar.

Cece smiled wryly. "Yes, Quentin. Surely you remember him? The gentleman you find so frustrating and confusing?"

"I know perfectly well who you're talking about. I haven't the vaguest notion where he is." Emily lifted her shoulders in a casual gesture of dismissal. "And I'm not particularly concerned either."

"You're not?" Cece said cautiously.

"Not a bit."

Cece cast her sister a speculative glance. "I thought you were in love with him."

"So did I," Emily said airily. "But that was long ago."

"Last week, I believe." A dry note sounded in Cece's voice.

"It seems very long ago." Emily's tone was firm. "Honestly, Cece, I see no reason why I should set my cap for any one man right now. Just, for a moment, consider the possibilities." Emily swept her fan in a gesture that encompassed the entire ballroom.

"Look at all these young men here. Handsome, exciting . . . why, a girl would be a fool not to consider all the options available. And not just here, either. There's still all of Chicago society that I've yet to really meet, as an adult anyway." She leaned toward her sister with a patronizing air. "It's not as if Quentin was my only chance for a good marriage. After all, I am only seventeen. It would be far different if I were your age."

"I see," Cece said slowly. "Then I gather you think I'd best snare Jared and haul him to the altar before he notices my failing eyesight, imminent wrinkles and deteriorating wits?"

"No, no." Emily shook her head impatiently. "I did not mean that at all. I am certain, even without Jared, you still have a few opportunities left."

"Thank you."

Emily blithely ignored her sister's cutting response. "It's of no consequence, at any rate. Whereas I have realized that my interest in Quentin was no doubt the result of close proximity and possibly even a still unknown malady, you are confident of your feelings for Jared." She raised a brow. "You are still certain that you love him, aren't you?"

Cece sighed in resignation. "Yes, that is one thing I'm confident of."

"Very well, then." Emily beamed. "We needn't worry about your fate. There shall be no more nonsense about working for a living. You and Jared will marry and live happily ever after, and I need no longer fear you'll end up old and feeble and alone."

"I had no idea you foresaw such a dire end for me," Cece muttered.

Emily nodded vigorously. "I did indeed. I have spent years hoping against hope you would come to your senses and finally develop some measure of decorum and rational behavior. At times I have even—"

"Pardon me."

The girls turned at the deep, resonant voice.

"I believe this is my dance." A tall, roguishly handsome, dark-haired man nodded to Cece and presented his arm to Emily. Cece had to admit, if Jared's charms had not already blinded her to the temptation of any other man, she would find this one quite inviting.

"How delightful," Emily said in a voice at once sweet and sultry. Emily cast her sister a smug smile, then turned her complete attention to the stranger, and the couple glided onto the dance floor.

Cece stared in astonishment. Where on earth had her quiet, proper sister acquired that flirtatious manner? From whom had she adopted that come-hither expression? Obviously, this trip to England had made an impact on Emily that Cece never would have expected. Why, Em seemed almost like . . .

The idea struck her with the force of a physical blow, and Cece's eyes widened with the emotional impact. Emily's behavior was not unlike her own at that age. Of course Cece's adventures had started long before she discovered the innate appeal of the opposite sex, but the tilt of Emily's chin and the rapt look in her eye that told the man she gazed at that he was, at that moment, her world, and even the mix of honey and spice in her voice was so like Cece at seventeen, it was nearly as if she'd just gazed into a mirror of the past.

My goodness! What had she done to the prim, docile child? Cece drew her brows together and tried to consider this new development rationally. Was this evolution of Emily's character really so bad? A slow smile spread on Cece's face. Of course not. She was merely following the example set by her big sister. Cece'd had some marvelous adventures in her life that she credited to her uninhibited nature. Only now did she truly understand the need to consider the consequences of her actions before leaping forward. But Emily had always had that sense of restraint. Tempering it with a bit of exuberance, perhaps a touch of intemperance, even a dash of outrageous abandon, would do the girl a world of good.

Cece's smile broadened into a grin. If Emily had long worried about her sister's fate, so too had Cece harbored concern over Em's future. It seemed there was no longer cause for concern. Emily was following in her sister's lightly trod, occasionally reckless, thoroughly enjoyed footsteps.

"I was so shocked to hear about Jared."

Cece spun around to meet Linnea DeToulane's mournful greeting. Her eyes widened and her heart stopped. Had something happened to Jared?

"What is it?" Cece asked sharply. "Tell me! At once!"

"You needn't take that tone," Linnea huffed. "It's not as if the man were dead or mortally wounded or anything like that."

Cece breathed a sigh of relief.

"He's not even mildly injured, as far as I know," Linnea said, adding in a dark tone, "although he might as well be, at least as far as his reputation is concerned."

The woman made absolutely no sense. "What on earth are you talking about?"

Linnea glanced to one side and then the other, as if making sure they were not overheard. "You do remember the discussion at dinner last week about Quentin's tinkering with that horseless carriage?"

"Of course I remember," Cece said impatiently.

Linnea leaned forward confidentially. "Jared's doing it as well."

Caution colored Cece's voice. "Doing what as well?"

Linnea sighed with exasperation. "Tinkering with automobiles, you silly goose."

At once Linnea's manner and the murmurs skittering around the ballroom made sense. Jared's secret was out. And, exactly as he had feared, it had not been well received.

Cece drew a deep, steadying breath and forced a cool, casual air. "Oh, that." She laughed lightly. "I think it's quite delightful of him to be so terribly creative."

Linnea shook her head in a pitying manner. "I suppose one really can't expect you to understand, being from America. You people simply don't have the same sort of standards we have. Standards that have helped us build an empire, while you . . ."

"Have carved out a completely new country?" Cece suggested sweetly, stifling the impulse to show Linnea precisely the type of damage one standardless American girl could do to one smug British face.

Linnea shrugged, as if there was no need to respond to a comment she clearly considered ludicrous.

"I will not debate the merits of my country with you, however." Cece smiled wickedly with unexpected inspiration. "There are a vast number of men in my country who have a great deal of ingenuity, exactly like Jared. With their creativity and inventiveness, those men have made a considerable amount of money."

She leaned closer to Linnea, as if revealing a confidence. "I have even heard it said that, today, there are more men worth millions in my country than anywhere else in the world."

Cece had no idea if her statement was true or not,

but it had a convincing ring. Her words hit their mark, and a speculative gleam appeared in Linnea's eye.

"And Linnea," she cast the widow a knowing smile, "a great many of them are . . . elderly."

"Mature," Linnea murmured vaguely.

"Old," Cece said with a firm note. She could see the gears and wheels of Linnea's mind working as clearly as she could see the inner mechanics of Jared's automobile.

"I think it's admirable that the British pride themselves so on their standards and their heritage. But it does make it all so much more lamentable, don't you think?"

"Lamentable?" Linnea's brow drew together in puzzlement. "Whatever do you mean, 'lamentable'?"

"Well," Cece sighed and shook her head in feigned melancholy, "it simply seems to me, in many cases, your fortunes are as old as your history. The inspiration that created the wealth originally is long gone. And without a continuing infusion of fresh funds," she shrugged, "some of your best families have already found themselves forced to sell family heirlooms and forge alliances through marriage with those with substantially lower standards. Americans," Cece struggled not to choke on the words, "like myself."

"Quite," Linnea said thoughtfully. "Do go on."

"Jared's automobile has unlimited potential. It could very well be the vehicle of the next century."

"And?" Linnea prompted.

"And . . ." Cece paused, drawing out the moment. The time was right to press home her point. "Everyone will want to buy one."

Linnea's eyes widened, and she fluttered her fan before her face. "Everyone?"

"Everyone." Cece nodded in confirmation. "It simply stands to reason. If Jared wishes to produce automobiles, there shall surely be a market for them. Why, look at how popular telephones and electric lights have become."

"And profitable," Linnea said under her breath.

"Indeed." Cece bit back a satisfied smirk. "As the inventor and manufacturer, Jared would doubtlessly double his family's fortune in no time."

"No time at all," Linnea agreed, a somewhat stunned expression on her face.

"Given all that, I can't imagine why every single one of these people here aren't slapping Jared on the back and applauding his British ingenuity. I should even think," Cece lowered her voice, and Linnea leaned toward her to catch her words, "some of those with a bit of business acumen and a little foresight would even wish to invest in this endeavor."

She fanned her face and studied Linnea with a surreptitious eye. The woman looked very much like a cat discovering the untold possibilities of delight to be found in a dairy barn. Cece couldn't resist one final jab to ensure that the woman understood her point. "My father says—you remember my father? He's the American with all that money?"

Linnea nodded mutely.

"I thought so." She smiled sweetly and mentally crossed her fingers against the tale she prepared to spin. "My father says anyone would be a fool not to invest in something with as much obvious potential for the future as automobiles. I'm fairly certain he plans on investing quite heavily."

"How very interesting," Linnea said under her breath.

"Oh, dear." Cece widened her eyes in a stricken expression of dismay. "I really should not have been discussing such things. Father will be furious if he thinks I've discussed important business secrets." And furious as well if he knew how very skilled his daughter was at fabrication. She pushed the guilty thought aside. Surely, given the opportunity, Henry White would indeed consider Jared's automobile a good investment.

She laid a pleading hand on the older woman's arm and gazed innocently into her eyes. "Please don't repeat this to anyone."

Linnea patted her hand sympathetically. "Of course not, my dear. Why, I shall simply forget this conversation ever took place."

Cece breathed a sigh of relief. "I would be ever so grateful."

"Now, if you'll excuse me?" Linnea cast her a polite but impatient smile and turned away, eager to do what? Corner her banker, perhaps?

Cece grinned to herself. At least she now had Linnea seeing Jared's work in a different, potentially profitable light. Hopefully, she would pass her newly acquired appreciation of his activities along and, with just the barest luck, others would feel the same way. All they really needed was to have their eyes opened. Determination filled her to do just that, even if it meant prying each and every eye open by force.

Still, Linnea was perhaps a bit more motivated by financial interests than most. Surely there was something else she could do to convince these people to see what Jared was doing not as menial and lower class but as fine and noble.

She cast her gaze around the room and caught sight of Jared sauntering toward her. The man moved with a stride cool, assured, even arrogant. A rakish smile skimmed his lips and his dark eyes danced in his handsome face. Relief battled with concern at his approach. Surely his behavior indicated that he didn't know of the rumors circulating. She hated to be the one to tell him. She drew a deep breath and squared her shoulders. But who better than she?

His gaze met hers and even at a distance she noted the blue of his eyes burning richer when it meshed with hers. Her resolve melted with her knees, and for the merest moment she wanted to forget all about rumor and scandal and even automobiles and let him wrap her in his arms.

"Forgive me, my love, for ignoring you." Jared took her gloved hand in his and brushed his lips suggestively across the back. Something deep inside her fluttered at his touch. "I had some . . . er, business to attend to."

His words brought back the matter at hand. "Jared," she said quietly, "everyone knows."

"I believe this is our dance." He pointedly ignored her comment, placed her hand in the crook of his arm and led her the few steps to the dance floor.

"Did you understand what I said?" Her terse tone belied the public smile she plastered on her face.

He took her in his arms and they danced together as easily as if one were made for the other. Cece barely noticed.

"I understood you perfectly," Jared said, his tone casual.

"You certainly are taking it well." Suspicion colored her words.

"It was inevitable that it would come out sooner or later, I suppose." He quirked a resigned smile. "I shall just have to make the best of it. It wasn't my idea to keep it secret in the first place."

Cece stared, surprised by the note in his voice. "Are you suggesting James's advice to keep your work quiet was wrong?"

Jared laughed shortly. "I have rarely thought my brother was wrong about anything. I never questioned him. Now I am beginning to see no small number of things he might have handled better, or at least differently."

She leveled him a curious gaze. "What kinds of things?"

Jared shrugged. "Nothing of any major significance. I've just found some items dealing with estate management, accounting, varied and sundry business practices that can be improved. No doubt James would have found them himself if he had lived."

"How did James die, Jared?" Cece said quietly. Jared pulled her a little tighter and his eyes darkened. She added quickly, "I apologize. If it's too painful—"

"It's not." A muscle ticked in the tense line of his jaw. "It was an accident."

He steered her to the edge of the dance floor, plucked two glasses of champagne from a passing waiter and escorted her to French doors that opened onto a terrace. They stepped out into the cool night air and walked in companionable silence for several moments. Finally Jared drew a deep breath.

"James drowned. In that same little pond you drove into that first day. He was alone. And he died."

The setting flashed into her mind: the road from the stable running along a modest ridge, the pasture falling away to the small valley, the water below. From what she'd seen the pond was not especially deep.

"How did it happen?" she said softly.

Jared's eyes appeared very far away, as if he were once again seeing the scene replayed in his mind. "No one knows for certain. It had been raining. We believe his horse slipped on the wet grass and threw him. He must have hit his head and rolled down the hill into the pond." Jared paused, as if choosing his words or his memories. "That's where I found him."

"You found him?"

Jared nodded.

"I see." She pulled her brows together and considered her next question carefully. "I thought the stables with your motorcars was the only building on that road."

"It is." He paused and shook his head. "I still have no idea why James was there. At first I thought he had come to find me. I used to spend a great deal more time working on the automobiles than I do now. But then I realized that James knew I was still in London. He didn't expect me at the castle for several days."

"So he couldn't have been looking for you?"

Jared shook his head. "No."

How very odd. What could Jared's brother possibly have been doing on that little-used section of the estate?

"I daresay we'll never know why he was there. At any rate, I suppose it doesn't matter anymore." Jared frowned and eyed her over the rim of his glass. "What does matter now is how to weather this storm of scandal."

"Jared, I don't care—" she snapped her fingers in his face "—that much about what these people think."

"Perhaps not." His tone was wry. "But if we are to live with these people, as you so charmingly call them, in this society—my society, I might add—I would prefer that the Earl and Countess of Graystone be respected, not forever haunted by the taint of manual labor."

She raised a skeptical brow. "And just what do you suggest we do?"

"I don't know," he said sharply. "I've never been in this situation before. Any other time I've been touched by scandal I've quite enjoyed it. I've never tried to repair the social damage I caused."

"Well, what have you done before?" she snapped.

He grit his teeth. "Usually I do something to make the problem a little worse by thumbing my nose at the lot of them."

"Why don't you simply do that now?" Her words were clipped with exasperation.

"Now, I'm the bloody earl!" He ground out the words, his voice barely under control, his eyes flashing. "Before, I was the second son. Nobody expected any better of me. I could do what I damned well pleased."

She cast him a glare of frustration. "Well, I'm not the earl and I can still do what I damn well please! I'm an American. They don't expect anything better from me. I can certainly thumb my nose at them if that's what I wish, and I should derive a great deal of pleasure from the act to boot."

"And just how do you propose to do that?" Ire and sarcasm dripped from his words.

"How?" Her mind grasped for answers. How, indeed? What one thing would show those sanctimonious snobs she didn't care one whit for their haughty, old-fashioned ways of looking at the world? At once the answer struck her with the clarity of fine crystal.

"That's it, of course. It's perfect. We'll show them you're not tainted and their absurd way of looking at the world doesn't mean anything at all. We can announce it tonight. It won't stop the talk altogether, I suppose." She paused to corral her ricochetting thoughts. "But it will give them all something else to gossip about."

"Announce what?" Jared's brows furrowed with apprehension. "What are you planning?"

"It is perhaps the most interesting idea I've ever had." She beamed with modest triumph. "I'll simply have to marry you."

"Marry me!" He gasped.

"Yes, thank you, I'd be honored," she said primly.

He glared, outrage shadowing his eyes. "That was not a proposal."

She shrugged and waved her fan lightly. "It certainly sounded like one to me."

"Well, it wasn't." He looked like a little boy about to stomp his foot in a fit of vexation.

"You don't want to marry me?" She widened her eyes and bit her lower lip in an excellent imitation of crushed feelings. "I thought you loved me!"

"Of course I love you. And I do want to marry you." Jared shook his head, as if to clear the confusion apparent on his face. "But when I ask you to marry me, it shall be my idea."

"I thought it was always your idea," she said innocently.

He stared for a long moment; then understanding dawned in his eyes. He pulled her tight against him, her hands flattened between his chest and hers.

"I had always assumed, when I asked a woman to wed, even an American, even you," he growled the words, and the intensity in his gaze muddled her thoughts and stole her will, "it would be at my instigation, not hers. The act would be in my hands alone."

"Everything seems to be very much in your hands," she said breathlessly.

"Is it?" The midnight of his eyes drew her into their depths until she wondered if she would glimpse his soul, and he would glimpse hers.

"Will you marry me?"

For once Cecily Gwendolyn White could only nod speechlessly.

"Excellent."

His eyes smoldered and his voice simmered with the rich promise of all her silent agreement meant. He bent to touch his lips to hers and she strained forward until their breath mingled.

"Oh dear," she blurted. "I nearly forgot." Her words brushed against his lips.

He groaned with obvious frustration and pulled back to stare at her. "What is it now?"

"Perhaps this is not the right time." She gazed at the desire on his face and wished she hadn't stopped his relentless progress toward another of his rather awe-inspiring kisses.

"What?" he demanded sharply.

"I simply wanted to say you really should talk to my father." Her voice was a sigh of longing. "To ask him for my hand."

Amusement glittered in his eyes. He pulled her closer, and she melted into his arms. And just before his lips claimed hers he laughed softly.

"I already have."

". . . AND I SHOULD therefore wish to propose a toast." Henry White lifted his glass in a salute to Cecily and

Jared. The hushed crowd in the ballroom followed suit. "May you find laughter, prosperity and joy. In life. In children. And, above all else, in each other."

Murmurs of agreement and approval rolled through the gathering. There certainly was nothing like the surprise announcement of a betrothal to soften even the stuffiest hearts. Oh, it hadn't quieted the snide jibes about Jared's inventive nature, but it had thrown the dogs of gossip a new bone to chew. It had also proven, once and for all, the worthiness of the soon-to-be Countess of Graystone.

Olivia surveyed the happy couple by her side and could barely contain her delight. Certainly when Jared informed her of his engagement, a scant few minutes before Henry White announced it publicly, she was taken aback momentarily. It was not precisely how she had expected Cecily to handle this last test. Still, she had to admit the girl had finally gained her complete admiration. What better way to display courage and loyalty to a man, and to a family, than to declare to all the world your pledge to stand by his side forever?

Olivia suppressed a satisfied chuckle. This was the last pea beneath the mattress for Cecily. She had passed every trial, every test. Olivia could now give the couple her blessing without reservation and look forward to a life of her own, knowing her son's future was in capable hands.

Olivia looked up into Jared's assessing gaze. "You appear quite pleased with yourself, Mother."

"I suppose I am." Olivia cast him an innocent glance. "You have finally selected a bride who, although American, is still suitable both socially and financially. I am quite happy for you both."

"Are you?" Suspicion underlaid his words.

"Quite." She smiled.

He studied her through narrowed eyes. "No more silly tests?"

"Jared," she said with indignation, "in the first place, it was all in your imagination. I would never subject Cecily to anything so ridiculous. Beyond that," she raised her shoulders in a dismissive gesture, "you did threaten me with the most dire of consequences should you even suspect me of any activity whatsoever.

"It really was not at all fair," she chided gently.

"Perhaps not." In spite of his words, distrust still lingered in his eyes.

She smiled back sweetly. With one last measuring glance, Jared stepped aside to greet the throng of guests eager to tender their congratulations. Olivia turned to find Cecily.

The girl was surrounded by well wishers and fairly glowed with happiness. It warmed Olivia's heart, and any remaining doubt she might have had as to Cecily's suitability to be Jared's wife vanished.

"My dear child." Olivia grasped both her hands and lightly kissed the air by each cheek. "I can't tell you how very pleased I am."

A flicker of surprise flashed through Cecily's eyes, but her expression remained pleasant and composed. "Thank you."

Something in her tone, the merest hint, the tiniest suggestion, caught Olivia's attention, and she considered the girl carefully. Cecily's gaze locked with hers, the look in her eyes direct and candid.

Reserved success colored Cecily's smile. There was no suggestion here of smug, self-satisfied triumph; only the honest victory of a battle hard fought and fairly won.

At once understanding dawned, and Olivia smiled slowly. There was no doubt whatsoever. The girl knew of her tests. The knowledge did not make the trials any less valid, but Cecily's perception raised her esteem a notch in Olivia's book and added a final check to the list in her mind.

"Someday," Olivia arched a brow, "we shall have to have a very long talk."

Unexpected pleasure shone on Cecily's face. "I should like that."

"I rather think we have quite a bit in common."

Cecily laughed. "I would not be at all surprised."

Olivia nodded agreement, then surrendered Cecily to the few waiting to offer their best wishes and the many eager to cast their own critical, assessing eye on the future countess. Olivia had not had this sense of serenity and fulfillment in years. It was as if, having assured herself her son's future was in good hands, she could relax and concentrate on other, less pressing matters.

She turned and surveyed the crowded ballroom, spotting Robert within seconds. Odd that she hadn't had this desire for a new life of her own before his return to England. Was it mere coincidence or fate? Olivia had never believed in either. But now, well, perhaps . . .

Olivia headed toward Robert with a determined step. Now that the course of her son's life was firmly set in the right direction, it was past time to take charge of her own.

Chapter 14

THE day dawned clear and crisp, bright and beautiful. It was a perfect day for an outing, for a picnic, for a race.

Cece stifled a discreet yawn behind a gloved hand. She had no idea what time she finally retired last night. It was long after the guests had left and long past the moment Jared kissed her good night. A shiver ran through her at the memory of that passionate embrace.

She glanced around the surprisingly large group that had gathered here at daybreak at this inn on the outskirts of London. There were not as many entries in this race as there had been in Paris; still, the variety of motorcars displayed was impressive.

While Jared hadn't taught her to drive, his instruction in the mechanics of automobiles was thorough, and she realized just how good a job he'd done. She recognized cars powered by steam, by electricity and by gasoline. Only a small number of the vehicles entered were of British origin. Many more were from France, Switzerland and Italy. She strolled along the grounds, her educated eye discerning the differences between the vehicles, the possible flaws and potential advantages of each design.

Jared and her father were engrossed in a discussion regarding some minor detail or other about his automobile, the only one of his three inventions housed in the stable that actually ran. After last night Jared had agreed to accompany Quentin in the race, and Cece could tell the man was delighted with the opportunity. And well he should be. She sighed in irritation. She would give a great deal to come along on this race. Goodness, she'd only spent one morning with the vehicle away from Jared's protective eye, but already she could start the machine on her own. Steering and driving could not be nearly as difficult as he would have had her believe.

Cece bobbed her head and smiled at those she recognized from last night or the various other social events they'd attended in London. Lady Graystone, Lady Millicent, her mother and Emily were here as well.

The older women had varying reactions to the news revealed at Emily's party. Lady Millicent seemed quite pleased to know Quentin's partner was not some disreputable cur. Her mother was apparently impressed with Jared's accomplishment. Lady Graystone's response was a bit more difficult to judge. She seemed neither particularly surprised nor especially shocked. Rather, the woman had taken the whole evening with a serenity that indicated she knew far more than she ever let on. Cece wondered if her future mother-in-law had anything to do with the gossip about Jared's invention that had swept the party. No, surely not. What possible reason would she have to reveal that interesting tidbit? Cece was certain, however, that Lady Graystone knew full well that Cece was aware of her series of tests. But

Jared's mother appeared more pleased than distressed by that knowledge.

Cece spotted Quentin talking to a short, wiry, dark-haired man and headed toward him. Really, he should be with Jared, preparing for the start of the race. Indignantly she started in his direction, then slowed and paused.

Even at this distance she could see Quentin's conversation was anything but cordial. The smaller man gestured furiously, waving around a sheaf of papers clutched in his hand. Anger colored Quentin's face, the sharpness of his words apparent from his expression. The stranger thrust the papers at him one last time, then turned and stalked off. Quentin glared after him, his hands clenched at his sides.

"Quentin"—Cece hurried toward him—"what on earth was that all about?"

Quentin drew a deep breath and cast her a considering glance, as if debating whether to answer her question or not. Her apprehension grew. Finally he nodded abruptly, grasped her elbow and led her farther away from the crowd.

"It's not at all good, Cece," Quentin said. "I'm afraid we have a rather difficult problem on our hands."

"What kind of problem?" Caution and concern underlaid her tone. "Who was that nasty little man?"

Quentin's eyes narrowed with disdain. "His name is Barton Sinclair. He's another so-called inventor. Sinclair's not especially clever, and I've had more than one occasion to doubt his honesty. But he's always displayed relatively sophisticated designs, very similar to those of mine and Jared's. I always wondered if he had someone else working with him. Now I know."

The serious tone of his voice tightened her stomach

with foreboding. She forced herself to ask the question she abruptly feared to have answered.

"Who, Quentin? Who was working with him?"

"James."

Cece gasped. "James? Jared's brother?"

Quentin nodded grimly. "It seems James was selling our designs, our drawings and blueprints. Sinclair paid James just before he died for the design of our carburetor. Jared and I have managed to come up with a—"

"I know all that," she said impatiently, reciting by heart, "the main problem facing developers is achieving the proper mix of gasoline to air in the carburetor. It all has to do with creating an explosion in some kind of sealed metal tube that forces the engine piston downward."

Quentin stared, shock mingling with admiration in his eyes. "How on earth did you know all that?"

She dismissed his question with an exasperated wave of her hand. "It scarcely matters now. All that's important is dealing with this Sinclair creature."

"I don't see a lot of choices." Quentin sighed in resignation. "We'll have to give him the damn carburetor—or at least the blueprints."

"You can't do that," she said quickly. "It would give him a competitive edge that simply isn't fair. The man hasn't earned it."

"No." Quentin's tone was glum. "But he did pay for it."

"Quentin," Cece said, her words slow and measured, "Jared doesn't know about this, does he?"

Quentin shook his head, his gaze meeting hers, and she could see her own realization of what this knowledge would do to Jared reflected in Quentin's eyes.

"We can't tell him." Her tone was urgent.

"I don't see how we can avoid it."

"From everything he's said I gather he adored his brother." Compassion for Jared mixed with a firm resolve to protect him. "This would devastate him."

"I know." Quentin's lips compressed in a grim line. "I just wish there was another way out of this."

The couple fell silent for a long moment.

"What would Nellie Bly do?" Cece said under her breath.

Quentin pulled his brows together in confusion. "What did you say?"

"Never mind," she said absently, still trying to come up with a solution to this dilemma, a solution that would prevent Jared from ever learning of his brother's duplicity. At once the answer struck her. So easy and obvious, she was amazed she hadn't thought of it sooner.

"Why don't we just give Sinclair back the money he paid James?"

Quentin cast her a look of disbelief. "And where would we get it?"

Her heart sank. "How much money are we talking about?"

"Three hundred pounds."

"Three hundred pounds?" She gasped. "That's a small fortune."

"Sinclair has more money than talent," Quentin said sarcastically. "I could perhaps get it from Aunt Millicent, or even my father, but not without telling them why. And I would not trust either of them to keep this from Jared, or his mother for that matter."

"Three hundred pounds," she murmured. She certainly did not have that kind of money readily available. But she did know one man who could easily furnish the funds. A man she had complete faith in to keep quiet, and a man who, hopefully, would have complete faith in her judgment without insisting on detailed explanations. "Will Sinclair be driving in the race?"

"No. He has hired a driver."

"Good, that gives me some time. I think I can take care of this, Quentin," she said firmly. "Just don't say anything to Jared."

"What are you planning?" Suspicion colored his words.

"I know where to get the money. I'll pay off Sinclair."

"I can't let you do that." Concern stamped his face. "Not alone."

"You have a race to run. Besides, I don't plan on doing this alone." She crossed her fingers behind her back. There was no way in the world she would allow anyone else to know about this. Besides, it wasn't actually a lie. She wouldn't be alone in spirit. Her gaze skimmed the crowd until it rested on her father.

"I have an interesting idea."

"WHERE IS SHE?" Jared glared at the assembly as if each and every person in his line of sight was somehow responsible for Cece's absence. "The race will be starting in just a few minutes."

"I'm certain she's here someplace," Quentin said, a slight nervousness apparent in his tone. Jared cast him a sympathetic glance. He could well understand Quentin's apprehension. Jared too was filled with a stomach-clenching mix of excitement, anticipation and sheer terror.

So much more rode on the outcome of this race than the mere satisfaction of winning. Jared had no doubt of the potential of automobiles; he simply needed to convince others. And this race could do that. If their machine showed well here, there was a distinct possibility of attracting investors who would put down good money in a gamble that someday it would be paid back tenfold or better.

"You really are pleased to be coming along, aren't you?" A crooked smile quirked Quentin's lips.

"I know I never said anything, but the thought of letting you do this without me . . ." He shook his head wryly and grinned. "I hated it."

"Well, you certainly hid it well," Quentin said mildly.

Jared shrugged. "I didn't feel there was much choice." His tone turned somber. "We have to do well today. We have a great deal to prove."

Quentin's solemn mood matched his own. "I know. This could be the break we've worked for. We have a good design. All we need now is a little bit of luck." He nodded toward the automobile and grinned. "This could be just the start. I can see it all now: The Bainbridge-Graystone Motorcar Company."

"The Graystone-Bainbridge Motorcar Company." Jared returned his grin. "It has a better ring to it."

Quentin cocked an eyebrow. "That, my dear friend, is up for debate."

"We have to win," Jared said, the urgent note returning.

"And when we do, investors will no doubt flock to give us their hard-earned money and we shall be on our way."

Jared's gaze skimmed the crowd once more. "I wasn't thinking of investors."

"Oh?" Quentin slanted his friend a quizzical glance.

Jared shook his head. "I was thinking of Cece."

"Come now, old man, there's no need to impress the girl now. You've both publicly declared your intentions. She's yours. Body, soul and, I might add, substantial wealth."

"I no longer care about the money."

"I find that difficult to believe," Quentin said skeptically. "For months you've been on a quest for an heiress. Now you have one, and one whose fortune is impressive by any standard, and you say it no longer matters?"

Jared laughed shortly. "It does sound absurd. It's a realization I've come to in the past few days."

He narrowed his eyes and tried to find the words to explain. "I find it difficult to understand myself. But Cece is the first woman I've ever met who cares nothing for my name or my title. The man she fell in love with was an impoverished inventor who had dreams of building motorcars. I suspect she would be as happy today if I were still nothing more than that dreamer." He shook his head in amazement. "She believed in my farfetched dreams. She believed in me. In Jared Grayson, not the Earl of Graystone."

"I see," Quentin said quietly. "Is there a difference?"

"There's a great deal of difference. There always has been. That's exactly why this is so important. Why we have to do well." Jared smiled wryly. "I have to prove myself—as much to myself as to her. I have to live up to those dreams."

The two friends stared at each other silently. Then Quentin extended his hand and Jared grasped it warmly. "Let's do it."

"Whatever are you doing?" Cece hurried up to stare accusingly at the men. "Shouldn't you be getting ready? The other automobiles are lining up."

Jared grinned and nodded confidently at Quentin. "We're ready."

"Then you really should take your places," she said impatiently, and Jared realized she was as excited and anxious about this race as he was.

He grasped one side of the vehicle, Quentin the other, and they pushed the automobile toward the starting position. Cece stepped briskly beside Jared, one hand clutching her skirts and the other clasped to a hat ridiculous even by Cece's standards.

"Are you at all nervous?" she said casually, as if the answer was of little importance.

"No," he lied. They pushed the automobile into its place. "Not at all."

"Excellent. There's no need for concern." She nodded vigorously. Something, some bit of feminine frippery, a feather or a ribbon or perhaps a flower, bobbed atop the absurd concoction that perched on her head. "I have every confidence in you."

He turned, and his gaze met hers. Abruptly it struck him anew, and the revelation inspired awe and more—determination. This woman did indeed believe in him. Her earnest expression coupled with her preposterous hat broke the tension within him.

"I have no fears at all about the success of this venture. The vehicle is in excellent shape. The route is relatively simple. The competition is stiff but not overwhelming." He grinned with assurance. "With any luck at all, we shall be back by dusk."

Quentin circled the car to join them and handed Jared his goggles and duster. "It does appear everything is under control."

Cece and Quentin traded glances so swift, Jared thought surely he was mistaken.

"Then I suggest you take your places," she said quickly.

The men donned their gear and Jared climbed into the vehicle. A surprising calm descended over him. He was definitely ready.

"It's a pity she can't give you some kind of favor for the race," Quentin said.

"Favor?" Jared raised a brow.

"You mean just as a lady would give a knight before a tournament?" Delight shone in Cece's eyes. "What an interesting idea."

Quentin nodded, a wicked twinkle in his eye. "We could attach it to the automobile."

Attach something to the automobile? His automobile? Jared opened his mouth to protest, but the eagerness on her face persuaded him otherwise.

"Very well." He sighed in defeat. "What do you suggest?"

"Let me think." A frown knit her forehead.

"It would have to be something she has with her," Quentin said, a helpful note in his voice. "There's no time to fetch anything else."

"How about a nice, simple, small handkerchief?" Jared said hopefully.

Quentin shook his head in a gesture of regret. "No, that won't do at all. It's far too discreet. Simply not a visible enough symbol of support."

"Oh dear," Cece said.

Jared brightened. "In that case—"

"Wait, I have it." Cece's hands seemed to fly to her head, and in less than a moment that thing she called a hat was in her grasp.

"Here." She thrust it at him triumphantly.

He stared at the frilly, delicate, female monstrosity

as if it were a carrier of some dire disease. "Here what?"

"Take my hat." She beamed. "It will be perfect and definitely declare my support."

"It will declare something, all right," Jared muttered. "Exactly what, I hesitate to say. I will not have that bizarre example of feminine excessiveness on my car."

"I think it's a charming idea," Quentin said, his manner mild.

Cece cast him a grateful look. Jared glowered. Quentin smiled innocently.

She turned to Jared, her voice firm. "I don't believe this is too much to ask. After all, I am not being allowed to come along on this race—" he opened his mouth, but she held up a hand to stop him—"and I accept that. However," she leaned closer to him. Sparks flashed amber in her eyes. "You have yet to teach me to drive as, if I remember correctly, you promised—"

"I never actually promised," he said sharply.

"Nonetheless, we had an understanding." Her eyes narrowed. "I would think taking something that means a great deal to me and is extremely fashionable in addition is the very least you can do."

He rolled his eyes heavenward and sighed. "Very well. Quentin, put the bloody hat on the vehicle."

With a quick twist of a wire the hat was firmly affixed to the front of the automobile.

"It looks ridiculous." Jared gritted his teeth.

"I think it's wonderful. I think," her voice softened, meant for his ears alone, "you're wonderful."

Their gazes locked for a long, silent moment. His irritation drained away.

"Wish me luck?" he said softly.

"I wish you everything." She extended her hand and he brushed his lips across the back. He raised his head and read all that he wanted to see in her eyes, and more.

Quentin cleared his throat. "As much as I hate to interrupt this touching moment"—he gestured at the gentleman serving as the official starter of the race— "it appears we are about to begin."

"Quite." Jared was abruptly all business. Cece backed away and Quentin took his place in front of the machine to crank it to life.

A gunshot signaled the start of the contest. Quentin turned the crank once, then again, and the engine sputtered to life. He leapt back into the vehicle, Jared pushed the lever for more fuel, and they were off.

He vaguely noted Cece blowing him a kiss. This was not the time to think of anything but the race ahead. Still, he could not put her completely out of his mind, and the sweet, hot passion he would soon claim through the legal means of marriage. Firmly, he pushed her image away. It was not easy.

Not with her silly hat fluttering in the breeze before him.

"Do YOU SEE them yet?" Irritation underlaid Emily's words.

"No." Cece squinted into the setting sun. "Nothing."

"Surely they'll be here soon," Emily said impatiently. "After all, it's been more than fourteen hours since they left. How long will this silly race take, anyway?"

Cece gritted her teeth and resisted the impulse to scream. She pulled a deep breath. "I believe I have explained this to you a number of times already. However, just to pass the time, I will endeavor to explain once again.

"The race last month from Paris to Bordeaux was accomplished in a little more than forty-eight hours at an approximate speed of just over fifteen miles per hour. A remarkable feat. Since the British are not quite as advanced as the French in motorcar development, generally we could not expect such speeds here. Yet there are many more foreign vehicles entered in this event than English automobiles so—" she shrugged— "it's impossible to say with any certainty how long this will take."

Emily pouted. "I, for one, am tired of waiting."

"Well, you'll just have to marshal all your resources and wait a little longer," Cece snapped and rose to her feet.

The girls shared one of a number of tables placed on the grounds by the owner of the inn for the express purpose of seeing a hefty profit from the beneficent gesture of allowing the race to begin and end from his property. It was apparently a wise move. The crowds were increasing with the expectation of an imminent end to the contest.

Cece crossed her arms over her chest and stalked off. Surely any activity, even pacing, was preferable to simply sitting here. Waiting. She sighed. She had never been terribly good at waiting.

This day had stretched to eternity. After the automobiles had gone Cece had managed to convince her father to supply the three hundred pounds she'd needed to pay back Sinclair. It was no doubt her earnest sincerity and her fervent promise that this was not some frivolous escapade that had persuaded the senior White to write a bank draft with the amount filled in but the payee's name left blank. It did, however, still rankle that her father had noted he was only trusting her judgment in this instance because she'd had the wisdom to select Jared for a husband and not some scurrilous fortune hunter.

Sinclair was an easy matter as well. Oh, the vile little man had whined and muttered and complained that the carburetor was his, bought and paid for, and the very least she could do was let him study the device. Cece pointed out, in no uncertain terms, that James was dead and since the apparatus in question never actually belonged to him in the first place, a good case could be made that both James and Sinclair were thieves and should rightfully hang at the end of a very short rope. She noted that that was how the situation would be handled in America, specifically in the West. The Wild West.

Sinclair actually turned a pale, rather sickly green color, muttered something about the "bloody aristocracy" and "Americans who stick their noses in places where they don't belong," snatched the check from her hand and stomped off. Nellie Bly would have been proud.

Still, the few moments of excitement were not enough to fill the long, dreary hours. Those gathered for the start of the race, including Cece and her family, had spent the day in London. There was certainly no reason to remain at the inn while the contenders were on the road. Only now were eager spectators drifting back to witness the last leg of the proceeding.

Cece gazed for the hundredth or perhaps the thousandth time to the west. The vehicles would be coming from this direction, driving straight out of the sunset. It would make a glorious picture, but only if they appeared soon. The sun was already barely above the horizon.

She turned away and glanced absently at the gathering crowd. Lady Graystone was here, accompanied by Sir Robert. More than once this morning and again tonight Cece had caught him tossing considering glances in her mother's direction, but as far as she could tell, neither of her parents had exchanged more than a few words with him. Cece pulled her brows together thoughtfully. There was definitely some kind of trouble brewing here.

Lady Millicent apparently agreed. She seemed to spend her time flitting from one couple to the other, as if she preferred not to have to declare loyalty to either old friends or family. Cece studied her for a few moments, then started toward the aging social butterfly. It could be well worth her while to have a little chat with Lady Millicent. The woman knew all the scandalous details about the past. Perhaps she knew as much about today's occurrences as well.

"Here they come!"

The shout echoed and swelled among the throng. Those relaxing on the grass or lounging in chairs leapt to their feet. Others surged forward. Cece pushed her way through to a vantage point she had noted this morning: a slight rise close enough to reach arriving drivers in a few seconds but still with an excellent overview of the winding road.

The sun dipped below the horizon. The last lingering light shone behind the approaching vehicles, nothing but black silhouettes in the distance. Cece strained to identify the shadows, but it was impossible with the dimming illumination and the considerable gap yet to be covered.

The automobiles drew nearer. The crowd grew louder. Cece could make out three machines, all very close together. If they were horses, they would be neck to tail. They disappeared behind a bend in the road, and she scrambled to a spot near the finish line.

At once they were in sight, barely a few hundred yards away. They rumbled toward the finish line. One. Two. Three. The gathering behind her roared their approval, but Cece barely heard.

The German motorcar crossed the line first, followed closely by the French vehicle and Jared's a scant few inches behind. Her heart sank.

He was third.

She swallowed her disappointment and shoved her way through the cheering throng. It was not at all difficult. Most spectators clustered around the winning automobile. She approached Jared's motorcar and forced a radiant smile to her face.

Jared and Quentin climbed slowly out of the vehicle. Jared pulled his goggles off his mud-spattered face and his gaze met hers. Defeat, cold and hard, shone in his eyes. He cast her a halfhearted smile, and she thought her heart would surely break for him.

"Jared," she cried and threw herself in his arms.

He held her in a grasp so tight, for a moment she thought she'd be crushed, but it was of no consequence. She needed to cling to him as much as he seemed to need her.

"Cece," he said, his voice muffled against her. "I tried. Bloody hell, I tried."

She pulled away and stared at him. At once she realized the truth. This was no defeat. "And you succeeded."

His wry smile matched his words. "I fear you're confused. We didn't win."

"You didn't have to win," she said, excitement growing in her voice. "Don't you see? You accomplished far more than anyone ever expected."

"But we lost." His voice was gentle, as if he was trying to bring understanding to a very small child.

"Jared, just look. What do you see?" She gestured at the commotion around them. "You finished before a score of other motorcars. We haven't even seen most of them yet, they are so far behind you. And you finished on the very heels of the best automobiles in the world."

"We lost," he muttered again, but she could tell from the look in his eye that he was considering her point.

"You have ranted time and again, in your interminable lectures on automobiles, about how terribly advanced the French and the Germans are, haven't you?"

He nodded grudging agreement.

She pressed her argument home. "And haven't you railed on and on about how the laws here in England regarding automobiles are so restrictive, it effectively dampens all but the most persistent inventors? And don't you and I actually break the law each and every time we ride in your vehicle without a man waving a red flag walking in front of us?"

"It's a stupid law," he said under his breath. "Besides, I can do as I wish on my land."

She cast him a skeptical glance. "Does that apply to murder and mayhem as well, or are only the laws regarding motorcars exempt from applying on the Earl of Graystone's land?"

"Whatever." He shrugged, but a twinkle appeared in his eye, and she noted with satisfaction that he had to fight the faint beginnings of a smile.

"And didn't the sponsors putting on this very race

require a number of variances and waivers and goodness knows what else, including the permission of an endless number of people ranging from the farmers whose fields you drove by all the way to Parliament?"

He laughed. "It did seem that way."

"Given all that," she drew a deep breath, "a third place finish is nothing short of miraculous. And I, for one, am quite proud of you."

He cocked an arrogant brow and pulled her close. "Are you?"

"I am." She nodded and grinned. Relief surged through her. She read it in his eyes: He understood now as clearly as she did that he'd lost nothing and might have gained quite a bit.

She threw her arms around him and he bent to meet her lips with his. She leaned eagerly into his embrace. Her blood quickened with desire and her skin tingled with anticipation and her nose tickled with . . . dust.

"Jared . . ." She pulled back and glared. "You are filthy. Really, quite disgusting."

He smiled proudly, looking very much like a small boy caught at playing too hard and too well, as if the dust and grime covering him was a badge won in battle. "Hazards of the road, my love."

Quentin joined them, a more than fitting match for his partner. "I daresay I didn't think she'd notice, given the lateness of the hour." A decisive note sounded in his voice. "Have you seen your sister?"

"Emily should be somewhere over there." Cece nodded toward the inn.

Quentin bid them farewell and hurried away with a resolute step. How very interesting. Although Emily had determined her interest in Quentin to be short-lived, perhaps Quentin had not.

"Now then . . ." In the misty gleam of twilight she could question his expression, but the carnal note in his voice was unmistakable. He pulled her close. "Where were we?"

"We were discussing how very successful this effort of yours was." Her breath caught in her throat.

"Which effort was that?" His eyes sparked seductively.

Her heart thudded in her chest. "The race, of course."

"The race . . . of course," he murmured. "That's precisely what I thought you were talking about." He bent his lips to meet the line of her neck and drifted his mouth across her heated flesh.

She gasped. "Did you?"

"I did." His solemn manner belied the gleam in his eyes and the increasing pressure of his body against hers. "Whatever else could we be talking about?"

He grinned. She smiled weakly. Slowly his lips claimed hers with a growing eagerness that tossed aside any concern over appropriate public behavior. She was in his arms and that was exactly where she wanted to be.

Just before she lost herself to the intoxication of his kiss she noted, with a vague sense of wonder and amazement: Dirt had never tasted so good.

Chapter 15

"JARED?" Cece said softly and squeezed through the barely opened door to the stables. "Are you in here?"

A lantern perched near the center automobile cast a pool of yellow light. Jared stood in front of the motor-car and glared as if he and the machine had come to some irreconcilable difference.

"Jared?" She stepped toward him. "Whatever are you still doing here? It's the middle of the night."

Jared glanced up, surprise on his face, as if he had only now noticed her presence. "What? Oh, Cece, it's you." He tunneled his fingers wearily through his hair. "Whatever are you doing here? It's the middle of the night."

She sighed and shook her head. Obviously, the man was dead on his feet. It had been a very long day. After the race they had transported the automobile back to the stable, the Whites once again taking up residence at the castle. With the upcoming wedding, it was only fitting that both families spend time together to work out details and plans for the event itself and the future.

"I came to find you."

"I'm afraid I'm not much worth finding right now." He pulled his brows together in a troubled frown and nodded toward the automobile. "There's an odd sound I noticed today. I meant to leave the machine here and study it further tomorrow—or rather I suppose now it is today—but I began tinkering and . . ." he shrugged, "here I am."

"Not for long," she said firmly. "This can definitely wait. It is past time you retired for the night."

Absently she reached her hand out to brush a dark strand of hair away from his face. Honestly, he was very much like a child at times. She could almost picture him as a boy, losing track of the hours, intent on catching frogs or climbing trees. One wondered if all men were as—

His hand caught hers abruptly and her startled gaze jerked to his. For a long moment they stared unmoving. Then, slowly, he brought her hand to his lips and placed a single kiss in the palm.

She sucked in air through her teeth, as if his touch burned, branding her as his forever.

He dropped her hand and quickly turned his back on her. "Go away, Cece." He fairly growled the words. "Go back to the castle and your own bed. Or I cannot guarantee your safety."

Cece stared, speechless. At once her decision was made. Her stomach fluttered with apprehension and excitement. "I have no fear for my safety."

He refused to face her. "You would if you knew what I'm thinking."

She laughed lightly. "But Jared, I do know what you're thinking."

He turned sharply and pulled her into his arms.

"Do you, Cece? Do you know how I long to savor

the taste of your lips on mine?" His gaze lingered on her mouth and instinctively she licked lips at once dry and heated. His eyes narrowed at the sight.

She gasped. "Yes."

"And do you know how my fingers yearn to explore every inch of you? To feel the heat of your silken flesh beneath my hands?"

"Yes, yes." The words were a bare breath of agreement.

He splayed one hand across her back, the other cradling her neck, and she stared up at him, wanting all that he wanted and more, much, much more. Surely the need revealed in her eyes mirrored his own?

"And do you know, my love, how I long to rip your clothes away and let my eyes ravage your innocent charms?" Her hands were trapped between his chest and hers and his blood seemed to throb beneath her fingers. "And do you know how I ache to join my body with yours and make you mine for all eternity?"

"I know. Lord, Jared, I know." A cry caught in her throat and desire pulsed through her.

He smiled in a wry manner and pushed her gently away with obvious reluctance. "But you are to be my wife and, as much as it pains me to resist, it shall have to wait until we are duly wed."

"What?" She widened her eyes and struggled to catch her breath. "Why?"

"Why?" He stared at her as if she had lost her mind.

"Yes, Jared." She fought the urge wrought by frustration to stamp her foot. "Why?"

"I just explained—" He glared as if his passion had suddenly turned to anger. "Do you have any idea that this is exactly what I had planned all along?"

"What are you talking about?" Outrage simmered

within her. A confession was the last thing she wanted at this moment.

"I thought if I seduced you, you would have to marry me."

"Well then, why on earth didn't you?"

His eyes widened with obvious annoyance. "You want to be seduced?"

"Yes, if it was by you," she snapped.

"Perhaps this will change your mind." He clenched his jaw as if he still debated whether to force the admission from his lips or hold it back. "I also believed that if I could seduce you, I would not have to teach you to drive. I intended to avoid that chore as long as possible."

"No!" She clapped a hand to her cheek in a sarcastic imitation of surprise. "Why, I never would have guessed."

He stared for a long moment. Then a smile played at the corners of his lips. "You knew?"

She heaved an exasperated sigh. "Jared, I would have to be a complete idiot not to."

"And you're not angry?" Caution shaded his tone.

The knowledge that she had, more or less, already taught herself to drive flickered through the back of her mind, and she shrugged. "Perhaps I will be at some point, but not now. Although if we are confessing all, I too have something to disclose. I suspect it would be best to start this marriage with as few secrets as possible between us."

He laughed, his mood now light, and she realized he must have been quite concerned at her reaction to his divulgence. "What kind of secrets can you possibly have to confess?"

"I'm not quite certain how to say this." She clasped

her hands together and gazed upward, searching for the right words. "Do you remember Marybeth Anderson?"

"Anderson?" A thoughtful frown furrowed his forehead. "I can't say that I do."

"She's a friend of mine, from Chicago. You met her several months before we arrived."

His expression cleared. "Of course. The one who would have gone to fat. Well on her way to two chins, I believe."

"Jared!"

"Sorry." He cast her a sheepish smile. "Mother's opinion, not mine."

She snorted disparagingly. "Now there's another surprise."

"If I recall, I quite liked her," Jared murmured.

"You broke her heart." Cece tossed the accusation like a weapon.

"Did I?" Genuine remorse crossed his face. "I had no idea. I didn't mean to."

"Well, of course you didn't," she said quickly. "I can see that now. But at the time I didn't know you at all. My plan would have worked quite nicely if I hadn't fallen in love with you." She heaved a sigh of regret. "It was such an interesting idea."

His eyes narrowed. "Cece, for the rest of our lives together, that phrase will strike terror into the very depths of my soul."

"What phrase?" she said with genuine curiosity.

"'An interesting idea,'" he said wryly.

"Yes, well . . ." She waved his comment aside as if it had no meaning. The dear man would no doubt get used to her "interesting ideas" sooner or later.

"Just what was this 'interesting idea'?" The expression on his face indicated that he was not at all convinced he wanted to know the answer.

"If I remember correctly . . ." She drew the words out, stalling for both time and inspiration, in hopes of her idea sounding somewhat less ridiculous than she now realized it was. It had, however, seemed so clever at the time. She pulled a steadying breath, then pushed the words out in a long, quick rush. "I was to meet the notorious Earl of Graystone and engage his affections—"

"You were to entrap the Earl of—or rather—me?" Jared raised a disbelieving brow. "To what purpose? Marriage?"

"Don't be absurd, Jared." She threw him a condescending smile. "First of all, I don't believe the term *entrap* is quite accurate. And secondly, the plan was merely to break your heart. I had no intention of marrying you."

"Bloody decent of you." Sarcasm dripped off his words.

She ignored him. "The purpose of this venture was to point out to a sanctimonious, stuffy, British snob—"

"That would be me," he said pointedly.

She continued without pause, "—that Americans are just as good as the English, if not better. That the standards of my country are as high or higher than yours."

"You came all the way to England to prove some convoluted, patriotic point?" Amazement shone in his eyes.

"Well," she hedged, "there was another purpose."

"Oh?"

"My, yes." Goodness, this was far more difficult to explain than she'd thought. With every word the entire proposal seemed to grow more and more preposterous. She squared her shoulders. "It's entirely likely that one of the reasons I was intrigued by you in the first place was because of your dreams."

"The automobile?" he said carefully. She nodded. "Go on."

"I have—or rather, I had—a dream as well." She hesitated, hoping to gauge the reaction on his face but his expression revealed nothing. She plunged ahead. "I wanted to travel the world, see all there is to see. I wanted to have adventures and experiences. And I wanted to write about them. I wanted to be a newspaper reporter. Like Nellie Bly."

He studied her silently. Long moments ticked by. What was he thinking? Was he annoyed? Angry? Did this change anything between them? Did it change everything?

"What do you want now?" he asked, his tone quiet and intense.

"What do I want?" She stared and considered him thoughtfully. This was perhaps the most important question of her life. Honestly, didn't he know the answer by now? She threw his own words back at him.

"I want to build a motorcar company and see an automobile in front of every manor house and cottage in England."

Relief shone in his eyes, the beginnings of a smile touching his lips.

"I want to be the Countess of Graystone. Not because of any desire for a silly title," she said quickly, "but because the Earl of Graystone is not nearly as stuffy and sanctimonious as I had originally believed—"

"Thank you." He grinned. "I think."

"And because whether he's an earl who needs to marry for money—which I still do not approve of, mind you—" she slanted him a pointed glance, "or an inventor without a penny to his name, I cannot envision my life without him.

"And that's not all I want." She advanced toward him with a purposeful step.

"What else do you want?" His brows drew together and he gazed at her with suspicion.

"I want you, Jared Grayson." She wrapped her arms around his neck. "Now. This minute."

"Cece." His tone rang hard and taut with restraint. "Don't tempt me this way. I refuse to seduce the woman who will be my wife. The woman I love."

"Very well." She gazed up at him. Regret mingled with desire in his eyes. Did the man really have a will of iron, or was the disreputable rake lingering just beneath the surface?

With a long, deliberate movement, she ran her tongue across her lips. The night sky of his eyes darkened at the sight. "What if the woman you love seduces you?"

He glared, as if to give her one last chance to escape. "You know nothing of seduction."

"Teach me, Jared." Exhilarating anticipation deepened her voice. Delicious apprehension roughened her tone. "Teach me . . . to drive."

Jared's gaze widened slightly, and in his eyes she saw the last traces of control swept away by a tide of passion. His lips crushed hers with an urgency that called to the very depths of her being. She opened her mouth beneath his and welcomed his tongue with her own. Her hands tunneled through his hair and she pulled him tighter, driven by a hunger she'd never known, never suspected. A hunger greeted and embraced with mindless jubilation.

She tasted of summer nights and promises kept and the richness of creation itself, and he could not slake the thirst she stoked within his body and his soul. He jerked his lips from hers and ran his mouth along her jaw to sample the sweet flavor of her flesh. Her head fell back, urging his lips down her neck, smooth and silken and scorching beneath his tongue. She moaned and clenched his shoulders with an instinctive grip, fingernails digging into flesh, causing prickles of pain and pleasure.

He swept her into his arms and she clung to him, her hands and lips exploring in a frantic search for fulfillment. He stepped around the motorcar and strode toward a corner of the stables, where the same canvas that patched the wall lay in a heap upon long-forgotten hay. They tumbled onto the makeshift bedding with an urgent disregard for comfort and a frenzied need for each other.

Her lips claimed his and they seemed to breathe as one. She found the buttons of his shirt and swiftly opened it to her inquisitive hands, her fingers running through the coarse mat of hair covering broad, hard muscles, and he shuddered beneath her touch.

His hands roamed over the bodice of her blouse, fumbling with the sentinel buttons guarding her secrets from his demanding desire. In the back of his mind he noted that he would have to forbid buttons on her blouses when they were married.

"Bloody buttons," he muttered.

"Jared," she murmured against his ear in a voice rasping with need, "tear them off."

He pulled back and stared. "Tear off your buttons?"

She lay beneath him, her chest heaving, her eyes dark with newfound passion, her lips parted slightly. "Tear the silly things off."

All hesitation dissolved with the searing urgency in her voice. He grasped both sides of her blouse and ripped. Satin-covered buttons flew, and she strained toward the freedom of his touch. Roughly, he yanked the ribbons of her camisole and pushed the delicate fabric aside to reveal her breasts to his eager gaze. He quirked an eyebrow.

"No corset?"

She bit her bottom lip and blushed, a deep pink that suffused her skin from the curve of her cheek to the rosy tips of her already pebbled breasts. He cupped first one and then the other, his mouth following his hands. She gasped at the first flick of his tongue. He took a succulent offering into his mouth and she moaned, her hands clutching his head. He lavished attention on one breast and then the other, until she whimpered at his touch and quivered beneath his lips.

Pure pleasure surged through her. She had never imagined, never dreamed, never dared to hope of sensations like this. His tongue trailed between her breasts and drifted lower, ever lower, to the waistband of her skirt. Desire scorched her skin, and his touch only served to fan the flames. Each moment brought a new intensity, a greater excitement, and still it was not enough. It was as if a spring wound inside her tighter and tighter and she wondered how any mere mortal could survive such exquisite joy.

With a deft touch he unfastened the closure of her skirt, sliding it, and all she wore beneath, down the curve of her hip to tangle at her feet. She lay beneath him clad only in the wisp of a camisole that barely clung to her shoulders. He pulled her close and ran his hand up the long length of her leg to her hip. Her hands roamed across his back and her fingernails clawed at the fabric of his shirt. In one swift movement, he sat up, tore off the restrictive garment and tossed it unheeded into the shadows.

She melted back into his embrace. His naked flesh pressed against her sensitive breasts, and she gasped at the shocking heat of his skin against hers. She twined her fingers in the silken hair at the base of his neck, pressing her lips to his, molding her body to him. His manhood pushed against her through the rough fabric of his trousers. Lost to sense and sensibility, she could only revel in the hard, strong feel of it.

His hand explored the curve of her waist, the flat of her stomach and downward, ever downward, in a relentless torture of aching desire and spiraling excitement. His fingers reached the soft curls between her thighs and hesitated. She arched against him, urging him on. Surely she would go mad if he did not continue. Surely she would go mad if he did.

He found the soft folds that guarded the key to her passion and she cried out at his unexpected touch. She was wet with wanting him and he fought the urge to tear away his remaining clothing and claim her for now and always. She quivered beneath his touch and he struggled for control. She had never been with a man and he could not take her with the hard, driving force he wanted, he needed.

She was fire and flood and as eager as he, and he did not know how long he could hold back. He drew a steadying breath and touched her with sure, gentle caresses, and she shuddered without thought or reason.

He found the bud of her desire and stroked until she thrashed blindly and moaned with mindless abandon.

"Jared . . ." she cried softly. "Please."

"Cece, my love." His voice was hoarse with frustration and restraint. "You are untouched and I—"

"Jared! I know full well what we are about here." Her eyes widened and she glared, the madness of unfulfilled passion in her eyes. "I am a modern woman and . . . I read!"

He needed no more encouragement. Swiftly he shed his trousers and for a moment towered over her, the glow of the lantern silhouetting him in the shadows of the stables. He was a god. He was a man. And she wanted nothing more than to know him as a woman knows a man.

He lowered himself over her and settled between her legs. His manhood throbbed between them and fear flickered for the barest moment and was swept aside by the pleasure that washed through her. Slowly he pushed against her, driving himself into her, filling her body, filling her soul.

He was immersed in flame, slick, tight and glorious. He moved with a prolonged, precise stroke until he hit the barrier of her maidenhood. He groaned and nipped the lobe of her ear. "I fear this will hurt."

Her hands gripped his shoulders. "Anything achieved too easily . . ." she gasped the words, ". . . is valued too lightly."

He nodded and thrust into her, plunging past the proof of her virginity and into heaven on earth.

She cried out at the pain, sharp and piercing. Her body throbbed around him and it was not at all what she expected, what she wanted. He moved within her, slowly at first, and she bit her lip to stifle the cry that rose within her. But he continued with long, even strokes that abruptly vanquished the pain and kindled sensations like those he'd provoked before. Instinctively she moved with him, matching his thrusts to hers, arching upward to greet him, each stroke more exquisite than the last.

With a joy born of the oblivion of sheer bliss, he plunged into her again and again, his passion fueled by an urgent ache for this woman, only this woman. She writhed beneath him and his exhilaration grew with the sure knowledge that her pleasure equaled his own.

She no longer knew her name, her country, anything but the delicious wickedness that pulsed through her blood, her body, her soul. Tension built within her with every stroke, every thrust, and she knew she would surely die from the sweet flame of ecstacy.

It was as if they were one being, no longer separate and distinct but joined in a ritual as old as time, as new as tomorrow. Together they spiraled upward higher and higher until each wondered if they glimpsed a promise of paradise or heaven itself. Finally, with one powerful thrust, he drove into her until it seemed he reached a forgotten or forbidden secret and she exploded in waves of quaking elation so intense, her body jerked with the strength of it. She screamed softly and he tensed and shuddered, and together they collapsed, drained of passion.

Fueled by love.

She rolled over, propped her chin in her hand and gazed at him. He returned her stare with a satisfied smile and a look of contentment in his eyes.

"You are an excellent teacher," she said with a soft laugh.

Idly, she trailed her fingers across his chest, over the rough mat of hair, across hard, strong muscles, to lightly flick a nipple with her thumb. He gasped and grasped her hand.

His eyes were again the color of midnight, the color of passion. He growled, and the sound sent shivers of renewed desire through her blood. "If you do not desist at once, I shall have no recourse but to take you in my arms and teach you a lesson you shall not soon forget."

"A driving lesson?" Her voice accepted his challenge and invited it.

He grinned. "A driving lesson."

"Why, Jared . . ." She reached forward to brush her lips across his. "What an interesting idea."

Chapter 16

"WHERE are we going anyway?" Emily panted in a vain effort to keep up with her older sister.

"To the stables." Cece strode two long steps ahead, setting a brisk pace. "I wish to drive Jared's motorcar, and I might need some assistance."

"Drive his motorcar?" Emily's question hung in the air behind her, and she ignored the blatant curiosity in her sister's voice. "I thought he—"

"Never mind that now," Cece said firmly. "Just stop your dawdling."

"I don't dawdle." Indignation colored Emily's voice. "But I still do not understand why you're dragging me out here at the crack of dawn."

"Motoring is ever so much better early in the day." Cece smiled to herself. Driving did indeed seem even more delightful in the morning. Why, at this time of day, the chances of running into anyone, particularly Jared, were extremely remote. After last night the dear man was probably still asleep. This was the perfect opportunity to finally drive his automobile. Even if he found out, he couldn't possibly get too upset. Especially . . . after last night. "Besides, Em, dawn was nearly an hour ago."

"Nevertheless," Emily grumbled, "it's far too early for either of us to be out and about, engaged in a ridiculous escapade that sounds very much like an 'interesting idea.' What time did you retire last night, anyway? I stopped by your room around midnight and you weren't there. Where on earth were you?"

Cece tossed a grin over her shoulder. "Studying."

"Studying what?" Emily said suspiciously.

"Driving." Cece laughed with delight. She drew a deep breath, drinking in the early morning air, fresh and exhilarating. The rising sun sparkled with a magical brilliance; the deep green of the rolling countryside seemed blessed with an artist's touch; the new-day calls of the birds rang out a sonata of sheer joy. "Isn't it a glorious day?"

"Lovely," Emily muttered.

Cece stopped and gestured at the lush landscape. "It's more than lovely, Em. It's magnificent and abundant with hopes and dreams and life." She gazed at the land around them. "Jared loves it here. It's his heritage and it pulses through his veins."

Emily studied her sister with a considering frown. "I gather all is going well between you and Jared? If you're planning on driving his machine . . ." She brightened. "Then he did finally teach you to drive?"

Cece laughed again with an effervescence she could not restrain. "In a manner of speaking."

Cece turned and set off once more, Emily scrambling to keep up. "Just smell the air here. Have you ever smelled anything more invigorating in your life?"

Emily shrugged. "Smells a little like wood smoke to me."

"Wood smoke?" Cece sniffed the air curiously. "Why, there is a faint smell of smoke."

Emily trudged along beside her. "Some farmer must be burning something."

"It seems to be getting stronger." Cece pulled her brows together thoughtfully. "How odd. There's really nothing on this road except—" she stopped abruptly and stared at her sister "—the stables. Em that's the only thing around here that could be burning."

Emily's eyes widened with realization and fear. "The automobile!"

"Come on!" Cece gathered up her skirts and ran as she'd never run before, pushing her feet faster, ignoring the stitch in her side and the burning ache in her chest. She reached the ridge, Emily hard at her heels, rounded a curve and sighted the old building at the end of the lane. Smoke poured out of the half-opened doors. There was no flame yet, but Cece suspected it was only a matter of moments.

They raced up to the stables. Smoke billowed from the entry, swirling around them with an insidious, acrid bite that turned every breath to a battle for air and sanity.

"Help me with the door," Cece cried, fighting to swing the heavy doors aside. "We have to get the motorcar out!"

"You can't go in there!" Emily screamed beside her sister, lending her assistance in spite of her protest. The door would not budge. "It's no use! It's stuck!"

Cece's gaze met her sister's. Determination rang in her voice. "It's Jared's machine, Em! I can't let his life's work go up in flames. I can drive it out. I know I can!"

"You can't get it out if we can't open the door!" Emily's eyes were wide with fright.

Cece brushed her hair away from her face in frustration and frantically tried to think. They couldn't open the doors without help and there was no time to waste. This was the only opening to the stables. There was no other way out. Or was there?

"I have an idea!" It was a huge gamble in an unforgiving game. The stakes were her life or death. There was no choice.

"What are you going to do?" Emily's eyes mirrored the fear in her own heart.

"I'll see if there's a way in from the other side. You go get help." Emily stared as if she didn't believe her sister. Cece pushed her roughly. "Go, Em, now. I'll be all right, I promise!"

Emily threw her a last worried look, turned and flew along the ridge and back toward the castle. Cece grabbed a handful of her skirt and ripped a long piece of the fragile fabric. She drew a deep breath, held the cloth over her mouth and slipped into the stables.

The fire raged to the left of the building, feeding on the very canvas and hay where she and Jared had lain only a few hours before. Had they forgotten to take the lantern when they left? She could see only in the area where the flames roared; smoke obscured all else. She dropped to her knees, the heavy, choking air lighter near her feet. Where was the automobile?

Sight would do no good here. Memory and touch were her only senses. She tried to think. The lone machine that worked was directly in front of the doors. She crawled toward the location, praying she was right. It was an eternity, or only a moment, before she grazed the wheels of the automobile. Her fingers led her along the spokes to the body and finally to the front of the beast. She wondered vaguely why it had always seemed so small before and now, with only the touch of her hands to guide her, it had grown to enormous proportions.

She fumbled until her fingers found the crank. She pulled a breath from the sweeter air at the floor and jerked to her feet. Jared had drilled her on the mechanics of the machine over and over. This was the real test of his long, tedious lessons. She summoned all her strength and turned the crank.

Nothing.

Panic filled her. She had to save his motorcar. It was akin to saving his life.

From some reserve she never dreamed she possessed, she tried once more, pulling with every muscle, every tendon, every surge of blood through her veins to snap this mechanical creature to life. The automobile sputtered and coughed and caught. She stumbled around the car, blindly groping her way until she found the seat. Her hand brushed a pair of goggles and she pushed aside what felt like Jared's coat and leapt into the seat. Fear clawed at her and she searched wildly for the levers that would fuel the vehicle and steer it to safety. Her breath was rough, rasping with a need for air, and only determination held her upright and spurred her on.

There was no time to consider whether her actions were right or wrong, no time to ponder which lever to push and which to pull. There was no time to think at all. She stared straight ahead, squinting in a futile effort to see. Somewhere in front of her was the back of the stable and the canvas-patched hole in the wall. Thank God Jared had never thought to make that ill-fitting covering permanent. The smoke obscured nearly everything, but she could make out the wicked flicker of the blaze, a vague whisper of glowing orange. Terror stilled her heart. Flames licked at the edge of the canvas.

With an instinct born of a soul-searing knowledge that if she was to escape it had to be now, she gritted her teeth, squared her shoulders, clutched a tiller and threw the car into motion. It lurched forward almost as if it had a life of its own and a primal need for survival. To one side she heard the unmistakable sound of collapsing timbers. Before her, the canvas loomed closer and closer. She braced herself for the impact. Ducked her head. Closed her eyes.

And prayed.

JARED'S FEET POUNDED the ground, pushing hard and fast in his desperate attempt to get to the stables. A farmer had reported the blaze a scant few moments earlier and already Jared was but a step or two ahead of the servants and neighbors racing to the scene. Some carried buckets and headed down the ridge to the pond. Others made straight for the old, rundown structure. There was no need to give directions; everyone in the neighborhood knew the only thing that could be on fire in this secluded area was the ancient stable.

He forced himself onward, his lungs straining for air, his legs bearing the hammering of the ground beneath his feet, his mind pushing away the inevitable meaning of the smoke billowing into the summer sky.

Damnation! The automobile. All he'd worked for, all he'd wanted was in that stable. Not irreplaceable, of course—he still had the skill that had brought him to this point—but starting over would be impossible. Even with a wife eager to share in his plans, the responsibilities of the life of an earl were not conducive to long hours reworking the finer points of a motorcar. No, if the machine was destroyed, so too was his dream.

He sprinted for what might have been forever, through long moments that moved like the somnolent molasses of a nightmare until finally the building appeared around the bend. Smoke streamed from the doors and surged from every chink and crack in the rickety structure, as if eager to escape to the clean air and blue sky. A boiling plume of black smoke eddied and swirled about the old structure in a macabre torrent of destruction.

"Jared!" Emily stumbled toward him. "It's Cece—"

He grabbed her shoulders with a harsh hand and stared into eyes reddened by smoke and a face pale with fear. Dread gripped him at her expression. "Cece! Where is she?"

Emily struggled to get her breath and waved frantically in the direction of the fire. "I left her at the stables. She sent me for help." Emily gasped and unbidden tears streaked down her soot-smudged face. "She promised she'd be all right."

"What do you mean?" Cold fear squeezed his heart. He fought the urge to shake the answer out of her.

Emily shook her head. "She said she was going to the other side of the building. But when I looked back I saw her." She clutched his arm, panic in her eyes. "She went in, Jared. She went into the stables! Into the fire!"

"Bloody hell! Why?"

"The motorcar, Jared. She wanted to save the motorcar!"

Shock coursed through him with the paralyzing import of Emily's words. For a moment images of Cece flashed through his mind: the spirit-freeing sound of her laughter, the righteous indignation and determination in the set of her shoulders, the rich, amber flash of her eyes in the throes of passion. He clenched his jaw. He refused to lose her. Even if it meant fighting the fires of hell itself, he would not give her up. Not even to death.

"Come on!" He released Emily and sprinted toward the stables. Flames leapt along the left side of the building. So far, the fire appeared to be contained to that one area, but with the age of the structure and the dry state of the wood, it would not remain in check for long. There was little time. He ran for the stable doors. Hot waves slapped his face and he staggered back at the intensity. Still he struggled forward.

He reached for the door, a scant few feet away, and it seemed to explode before him, heat biting the tips of his fingers. Flames leapt along the timbers of the frame, consuming the planks with a voracious hunger. Still, if he could slip through the opening quickly enough, he could get inside and—

A strong hand jerked him back.

"You can't go in there!" Quentin yelled, his voice barely audible above the roar of the blaze.

"Cece's inside!" Jared tried to shake off Quentin's firm hold.

"You can't make it!" Quentin's grip tightened.

"I have to!" Jared glared, fury and fear welling up within him. He grabbed Quentin's shirt. "I must find her, and if I have to go through you to do it, old friend, I will!"

"No. It's too late, Jared." Amid the hellish scene around them, Quentin's voice rang firm. Distress and sympathy filled his eyes. He shook Jared roughly. "She's gone. Look!"

Jared whirled back toward the stable. Flames engulfed the doorway. The blaze climbed the wall before him and all but the right side of the building was obscured by clouds of smoke and rivers of snapping flame, vibrant with color and blistering heat. The left side of the structure collapsed, and Quentin dragged him to a safe distance. There was no possible way in.

And there was no way out.

He stared mesmerized at the consuming flames. The realization of his loss struck him with a force as intense as the heat from the blaze, a burning, blinding anguish that scorched his mind and seared his soul. He clenched his fists, his nails biting into his palms with a pain he ignored. Nothing could match this agony. Not now. Not ever.

How could he live without her? Without her wit and her smile and her passion? How could he go on? And all for what? For his automobile? A harsh, bitter laugh curled within him. She had sacrificed her life for his vision, but without her there was nothing left except the dry, empty chill of a nightmare.

"Jared!" Her voice echoed in his mind, obscured by despair and the violent din of the blaze.

"Jared!" Would her voice linger in his memory forever? He stilled, pulling his brows together in an attempt to concentrate his thoughts. Odd; why didn't he remember her voice filled with joy and love? Why did he only recall a tone colored with insistence and impatience and urgency?

"Jared!" This time his name was a scream, and it was no memory. He jerked his gaze away from the flames and frantically searched the grounds.

It was a scene set in hell and a gift straight from heaven. His automobile burst through the smoky haze, Cece at the helm. Was she real or was this some illusion brought on by a mind numbed by desperation? He sprinted toward her. She stopped the motor-car and he pulled to a halt, his mind struggling with disbelief.

For a long moment their gazes locked. A slow grin spread over her smoke-blackened face and she shrugged. "I knew I could drive if given half the chance."

Joyous laughter erupted from him and he swept her into his arms, half pulling, half dragging her from the machine. A scent of charred wood and scorched metal and fear clung to her, and he had never smelled anything so delightful in his life.

"I thought you were dead." He cupped her face in his hand and stared into her eyes. "I thought I'd lost you."

She laughed. "Jared, it would take more than a little fire to get rid of me."

"A little fire?" The woman was insane. Had she no idea of the danger she'd faced? "Look at the stables."

They turned as one toward the building, now consumed by the blaze. Those fighting the fire with feeble buckets of water could do nothing more than wet the grounds around the structure to keep the flames from spreading. They watched as the few walls still standing slowly collapsed with a flurry of sparks and glowing embers.

"Oh dear," she said faintly, and he cast her a sharp glance. Her face was ashen beneath its smudged coat of black. "I had no idea it was quite that bad."

"Whatever were you thinking?" Anger washed aside his relief at her escape. "How could you run such a deadly risk? You could have been killed. I thought you had."

"I didn't think—"

"No," he snapped, "you certainly didn't think at all."

She stared at him, her expression quietly defiant. "I wanted to save your automobile. I know how much it means to you."

His voice was rough with remembered fear. "It means nothing compared to you. It's only metal and rubber and wire—"

She glared indignantly. "It's your dream! Your life!"

"You're my life." He pulled her tightly to him and crushed her lips with his in a kiss born of a compelling need to convince her without words how she, and only she, was what made his existence possible and his spirit soar.

He pulled away and awe glimmered in her eyes. He grinned down at her. "Nothing to say?"

"Of course." She sighed and smiled, staring at him with widened eyes. "Now you have the motorcar and me as well. It seems to me you have all you want in life."

He threw back his head and laughed. "And with you in it, Lord knows, it will never be dull."

Her eyes twinkled. "I should certainly hope not."

SPIRES OF BLACKENED timber climbed skyward, the only still-standing remnants of the stable. The structure was gone, burned to the ground. Nothing remained but charred, smoking rubble.

Cece wandered aimlessly through the area, nodding to a servant here, an acquaintance there. Her voice rasped and her throat ached from the smoke, but she'd tried to help battle the blaze as best she could. Still, even a well-trained Chicago fire brigade could not have saved this building. The loss was such a shame. Both spare machines were burned beyond salvage, any number of tools were missing and all drawings and plans had been destroyed. At least she'd recovered the automobile.

She stared at the smoldering wreckage. It could have been so much worse. Thank goodness Jared and Quentin had learned from their past mistakes. Previous incidents with highly flammable fuel had taught them to store the petrol in a shed some distance from the stables. It was untouched. Cece shuddered at the thought of what would have happened if the flames had found the fuel.

Emily, of course, had dressed Cece down for her actions, claiming she always knew her older sister's impulsive nature would lead her astray some day. She railed for long moments over the sheer stupidity of what she called Cece's "stunt" until she burst into tears and threw herself into her sister's arms. Finally, her emotions spent, Emily looked at her and said solemnly, "Nellie Bly couldn't have done better." Cece grinned at the memory. It was indeed a high compliment.

She glanced around at the thinning crowd. Now that the fire was essentially extinguished, many who had come to help had drifted back to their own concerns. Her parents had already come and gone. Her mother grew faint at Emily's somewhat embellished telling of her older daughter's exploits. Her father expressed his opinion in no uncertain terms, and his blistering words still rang in her ears. Even so, with the look in his eye, she wondered if he wasn't at least a little proud of the initiative she'd shown. He'd muttered something to Jared as well that she couldn't quite make out. It sounded suspiciously like, "Good luck. You'll need it."

So far, Jared had said nothing about her driving the motorcar. She'd caught a few considering glances tossed her way and she'd responded to each with an innocent smile. But she had little doubt he would broach the subject eventually. Her gaze fell on the automobile standing alone like a cocky warrior who had defeated a powerful enemy, and she grinned to herself. It was nice to learn the way to truly disarm a man was to allow him to believe you were in serious danger, or better yet, dead. Relief appeared to wash away any vestige of anger at one's actions. Perhaps it was a trick that would not work every time, but it was useful knowledge to have.

Lady Graystone was still in the vicinity somewhere. She was the quintessential lady of the castle today, lending assistance and support with words of encouragement and gratitude. Cece could not help but admire her.

"Are you ready to go home?" A thoroughly grubby Jared trudged toward her. "There's nothing more to be done here." He and Quentin both had joined in fighting the blaze, and the man now standing before her was a picture of soot-covered weariness.

She laughed softly. "You look as bad as the stables."

He arched a brow and tossed her a tired grin. "I would not cast stones, my love. Perhaps you've forgotten your own state?"

She glanced down at the charming frock she had donned only a few hours earlier. The pale apricot dress was streaked with grime. A long tear exposed her no longer white slip. Her hands were black with smoky grit and she suspected her face had not fared much better. "We do make a pretty pair."

Jared wrapped a strong arm around her. "We do indeed." They started toward the castle. He heaved an exhausted sigh. "Let's go home."

Home. The castle. It struck her that it would indeed be home soon. Her home and his and, someday, their children's. The thought was as warm as the arm around her.

Slowly they walked down the lane, a content silence between them.

"Your lordship." A voice called from behind and they turned. A pair of servants tramped toward them, a small weasel of a man gripped between the two.

Cece gasped. "Sinclair."

Jared threw her a puzzled look, then turned to the men holding Sinclair. "What is this all about?"

"Beggin' your pardon, milord." Cece recognized the taller man as one of the servants who had played the fiddle. Andrew, she thought. "We found this bloke skulking about. He tried to make a break for it, but we caught him."

"Right after the fire started, it was, milord," the second man said. "He looked suspicious, so we thought we'd bring him to you."

"We're nearly certain"—Andrew threw Sinclair a disgusted glare—"he started the fire."

Jared's eyes darkened. "Is this true, Sinclair?"

Sinclair shook off the hands gripping him. The servants took a short step backwards. Sinclair straightened his jacket and glared coolly as if it was Jared, and not he, who was in the wrong. "It was an unfortunate accident. My apologies. I will, of course, make financial restitution for the loss."

A muscle ticked in the clenched line of Jared's jaw. His voice was icy, calm and dangerous. "What were you doing at the stables? On my property?"

Sinclair's beady, ratlike eyes narrowed and he stared at Jared for a moment. His oily gaze slipped to Cece, and she shuddered. This was indeed a wicked creature doubtlessly here to steal the carburetor. What was he going to say? Fear caught her breath. Surely he would not tell Jared about his arrangement with James?

A slow, hateful smile creased Sinclair's face and he nodded at Cece. "Ask her."

"Me?" Her voice squeaked.

Jared's eyes hardened, his gaze still on Sinclair. "Why?"

Sinclair cocked an insolent brow.

"Jared . . ." Cece said, a rising note of concern in her voice.

"Why?" Jared repeated sharply.

"Why?" Sinclair leered. "Why, my dear sir, because she knows my purpose here."

"I doubt that your presence has anything to do with legitimate matters," she snapped. Misgiving flashed across his face, as if he had just remembered her threat of legal prosecution. She suspected he would not take that risk.

Sinclair shot her a spiteful glare, the look of someone who realizes he's lost. Then his eyes widened, as if a new strategy had occurred to him. Apprehension gripped her with an iron grasp.

"And who would know better than you about legitimate matters?" He sneered with pure malice. His vile gaze lingered on her, but he directed his words to Jared. "Did you know she paid me off?"

Cece gasped.

Jared slanted her a quick glance of surprise but returned his attention to Sinclair. His voice was deceptively mild. "I find that extremely hard to believe."

"Believe it or not, as you wish. But your charming little American fiancée indeed paid me three hundred pounds." Sinclair shrugged. "She wanted to make certain your automobile would beat mine."

"That's not true!" Cece said with indignation.

"It is quite farfetched, Sinclair," Jared said. "Your machine has never been the equal to mine. If Cece wanted to ensure my success, there are far better competitors to bribe than you."

"Perhaps I was mistaken then." Sinclair smirked at Cece. "Are you saying you didn't give me three hundred pounds?" He patted his waistcoat. "I could have sworn I had the bank draft on me here somewhere."

"Cece—" Jared said, a warning in his voice.

She wanted to lie through her teeth and deny everything, but she couldn't contradict one part of Sinclair's statement without admitting to the other, and the disgusting little man obviously had the proof still on his person. If she told Jared she had paid Sinclair, she would also have to tell him why. It was best for him to be angry with her, rather than know the truth about his brother.

"Jared, I . . ." She stared, powerless to defend herself.

The emotions that flickered through the stormy seas of his eyes nearly broke her heart. Disbelief. Shock. Disappointment. Anger.

A controlled fury underlaid his words. He turned to the servants and jerked his head toward Sinclair. "Remove him at once and deliver him to the proper authorities. Make sure he's charged with something. Arson, trespassing, I don't care."

Sinclair cast them a smug smile of triumph and turned to accompany the servants, as if he was leaving of his own accord. He had distorted the truth just enough to put her in the position of destroying Jared's faith in his brother or his faith in her.

Jared turned and stalked toward the castle. She scrambled to catch up with him. "Jared!"

He ignored her and continued. She reached out her hand and grabbed his arm. "Jared, please."

He stopped and turned to face her. His midnight eyes glittered like dark jewels on a winter night, cold and hard and unfeeling. He studied her for a long moment and her heart sank. "Tell me the truth, Cece: Did you pay him three hundred pounds?"

She stared helplessly and struggled to find an answer. Nothing came to mind. No clever rejoinder. No keen evasion. Not even an intelligent, outright lie. She pulled a deep breath. "Yes."

"Why?" He spat the word as if it were obscene.

Again defenselessness washed over her. She could only shake her head mutely.

He seized her arms, his gaze boring into hers. Betrayal shone in his eyes. "I thought you believed in my machine. In my aspirations. In me."

"I do, Jared, I do." The words came from the depths of her heart, and she prayed he'd believe her.

"It would seem your actions contradict your words. If you had faith in me, you would not find it necessary to resort to paying off a scoundrel like Sinclair. Really, Cece." He released her and cast her a look of disgust. "If you were going to squander good money on my behalf, you might at least have found a more worthwhile competitor than Sinclair." His eyes narrowed. "Or was he the only one willing to take your bribe?"

"It wasn't that way at all," she said, a beseeching note in her voice.

"Wasn't it?" He ripped the air with a short, bitter laugh. "I find the irony in all this quite amusing."

"Amusing?" She stared in disbelief.

"Indeed." Sarcasm weighted his words. "I find a great deal of amusement in the fact that you, who are so fond of regaling me with the American appreciation of ingenuity, would bypass that process altogether and simply purchase victory. Although, I suppose"—he shrugged—"depending on one's point of view, and tossing aside all thoughts of morals, standards and basic honesty, it could be considered extremely clever."

"Jared!" She gasped. "That's not—"

"Not what?" He arched a scornful brow. "Not funny? Oh, but it is, my dear. And it's not the only thing.

"There is something exceedingly humorous in the delightful way you have gone on and on about how a man shouldn't marry for wealth. How a man should earn his money. Yet, you are willing to spend a small fortune on deceitful methods to ensure my success. Is that how this marriage will work, Cece? You will spend your resources behind my back to guarantee my triumphs?"

She shook her head vehemently. "That's not it at all."

"Then what is it?" He stared angrily. Fury battled desperation in his eyes, and she couldn't bear the anguish she saw there. She wanted to tell him everything, all about Sinclair and James. But the pain that gripped him now at her perceived treachery was nothing compared to how the truth about his brother would tear him apart.

She placed a hand on his arm. "Jared"—she dropped her hand—"I don't know what to say."

"Say something, Cece." His gaze was hard, his jaw set, his fists clenched. "Say anything."

She swallowed the lump lodged in her throat. "I . . . can't."

It was as if the warm flesh of his face changed to

stone, as if a shutter snapped shut over the simmering depths of his eyes, as if he closed himself off from her. He stared with a cold disdain that chilled her blood. He nodded sharply.

"Very well, then." He swiveled to leave, hesitated, then abruptly turned back. "When I did not meet you in Paris, when I sent you that note, I thought I had lost something rare and precious. Oh, certainly, I expected I would find an heiress eventually and marry. But the woman I left waiting at the Eiffel Tower had claimed my soul and I knew my life would never be the same."

His voice was low and intense and held her spellbound. "You see, she had not fallen in love with the Earl of Graystone or a respected position in society or even a castle in the country." For a moment the mask over his eyes lifted, and they burned with the anguish of betrayal. "She wanted Jared Grayson, an impoverished inventor. And for the rest of my days I would cherish the memory of that one woman who loved not the title but the man."

"What are you saying?" She squared her shoulders and fought the tremor in her voice.

"I don't know." He shook his head and ran his fingers through his hair in a gesture of exhaustion. "I suspect we would have all been better off if I'd settled for your friend from Chicago. Multiple chins aside, I was prepared for a marriage based on my family's need for funds. I was prepared to accept my responsibilities to my heritage. I was even prepared to cast aside all thoughts of automobiles." His gaze meshed with hers, and she could hardly breathe for the deep sorrow simmering in his eyes. "But I was never prepared . . . for you."

"I love you, Jared," she said quietly.

"No, my dear, it's just as you've said before. Love"—a bittersweet smile quirked his lips—"has nothing to do with it." He turned and strode toward the castle.

She watched his retreating figure, struck numb by shock and the certain knowledge that he might never forgive what he perceived as her betrayal.

"No, Jared," she whispered, "love has everything to do with it."

"How could you?" Lady Graystone's indignant voice rumbled behind her.

Cece heaved a weary sigh and turned around. A glowering Lady Graystone stood beside Emily and Quentin. She arched a brow. "Forgive me. I didn't know we had an audience. Did we speak loudly enough for you?"

Olivia shot her a cutting glance. "Sarcasm is not becoming in a countess."

"Oh?" It might have been her tone, it might have been the look in her eye or it might simply have been the end result of the long, tiring hours just past and her devastating confrontation with Jared, but something deep inside Cece snapped. She glared at the woman who might, or might not, become her mother-in-law. Cecily Gwendolyn White had had just about enough of the Countess of Graystone and her tests.

"And what else is not becoming in a countess?" she said sharply. "Is there a list somewhere? An instruction manual I could study? Or is it just one of those learn-by-experience sort of things?"

"Rudeness is not acceptable under any circumstances." Lady Graystone's voice was icy.

"I see." Cece glared, too tired to think before she spoke, too worried about Jared to care. "But placing the woman who has the nerve to wish to marry your son in humiliating and embarrassing and possibly even dangerous situations in some arrogant test of worthiness is acceptable? What would you have me do next to prove myself to you?"

Lady Graystone's eyes widened with obvious shock at Cece's outburst.

Cece plunged ahead, her thoughts rushing forward without restraint, as if a pent-up dam of emotion had finally burst. "What else is in your little book of tricks? Must I scale a mountain? Swim an ocean? Slay a dragon?"

"I had thought a simple pea under your mattress would suffice," Lady Graystone murmured.

"What?" Cece pulled her brows together in confusion.

"She said a 'pea,'" Emily said helpfully. "Under your mattress. Just like in the fairy tale. You remember?" Emily smiled her encouragement. "The princess and the pea?"

"Yes, of course I remember, vaguely." What was this nonsense about a story? What did it have to do with anything?

"It's a charming tale," Emily said.

"It's always been one of my favorites." Lady Graystone nodded her agreement.

Cece glared in disbelief. Quentin shrugged and rolled his eyes heavenward, as if to remove himself from this ridiculous conversation altogether.

"We are not talking about some silly story here," Cece snapped. "We are talking about your actions, Olivia—"

"It's Lady Graystone," Emily said under her breath.

Cece narrowed her eyes. "Well, I for one have had

more than enough of 'lady' this and 'your lordship' that. We don't have such nonsense in my country."

"Pity," Olivia said sweetly.

"Bravo!" Quentin grinned his approval.

Olivia cast him a quelling glance and returned her gaze to Cece. "Nevertheless, when you and Jared marry you will be Lady Graystone."

The thought of being called Lady Graystone jerked Cece back to the matter at hand. For a brief moment the absurd conversation had distracted her. Now the very real possibility that she had lost Jared forever loomed ahead, and pain ripped through her.

"How could you?" Olivia said again.

Cece's gaze met hers, and the younger woman was surprised at the sympathy she read there. "It's not what you think."

"My dear child," Olivia said quietly, "it matters very little what I think. It's what Jared thinks that counts. And there are several things you must remember about my son.

"He has always believed his older brother to be more competent and capable than he. Perhaps it was true when James was alive, but since his death I have seen a change and growth in Jared I never expected. He is quite remarkable."

She drew a deep breath. "However, because of his feelings about his brother, this automobile nonsense has become far more important to him than perhaps is warranted. He sees it as the one thing in life that is truly his accomplishment."

Cece stared in surprise. "I didn't think you knew about his motorcar."

"I have known nearly from the beginning." Olivia smiled benignly. "I am his mother."

Cece and Emily traded swift glances. Olivia continued without interruption. "From what I overheard just now, it appears you gave a considerable amount of money to a competitor in the race to ensure Jared's victory."

Cece opened her mouth to protest, but Olivia waved her aside. "No, please, I do not wish to hear the details. I simply have some advice. Should this situation ever arise again—not that I would encourage such activity, mind you; still I can see the temptation—choose where you put your money wisely. For goodness sakes, Cecily, if you are going to spend that much money, make certain Jared wins."

"Olivia, I—"

Olivia held up a firm hand. "I am not finished yet. Secondly, never, ever, under any circumstances, let the boy find out what you've done." She leaned toward her, as if to share a confidence. "Men are so much happier believing they know everything than when they actually do."

Quentin snorted in disgust. Emily grinned.

Cece stared at Olivia and at once realized the woman had just given her approval, and more, her support. But was it too late? Now that she had the respect of the mother, did she have nothing more than contempt from the son?

"You have to tell Jared the truth," Quentin said quietly.

"I don't know." Cece shook her head. She couldn't seem to think past the searing ache that enveloped her every time she remembered the devastating look of betrayal in his eyes. She clasped her hands together and noted the black soot still covering her skin. Her state of disrepair had completely slipped her mind.

"I can't, Quentin." She cast him a tired smile. "That's the one thing I do know right now." She held her hands out in a gesture of dismay. "I also know that I am nothing short of a disaster. So, if you will all forgive me, I shall return to the castle in hopes of finding a hot bath and clean clothes."

She nodded pleasantly to the trio and strode off toward the castle, head held high, back ramrod straight and step brisk. From this angle she was certain no one would notice the tears trickling down her face, or the trembling of her chin.

Or the crack in her heart.

"SHE CERTAINLY DOES carry herself like a countess," Olivia said approvingly, her gaze on Cecily's determined march back to the castle.

"I'd say Jared's a lucky man," Quentin said.

"Indeed." Olivia nodded.

"A very lucky man," Emily said staunchly. "He does not deserve her."

"Loyalty is to be commended, my dear." Olivia's voice was deceptively mild. "However, you should take care as to when and where you display it."

Emily blushed, and Olivia smiled forgivingly. "However, in this case I certainly can understand your point. Quentin"—she cast him a steady gaze—"I believe you have some information I might find useful."

He stared, his gaze searching hers. Finally he sighed in defeat, as if he knew any protest would be futile.

"It's about James," he began.

It was worse than Olivia had suspected. Cecily and Quentin were right: This would devastate Jared. But there was no choice in the matter; Jared had the right to know the truth. As difficult as it was, Olivia refused to sacrifice the future happiness of a living son for the reputation of a dead one.

Telling Jared would not be easy. Quentin's story was not an easy thing to hear. She would have to deal with her own reactions to James's treachery privately.

A wry smile touched her lips at the odd twists this day had taken. After all her scheming and plotting and planning to test Cecily's worthiness to be Jared's wife, there was one test she could not devise. One quality she could not control. One attribute, above all others, she would wish for in her son's wife. And the girl had passed without question.

It was the final test.

The ultimate test.

The test of love.

Chapter 17

CECE paced back and forth in her room in the castle. A soothing bath and a change of clothes had refreshed her body, but nothing could revive her spirit. Her mind was a turmoil of emotion and thought and pain.

There was only one real solution to her dilemma, only one way to resolve this crisis with Jared. But telling him the truth was not an option. No, she had to think of some other way to reach him. Some other way to convince him she did indeed have faith in his motorcar and in him. Some other way to prove her love.

She stopped short and stared unseeing at a point far beyond the walls of her room. What if she failed? What if Jared could not forgive her? What if the love he held for her had vanished? What then? Would he abandon her? Would he break off their engagement?

A sudden thought struck her and her breath caught. Surely Jared would believe it was his duty to marry her. He had committed himself publicly, and honor forbid his retracting now. But what kind of a marriage would it be? Cold and lifeless and without love? She would not, could not, condone such a state.

And why not, if that is the only way to spend my life with the man I love?

She slumped onto the bed at the devastating revelation. Were these the depths to which she had sunk? Was this the woman who wanted to forge into the twentieth century in the footsteps of Nellie Bly? Had love turned her into a silly twit of a girl more than willing to marry a man who might possibly despise her because she could not bear the thought of living without him? A girl weak and cowardly and pathetic.

Dear Lord, what had happened to her? She could never abide such a life. She buried her face in her hands. No. Even if it meant struggling with the agony of his loss forever, she would not submit to a lifetime in his presence but without his love.

She rose to her feet and wrapped her arms around herself. Think! There had to be a way out of this. A logical, rational solution. She racked her brain for an idea, any idea. At this point it didn't have to be particularly interesting, just viable. But her mind was too filled with the bitter ache of his final words to concentrate.

Perhaps if she got out in the fresh air? It was only midafternoon. So very much had happened in such a short time. A long walk might clear her head. It would at least give her something to do, something to ease her restlessness, something to keep her busy. She always did think better when she was busy.

She stepped to the door with newfound determination. She would come up with an answer. After all, she was an American, and Americans never accepted defeat. Why, no one enjoyed a good fight better than a patriotic American. Cece was nothing if not patriotic. And this would likely be the fight of her life.

She squared her shoulders and flung open the door.

She would do whatever she must to win back Jared's love, and better, his respect.

She nodded firmly and marched through the doorway. Yes, a long walk would do it.

Or, better yet, a long drive.

"I CAME AS soon as I heard."

Phoebe glanced up at the well-remembered voice. She'd selected this bench in a relatively secluded spot in the castle garden to savor a quiet moment alone and collect her tumultuous thoughts. Her hands still trembled at how close she'd come this morning to losing her daughter.

Robin strode toward her, and she suppressed a sigh of resignation. He was the last person she wished to see now, and a confrontation the last thing she wanted.

He sat down beside her, his worried gaze searching her face. "I've just returned from London, and Quentin told me about the fire. I hope your daughter has not suffered any ill effects from her escapade?"

Phoebe noted a slight shade of disapproval in his tone. "She's quite well, thank you. I find myself today marveling at her courage."

"Courage?" Robin raised a condescending brow. "Recklessness is the more appropriate term, I should think."

"Do you?" she murmured, surprised by her own annoyance at his attitude.

"It scarcely matters. My purpose here has far more to do with you than your daughter. The fire simply provided an appropriate excuse." He took her hands in his. "I have come for your answer, Phoebe."

"Robin . . ." she said, her words measured. She tried to withdraw from his grasp, but his fingers held firm.

"I don't know why you feel any relationship between us is even possible—"

"I love you, Phoebe." His blue eyes burned with desire. "I always have. I always will."

"Robin—"

"And you love me as well." His voice was intense with certainty. "I know it."

She jerked her hands from his and rose to unsteady feet. He jumped up, as if unwilling to let her put so much as a few inches between them. Why did his mere touch still take her breath away? "I did once, but that was long ago."

"And have you forgotten?" He stood so very close, she could see the rise and fall of his chest. "Have you forgotten how it was between us? The sweet sparks of passion we never allowed to flame?"

"I remember," she whispered and shivered with the memory.

"And do you remember this?" He pulled her unresisting into his arms. "Do you recall how you fit into my embrace as if we were made, one for the other?"

"Yes." She sighed.

"We still fit together, Phoebe." His mouth trailed along the lobe of her ear, and she shuddered at his touch. "Leave him, Phoebe; leave your husband. We should have been together long ago. We can still be together now."

His lips crushed hers and she surrendered to the overwhelming rush of emotion pent up within her for years. This was mere lust, a voice in the back of her mind cried, plain and simple. It was indeed but, oh, for one, long, magnificent moment, wasn't it glorious?

Still, as much as this man made her senses pound and her body tremble, there was something lacking here. As swiftly as the urgent need to cling to him swept over her it vanished. Abruptly, realization struck her, and she knew with the certainty of life itself that whatever desire still lingered for him, whatever questions still haunted her, whatever remnants of a long-ago love still remained were purged with this encounter as surely as if they'd been washed aside by raging waters.

She pulled away from him and stared into azure eyes darkened by passion. "Robin, I am sorry, but"—she shrugged as best she could in his embrace—"there really is nothing left between us."

"Nothing left between us?" His eyes widened incredulously. "But you are in my arms."

"Robin," she said firmly, "this is a mistake."

"It's no mistake." He glared down at her. "The only mistake here is the one you made twenty-three years ago when you left me. When through sheer stupidity you chose to marry some insignificant, provincial," he sputtered as if searching for an appropriate word, "cowboy!"

He released her and she stepped back, shocked at the vehemence in his words. "Have you ever considered what you gave up by that rash act?"

"I know what I gained," she said quietly.

"Hah!" He snorted in disdain. "What could you possibly have gained? Look at your life. Of your children, at least one is a headstrong hellion who will no doubt come to no good, regardless of whom she marries. You move in the limited society of a city whose very existence is scarcely acknowledged in the civilized world. And your husband has certainly progressed far in the years of your marriage, well beyond the dubious skills of herding cattle to something a bit more down to earth."

He raised his brow in a gesture of contempt. "I believe now it would be accurate to refer to him as a glorified . . . butcher."

For less than a moment shock held her helpless. Then rage surged through her with a blinding force that shattered years of polite behavior and self-control.

"How dare you insult my husband and my family!" Phoebe cracked her hand across his cheek with the power born of the indignity of today and the bitter betrayal of yesterday. "You arrogant son of a bitch!"

"Phoebe!" He gasped, whether more at the slap or at her language she didn't know.

She clapped a hand over her mouth. She'd never used such language in her life.

"I daresay, I never expected—" Robin stammered "—what I mean to say is—" He drew a deep breath. "I do apologize, Phoebe. Please forgive me. My comments were both uncalled for and untrue. My only excuse is that the thought of losing you once more was more than I could bear. I'm afraid I was simply trying to soothe the pain in my heart by hurting you."

"You no longer have the power to hurt me, Robin." With her cool words came the surprising discovery that they were true. Her feelings for this man were at long last spent.

"I must tell you, Robin, I have done a great deal of thinking since meeting you again. While I may well have loved you once, it was the emotion of an untried girl, a child. The passion I felt for you then was as intense as a summer cloudburst and, no doubt, just as fleeting."

She stared at him for a long considering moment. 'True love, Robin, has more to do with living than lust, with sharing hand in hand the day-to-day joys and tragedies of life, and with the unquestioned knowledge that the one nearest and dearest to your heart will always be by your side. It has to do with faith, Robin, and trust, and a certain, quiet passion that springs to life with a gentle kiss or a chance brush of his hand or the meeting of his eyes across a crowded room."

Robin heaved a sigh of defeat. "We never had the chance to know that, did we?"

"No, but I suspect it has all worked out for the best." She smiled. "I find I am not merely content with my choices but happy as well."

"Then this is good-bye?" A last, hopeful look lingered in his eye."

"Indeed it is," she said softly.

"As well it should be."

Phoebe turned sharply at the familiar voice. Henry stood tall and strong and handsome, with the power still to make her blood pound and her heart flutter. How could she have lost sight of that, even for a moment? He was her rock and she would love him forever. His voice was mild, but menace simmered in his eyes.

Robin's glance slid from Henry to Phoebe and back to her husband. A wry note sounded in his voice. "No doubt my presence is no longer welcome; therefore I shall take my leave. Phoebe, I . . ." He drew a deep breath. "I wish you all the happiness in the world."

"Thank you, Robin." She cast a quick glance at her husband. "I believe I already have that."

Robin nodded. "Indeed." He turned to Henry. "You are a lucky man. Take care of her."

Henry's smile never reached his eyes. "I always have."

Robin stared for a moment, then nodded, turned

and strode off. Henry's gaze never left the retreating figure, and Phoebe studied him thoughtfully.

"How long were you standing there?" she said.

His gaze met hers, the hard chill in his eyes softening. "Long enough. I arrived just in time to see Bainbridge take you in his arms." A rueful smile touched his lips. "It was all I could do to keep from ripping him apart limb by limb, but I was afraid that might upset you so I refrained."

"Extremely thoughtful of you," she murmured.

He heaved a heavy sigh. "It wasn't easy. But I decided if he was what you wanted," he shrugged, "then I would have to let you have him."

Surprise coursed through her. "Why?"

"Why?" He pulled his gaze from hers and stared at a far distant point, as if he couldn't bear to meet her eyes. "It's not an easy thing to admit, Phoebe, but I have found myself evaluating our life together in recent days, and I have come to realize a number of things. I believe I have taken your presence for granted and treated you somewhat shabbily through the years."

"Henry . . ." Her eyes widened with astonishment. "I don't—"

"No." He shook his head firmly. "Please, allow me to continue."

"Very well." She stared, fascinated by the tension in every line of his body. Apparently this admission was far more difficult for him than she would have imagined. She bit back an inadvertent smile. It was altogether charming of him to worry that anything he said would make any real difference in her feelings.

He pulled a deep breath. "I have paid far more attention to business, to achieving what I believe is a respectable amount of success, than I have to your happiness."

"Why, Henry, I—"

"Phoebe." His gaze again locked with hers. "Since your renewed acquaintance with Bainbridge I have worried that I would lose you to him, to your first love." His dark eyes flashed with an intensity that stole her breath and weakened her knees. "But a few moments ago, when you told him . . . well . . . that you were happy, did you mean it?"

"With all my heart," she said with earnest conviction. Relief and joy broke in his eyes and he swept her into his arms.

"Phoebe . . ." His lips claimed hers with all the passion of a new love, and she met him just as eagerly.

He drew his mouth from hers and drifted it along her neck. Shivers of pure delight coursed through her. Goodness, what would people think? Such scandalous behavior, here in the garden, with her husband? She wanted to laugh aloud.

"Phoebe," his words whispered against her skin, "I want always to share life's joy and tragedies with you, to be always by your side, to be forever the gaze you meet across a room."

She sighed with pleasure. "So you heard all that, did you?"

"Indeed," he murmured. "And more. It was extremely informative. I never suspected . . ." he feathered kisses along her neck ". . . you even knew the term 'arrogant son-of-a-bitch.'"

"Henry!" She jerked back, heat flashing up her face.

He laughed and refused to let her out of his arms. "As surprising as it was, I must say it was also appropriate."

"He was being quite horrid," she said defensively.

"Quite." Henry grinned, then pulled her close, a

serious light in his eye. "Things will change between us, Phoebe; I promise. I can well afford to leave my affairs in the competent hands of trusted employees. After all, their fortunes are tied to ours. You have always wanted to travel. Paris shall be just the beginning." He stared down at her and her heart stilled, and she wondered just how wicked it would be to retire to their bed in the middle of the afternoon. "Where would you like to go first?"

"I should very much like to go home, Henry. As for now," she bit her bottom lip and prayed he would not think her too wanton, "perhaps we are both in need . . . um . . . after the stressful hours of this morning, that is . . . I should think a rest . . . ?" She gazed at him hopefully.

He stared for a puzzled moment. Then a slow grin spread across his face. "A rest?"

Dreaded heat again flushed her cheeks, but she lifted her chin to meet his gaze directly. She nodded. "A rest."

Henry tucked her hand in the crook of his arm and started toward the castle. "My only desire is to ensure your happiness. And if a rest is what you wish, a rest is what you shall have." A low chuckle rumbled through him. "I can't think of a more delightful way to spend the afternoon."

"Frankly, Henry"—she stopped and cast him a bold smile—"neither can I."

It was his third whiskey, or his fifth or more. Jared had lost count long ago. It didn't matter and he didn't care. In one hand he gripped a glass, in the other a decanter with steadily shrinking contents. Scottish whisky was not generally his drink of choice, but it had been his experience in the past that, when oblivion was the goal, this liquor was the method. And oblivion was what he sought now.

"Bloody hell," he muttered to the world in general and no one in particular. He'd come straight to the castle library on his return home, straight to blessed solitude, straight to the pungent, powerful liquor. Soot still covered him, a gritty, uncomfortable coating that chaffed his skin and filled his nostrils with the lingering scent of wood smoke and treachery.

How could she?

The words pounded in his head in an unceasing refrain. How could she have so little faith? So little trust? After all her fine words about a man making his own fortune, about a man laboring to achieve his goals, to resort to using her wealth to ensure his success was the height of hypocrisy and betrayal.

Obviously that was all her high-and-noble speeches were: mere words without a shred of truth behind them. He was nothing short of a fool to have thought she could truly have considered him capable of achieving his dreams on his own.

He pulled another swig of the potent alcohol. The whisky did nothing to dull the hard, hot pain that simmered within him. The irony of it all drew a bitter smile to his lips. He had so ardently believed in her false vows of confidence, he had even threatened to give up his home, his heritage, to return with her to America and build a life with her there, a life of struggle and hard work in a gamble that it would someday pay off with prosperity. Prosperity achieved by his own two hands, with her at his side.

How could he have been so wrong about her? In spite of her words, he should have known she could never live without the vast wealth that was her birthright. Hadn't she just proved to him that when it came to getting exactly what she wanted, she would not hesitate to use her fortune? It didn't matter that she used it for him.

"Do you plan on hiding in here all day?" Olivia's voice sounded from the doorway.

"I am not hiding." There was a warning beneath his words. "Leave me alone, Mother."

She ignored him. "You look frightful. Why, you haven't even cleaned up from the fire."

He stared sightlessly before him. The last thing he wanted now was companionship, especially his mother's. "I have other things on my mind."

"So I understand," she said mildly.

Her words caught his attention, and he jerked his gaze to hers. "What do you mean?"

Olivia stepped closer and settled herself in the overstuffed couch near the wing chair in which he slumped. "I know about Cecily."

"Oh?" He narrowed his gaze. "And just what do you know?"

"I know you believe she tried to pay that disgusting little man, Barton Sinclair, to lose the race to you."

"Excellent, Mother." He raised his glass in a toast. "You do indeed know all regarding my lovely fiancée. It seems I chose the right heiress, after all. She has more than enough money to preserve what is left of this wretched family's past and buy the future for her husband as well."

"I hardly think—"

"Frankly, Mother, at this point it no longer matters

what you think." He drained the last dregs of whisky in his glass and stared at her over the rim. "As to what I think . . . well, that's an interesting tale."

He poured another glass and carelessly thudded the decanter onto the table beside his chair. The crystal tottered on the edge before settling and Olivia twitched, as if restraining herself from leaping to the fragile container's rescue.

"Please do continue, Jared." She was quite good, his mother, quite under control, calm and collected. Did nothing ever shock her?

"Very well." He paused for another long sip. "I think we have achieved precisely our purpose when we started, you and I. We needed an heiress to refresh the family coffers. That was the only requirement for a suitable marriage. Affection, respect, even love played no role in our quest." He paused and stared into the bottom of his glass. "It seems we have accomplished our goal far better than we ever expected. I am engaged to the heiress of a considerable fortune and love plays no role. No role at all."

"Cecily does love you, Jared," Olivia said softly.

His voice was bitter. "Love has nothing to do with it."

"I believe love has everything to do with it." Olivia drew a deep breath. "Love is precisely why Cecily is allowing you to continue under the erroneous impression that she has done something wrong."

"She paid Sinclair." Jared glared, narrowing his gaze. "She admitted it."

"Did she tell you why?"

"She didn't need to," he said darkly. "Sinclair confessed everything."

"Indeed." Olivia raised a skeptical brow. "And you believed him?" Jared nodded.

"I see." Her words were measured and precise. "From everything I have ever heard about Sinclair I am surprised you would take his word so readily."

"Your point, Mother." Sarcasm colored his voice.

Olivia studied her son thoughtfully. "My point, Jared, is that, until this incident I don't believe Cecily has lied to you. Has she?"

"No," he conceded grudgingly.

"Neither has she sought to deceive you—at least not in any significant manner. Has she?"

"No. Although, she did come to England originally to entrap . . ." He sighed. "No. Not really."

"Then why on earth would you take the word of a man you distrust over the word of the woman you love?"

"She refused to say anything," he muttered.

"Goodness, Jared!" His gaze jerked up to meet hers at her forceful outburst. "I never suspected I had given birth to a complete idiot before this very minute. Think, Jared; what does her silence mean?"

"Nothing." He shrugged. "I don't know. That she didn't wish to admit her actions?"

"Jared!" she snapped

"Very well." He pulled his brows together in an effort at concentration, ignoring his mother's impatient glare.

Jared pulled himself to his feet and paced the room. "I have no idea what her silence means. If she's not hiding her own actions from me, protecting herself, then . . ." he stopped and stared, struck by the obvious possibility, "perhaps she's protecting someone else?"

Olivia nodded.

"Who is she shielding, Mother?" Jared said with a controlled intensity, needing to ask, fearing the answer.

Heartfelt regret shone in her eyes, and his stomach clenched. She clasped her hands in her lap and drew a steadying breath.

"James."

"James?" Doubt flooded through him. "But James is dead. How can she be protecting James?"

Olivia studied her intertwined fingers, as if she'd never seen them before. "It seems that for quite some time James had been selling plans and parts that you and Quentin had developed regarding your automobile. Sinclair was insisting on the item he had paid James for before his death. Instead of surrendering the part, Cecily returned his money."

She lifted her gaze to meet her son's. "I believe that's why James was near the pond the day he died. He had gone to the stables to—" she hesitated to say the vile word "—to steal your inventions to sell."

Jared stared, shaking his head in stunned disbelief.

"I'm quite afraid it's all true," she said quietly.

"But . . ." Betrayed? By his own brother? The brother he had respected and admired and loved? "Why?"

"Money." She shrugged. "It's as simple as that. Your brother apparently believed in your abilities enough to know he could raise money with your work. As for Cecily—"

Jared groaned and sank back into his chair, burying his face in his hands. "She'll never forgive me, and I can't say I blame her." He raised his head. "I said some horrible things to her."

Olivia favored him with a motherly smile. "She'll forgive you. She loves you. You've done quite well, my boy; a young woman who meets all of my standards and loves you as well. Surely you can't ask for anything more."

"She meets your standards?" Jared stared incredulously. "That's right, I'd nearly forgotten, your tests. She's passed them all, hasn't she?"

Olivia cast him a relieved smile. "Yes, indeed. Now all you have to do is apologize—"

"Apologize?" He leapt to his feet. "It's not that simple. You have put this woman through a course of trials and tests that the hardiest competitor would be hard pressed to accomplish."

"I never . . ." He cast her a scathing glare and she clamped her lips closed.

"And I . . ." Pain shadowed his heart. "I have charged her with a lack of faith and trust. I was the one who didn't believe. The one lacking in faith. I should have known better. I thought I was a fool to have trusted her. I was only half right."

"She will understand," Olivia said with conviction in her voice.

"Will she?" He shook his head in disgust. "I didn't. I have treated her with complete contempt. Even excluding the events of today, I have taken for granted that she would give up her home, her country and her own dreams to marry me. I have blithely expected her to sacrifice everything she holds dear and for what? What do I offer her in return?"

He paced the room, talking more to himself than to her. "A title she cares nothing about? A future in a country more mired in the past than striving toward the future? A life amid people she believes place far too high a value on traditions and appearances than on ingenuity and progress?"

Contempt for his own selfish behavior swept through him. "I could have given her more of what she wants, what she respects, what she deserves, when she thought I was a penniless inventor than I can offer her now as the Earl of Graystone."

For a long moment heavy silence hung between them. The abject sorrow that surrounded her son nearly broke Olivia's heart. Certainly there were other prospective brides for Jared, but Cecily had met all the requirements and more. Cecily loved him. She drew a deep breath and prayed that after all these years spent preserving this family, its name and its heritage, she was not about to make the biggest mistake of her life.

"Would she be happier, would you be happier, as a"— she shuddered at the words—"penniless inventor?"

He laughed, a short, mirthless sound. "It sounds absurd, doesn't it? But with her by my side, striving to achieve something by my own, hard work, yes."

"How very American of you," she murmured.

"Perhaps." He shrugged. "We shall never know."

Olivia studied him and heaved a sigh of resignation. The foolish things one does for the love of one's children. "I believe you threatened to do just that should I put Cecily to one more test."

His gaze narrowed. "Yes?"

"Well," she paused, intent on studying her fingernails and choosing the proper words, "I did."

"You set the stables on fire!" He gasped with astonishment.

"No, of course not. Don't be ridiculous." She cast him a chastising frown. "I would never do such a thing."

He ran his fingers through his hair in a tired gesture of relief. "Thank God. For a moment—"

"I did, however, reveal your involvement in the automobile at Emily's ball." She gritted her teeth and waited.

"What?" The word exploded from him. "Why?"

"To see what Cecily would do. Would she abandon you to the vicious web of London gossip? Or would she stand by your side?" She smiled hopefully. "She did show a great deal of courage, you know."

He stared, anger darkening his eyes. "Did you think my warning an idle one? Did you believe for one moment I was not fully prepared to do exactly what I threatened?"

She straightened her shoulders and met his gaze directly. "It was a gamble I was willing to take."

"It is a gamble you've lost." Jared's voice rang strong and stern. He stalked to the doors and threw them open. "Watkins!"

"Yes, milord?" How very prompt Watkins was. He must have been listening at the keyhole again.

"Is Miss White in her room?"

"I believe she left the castle, milord, quite some time ago." As usual Watkins's face remained expressionless. Olivia wondered vaguely what family secrets lay hidden behind that carefully concealed facade.

"Very well. I'll simply have to find her." He nodded sharply to his mother and strode from the room.

All strength drained from Olivia. She sank into her chair, rested her head against the back and stared at the ceiling. Nothing had turned out even remotely as she had planned. It was all so muddled. They would no doubt need to sell the castle at some point if Jared was going to America. But she did so wish to keep the house in London. Still, her son's happiness, while admittedly not completely worth throwing away centuries of history and heritage, was worth some sacrifice.

She was pleased he'd found love and pleased with Cecily as well. If the girl had been another milksop heiress Jared would never have fallen for her. Olivia snorted to herself. If the girl had been like the others, she certainly never would have passed her tests. Marriage to money was such an excellent idea. It had worked for so many other families as well; why was hers—

The thought struck her with a startling clarity, and she sat bolt upright in her chair. Marriage! For money! Of course! What a delightful idea. What an interesting idea. Why on earth hadn't she thought of it sooner? Jared was not the only marriageable member of the family.

She sprang to her feet and headed toward the door, deep in plans and plots and sheer excitement. First she would need to change into something a bit more—

"Mother." Jared reappeared in the doorway so abruptly, she nearly ran into him. She stared with speechless surprise.

"I neglected to say something before I left."

Oh dear. What now? "Yes?"

He cast her an exuberant grin and dropped a kiss on her cheek. "Thank you."

He swiveled and disappeared into the shadows of the corridor. Olivia touched her fingers to the spot his lips had brushed and smiled. Perhaps everything was not nearly as muddled as she'd thought after all.

OLIVIA'S GAZE SWEPT Millicent's drawing room. Her friend's butler had informed her that she would find Robert here. He sat at Millicent's writing desk, looking quite large and extremely out of place behind the fragile piece of furniture.

"Robert?"

He glanced up and rose to his feet, a smile of obvious

delight on his face. Excellent. That would make this so much easier.

"Olivia!" He took her hand and brushed his lips across the back. "What a charming surprise. To what do I owe this unexpected pleasure?"

"Robert." She gazed straight into his eyes. Blue, she noted, and very nice. "I am here to offer you a proposition."

"A proposition?" He quirked a brow. "It is far too seldom I receive propositions from enchanting women these days. Dare I hope it is quite scandalous?"

"Robert!" Heat flushed her cheeks. He was far more accurate than he knew.

He laughed. "So what is this proposition of yours?"

She pulled a steadying breath. "I have given this a great deal of thought. With your new position in the government, I believe it would be of great benefit to you to have a home and . . ." she summoned all her courage, for broaching this subject was far more difficult than she'd expected, "and . . . a wife."

"A wife?" Surprise flooded his distinguished features.

"Indeed." She nodded firmly.

"Well . . ." A poignant look crossed his face, and Olivia knew he thought of Phoebe.

"No, Robert," she said sharply and prodded him in the chest with her finger. "I mean, a wife of your own."

He sighed. "I have no further illusions on that score. Phoebe was a dream of my youth, and when I saw her again it was as if the years separating us were no more than mere moments." He shook his head. "I fear I was something of an old fool. Whatever Phoebe and I once shared was over a very long time ago and is best forgotten. The past is now firmly in the past."

"Excellent." She poked him again. "Now, regarding your need for a wife—"

Caution edged his voice. "Did you have a candidate in mind?"

"Yes." She pushed once more and he tumbled back on the sofa. She dropped down beside him. "Me."

"You?" He stared with amazement.

"It seems to me," the words rushed out in a swift, unstoppable torrent, "that we have always gotten on quite well together. In fact, if I recall correctly, during my first season—before I married Charles, of course— we shared several, shall we say, flirtatious moments, and had circumstances—"

He placed a finger on her lips, effectively cutting off her comments, and chuckled wryly. "I did say you had a direct nature."

"If you don't go after what you want, you will very likely miss it altogether," Olivia said breathlessly, staring up at him. Odd; Robert's touch on her mouth brought the most peculiar fluttering sensation to her stomach.

"And what do you want?" His voice was at once quiet, his eyes intense.

"To be perfectly honest, I need funds to restore the castle and the estate. You have a significant fortune." Goodness, the man's eyes were startlingly blue and deep, with some hidden fire that seemed to draw her toward him.

"Is my fortune all you're interested in?" The words fell from lips firm and full, and she wondered if they would feel as delightful on her mouth as they had on her hand.

"I . . ." Longing such as she hadn't known for years swept through her. The sweet ache of desire she'd nearly forgotten existed filled her, and she wanted nothing more than to throw herself into his arms. "No."

She stared for a long moment. He studied her closely, with an expression that concealed his thoughts. Her heart sank. She had been far too brazen. Why, she'd behaved like a common tart. Disappointment shot through her, and she realized with a start of amazement that the idea of marriage to Robert meant far more to her than a way to save her family's heritage. For the first time in years she desired a man. This man.

Embarrassment pulled her to her feet. "Robert, you must accept my apology. I have no idea what came over me. What you must think of me!"

She turned away, her manner brisk, determined to hide the surprising pain that stabbed through her. It would be best if she left, at once.

"I think . . ." His voice was soft, near her ear, and she realized he stood directly behind her. He laid his hands on her shoulders and gently turned her to face him. A bemused smile hovered on his lips. "I think you are quite refreshing, Olivia Grayson. I think I was a fool all those years ago not to have pursued that flirtation. I also think you are no doubt correct; I do need a wife."

"Do you?" Her blood pounded in her ears.

His solemn nod belied the twinkle in his eyes. "I do."

"And will I suffice?" Her heart caught in her throat.

He pulled her into the warmth of his arms, against the hard, broad expanse of his chest, and she marveled at her own urge to melt against him. "I should think you'll do very nicely, my dear; quite nicely indeed."

"Excellent." Were his eyes getting bluer, darker? "In that case . . ." she couldn't seem to quite catch her breath ". . . perhaps it would be acceptable if you were to . . . shall we say . . . what I mean is . . ."

"Kiss you?"

She gazed up at him, her reply little more than a sigh. "Indeed."

He bent his lips to hers and she lost herself to the rich, warm currents coursing through her. Her arms slipped around his neck and she met his embrace with an eager need that would have shocked her had it not seemed so natural, so wonderful. He pulled her tighter and her breath mingled with his, and she reveled in a passion she'd thought she'd never know again or, perhaps, never really had.

He pulled back and stared down at her, the surprise on his face mirroring her own. "My—"

"—goodness," she said, her usual serenity only a dim memory. "That was certainly . . . most definitely . . ."

"Most definitely." He nodded firmly and kissed her again.

"I had no idea," she murmured, "no idea at all."

Robert laughed. "Neither did I. Believe me, my dear, had I even suspected this was a possibility I would not have waited so long to return home. What a great deal of time we have wasted."

She pulled her brows together in a frown of concern. "You don't think we are too old for this kind of . . ."

"Passion?" He trailed his lips along the side of her neck and she shuddered with unexpected pleasure. "No, I think we are both just about perfect. It is such a shame to waste passion on the young."

"Robert?" She pulled back to lock her gaze with his. "About Phoebe; have you truly put your feelings for her behind you?"

"I spoke to her earlier today, and we have finally resolved everything between us. It simply took me some time to realize it." He smiled ruefully. "She called me an arrogant son of a bitch."

She reached up and brushed his fair hair away from his face. "But my darling Robert . . ." Olivia cast him a teasing look and brushed her lips against his. "You and I both know she was very probably right."

CECE WAS NOWHERE to be found. Servants confirmed she had left the castle, but her belongings remained in her room. Good, she had obviously not taken it into her head to return to London—or worse, to America. She could not have gone far.

Emily had not seen her. The maids said she was not with her parents, who had retired to their rooms for a rest before dinner. Odd; Henry White did not seem the sort of man who required a late afternoon rest.

Jared checked with the stable boys and the grooms. Cece had not taken a horse. He stifled a rising sense of panic. Where could she have gone? There were few places on the estate with which she was familiar.

The answer struck him abruptly and he cursed under his breath. Of course: the ravaged stables. No doubt that was where he would find her. For the second time that day he set off for the distant site with a speed driven by apprehension and concern.

What would he say when he found her? His pace slowed with the thought. This would be the most important speech of his life. The proper words and phrases ran through his head like so many birds scattering at the approach of a vehicle.

"Cece." His voice echoed on the lonely trek. "I have been a fool."

Excellent way to begin. She would no doubt agree with that admission. He nodded and continued with renewed confidence. "I was wrong not to accept your actions without question. I should have known better. I was a complete fool."

No, no; he shook his head in irritation. He had already called himself a fool once. It was not necessary to belabor the point.

"Cece," he began again, "I believe—" His words caught in his throat. The ruined stables stood in the distance, a sorry sentinel against the setting sun. The scene appeared precisely as it had earlier in the day with one notable exception.

His automobile was missing.

"Bloody hell!" He picked up his step and sprinted toward the site. Perhaps he had simply forgotten precisely where the car had been left? He searched the area to no avail and strode to the shed where the petrol was stored. His worst fears were confirmed; several cans were missing. His stomach tightened and his fists clenched. The blasted woman had taken his motorcar.

He struggled against the immediate impulse to return to the castle stables, saddle a horse and pursue her. The urge was useless; he had no idea in which direction she might have headed. There was nothing to do but wait. He only hoped he would not have to wait long.

He sank down beneath an ancient oak and rested his back against the bark. Fear and anger boiled within him. It was fast growing dark, and anything could happen to her alone on the road. What if the automobile broke down? What if she were accosted by thieves, or worse? What if she never returned?

He would not lose her. If—no, *when* she came back,

he would get down on his knees and beg her forgiveness if necessary. He would even—he swallowed dryly at the thought—allow her to drive his machine whenever she wished, now that she obviously knew how. And he would vow to return to her country and do all in his power to make his automobile a success.

His gaze traveled over the fields spread out below the ridge, painted gold with the last rays of the sun, an artist's feast for the eye and soul. His heart tripped at the sight. How could he leave this behind? He was the steward of this land, entrusted to him for safekeeping by a legacy stretching back through the centuries. He gritted his teeth in determination and pushed the odd ache that stabbed him aside. It was high time to give up the past in favor of the future, in favor of progress.

What would his brother have done? The unbidden question surprised him. He'd had no time to ponder James's action since his mother's startling revelation. Considering his brother now, he was more saddened than angered at his treachery. It appeared James was not as competent as Jared had thought. The disloyal idea had grown within him for some time, and this discovery only solidified his opinion. A strong sense of relief flowed through him. He was at least the man his brother was. It was such a shame he hadn't realized it when James was alive.

Jared's anxious gaze searched the long lane stretching into dusk and beyond. Where was she? Bloody, impulsive, unthinking American. Would he have to spend the rest of his life mad with worry about what she might be getting into? Lord, he certainly hoped so.

Night fell with the soft, satisfying comfort offered only by a late summer eve. He sat for hours, gazing into the strange shadows of the night, grateful that at least the full moon filled the evening with its white-blue brightness.

Fatigue plagued him, and he struggled to remain awake and alert. He couldn't remember when he'd last slept—long before the revelations of the day and the morning spent battling the blaze at the stables. Concern for Cece's safety sparred with his own emotional and physical exhaustion. He started time and again at the scamper of rabbits or the screech of a night bird. Finally he dozed, a fitful, restless sleep, and when he dreamed he dreamed of her. Of dark hair and darker eyes. Of full, lush lips made for him and him alone. Of a spirit of independence and a soul of passion . . .

The unmistakable sound of his motorcar jerked him to his senses. He shook his head to clear his mind and staggered to his feet. Relief surged through him at the sight of Cece driving toward him. She was whole and well, and he wondered how long he could restrain himself before he was compelled to wring her lovely neck.

He stood straight and tall and folded his arms over his chest, knowing full well that the rising sun behind him would obscure his features and he'd appear as an appallingly stern silhouette. As grateful as he was to see her unharmed, as determined as he was to beg her forgiveness, he could not let her think he condoned her shocking and dangerous behavior. It would not be the best way to begin a marriage.

The motorcar puttered to a surprisingly smooth stop a mere few inches from his feet. His gaze narrowed. Not only did the woman have the nerve to take his automobile but she wore his duster, gloves and goggles. Yet, even with the oversized garments Cece stepped from the vehicle with the grace and ease of one who'd been driving all her life.

"Good morning," she said coolly, pulling her goggles from her face and stripping off his gloves.

"Where have you been?" He ground out the words.

She shrugged off his coat and tossed it into the automobile. "I simply went for a little drive."

"A little drive? Hah!" He glared with irritation. "You've been gone all bloody night."

"It did take longer than I thought." Her manner was infuriatingly casual. "But once I was on the road I found myself on the way to Bath."

He gasped with disbelief. "Bath?"

She nodded. "Indeed. I have a knack for remembering routes and had no problem navigating the journey."

"Bath." Was the woman truly deranged?

"You said that, Jared." She frowned with annoyance. "As I was saying, taking into account the difference in distance between here and London, I believe I made the run in a bit better time than the competitors in the actual race."

"You did?" She was truly mad.

She heaved a sigh of irritation. "If you plan to comment on everything I say, we shall never complete this conversation."

He clenched his teeth in surrender. "Please, do go on."

"Thank you," she said primly. "It was quite enjoyable, but I did notice that noise you mentioned. I believe one of the chains is loose."

"The chain? Possibly that would account—" He frowned sharply. "I don't care about the blasted chain. You are evading the subject."

"Am I?" she said innocently. "And just what is the subject?"

"The subject?" What was the subject? The woman had muddled his mind as surely as she'd muddled his heart. "The subject is your taking off, without a word to anyone."

"Oh, that." She waved a dismissive hand. "I had a great deal of thinking to do."

His heart stilled. "And what conclusions did you reach?"

"First of all, I believe you owe me a rather extensive apology." He opened his mouth to speak. "No, please, allow me to finish. You ranted quite a bit about trust and faith, but you have had neither in my case. You had very little faith in my intelligence, my abilities and my principles."

"Cece, I—"

She threw him a stern glance. "In addition, you did not trust that I would never do such a thing as Sinclair accused me of. And you failed to understand that your dreams are as precious to me as my own. If for no other reason than that they are your dreams."

She pulled a steadying breath, and at once he realized his confident American was more than a bit nervous. "Furthermore, I would never betray you. And if I cannot always explain my actions fully, there is a very good reason. Trust, Jared, goes both ways."

She stared at him, chin held high and shoulders squared, as if daring him to dispute her words. Lord, he loved her.

"I know, Cece," he said quietly.

"Know what?" Caution hung in her voice.

"I know about James."

"Oh, dear." Her expression crumpled. Sympathy shone in her eyes. "I am so very sorry. I did not want you to find out. Did Quentin tell you?"

"Quentin?" Did everyone know about James except him? "No, it was my mother."

"Your mother? How very interesting," she said thoughtfully.

"And you're right, you know."

"I am?" She drew her brows together in a puzzled expression.

"Indeed." He nodded. "I do owe you an apology and much more."

She smiled. "An apology is sufficient."

"No." He shook his head ruefully. "It is not nearly enough. I too have been doing my share of thinking."

He stepped closer and took her hands in his. "I have decided to spend the rest of my life making you happy. To do that, I need to be the man you first fell in love with. The man you kissed in Paris."

"Paris?" Confusion clouded her eyes.

"I have decided," he drew a deep breath, "to return with you to America, where I can pursue development of my automobile."

For one stunned moment she stared, speechless. Shock washed across her face. She jerked her hands from his and stepped back sharply. "Don't be absurd!"

"Absurd?" Wasn't this what she really wanted?

"Absurd! Insane! Ridiculous! I cannot believe you would even suggest such a thing!"

"But I thought—"

"Obviously you have done what you have so often accused me of doing. You didn't think at all." She stepped closer and glared into his eyes. "Think now, Jared. This is your home, your heritage. You belong here. You would not be happy anywhere else."

"What about your happiness?" he said softly.

Her expression eased. "I would be happy anywhere with you."

At once a weight lifted from his shoulders, and he realized how very much he did not want to leave. He wrapped his arms around her and pulled her close. "Then we shall stay."

She nodded happily. "And you shall still work on your dreams, and my money will restore the estate and—"

"No," he said firmly.

She gazed at him with surprise. "Whyever not?"

He groaned at the words he was about to say. "Because, my love, a man should not marry for wealth. He should have to make his own fortune."

"Jared!" She grinned with pleasure. "I am impressed. Obviously I have already been an excellent influence on you."

He quirked a brow. "Obviously." He shook his head. "It will certainly not be easy, but we will continue to sell off the family heirlooms and hopefully, someday—"

"Someday," her eyes sparkled, "we'll have a motorcar in front of every manor house and cottage in England."

He laughed. "God help the British." He bent to touch his lips to hers, then abruptly stopped. "I do feel, though, that I am asking you to give up a great deal for me, and I have little to offer you in return."

"Jared," she chided, "you offer me love."

"Indeed, still . . . I simply wish there was something more I could give you. One thing I could sacrifice for you."

"You do mean that, don't you?" There was astonishment in her eyes.

"I do," he said solemnly.

"Very well," her words were measured and thoughtful, "in that case, if you are certain?"

"I am." He nodded.

"I should very much . . ." Her eyes twinkled, and the corners of her lips quirked upward ". . . like to be the proud owner of my very own . . . automobile."

"My automobile?" he said, shocked by the very thought.

"Indeed." She bobbed her head. "It is the one thing you can offer me that would mean something."

"It is technically half Quentin's, you know," he said hopefully.

"Quentin will not care."

"My automobile." Surrender crept through him.

"Your automobile." Even the teasing light in her eye could not vanquish the sinking sensation in his stomach. He shrugged. "Then, my love, it's yours."

"Thank you." She snaked her arms around his neck. "Kiss me, Jared, and then," she grinned, "I'll take you for a drive."

He laughed and his lips met hers, and he knew for now and forever he would drive off into the sunset with this American princess who could hold her own with everyone from scoundrels to interfering mothers. And he further knew, and perhaps had always known, or possibly just hoped, that the true test, the final challenge, the real pea beneath the mattress . . . was love.

Epilogue

"I THINK you're being ridiculous." Emily glared at Quentin. "Why, there is no reason on earth why women are not just as capable as men of handling such a craft."

"It's far too dangerous for a woman," Quentin said loftily. "And altogether improper."

"For goodness sakes, Quentin, it's 1905, and your ideas of what is proper and improper for women are positively antiquated."

"I think I tend to agree with him, my dear," Jared said dryly. "Although I will admit I was once wrong about the abilities of women to drive motorcars, this device is a far different matter."

"Jared." Emily turned her ire to her brother-in-law. Cece laughed to herself and continued past the knot of friends and family arguing the virtues and dangers of that fascinating new invention, the flying machine.

The scent of roasting beef drifted on the wind. Since that first party a decade earlier, this evening of outdoor entertainment had become an annual tradition at Graystone Castle.

Odd how life turned out. She'd always thought she was the adventurous one, the one to climb mountains and conquer frontiers. But, in truth, it was Emily who ultimately slashed through the years with high spirit and a reckless disregard for what was expected and proper. The family had been stunned when she'd fled to Paris to seriously try her hand at painting. Then there had been her disastrous, though thankfully short, marriage to the person the family had only referred to as "that dreadful man." Perhaps, at long last, she and Quentin would now find each other. Quentin had never married, and Cece always suspected Emily was the reason why.

Dear Quentin. He had not taken well to the demands of producing motorcars, selling his share of the company to Jared within the first year of operation. There still wasn't a Graystone Motor Car on every drive in England, but it was the country's favorite.

She nodded to old friends and new acquaintances and made her way around the grounds, checking, as any good hostess would, on the enjoyment of her guests. Perhaps she was more nostalgic this year because it was a milestone of sorts. In the past few months Jared had reimbursed Robert for all the funds he had poured into the castle and estate. He had further paid back Cece's father for the loan he'd insisted they accept when Jared refused any sort of dowry. Today the Earl of Graystone's financial footing was as sound as the Bank of England itself.

Cece waved to her parents, chatting with neighbors. On hand for the party this year, their visit here was a brief stop on their way to see the pyramids of Egypt. They traveled a great deal these days.

Olivia and Robert had left just moments earlier. The couple lived in the mansion in London, sharing it with the rest of the family when Parliament was in session. And rumors were ripe in the City that Robert could become the next prime minister. Still, if there was one thing she'd learned through the years, London gossip was more often wrong than right.

Cece spotted Lady Millicent engaged in enraptured conversation with an older gentleman and grinned. Would he be husband number four?

Her own life was exceedingly dull in comparison to her sister's. Oh, certainly she kept an active hand in the business. And she was one of the founders and directors of the Ladies Motoring Society. Politics occupied more and more of her time, with Jared's increasing interest in Parliament. And then there were the children. Two girls and a boy were a handful, even with the help of a governess. Cece chuckled. Perhaps her life wasn't so dull after all.

She paused, and her satisfied gaze skimmed the manicured lawns, carefully groomed gardens and the crowd of partygoers. She rarely thought about Nellie Bly these days. Cece had taken a far different path than she'd orginally expected, but it had led her to a life she wouldn't trade for a page-one byline. A good life, filled with joy and laughter and love.

She studied the brown paper-wrapped parcel she still clutched in her hand with idle curiosity. Olivia had given it to her, along with a twinkle in her eye and a warning that she would need it with children of her own. Cece never would have dreamed how well she and her mother-in-law got along. Of course, Olivia had her own life to live these days.

Cece ripped off the wrapping and stared at a worn, threadbare copy of children's fairy tales. A faded blue ribbon dangled from a page somewhere near the center of the book. The volume seemed to fall open naturally at the page it marked, and she smiled.

It was "The Princess and the Pea."

Her gaze fell to the final lines. Hans Christian Andersen had ended his tale with the words, "and this is a true story." But beneath the printed lines someone, no doubt Olivia, had added her own ending.

Cece laughed aloud. Whoever would have thought, back in the last years of the last century, that the mother so determined to ensure that the woman who would carry her family name into the future be worthy of the honor, would have penned her own ending to their story. In Olivia's still strong, decisive hand, the flourishing script swept across the page.

"And they lived happily ever after."

Author's Note

THERE was indeed a race from Paris to Bordeaux and back in June of 1895. The round-trip course stretched 732 miles. Emile Lavassor won the race in just over 48 hours, a remarkable feat. However, a race in Britain that year would have been difficult, if not impossible. It wasn't until November 1896 that the law requiring that a man waving a red flag walk in front of an automobile was repealed. That prompted the first London-to-Brighton run with thirty-five motorcars. The run is still held today on the first Sunday in November. Attracting hundreds of cars, it's restricted to those built before 1905.

Also in 1895, nine American heiresses married British lords.

Not all of them lived happily ever after.